BRIDE OF STARS AND SACRIFICE

SACRIFICE

HR MOORE

Titles by HR Moore:

The Relic Trilogy:
Queen of Empire
Temple of Sand
Court of Crystal

In the Gleaming Light

The Ancient Souls Series:
Nation of the Sun
Nation of the Sword
Nation of the Stars

The Shadow and Ash Duology:
Kingdoms of Shadow and Ash
Dragons of Asred

Stories set in the Shadow and Ash world:
House of Storms and Secrets
Of Medris and Mutiny

The Cruel Goddess Series:
Bride of Stars and Sacrifice
Daughter of Secrets and Sorcery
Book 3 – coming soon

http://www.hrmoore.com

CONTENTS

Map	V
Rule One	VI
1. Maria	1
2. Ava	19
3. Maria	25
4. Ava	35
5. Maria	41
6. Ava	55
7. Maria	61
8. Ava	71
9. Maria	76
10. Ava	84
11. Maria	95
12. Ava	102
13. Maria	107
14. Ava	117
15. Maria	126
16. Ava	133

17. Maria   140

18. Ava   144

19. Maria   150

20. Ava   158

21. Maria   170

22. Ava   175

23. Maria   179

24. Ava   186

25. Maria   192

26. Ava   207

27. Maria   216

28. Ava   234

29. Maria   237

30. Maria   251

31. Ava   267

32. Maria   270

Connect with HR Moore   277

Acknowledgements   278

Titles by HR Moore   279

MAP

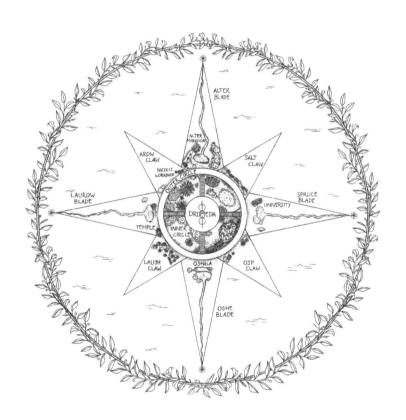

RULE ONE

The first rule of Atlas:
Take what you give. Give what you take.

CHAPTER ONE

MARIA

TODAY WAS THE DAY Maria's life would end. Or begin. It wasn't clear yet which.

'Make way! Make way!' The guard clad in light blue at the head of the procession was forcing the crowd apart, and Maria slunk back, hiding herself in the crush of bodies. Everyone was desperate for a glimpse of the first family of Oshe Blade, and Maria was no different, but she cared to see only one member: the man colloquially known as the Black Prince—her betrothed.

She went up on tiptoes, but it was useless, she could see little, and she hadn't risked being late to her formal introduction for this. She moved to the far side of the crowd, to where her brother, John, sat on horseback dressed in patriotic purple, surrounded by a formal guard from their homeland, Alter Blade.

John would escort the Black Prince and his entourage around the Outer Circle and into their home territory, all the way to their uncle's impressive fortress. It wasn't far, and Maria would have to sneak back across the neighboring Claw to get home before them.

She moved to the creamy stone wall behind John, which was heaving with bodies, and slipped a vial of lavender oil into the hand of a tall woman, who immediately relinquished her spot. Maria knew many of the people of Alter Blade and Arow Claw because she could get them things. In return, they would get her things, do things for her, or even better, share information.

She lifted her foot to the top of the wall—which came halfway up her thigh—and pushed up onto it in a single lithe movement, her balance and confidence honed through years of climbing trees, the task made easier because she insisted on a practical wardrobe. She wore sturdy leather boots and a split skirt with breeches beneath, just fashionable enough to be acceptable to her uncle and just sensible enough not to make her stick out in the Claws.

She could finally see the travelling party, made up of foot soldiers, guards on horseback, and three glittering carriages. She glimpsed a woman swathed in delicate blue fabric through one of the carriage windows, and Maria thought for the thousandth time how glad she was to be from Alter Blade. If rumors could be believed, the wealthy women of the other Blades were only ever seen in elaborate dresses. If the Black Prince thought he could force her into some straight jacket of a gown, their marriage was doomed from the outset, but she was very much hoping for something more ... companionable.

'Don't think you've fooled me, sister,' John called from his perch atop his prized chestnut mare. He wore his military uniform, his gold buttons and cuffs polished to a shine, black riding boots gleaming in the sunlight.

He turned to look her in the eye, and she smiled sweetly at the man whose features so closely matched her own. Warm beige skin, strawberry blond hair, prominent cheekbones, and violet eyes. He was lithe, boyish, and mischievous, and Maria had never been able to take him all that seriously, probably because he'd never taken himself seriously, at least, not until the marriage pact had come about.

'Oh, I wasn't trying, brother,' she said with a wide smile.

'Haven't you somewhere to be? Like in a dressing chamber putting on a pretty frock and coiffing your hair?'

'Can you blame me for wanting a glimpse of my future husband? Which do you think he is? Surely not the painted peacock?'

John turned his eyes to the man in black near the head of the procession, his plume of light blue feathers floating back and forth atop his helmet, garish in the extreme. The whole display was ostentatious, a sea of dazzling gold with horses fine enough to rival John's or her own.

'Looks like it,' said John. 'No other obvious candidate. Unless the great Black Prince travels in a golden carriage like an old woman.'

He wouldn't. She knew that much of him. Not unless there was some reason for him to hide himself away. Which meant this man with the proud brow, sun yellow hair, and haughty demeanor would be her lifelong partner. Not what she'd imagined, but one mustn't judge a book by its cover ... Urgh, who was she kidding? What other option did she have?

But it mattered little. Maria knew her role, and she would perform it with a smile. Being sullen would only make things worse for everyone. Her uncle, the head of their family, had been very particular in his expectations, and she would see no pity from his quarter if she exhibited anything less than gracious delight. Not that she ever would. She would do her part to end the bitter war that had torn Celestl to pieces for almost three hundred years.

'Maria, if you dally any longer, you'll be late. Don't expect mercy from me if Uncle—'

'Don't fret, I have plenty of time, especially because this convoy is travelling so slowly it's almost going backwards. But if needed, you *will* delay them, or your own betrothed may discover ...'

'Yes, yes,' he said, waving his hand dismissively.

'See you at home, brother,' she said, then dropped down from the wall and let the crowd swallow her. It wasn't the first time she'd successfully used that threat on John, and his wide-eyed feigned nonchalance made her chuckle every time.

Maria wove through the crowd, careful to keep her head down and her ears open because knowledge was power, and people especially loved to talk at moments like these.

'He's 'andsome but not what I expected.'

Maria followed a small group as they headed from the Outer Circle, which belonged to no one, towards Arow Claw.

'Six arranged marriages! 'Ave you ever 'eard anything so ridiculous?'

'And what about the Claws, eh? The Blades can play around all they want with tea parties and marriages, but 'ave they forgot who it was saved their arses? Arow Claw, that's who.'

'Too far past, love. They've long forgot.'

'Well, maybe we should remind 'em.'

'Or maybe we should rejoice at the peace. 'Ow many 'ave we lost, same as them, even if they think we paid no cost? We might 'ave no marriages to bind us to their peace pact, but I'll sleep 'appier in my bed knowing soldiers won't be racing round that there Circle no longer.'

Maria took a long inhale. She'd implored her uncle to include the Claws in the peace treaty, but her uncle had simply laughed and waved her off as though the notion were a childish fancy.

The people of the Claws were people too, living just beyond the borders of every Blade. They'd wisely stayed out of the war, and had no formal armies of their own, but if they finally decided to rebel against their poor treatment and took up arms against the Blades, many would die.

Not to mention, the people of Arow Claw were clever and should not be underestimated. Arow had saved every soul alive when the world had stopped turning. But these people were right, the Blades' memories were short.

The woman's voice pierced Maria's thoughts. 'And they own the water. What we gonna do without that, eh?'

Maria looked down at the line of red cobbles separating the grass of the Outer Circle from the grass of Arow Claw. The moment she crossed that line, she would be trespassing, at the mercy of the people of the Claw, and every time she entered their territory, that knowledge gave her pause. It was unlikely they'd harm her, not only because of her friendships, but also because her uncle controlled their water supply, but it was still a possibility, especially with tensions running as high as they were.

But Maria had no choice. If she wanted to make it back in time to formally greet her future husband, she had to cut across the Claw; there was not a moment to dally. She hurried over the line and didn't look back, disappearing between two wooden buildings. She wove between the hodge-podge of houses and taverns and shops as she had many times before, the buildings leaning this way and that, not a single one seeming to stand straight.

Considering the Claw had no water of its own, relying on the Blades on either side to supply what it needed, the streets were tidy and absent of waste. She'd heard it was different in other Claws, but Arow had always been inventive. They'd created a system of pipes to keep their streets clean—one the Blades had been so jealous of, they'd commissioned Arow to build the same in their own lands.

Maria rounded a sharp corner, close now to her destination, but a short, stocky woman with long dark hair tied in a high ponytail stepped into her path, bringing Maria up short.

'Where are you going?' demanded the woman—Gabriele—who crossed her arms over her chest. 'This is not the quickest way to Alter Blade.'

'You know where I'm going,' said Maria. 'I need to see him before—'

'Before you abandon my cousin for a Blade's first son?'

Maria scowled. She wasn't abandoning Nicoli—she never would. Nicoli had made no secret of despising the pact, but none of it was Maria's doing. Maria would hardly have chosen this course for herself ... Not that it was any of Gabriele's business. 'It's not like that.'

Gabriele lifted her hands to her hips. 'Then what is it like?'

Maria bit the insides of her lips together. She took a long breath, then said slowly, 'Nicoli is my oldest friend.'

'You should never have given him hope.'

Maria recoiled. *What the actual fuck?* 'I never ... It's not like ... It's none of your ... I have no choice in any of this!'

'Liar,' the infuriating woman sneered.

Maria closed her eyes for a beat, tamping down her rising agitation, then started forward. 'I don't have time for this today.'

Gabriele held up her hand, something about the movement worryingly assured, so much so it stopped Maria in her tracks, her stomach scrunching into knots as she met Gabriele's gaze. 'You are no longer welcome in Arow,' Gabriele said triumphantly. 'Next time you set foot in our territory, you will not make it out alive.'

Maria froze as the words sank in, a part of her wanting to cry. She'd visited Arow every other day for years, considered it her second home—her spiritual home, maybe. She'd thought the people were fond of her, that they knew she had their best interests at heart, that she respected them. 'I understand,' she said, looking away, trying to push aside the forlorn nostalgia seeping into her soul. She didn't understand—Arow cutting ties with their friends in the Blades was diplomatic madness—but she wanted to see Nicoli more than she wanted to argue with his cousin, and her available time was short.

The woman nodded officiously and finally stepped out of Maria's path, but as Maria walked away, Gabriele called after her, 'Oh, and you should know, you're being followed.'

Maria wanted to ask by whom, but she neither had time to spare nor wanted to give Gabriele the satisfaction. She wove faster and faster through the streets until she came to Nicoli's workshop, the same workshop where his ancestor had created the mechanisms that saved their world from destruction. Nicoli saw to the upkeep of those mechanisms now, alongside inventing new creations of his own.

She stepped inside, finding Nicoli's messy, dark-haired form hunched over his desk, sketching atop a map of Celestl. The eight points of the four long Blades and four shorter Claws protruded into the sea, their bases stuck to the Outer Circle. Inside that sat the Inner Circle—once filled with water but now a lush garden canyon—and beyond that, Dromeda, now still, but once the spinning center of their world, the realm of the Goddess creator herself.

Nicoli spoke without raising his eyes. 'Four Blades, four Claws, and yet only six marriages,' he said, his tone sending a shudder down her spine. In all the time she'd known him, he'd never been so cold.

He touched the uppermost Blade. 'Alter to Spruce,' he said, jumping to the Blade to its right, skipping the shorter Claw between. 'Spruce to Oshe.' He slid his fingers to the bottom of the star. 'Oshe to Laurow'—the point to the left. 'Laurow to Alter.' His fingers completed the circle, now back at the top. Then he drew two lines across the world, first from right to left—Spruce to Laurow—then from bottom to top—Oshe to Alter—the last line signifying her own betrothal to the Black Prince. 'Six marriages to bind Celestl as one, as if the Claws did not even exist.'

'You know I tried,' said Maria, walking to the desk and tracing her pointer finger around the Outer Circle. 'We are one world in my eyes, Blades and Claws together, but I do not control my uncle or the leaders of the other Blades.'

'They should have wed Claw to Blade, Blade to Blade, and Claw to Claw.'

'And how many marriages would that have required?' she asked, her tone harsher than she'd intended. She paused for a beat then exhaled loudly, forcing her shoulders down, softening her tone. 'How many men and women tied in ways they had no desire to be?'

His eyes finally met hers. 'You wish for me to feel sorry for you, oh pampered child of the first family of Alter?'

'Nicoli!' exclaimed Maria. He'd always been practical, pragmatic, realistic. This was not like him at all.

He shot to his feet. 'If they cared about peace, they would have bound us all.'

'They care only for power,' said Maria, her tone matter of fact, 'as you well know.'

'The Claws inconsequential next to the great Blades.'

He rounded the desk, and Maria shook her head. 'You know that's not how I see it. We are equal in my eyes.'

Nicoli scoffed. 'Equal? You are not stupid, Maria, and I've never thought you delusional.'

'Your people saved us,' she said, placing a hand on his arm. 'If that doesn't make you our equal, I don't know what ever could.'

He looked down at her fingers. 'We will never be equal; not until the Claws have water of our own.'

Maria was forced to drop her hand as he turned to face the map. Nicoli pointed an accusatory finger at Alter's great lake, set slightly back from the Outer Circle. He traced the river snaking from it all the way to the Blade's tip and into the sea.

Maria leaned across the desk and caught his hand as it skated over the tiny circle at the Blade's point. 'Your ancestors saved us with these,' she said, pressing his finger into the parchment. 'You keep our world spinning. That makes you equal—more than equal—in any world that is fair.'

'Such crafty words,' he said, entwining their fingers and standing straight. 'This world is not fair. You know that, I know that, and your twisting, pretty words mean nothing at all. You try to flatter me? Soften me? Seduce me with notions of equality? Convince me you care?'

'I do care,' she snapped. 'You know I do; I always have.'

'Yet you will marry your Black Prince. Your pretty words will serve you well in his court, for the court of Oshe Blade is the most devious of them all.'

'Nicoli, please don't be like this. How long have we been friends? That needn't change.'

He huffed a cruel laugh. 'Everything is changing, and you said yourself, we do not have the power to prevent it.' He lifted her palm to his lips and met her gaze as he kissed it, but his clear, clever green eyes had none of their usual warmth. 'We are done,' he said. 'A clean break is the best kind.'

Maria bowed her head and leaned towards him, pressing her forehead to his shoulder, wrapping her free arm around his waist. 'I love you, Nicoli,' she said into his shirt. 'I always will.'

'Go.' He released her hand and pulled back. 'Your betrothed will be waiting.' He rolled up the map and dropped it into a basket full of similar pieces of parchment, then sat in his chair. 'It is no longer safe for you here,' he added, slowly sliding his fingers together, then dropping his joined hands into his lap.

Maria squared her shoulders and nodded once. He was her dearest friend and most cherished confidant. They had been close since they were children, both audacious enough to explore each other's lands.

When she was young, she'd been convinced they would marry, unable to imagine a better partner, but as she'd grown, she'd known that future could never be. And he'd known that, too. Their lives were boats on separate rivers, destined to follow divergent routes to the sea. Maria had no choice but to perform her duty to her people, and she would do it without apology.

'I'll always be here if you need me,' she said, then turned slowly for the door.

As she stepped through, she could have sworn she heard the words, 'I love you, too,' but when she turned back, he was gone.

Maria sped for the border with Alter, knowing she should not have tarried so long. She untied her waiting horse, which she'd left outside the border tavern, and slipped a vial of orange oil into a nook near the ground.

When she straightened, she started, surprised to find a man watching her from atop an enormous black stallion. He had short, raven black hair, broad shoulders, and thick arms arranged in a relaxed, confident manner. He was dressed head to toe in black, his doublet tailored so it tapered as it traveled down the trim line of his torso.

His head was tipped to one side, seemingly amused, and her gaze snagged on his sharp cheekbones and strong jaw before meeting his deep brown eyes.

Her breath quickened, but she swung up into her saddle because whatever this man wanted, she had no time to delay.

'You are supposed to be elsewhere, are you not?' he said, his lilting accent giving him away as a native of Oshe.

'Oh?' she said innocently, gathering up her reins. 'Where is that?'

A broad smile took hold of his full lips, and it made his eyes sparkle. Maria found herself returning the gesture. She lingered a beat before schooling her features and pulling her eyes away, urging her mare forward.

'You've missed the buzzing about six sets of nuptials?' he asked, falling in beside her, his warhorse several hands higher than her own, so he towered above her.

'Why did you follow me through the Claw?' There was no other way he could have found her, and Nicoli's cousin had said someone was on her trail.

'I saw you talking to John Alter and wanted to find out who you were.' *Liar.*

They rounded the side of the tavern, and lush parkland rolled out before them, the only significant features a few trees and grazing sheep.

The weather was warm, the air clear, so Maria could see her family home perched atop a cliff in the distance. She could also see the procession from Oshe making their way along the trade road that led directly from the Outer Circle to her home. They were already halfway, and she swore under her breath.

'It was a pleasure making your acquaintance, sir.' Maria squeezed her horse's flanks, and her mare leapt forward, taking off at a gallop, leaving the man behind. Her beaming smile returned as the wind whipped her hair and the fabric of her skirts flew out behind her. She turned her head and wasn't surprised to find the man in hot pursuit, his horse surprisingly fast, given its size.

She urged her mount faster, flying first over a fallen log, then a boulder she almost didn't see in the grass.

'Slow down!' the man bellowed, steering his own steed around the obstacle. 'You'll hurt yourself!'

A laugh bubbled up through her chest, then spilled free as she turned her head to look at him once more. 'You think a little gallop a danger?' she shouted, adjusting her balance as her mare jinked around a sheep.

'I'm trying to help you!'

'No one can help me now,' she shouted, pushing her horse until she could go no faster.

'And what if you die?' He came up alongside, standing in his stirrups.

She huffed a laugh. 'Then my betrothed will have to make do with someone else! I can't imagine he'd mind; it's not like we've ever met, and there are plenty of women far more charming than I.'

'You care not for your life?' he asked, his features scrunching with a mixture of surprise and concern.

She had to pull her eyes away to jump a fallen tree. They cleared it together, landing with barely a check. 'Oh, I care. I just can't imagine any other would, and certainly not my betrothed.'

'You do not wish to marry?'

She barked a loud laugh. 'Since when were the wishes of those involved in the marriage pact of any consequence? I will do my duty, and I will not complain, but let us not stand on ceremony!' She gave him a sly smile. 'I am quite sure the Black Prince must feel the same.'

The man shrugged, and Maria chuckled to herself. She was surer by the second who he was.

They were comfortably ahead of the procession now, so she reined in her horse, slowing to a steady canter.

'You have no fear of your betrothed, then?' the man asked.

'I have plenty! Chiefly that he's a pig-headed oaf who might refuse to see what's right in front of him.'

He laughed, sounding surprised but maybe also a little delighted. 'And what will he find right in front of him?'

'Someone who is useful to him, and who wants him to be useful in return. An asset. A teammate. An equal.'

'Oh, I'm sure he will be able to see all that in an instant, or he is, as you say, an oaf.'

'A pig-headed oaf,' she corrected, then almost guffawed at his expression. They reached the moat marking the boundary to her home, and she pulled her horse to a stop. 'You should go that way, sir.'

'You're not planning to join me?' he asked with a start.

'Don't worry, I have no plans to flee, but I must be inside when the procession enters, or my uncle will combust.'

She took off without another word because the procession was already crossing the main bridge and, even if he'd wanted to, there was nothing her brother could do to stall them now. She raced around the back and steered her horse over the hastily lowered rear bridge, waving to the guards in thanks as she ducked through the tiny gate that granted entry into the cliff itself.

Around the front, the procession would travel back and forth up the switchback road that would deliver them into the courtyard before her uncle's imposing mansion. That road was wide and lined with shops and taverns and market stalls, but this entrance was narrow and dark. Maria prayed to the Goddess that she wouldn't snag a limb on a jutting rock and be torn from her horse as she travelled too fast in the gloom.

She burst out into a small, enclosed garden at the top, and three maids raced forward to meet her, their relief palpable as she slid to the ground. One grabbed her horse, a second untied her dress, and a third took a cloth to her face and hands.

The first quickly tied her horse to a tree trunk, then pulled at her hair, dragging the pins free so Maria's long blonde locks hung down her back in waves. The other two helped her step into a new dress as the first pulled back sections of hair on either side of her head and pinned them in place, which no doubt gave her the exact look of innocent serenity her uncle had demanded. He'd been specific that Maria should look girlish and naïve and that she should hide her intellect altogether, so as not to give her betrothed the *wrong impression*.

'Boots,' said the first maid, tapping Maria's leg until she lifted it. The maid replaced her sturdy riding boot with a delicate silk slipper.

One of the others spritzed Maria with her preferred perfume of eucalyptus and laurel, and then the mansion's summoning bells began to toll, and the color drained from all their faces.

'Your vials are in my saddlebag,' said Maria, already halfway to the door at the edge of the garden.

She flung it open, hurrying through the dense network of tunnels that crisscrossed the cliff until she skidded to a halt beside a peephole overlooking the main courtyard. The guard at the head of Oshe's procession was just entering, and Maria raced to the door behind which her uncle and his courtiers stood.

Maria slipped through, everyone thankfully distracted trying to get their first glimpses of the Black Prince. She stood at the back and took a moment to catch her breath as the captain of her uncle's guard called his soldiers to attention, but a small, bony hand closed around her wrist—her grandmother, Dio—and dragged her forward to stand beside her uncle.

'Where have you been?' her grandmother asked, somehow getting the words out with not a single crack in her courtly mask, hands now curled around the bulbous purple orb at the top of her walking stick. Despite her slightly hunched form, Maria wasn't convinced Dio needed the stick for stability, but she liked to give things a good whack every now and again, and wielded it most effectively as an intimidation tool.

'Here and there,' Maria said cryptically, joining the others in a low bow as the first man and woman of Oshe climbed down from their gold-trimmed carriage. The couple swaggered along the purple carpet that had been rolled out especially for the occasion, then came to a halt before Danit, Maria's short, rotund, bald uncle.

'Barron Oshe,' said Danit, who was different to Maria's dead father in every way.

'Danit Alter,' said Barron, bowing to his host. Barron was a tall barrel of a man with grey streaks in his brown hair that did nothing to diminish his good looks.

His wife, Erica Oshe, could not have been much older than Maria's twenty-eight years and was not the mother of Barron's children. She was a tiny thing with flowing blonde hair, large breasts that her skimpy blue dress put proudly on display, and a heart-shaped face that made her look kind, although Maria wasn't fooled, because her eyes were cold, icy, ambitious chips of blue. Maria would be sure to give the woman a wide berth.

Maria's mother, Bianca, was nothing like Erica, and Maria wished her mother were there now, not in Spruce Blade, preparing her younger sister, Pixy, for her own part in the marriage pact. It wasn't that Bianca was motherly—quite the opposite—but she drew others like a forceful magnet, sucking the attention of any room towards herself, meaning that when she was around, Maria never had to deal with the likes of Barron or Erica.

'It is such a great pleasure to host you in our home,' said Danit. 'Especially on this most profound occasion.'

Barron acknowledged the sentiment with an agreeable nod.

'But our dear Maria is eager to meet her betrothed. Come, bring forward your son.' In reality, Danit was even more eager than Maria, his sharp eyes scanning the courtyard, which was now emptying of horses and carriages, leaving only guards behind.

Danit turned questioning eyes on Barron when he found no evidence of Maria's betrothed, but before he could give voice to his question, three more horses clattered under the portcullis, first her brother, John, and then two other men, both dressed in black.

Maria's heart leapt as her suspicion was proven correct because although one was the painted peacock she and John had judged so harshly, the other was the man who had ridden through the parkland by her side. Maria fought to keep her features neutral as the two men dismounted, then approached, looking absolutely nothing alike.

'Maria Alter,' said the tall, slim peacock, 'I am Cane, First Son of Oshe. A pleasure to make your acquaintance.' He took her hand and bowed over it, and a flutter of panic beat against her ribcage. Wasn't she supposed to marry the first son? What was her betrothed's name? She should know, but everyone called him the Black Prince. It wasn't Cane, she was sure of it. Well, almost sure, but the way this man had so confidently stepped up first …

'And I am Elex Oshe, your betrothed,' said the second man, shouldering his brother out of the way and rescuing Maria's hand, taking it in his own, which felt solid and soft and assured after Cane's clammy, spiny grip. Elex was confident and handsome, and Maria's breath caught as her panic evaporated.

'A pleasure to make your acquaintance,' she said, having to pout a little to keep her features from showing her relief.

'Only if her uncle agrees,' said Barron. 'For you see, my oldest son, Cane, is already betrothed.'

'But I will break the betrothal if necessary,' Cane said seriously.

Danit frowned, and Maria knew he was weighing the pros and cons of each option. In one light, Maria's being wed to the second son of Oshe could be considered a slight and was not strictly in line with the marriage pact, but on the other hand, the assumption that Maria would marry the Black Prince had travelled ahead of the party from Oshe. The people of Alter had been whispering for days about the match, keen to lay eyes on the infamous man, and to be tied to a man with a reputation like that was valuable for Maria and Danit both.

Maria knew which option she preferred. 'I have heard of the Black Prince,' she said, refusing to release Elex's hand, 'but Cane, your reputation does not precede you.'

Danit coughed in warning as Cane pulled back and spluttered a little. 'No, well, unlike my brother, I keep my escapades to myself.'

Maria cocked an eyebrow at his blundering mention of *escapades* and swiveled her head to look at her uncle, who seemed to be coming to a decision. 'I should help Elex settle in, don't you agree, Uncle?'

Danit's watery grey eyes met hers, and he nodded slowly. 'Yes, an excellent idea, Maria. Help your betrothed settle in.'

Her uncle agreed then, Elex was the better choice. Maria didn't hesitate before stepping out of line and wrapping her arm through her betrothed's, keeping her movements carefully businesslike.

'It was a pleasure to meet you,' said Elex, nodding to Danit and the rest of the receiving line before allowing Maria to lead him up the long set of shallow steps behind them. She glanced up, as she often did, at the small, long-silent bell tower that protruded from the top of the building like a threatening limb, then sent a silent prayer to the Goddess as she stepped through the grand double doors at the top.

'This place is a fortress,' said Maria, her voice low enough that only Elex could hear. 'A luxurious mansion perched atop a cliff riddled with tunnels and secret chambers.'

He raised his eyebrows. 'And with a moat to wrap it all up in a bow.'

She smirked as they stepped into an enormous ballroom, the walls covered with portraits and woodland scenes, scrollwork ringing the places where crystal chandeliers hung from the ceiling. 'Exactly,' said Maria. 'An audacious symbol to remind the Claws of what we have and they do not.'

He nodded his head heavily.

'Do you have something similar in Oshe?'

'Something that rubs our abundance of water in the Claws' faces?' he asked, the hint of a smile on his lips.

'A moat,' she said defensively, 'or other protections around your home.'

'Of course. We live at the top of a cliff, too, and the only way in is across a bridge made of wood and rope. No defensive water, though.'

She considered his words for a moment. She'd never been allowed to visit the other Blades, and she wondered then if all the first families lived atop cliffs ... not that it mattered, she supposed.

'Come,' she said, leading him to the balcony and the wide, stone steps down to the garden below, 'I'll show you to the Rose Wing. Your family has the run of it while you're here.'

Elex nodded, then offered her his arm, which she accepted, although it felt strange, descending the steps so close that their legs accidentally brushed as they moved. They'd only just met, and with any other man such casual intimacy would be considered, if not scandalous, then certainly cause for gossip among the staff. But then, in only a few short days, this man was to be her husband, which meant they would soon be more intimate still ...

Maria bit her lip as they turned right at the bottom of the steps, feeling suddenly hot. 'Your brother seems like an ... interesting character,' she said, trying to move her thoughts to safer territory.

He huffed a laugh. 'My brother is just the painted peacock you pegged him to be.'

Maria stopped and whirled to face him, her eyes wide.

He smiled cockily. 'I can read lips really quite well, not that your words presented much of a challenge—you were enunciating beautifully.' Her mouth fell open, and his smile grew wider. 'I do hope I was not such a disappointment.'

Her own lips quirked upwards, forming a playful pout that she felt all the way to the top of her cheekbones. 'Are you fishing for compliments, Elex?'

He bowed his head low, suddenly close. 'What if I am?' His brown eyes bored into hers. 'Would you think less of me?'

'Certainly,' said Maria, although her voice was breathy. 'Narcissism is a terrible quality.'

He chuckled, shaking his head a little, and when he stopped, his eyes seemed to assess her anew. Then they dipped to her lips, and for a heart-stopping moment, she thought he might kiss her, everything around them fading away, nothing existing but their breaths and her racing heart. But he broke the spell, pulling back, sucking in a loud breath as he turned his eyes to the garden.

She didn't want the moment to end, desperate to remain the sole focus of his attention, craving it with surprising force. 'But I will tell you my assessment of you,' she said, 'if you do the same in return.'

His eyes returned to her, and something flipped in her chest at what she saw there. Joy, perhaps, mixed with something she truly hoped was respect.

He slid his hand into hers and squeezed, making everything inside her tighten. 'You are a most welcome surprise,' he said sincerely.

Her ribs seemed suddenly too small.

'And you're very beautiful.'

She laughed because the rest she'd bought, but not that. 'I am not! I am perfectly fine looking, but I'm certainly not a great beauty. That accolade is reserved for the likes of my sister, Pixy, or your stepmother.'

Her words seemed to shock him. 'Don't say that.' They resumed their stroll towards the Rose Wing, and she slipped her arm through his once more. 'That woman is ugly inside and out, whereas you are ... not.'

'That's it?' she said, forcing her tone to be bright as she squeezed his arm, although her chest cratered a little. 'False flattery and cryptic words?'

'Maria,' he said, candor shining in his eyes, 'my flattery is not false. You are beautiful.'

She looked away, her cheeks burning.

'And I suppose,' he said, 'if I am required to provide a more detailed assessment—'

'Which you are.'

He chuckled. 'Then I would also share my observations that you are intelligent and forthright and ... what was it again? An asset and a valuable teammate and most probably my equal.'

'Most probably?' she said, swatting him. 'Don't make me call you an oaf.'

'Well, I suppose you left off the *pig-headed* bit this time.'

She giggled, and the sound shocked her because she hadn't known she was still capable of it. It had been years since she'd laughed like that.

'Your turn,' he said, giving her arm a squeeze.

Maria tried to clear her mind and think. She shouldn't let his sweet-talking sway her better judgement, but regardless, her judgement was favorable. 'My first impression was that you're very big and your horse is a giant.'

'And?' he pressed.

'You have a sense of humor, and you share my contempt for your brother and stepmother.'

He cocked an eyebrow, gently chastising her for such a blatant attempted sidestep. 'That was your second impression, not your first.'

Maria couldn't suppress her broad smile. Of all the things she'd imagined for her marriage, this was certainly not it. She'd hoped for a respectful rapport or quiet friendship, but she had never dared hope for *flirting*. 'You are very ... manly,' she said and then clamped her lips together, not wanting to believe she'd uttered that word.

'I am?' he said teasingly. 'Manly? Please, go on.'

'And I fear you are vain.'

'Vain?' He clutched a hand to his heart as though wounded.

'Practically consumed by it.'

He slowed them as they approached their destination and leaned close, so they once again breathed the same air. 'Is it vanity if you care for the good opinion of only a single person?' His voice was a low, intense rumble she felt all the way to her toes.

'Oh, it's coming back to me now ...' she said, looking deep into his warm, inviting eyes, her heart galloping, her mind demanding sustenance to keep spouting clever retorts, 'your charming mouth is very much a part of your questionable reputation.'

They stopped abruptly before the external doors of the Rose Wing, her words sobering them both, coming out pointed, not coquettish as she'd intended. Maria pulled away, suddenly uncertain because she was right, his reputation was that of a brutal man, a gambler, and a cad. She should not believe his pretty words so easily, no matter how well he sold them.

'Maria—' he said, but the door swung open and an Oshe guard appeared.

Maria began to turn, wanting to escape, but Elex caught her arm and invaded her space, his presence overwhelming, his scent of oak moss and dry cedar filling her lungs. He brushed his cheek against hers, his skin rough, the feeling foreign and disorienting and doing strange things to her insides. 'My reputation is not without base, but it's also a façade,' he whispered, his tone fearsome, 'a carefully crafted mask I allow few to see behind. But make no mistake, I very rarely lie.' Elex stepped back just as his brother appeared in the doorway, his eyes narrowed suspiciously. Maria took a moment to regain her senses, dizzy as though she'd spun too many times in a circle.

'What took you—' Cane began.

'See you at dinner,' Maria blurted, then refused to look at either of them as she bobbed her head and ran.

CHAPTER TWO
AVA
AVA'S FOURTEENTH BIRTHDAY

AVA WAS USED TO the rhythmic banging. It was a feature of taverns like the one in which she dwelled. It wasn't her choice to reside in a pit such as the Cleve Arms, merely a by-product—perhaps intentional, perhaps not—of her parents' murder. But that was a long time ago now, and it wasn't helpful to linger on thoughts of the past because the comfortable existence of her youth was long gone and it wasn't coming back.

So she was used to the banging, along with cursing, nefarious dealings, and thieving. She'd seen it all, she supposed, at the ripe old age of fourteen. Or maybe she hadn't ... not that it made any odds; no one cared about her.

'Ava!' yelled Mrs. B.

Ava jumped to her feet and rushed from the cubby she liked to hide in outside one of the grimier bedrooms on the ground floor, pushing through the swing door into the kitchen. 'Yes?' she said to the short, wiry woman with greying hair and light green eyes that seemed to pierce Ava's skull, opening her brain to scrutiny. Mrs. B wasn't like the other tavern owners. They were all round and ruddy, enjoying a drink or two as they set the world to rights with their patrons. Not Mrs. B. If she ever drank a drop, Ava had never seen it. And she was particular, too. Meticulous. Unforgiving.

'Wipe your hands, change into a fresh apron, then go pick up the linens.'

Ava's eyes went wide. She'd never been given an important job before. Pot washing, stripping sheets, clearing tables, but never had she been allowed to touch anything on its way out of the kitchen or into a bedroom. 'Ah ...'

'Don't stand there with your mouth open,' snapped Mrs. B. Her bark was bad, but her bite wasn't as cruel as others. Ava counted herself lucky because not all orphans were so fortunate.

'Yes, of course,' said Ava. She hurried to the sink, then grabbed a freshly washed apron that was drying on the rail of the cookstove.

The kitchen was large for a tavern with only ten bedrooms and a medium-sized taproom, and it was always warm from the stove, with light pouring in from the many windows. It was a pleasant enough place to spend her days, even if the cook cursed and blasphemed his way through life and wasn't averse to kicking Ava when she got in his way.

It always smelled of fresh bread and garlic, which was perhaps the worst part of her circumstances because she wasn't allowed to eat anything that smelled anywhere near that good. Her rations came strictly from what others left on their plates.

She remembered the time before, when she'd been one of the lucky children sitting at a table by the fire, taking for granted the warm rolls and melted butter. Now the smell of those delights was a special kind of torture, so close and yet so far.

'Do not dally,' said Mrs. B, as she shooed Ava through the back door. 'Mrs. Kelly's expecting you. And don't let them give you any tosh about payment. It'll go on our bill, as usual. And watch Mrs. Kelly's son—he's handsy, and once he gets going, he doesn't easily stop.'

Ava nodded, taking the warning seriously because she knew only too well about the handsy ones; another reason she was happy in the kitchen.

'The linens are heavy. Go carefully. Dirty them and you will pay.' Mrs. B's eyes were hard as granite, and Ava nodded her head up and down as though her life depended on it, because Mrs. B never made idle threats.

'I'll be careful. I promise.'

Ava slipped out of the kitchen door and took off at a brisk but precise pace. She'd long ago worn away what little tread her shoes had had when Mrs. B had thrown the holey cast-offs at her, and it had rained recently, meaning the cobbles were slippery, the grime wet. If she fell, her clean apron would not fare well.

As always, she stuck to the shadows as she moved through the filthy streets, her eyes taking in every tiny detail. The blacksmith used his large hammer today. The street children were unusually thin on the ground. The man in black standing guard outside Malik's lair had a particularly deep scowl on his face. Best to avoid him—or risk losing a tooth.

As she approached the washerwoman's shop, the streets became cleaner. Not clean but cleaner, and the women there made more of an effort to keep their hems out of the muck. Ava didn't have to worry about her hem, because she hadn't had a new dress in two years, and given her recent growth spurt, the thin fabric reached no farther than the underside of her knees. It meant the men in the tavern regularly tried to see up her skirt, which was happening more and more frequently of late, seeing as her breasts refused to stop swelling and her hips had widened despite her lack of food. Another reason she was happy in the kitchen.

Ava stepped inside the small walled area around the laundry, where mangles and barrels of water and washboards lay about the place along with creamy bars of soap. Linens and towels and shirts hung from high lines, and above those, wisps of smoke danced about the chimney, then puffed up into the cloudless blue sky on the fickle, intermittent breeze.

Outside the stone wall was dirty, but inside was spotless, with fresh straw on the ground, brushes for customers to clean their shoes, and the watchful eyes of Mrs. Kelly's skinny son making sure they did so. Ava gave him a wide berth and stepped inside the shop, eyeing the bundles of neatly folded fabric piled up along the walls and sheets billowing by the fire.

'And you are?' asked Mrs. Kelly, eyeing Ava skeptically from the recesses of her round, ruddy face.

'Ava,' she said confidently. 'Mrs. B sent me for the linens for the Cleve Arms.'

'Never seen you before,' said the woman, taking a deep breath in, then blowing out so her lips vibrated. 'Hold on.' She limped her large frame to a set of deep, sturdy shelves, then hauled an enormous bundle into her washer-woman's arms.

Ava's breath stood still in her lungs. Was she really supposed to carry that whole load back by herself? Mrs. Kelly had muscles the girth of a beer barrel, and Ava did not. She was strong, having lifted more than her fair share of flour sacks and overloaded trays, but if she got a single speck of dirt on the pristine bundle, even plate scraps would seem like a luxury.

Mrs. Kelly seemed to sense her apprehension but didn't care one jot. She laughed. 'Don't go getting those dirty now, will you. Your Mrs. B's too tight to pay for a cover.'

Ava looked blankly at the woman, who laughed harder, seeming to think Ava's misfortune a great joke. The sound snapped Ava's spine straight, and she leaned forward a little, narrowing her eyes and studying the woman, working her out, as was Ava's way. She did it as often as she dared, and it mostly made people uncomfortable, but Ava liked that, relishing the power of something so simple as an extended stare. A study. An assessment. Her mother had taught her the trick, one of the few things Ava remembered from her life before.

And what Ava saw when she looked at Mrs. Kelly was a woman who'd worked all her life, who'd built a reliable business by breaking her own back, and who cared little for others. Maybe that was why her son took liberties with women.

Mrs. Kelly fidgeted, clearly at a loss, seeing as Ava hadn't moved to take the washing, but an excited shout from outside cut Ava's appraisal short. She turned to look through the open door, where Mrs. Kelly's son greeted a man only a few years older than Ava—a handsome man with warm, caramel skin, dressed in a perfectly pressed white shirt beneath a knee-length leather coat and with expensive, supple leather boots. He was tall, lean, and almost gangly, not yet wearing his wide shoulders quite right, although his dark chestnut hair lay perfectly across his head in waves.

The newcomer looked uncomfortable with the animated welcome, but Mrs. Kelly's son didn't seem to notice.

'I'm just here to collect my mother's washing,' said the stranger, his voice surprisingly deep.

'Take a seat,' said Mrs. Kelly's son. 'I'll fetch refreshments.'

'No, thank you,' he said with the authority of someone used to being obeyed. He was young for someone with that tone. 'Just the washing.' And then he looked up, and his eyes locked with Ava's through the door.

A shiver ran down her spine as his deep blue orbs sucked her in and held her hostage. Was it fear or elation that coursed through her? Or maybe a bit of both because, in the ordinary course of her current life, she never crossed paths with the likes of him. Powerful people, wealthy, perhaps even a little magical. Or had she imagined the ripple of something almost silver in his enchanting blue eyes? *Dangerous.*

His brow creased as though trying to figure something out, but then Mrs. Kelly's son stepped into his eyeline.

'Who is that?' Ava asked, turning back to face Mrs. Kelly, who'd dumped Ava's linens on the counter and was now frantically pulling out those belonging to the intriguing man.

'Ha!' Mrs. Kelly carefully hoisted a wrapped and scented bundle into her arms. 'Not for the likes of you, that's who.' She bustled out of the shop, practically bowing to the man as she handed him the washing. He took it, then glanced over the woman's shoulder as she wittered on about what an honor it was to have him in her humble place of business.

Their eyes met once more, his hungry and curious, and after a beat, they widened a fraction, as though he'd figured out whatever he'd been working on. His full lips parted, and she expected him to speak, but then Mrs. Kelly paused, finally realizing the man wasn't paying her the least bit of attention.

'Sir?' she said, and the intelligent spark in his eyes dulled, a mask falling across his features before he turned sharply away.

Ava's lungs began to work once more, and as she slowly spun to face her impossible task, she couldn't help the smile that tugged at her lips. That was the most exciting thing that had happened in ... well, months, probably ... maybe even years. Her heart fluttered in her tight chest, and a strange, giddy feeling spread through her. She bit her lip, chastising herself; it had only been a look.

Two looks, the foolish part of herself sang.

She shook her head at her own silliness, then carefully hefted the linens up onto her shoulder—the only way she could possibly make it back without dropping or dirtying them—and prayed to all the Gods that her neck could take the strain. Her muscles were underfed and certainly not trained to carry heavy, awkward loads over long distances. No shadows for her on the return, or the fabric would brush the bricks of the filthy, sooty buildings. But if she did her job well, maybe Mrs. B would reward her with fresh bread or the lukewarm leftovers of someone else's hot bath.

The handsome man was a way down the street by the time Ava stepped outside, heading in the opposite direction to the Cleve, and as she crossed the threshold from clean to dirty, her face hidden from the washerwoman and her son, their hushed voices floated to her sharp ears.

'Why's he back?' whispered Mrs. Kelly.

'Didn't seem keen to share the particulars ...'

'Curious. Such a scandal when he went, an' he's only been away a short span of months.'

'Doubt he'll hang around.'

'Whyever not?'

'What's there for him here?'

What was there for any of them? Ava turned her feet towards the tavern before they chastised her for loitering, but something about the man, about the way he'd looked at her—really looked—like no one had in years, buried deep into her mind and rooted there.

The memory of his eyes, blue and magical and astute, tugged like a string around her bottom rib, dredging up long-forgotten memories of other well-dressed strangers.

She shivered. Who was he? Why was someone like him picking up his mother's washing? And what scandal was he involved in? Perhaps he was someone important, someone who could help her ... Ava half floated on that thought as she returned to the seedy part of town, silently praying to the Gods that their paths would cross again.

CHAPTER THREE
MARIA

MARIA TRIED NOT TO put more effort into her appearance than she ordinarily would, but when her maids offered to apply powder to her cheeks, kohl to her eyes, and rouge to her lips, she shamelessly accepted. She also allowed them to sweep her hair into an elegant knot, adorn it with glistening pearls, and then poke small gems through the five holes along each of her earlobes.

She selected gold cuffs for the tops, matching rings for her fingers, and a long gold chain for her neck, from which hung a round disk of purple nightstone with a fine gold seam running through the middle. It sat lower on her cleavage than was her usual style, but she told herself the dainty dress required it.

Layer upon layer of light blue fabric—the color of Oshe Blade—cascaded from the dress's high waistband to the floor, the delicate silk so different to her usual practical attire, swirling around her legs as she moved. She felt as though she watched herself from the outside, like she'd switched places with another—her alluring, decadent sister, perhaps—as she padded on light, silk-slippered feet down the wide, portrait-lined corridor to the banqueting hall, only just resisting the temptation to twirl like an excited little girl.

'You are almost late,' spat her uncle, completing an appraising sweep over her outfit, bringing her back to reality with a bump.

'Sorry, Uncle,' she said, but they both knew she didn't mean it, and he narrowed his eyes.

Luckily, before Danit could chastise her further, dinner was called, music filled the air, and through doors on opposite sides of the hall, in processed the first families of Oshe and Alter. The dinner was to be an intimate one, with only the families and a few of their most senior guards.

Even so, they followed the traditional greeting reserved for formal occasions such as this, the two families linking arms and snaking between one other as their lines passed.

Maria was twirled by Barron, Erica, the painted peacock, and then Elex, who squeezed her arm a moment too long before letting go. Her heart raced, and by the time she reached her seat between her uncle and Elex, her face was flushed and an easy smile adorned her lips.

'I like you in Oshe colors,' Elex said in a low voice, leaning in and consuming her whole attention from the very moment her rear landed on her seat.

Their eyes met and held, and the smile evaporated from Maria's lips as a strange sensation coiled low in her belly, one she'd rarely felt.

A servant stepped between them, forcing them apart as he filled their golden goblets with pink wine, and Maria dropped her gaze to her lap, collecting herself. She peeked from the corner of her eye at her uncle and found him observing them closely. *Shit.*

'I'm sorry,' said Elex, when the servant stepped back, his voice still low, thigh bumping hers under the table.

'Sorry?' she asked, struggling to think past the impression his touch had left on her leg. She turned once more to face him, making an effort to stiffen her spine. 'You've already done something you need to apologize for?' She couldn't help the edge of flirtation that crept into her tone.

His eyes sparkled, then turned serious. 'My behavior in the garden. I suppose I got carried away, given, by some quirk of fate, this ludicrous arrangement has resulted in a match better than any I could have selected for myself.'

Maria faltered for a moment as his words landed. 'That is a ridiculous thing to say,' she snapped, her tone sharp, seeing as her uncle was now unashamedly leaning towards them from her other side. 'You've known me less than a day.'

He paused, then flicked his eyes over her shoulder before returning them to her. 'I'm an excellent judge of character.'

'And so very modest.'

'Naturally,' he said, then bowed his head, dropping his voice to little more than a whisper. 'Probably because I'm so especially *manly.*'

Maria flushed and gave a little cough, turning her attention to the plat-ters of food being placed up and down the table. Two servants set a suckling pig before her uncle, and stuffed birds, rolled herb-crusted joints, and whole fish followed, along with potatoes layered with cream, mountains of carrots and braised cabbage, and piles of fresh, green salad from the kitchen gardens. Maria loved to see the things they'd grown on the table. She reached for a bowl of crisp lettuce tossed in a sweet, acidic oil she'd created herself.

'Wow,' said Elex. 'Quite a feast.'

Maria shrugged. It was, but they ate like this a lot, and it wasn't her favorite kind of food. The gently spiced dumplings served in the street markets of Arow Claw ... now they were a treat. And she might never sample them again.

'Did I say something wrong?' asked Elex, holding a platter of pink fish between them.

She helped herself to several large flakes. 'No.'

'Are you angry I concealed who I was when we met?'

She smirked. 'I knew who you were.'

He tilted his head. 'You knew, and still you spoke so candidly?'

'You doubt it?'

His lip quirked as he placed the fish back on the table.

A servant leaned over and put a basket of bread rolls between them, and Maria slipped a vial of rosemary oil into the woman's hand as she retreated.

The servant didn't so much as blink, but Elex cocked an eyebrow. 'I think we shall get along quite well, you know.'

'I agree.' She smoothed her embroidered napkin across her lap and turned her head enough to check on her uncle, relieved to find he was deep in conversation with Erica Oshe, who sat on his other side. 'So long as we are open and honest with one another,' she added, reaching for her goblet.

He nodded. 'Then tell me this: how do you feel about our marriage? About the pact?'

She paused, considering just how far she could trust the Black Prince, then leaned close and whispered the truth because she could not expect openness from him and not give it in return. 'For now, know I do my duty gladly. Even if my betrothed had been less ... agreeable, I would have done what was expected with a smile. I abhor the war; there is no reason for it but greed.'

'I feel the same,' he said, and the sincerity in his tone made her believe him.

She gave a curt nod and pulled back a little. 'I just hope John is as lucky with his match. And my sister, Pixy. She's gone to Spruce with my mother.'

'I met your brother's future wife on our journey here, and her parents.'

'What are they like?' Celestl had been at war Maria's entire life, so she'd had little opportunity to socialize with the first families of the other Blades.

'The place was in a furor preparing for the weddings, and Sophie—John's betrothed—barely spoke. Her father seemed reasonable, although distracted. Her brother was fixated on my sister, his own betrothed, so I barely spoke to him.'

Maria groaned. 'It's all so complicated.'

'It's ridiculous,' he agreed. 'If it brings peace, it's worth it, but why, in the name of the Goddess, did they insist on all the marriages taking place on a single day?'

'Because our leaders aren't saddled with the organizational hassle and they adore symbolism.'

'Do your people still celebrate Toll Day?' asked Elex, picking up his goblet. He angled farther towards her, and again his leg pressed against hers under the table, but this time it didn't move away.

Her heart fluttered, not used to being the object of a man like Elex's attention. She'd never even met a man like him, aside from her brother, Hale, she supposed. A pang of longing hit her hard in the chest because she hadn't seen him in years, and she so wished he was there with them now, with his adventurous spirit and blunt, no-nonsense approach to life.

'Maria?' Concern edged Elex's tone.

'Yes,' she said quickly. 'Toll Day is the most sacred day of our year. We sing, dance, eat, decorate. Don't you?'

'We do.' He swirled his wine, then lifted his eyes and watched her closely. 'Do you still choose a ceremonial sacrifice?'

Horror gripped her. 'No! Do you?'

He laughed. 'Yes, but it's not as bad as it sounds. We doll my sister up every year and walk her to the Toll Gate, which she loathes. Although, given this is a real Toll year, she's a little more nervous than usual, worried the bells might actually ring ...'

Before the Goddess had abandoned them, she'd demanded a sacrifice once every hundred years. 'The Goddess hasn't rung the bells in almost three centuries,' said Maria, although her stomach dropped at the idea regardless. Who would her uncle send through Alter Blade's gate if it opened? Her? She was the obvious choice, seeing as her younger sister was away in Spruce Blade, besides being the apple of everyone's eye.

Elex slid his hand over hers under the table. 'They won't chime. And anyway,' he said, leaning in, a new intensity shining in his eyes, 'if anyone tries to sacrifice you to the Goddess, they'll have to go through me, and some parts of my reputation are entirely accurate.'

Maria's pulse ratcheted higher, her breaths becoming shallow as their eyes remained locked. Heat pooled in her core, and a reckless part of her urged her to lean in and brush her lips against his, just to see if it would feel as she imagined, soft and firm and dazzling. But if she did, it would reflect badly not only on her but her whole family and her people. It would be selfish, so she pulled back as her uncle jumped to his feet, seeming agitated.

'Friends,' Danit began, then gritted his teeth, making little attempt to hide his irritation, 'it is a pleasure to host you all in my humble abode, in the ancient Blade of Alter, at this most important time in our history.'

He seemed to relax as the eyes of the room settled on him.

'Almost three hundred years ago, the Tolls chimed for the last time. Shortly afterwards, Dromeda, the home of our Goddess Creator, stopped turning. The Inner Circle drained of water. And then the unthinkable happened, and the whole of Celestl ceased to turn.'

Danit paused, and a somber silence fell over the room. Those had been their darkest days, all believing they would die.

'But in the face of this adversity, and against all odds, we prevailed. We found a way to make our world spin once more.'

Arow Claw had prevailed, not the Blades, who had fought and postured and looked to sacrifice everyone but themselves. How Danit could stand to lie so brazenly, Maria couldn't fathom.

'But the strain on our great Blades was vast. Food shortages, uncertainty, disease ... Was it any wonder war ensued? A war started by our ancestors, which has lasted for too long.'

'Hear! Hear!' called Barron, slamming his hand on the table in time with his words.

'So we will rectify the poor decisions of our ancestors with good decisions of our own. We will bring peace to our lands for the first time in three hundred years. We will work together, all four Blades united, and the children of our children will belong to us all.'

Barron and Erica cheered while the others politely applauded.

Arow had saved Celestl, yet Danit's account made it seem as though the Claws had had no part to play at all. Her uncle, and the men like him, were only too happy to write the Claws out of history and steal their glory. The Claws had stayed out of the wars, too, the only ones wise enough to know no good would come from fighting.

'So I raise a toast,' said Danit, lifting his goblet, his shoulders low, features triumphant. 'To the Blades of Celestl. To the marriages of our children. To the end of this bloody war. And to the dawn of a new age, where we look to the promise of our future and forget the troubles of the past. To the Blades!'

'To the Blades!' they parroted, raising their glasses. Maria dutifully joined in, even if she had to swallow the bile in her throat.

Maria turned back to Elex, glad the pomp was over, but to her surprise, Danit continued. 'And from this year forward, Toll Day will be known as the Day of the Blades. We will celebrate not an absent Goddess but the joining of our children and the continuance of our lines.'

A stunned silence stole all movement from the room, and Maria clamped her lips shut to stop the protest that rose inside her, fighting to get out.

'To a new age!' cried Danit, but only Barron and Erica repeated the words with gusto because everyone else was still in shock.

Maria shared a look with John across the table, each silently asking the other if they'd known. Neither had. She shot a covert look towards her grandmother, but her face was, as usual, a mask, and it was only when Elex squeezed her hand that she realized she'd taken hold of his fingers and was gripping altogether too hard.

She eased off and twisted her face towards him. 'Did you know?'

He exhaled heavily. 'No.'

Something sad but ferocious in the depths of his eyes made her believe him. 'No,' she said. 'Nor I.'

The mood was mixed for the remainder of the evening, some elated, others doing a poor job of hiding their shock and worry. Danit instructed the men to move over two places after the first course was cleared, which meant Maria was stuck with the painted peacock on one side and Barron on the other for the rest of the meal.

She was congenial. She tittered and generally did what was expected, politely ignoring their impertinence when they leaned in a little too far or placed a hand on her arm, but by the end, her face hurt from her forced smile. She couldn't wait to get away, to hide the skin her dress displayed and banish the two men from her mind.

Maria had no further opportunity to speak with Elex, but his image plagued her thoughts, along with the phantom feel of his hand, the press of his thigh ...

Her preoccupation meant she didn't notice her uncle lying in wait when she finally fled the banqueting hall. He grabbed her arm and hauled her into an anti-chamber, then pushed the door closed behind them, careful not to make a sound.

'What are you playing at?' he hissed, trying to look down his nose at her, but it was difficult, considering she was the taller of the two.

Maria always found it strange to think this man was her father's brother, because her father had been tall, with a thick head of hair and an easy, mischievous disposition, even if his temper had been quick, and he'd been stubborn as a mule. He'd been dead many years, and Danit had succeeded him to lead Alter Blade because her brothers had been too young. And then Hale had gone adventuring and never returned to pick up the mantle.

He was probably sunning himself on an island somewhere, or at least that's how she preferred to think of him, refusing to entertain the idea that someone so capable and full of life could be dead. And in the meantime, Alter Blade was stuck with Danit because John didn't have a taste for leadership, and Maria had been laughed down when she'd suggested she could take on the role.

'Answer me,' Danit snapped. 'You embarrassed yourself tonight. Embarrassed *me*. The whole of Alter ... What were you thinking? Acting that way with the Black Prince? He had you eating from his palm, and what did you do? Leaned in and *giggled* like a child. You forgot yourself and your duties.' He moved even closer when she didn't immediately reply, his features dark. 'Well?'

Maria gave him a benign, softly quizzical look. 'I was playing him the same way he was playing me, Uncle. I am glad you think those things of me, because if you were fooled, then so was he. I am sure he thinks me an airheaded woman, head over heels in love with him. He thinks he has the upper hand. And good, I say, because that is how I will get him to reveal his true self. To trust me enough to tell me his plans and secrets.'

Danit faltered in the face of her unwavering confidence. 'Do not forget yourself, Maria. Remember your duty.'

'I am loyal to you and the people of Alter,' she said fervently. 'I love my people. I love my family.' It was true, although Nicoli was also her family, and soon Elex would be too, but she showed Danit the unwavering face of devotion he needed to see.

Danit held her gaze for a long moment, then nodded. 'You may not understand why I do the things I do, but it is not for you to understand—it is for you to obey. This is our one chance at greatness. Our one hope.'

'Our one hope of what, Uncle?'

She immediately regretted her words, for her tone held an accusatory edge she hadn't meant to be there, and his features turned suspicious.

'I only want to make sure I act in accordance with your wishes,' she added. 'I would hate to inadvertently work against you.'

'It is not for you to know,' he said through gritted teeth.

Maria bowed her head. 'Yes, Uncle, of course.' She took a step towards the exit, but he stopped her with a tight hand on her arm.

'Tomorrow, you will take our guests triffling in the Inner Circle, and then you will slip away and get a message to your friends in Arow that I require a meeting with Nicoli.'

He released her and stepped away, as though that were the end of it, but Maria was frozen in place, her mind trying to decipher why he would need such a meeting. 'I wish I could, Uncle, but I am no longer welcome in Arow Claw. They don't like the peace pact. They're unhappy the Claws were not included ...'

Danit, who had started pacing, suddenly stilled. 'They think we would sully our lines by marrying them?'

Maria gasped. 'Uncle, they merely—'

'Then it is worse than I thought. They have ideas so far above their stations as to consider themselves our equals?'

She would never understand how he could think of them as anything other. 'If it weren't for the people of Arow Claw, we would all be dead!' She'd never been so bold, and as soon as the words were free, she clamped her lips shut, dread chasing them up through her chest.

'They are nothing without us,' he sneered. 'They have no water without us. They die without us. I don't care how you do it, but I need a meeting with Nicoli and you will see to it that he comes.'

A wave of nausea washed over her. 'They'll kill me if I ever go back.' Gabriele's lookouts would spot her before she had any hope of reaching Nicoli.

He exhaled a dismissive huff.

'I'm serious! And they still worship the Goddess; they won't like our changing Toll Day.'

'That is because they live in hope that the Goddess will finally take pity on them. She will not. It has been three hundred years, and it is time for even the most devout of them to admit they were wrong. We are alone. The Blades have the only water, the Inner Circle will never again be full, and the Claws are at our mercy.'

'We're only alive because of them,' said Maria, her tone sharp, but she didn't care, her temper having slipped its leash. 'They control the turbines that keep Celestl spinning. They built the pipes that carry water to our home. They are the ones who maintain everything ... who keep us safe!'

'And?' he snarled, stepping closer as he mocked her. 'What is it you think they can do? They rely on the turbines, too. And anyway, we have guards at the Blade tips; the Claws can't get close.'

'You rely on Nicoli to maintain the mechanisms. He is often close.'

'We will learn to do that ourselves, and then the Claws will have no leverage at all.'

'Why?' said Maria, digging her fingernails into her palms. 'Why not just work with them?' If she had her way, it would be nothing like this, but she did not have her way. She was powerless, hopelessly so.

'You are naïve, Maria, to believe things could ever be so simple.' He stepped into her space, making her uncomfortable. 'Leave the thinking to me and do as you are told. Now be a good girl and run along.' But as she moved to step past him, he grabbed her hair and yanked her closer still. 'Do not test me, child.'

'Yes, Uncle,' she whimpered, averting her gaze like a meek little mouse, but only because if she looked at him, he would surely see the hatred in her eyes. Soon she would marry the Black Prince and she would leave her uncle's home, and he would never treat her this way again. Until then, she would hold her tongue and bide her time and ignore how the fire of her resentment wounded as it burned.

Chapter Four
Ava
Ava's Fifteenth Birthday

Ava tore a tiny piece of bread from the small, precious loaf she held in her hands, trying to ignore the rhythmic thumping and loud moans coming through the door against which she sat. She banged on the wood, and the moans quietened, but she scowled nonetheless because they were making her job dangerous. If Mrs. B found out one of her girls was whoring, and that Ava was the lookout, Ava would be on latrine duty for a solid month, and things were already bad enough.

She popped the piece of bread into her mouth and savored the warm, yeasty flavor, her tastebuds tingling with delight. The danger was worth the payment, especially as she lived off gruel these days, ever since Mrs. B had labelled her uppity and entitled, deciding she needed to learn her place after the linen incident of the previous year.

She'd almost made it back without a mark. She'd practically tasted whatever morsel Mrs. B would have given her in reward, but then Malik had turned up on his disobedient horse. The goon guarding his den hadn't come forward to take the reins. Two street kids had rushed past, and the horse had spooked, swinging around and rubbing grass stains, slobber, sweat, and mud across Ava's precious load.

Mrs. B had stepped outside at that very moment, and even though Ava had rushed inside and pulled off the outer sheet, making sure it was the only one marred, it had spelled the end of the miniscule comforts in her life.

Shortly afterwards, Mrs. B had taken another girl, Tasha, off the street and had cast Ava back into the shadows. Mrs. B barely spoke to her now. Not that Ava cared about the attention, but she did care about the food and secondhand baths. She was lucky if she ever got to wash these days, and the water was always freezing cold and filled with filth. She occasionally snuck away to the stream in the field behind the prison, but she couldn't manage it often.

She took another small bite of bread as the noises in the room behind her ratcheted higher. They'd be out in a minute, and Ava's break from washing pots would be over. She sighed and finished the bread, then picked the crumbs off her threadbare skirt and relished those too.

She wondered when Malik would next return. It had been a while since his last visit, and Ava had feared he'd lost interest in Tasha. If that happened, she might never taste fresh bread again.

The noises stopped, so she got to her feet and smoothed down her skirts as confident footsteps sounded on the bare wooden planks of the bedroom. The door swung open, and Malik stepped through, casting an eye over Ava, then leaning against the doorjamb in his usual cocksure way.

He had every right to his swagger, she supposed, because he was King of the Cleve. Not quite the poorest area in Santala, but almost, with the docks on one side and the prison on the other.

Everything about him was dark. Dark hair that stuck up in spikes from the top of his head, dark eyes, dark bushy eyebrows, brown skin that seemed to shine with a luster Ava could only dream of. And a dark soul. Ava had appraised him once, looking deep into his eyes as silence settled around them. He'd seemed to find it amusing and hadn't flinched or shuffled or looked in any way uncomfortable, as most others would have. But she wouldn't do it again, because despite his cheeky, almost boyish good looks, he was terrifying and brutal, and although capable of kindness, especially if it got him what he wanted, he was mean.

Tasha came up beside him and wrapped her arms around his neck, giggling as she pulled his lips to hers. He let her, kissing her back in a way that made Ava uncomfortable, all tongues and teeth, his hand groping Tasha's breast. But making Ava uncomfortable was the point, she realized, as Malik pulled back and turned his head to her, his hips still pinning Tasha to the door frame. He pulled a coin from his pocket and placed it in the cleft between Tasha's breasts. A crown. Enough to keep Tasha in good food and clean blankets for a week. Longer, if she was careful.

Tasha giggled again as she looked down at the coin, and a stab of jealousy knifed Ava in the chest. Where Tasha had ample flesh, Ava was skin and bone, even her large breasts having finally stopped growing given her current predicament. Tasha's hair gleamed from good food and a recent wash; her nails were strong, with only a little dirt under them; her dress had only a few patches. Ava was like an insect, scrounging crumbs from the floor, but Tasha was a favored dog, too important even to notice the creature by her paw ... unless she was bored and wanted to play.

'You could be pretty, you know,' said Malik, his eyes still on Ava. 'With a few good meals and a nice new frock.'

Ava said nothing. Did nothing. She barely breathed. Because if Tasha was a dog, Malik was a feral cat, and in his games, the insects never survived.

'Good round pair of tits on you. Nice sandy hair, good teeth—'

'Malik!' said Tasha, swatting him playfully on the chest. 'Leave her alone; she's never done it!'

Malik's eyes narrowed, and Ava inwardly retreated. 'Is that right?'

'I should get back to work,' said Ava, backing away, but Malik moved like lightning, catching her arm.

'Not so fast,' he said, and Ava closed her eyes for a second, steeling herself. When she opened them, he was holding up a copper. 'Want this?'

Yes ... more than anything. She salivated at the thought. 'Depends.'

'Malik!' said Tasha, trying to pull his attention back to her. Malik ignored her.

'Depends on what?' he said.

'What you expect me to do for it.'

Malik chuckled. 'You're not stupid, then. That's good, I don't like them stupid.' He swung his head towards Tasha. 'What does a man get for a copper around here?'

'Not much,' she said through a pout.

Malik put his hand on Tasha's face and pulled her roughly to him. 'A kiss?'

'Sounds about right,' she breathed, plastering a brave face over her obvious unease, no doubt concerned Ava might steal her patron ... as if she ever would.

Malik kissed her. A quick thing, nothing like the one before, then slid the copper into the space below the crown. He turned back to Ava. 'Want this?' he asked again, holding up a second coin.

Ava's eyes flicked to the tiny piece of tarnished metal, and Malik smiled a triumphant smile. It would be enough for an apple or a couple of carrots. Maybe both if she played her cards right.

But what Tasha did with him ... it wasn't what Ava wanted. A kiss was one thing, but ... 'I won't do more,' she said. 'So if that's what you're after, no thank you.'

'Polite as well,' said Malik. 'Makes a change around here. Shame. You're shorter than Tasha ... you'd fit right nicely—'

'Malik!'

He ignored Tasha, and she removed the coins from her cleavage and folded her arms across her chest. 'For the love of the Gods, just kiss her and let this be done. Before Mrs. B comes along and has both our hides.'

Ava's heart stopped. It wasn't bad so bad ... A kiss for an apple. 'Just a kiss,' she said again, 'and don't stick your tongue in my mouth either.'

Malik chuckled as he stepped into her space, and she fought the urge to wrinkle her nose at the smell of stale sweat and last night's alcohol. She kept her eyes open, watching as he closed his and puckered his lips, his hands closing around her waist.

As he pressed his mouth to hers, Ava's eyes flicked to Tasha, who studied them closely. Tasha seemed to relax when their eyes met, a smug smile spreading across her features. Ava refocused on Malik, whose lips were hard and moist and certainly not enjoyable, like kissing a snake. He pulled away—after what felt like an eternity—and she fought the intense urge to wipe away all traces of him. But he wouldn't like that.

'Can't say you're a natural,' said Malik, pressing the copper into her hand. 'And I have no patience for teaching. See you round, Tash.'

As soon as he left, Ava vigorously scrubbed her lips.

'Are you okay?' asked Tasha. 'You look ... I don't know ... you most always look ill, but you're paler even than normal.'

Ava dropped her hand and inhaled, fixing Tasha with her customary stare. Tasha shuffled and averted her eyes, and a small pang of satisfaction pulsed through Ava's chest.

'I'm fine,' Ava said eventually. 'Are you?'

Tasha giggled. ''Course.' She held up her coins like two tiny trophies. 'I'll eat like a queen 'til next he calls!'

Ava couldn't imagine doing what Tasha did, although no judgement came along with the thought. And Tasha was a few years older than Ava's fifteen years. Maybe she'd change her mind if she had to endure near starvation much longer, but still ...

'Do you like him?' Ava asked, genuinely curious.

'Yer what? Malik?' She shrugged. 'He's not as bad as some, I suppose.'

'And if he proposed tomorrow?'

Tasha cackled. 'If he proposes tomorrow, you'll see unicorns flying past that there window.'

Ava nodded, but she didn't miss the flicker of—was that hope?—crossing her features. 'You didn't answer the question.'

Tasha rolled her eyes and leaned in close, dropping her voice to a whisper. 'The walls have ears. Remember that.'

Ava fought a laugh of her own. Who would bother listening to them? But Tasha was already heading down the stairs, leaving Ava to change the dirty sheets alone.

She stepped into the room and closed the door, leaning back against it, glad for the rare moment of solitude in somewhere other than her bedroom in the cellar. She sucked in a deep breath, held it, then exhaled.

Her first kiss had been with Malik.

It had been okay, she supposed. Not unpleasant, necessarily. But she wouldn't hurry back. She ran her fingers across the copper in her pocket. A kiss for a carrot. How romantic. Although a carrot wasn't to be sniffed at ...

The King of the Cleve; how far she'd fallen. Once upon a time, she'd lived a short walk from the temple. Perhaps close to the handsome man she'd locked eyes with at the washerwoman's shop almost a full year before.

She'd thought of him often, wondering who he could be and why his return had been curious. She'd asked around as subtly as she could, trying to uncover some scrap to go on, but no one had known whom she'd meant, or if they did, they hadn't admitted it and had done a good job selling their lies.

She pushed off the door and set to work pulling the linens off the bed, then scrunched the fabric into a tight ball, barely resisting the temptation to hurl it through the window. The damn linens had caused her constant hunger and discomfort. She'd had it bad before the incident, or so she'd thought, but now she longed for that sorry life. If only she'd taken greater care ...

It was all the handsome man's fault. She'd been daydreaming about him when the street kids had run past. If she'd been paying attention, she would have easily sidestepped them and ducked out of the way of Malik's horse. If she'd done that, she'd still be in lukewarm baths and discarded crusts. Oh, the luxury.

His inquisitive blue eyes flashed across her mind once more, and her heart gave a thud. Tasha might not entertain the fantasy of Malik rescuing her from this life, but Ava never stopped dreaming. She dreamed of long-lost relatives and family friends and even the handsome man stepping through the door and whisking her away.

It was lunacy. Ava couldn't even remember her surname, and no one in the Cleve knew she'd come from a life on the other side of the temple—one of the conditions of Mrs. B's *charity*—and anyway, she didn't remember any relatives and she didn't know the names of her parents' friends. The handsome man was a folly, nothing more. He wouldn't even remember she existed, and she only thought of him so often because she had nothing else to occupy her thoughts.

But who was he? Where had he gone? Why had he come back? Why was a man like that picking up his mother's washing?

When no one in the Cleve had answered her questions, she'd snuck farther afield as often as she could. She'd travelled as far uptown as she dared, where the well-to-do had glared and pulled their children behind their skirts as though Ava might contaminate them with her dirty clothes, holey shoes, and sallow skin.

She'd found neither hide nor hair of the mysterious man, so eventually she'd stopped trying, using her precious free time to bathe in the icy water of the little-known stream instead.

But perhaps one day their paths would cross again, and then she'd get her answers, and perhaps she'd even make him pay for all the times she'd gone to bed hungry.

CHAPTER FIVE
MARIA

THE PAINTED PEACOCK MONOPOLIZED Maria for the whole ride to Alter's precious lake. The young members of each first family had been given little choice but to participate in the triffling, and Cane had made a beeline for Maria's side as soon as they'd crossed the moat. Elex was close behind, chatting easily with John, but despite her best efforts to involve herself in their conversation, Cane worked hard to keep her engaged.

When they reached the oval lake, however, she was granted a blissful reprieve, because they'd timed their arrival to perfectly coincide with the Mid-Sun Fall. A telltale clunk reverberated up through the lake, then spread out around them as they reined in their mounts, and a familiar prickle of awe and excitement shot down Maria's spine, spreading bumps across her skin.

Parkland surrounded the lake, the trade road cutting through on one side, leading to the Inner Circle beyond, and a handful of modest houses dotted the landscape, along with sheds, barns, and a few magnificent old trees that stood like proud monuments, branches sweeping low, begging to be climbed.

Past the parkland, where wildflowers swayed gently in the breeze, sat fields in one direction and woodland in another. It was cultivated yet haphazardly arranged, no straight lines to be found, trees interspersed among the crops, and sheds placed in what seemed to Maria to be bizarre locations.

The place went still, full of anticipation, no one making a sound. The birds' chatter faded into nothing, and even the humming insects paused. Maria's horse tensed against her thighs, and she sat quietly in the saddle, sliding a reassuring palm across her mount's shoulder.

She glanced back at Elex, whose gaze was aimed skyward, like most others in their party. Her attention snagged on his strong jaw, his relaxed shoulders, and the inquisitive quirk of his lips that looked almost like a smile. His eyes flicked to hers, and her chest constricted as their gazes held, his scrutiny open and disarming.

Her horse snorted, then stepped sideways, and then from the clouds above came a terrific rushing sound, followed by a thundering torrent of water plunging down into the lake with ferocious power.

A billowing cloud of mist flew up into the sun-drenched sky, prisms of light appearing in the air as the water frothed and boiled. It fell and fell, a liquid weight that none could ever hope to stand under and survive, terrifying and beautiful and life-sustaining. Their advantage over the Claws. Without this, they were nothing.

'Just the same as ours!' Cane shouted above the roar of water, looking to his brother for confirmation. Elex finally tore his eyes from Maria, but he ignored his brother.

'Just the same as the falls and lakes in all the Blades!' John shouted back. 'It is well-documented they are alike in every way.'

Cane nodded. 'Still, a magnificent sight to behold!' He looked far up into the sky, to where the tumble of water emerged from the clouds. There were always clouds shielding the top from view, and none knew what was up there. Some believed Water Gods dwelled there, but most believed the Goddess of Creation was the only power in their world. Maria was inclined to agree because the water in the Inner Circle had disappeared when the Goddess's home, Dromeda, had ceased to turn.

The fall stopped as abruptly as it had started, and a *thunk* sounded as the land began to gently turn once more, powered by Nicoli's turbines. Maria swept her eyes across where the water butted up against the edge of the lake, higher after the top-up from above, but not all the way to the top, where a historic line ringed the edge.

'Come,' said John, 'we shouldn't dawdle, or we won't be back by nightfall.'

'Then we should race,' said Maria, with a mischievous smile. The air was quickly heating in the warm sunshine, sweeping away the freshness from the fall and lifting the light floral sweetness of the wildflowers to their noses. It buoyed her soul, unleashing a childish exuberance, and she kicked her mount into a gallop before anyone had time to protest.

The servants accompanying them wouldn't have a hope of keeping up, their horses slow and weighed down by tents and picnic food, but Maria couldn't face another moment trapped in Cane's dull company—not when she felt so full of life—so she spurred her mount on.

'Maria!' John called after her, scolding and exasperated. 'Why are you always like this?'

Maria swiveled in her saddle and found John and Cane watching with matching chastising looks, but Elex was in hot pursuit, a delighted smile on his lips.

Maria whooped as a shot of adrenaline pumped into her blood, then turned her attention forward, urging her horse to run faster.

It was inevitable Elex would catch her, seeing as he'd already proven his horse was faster, so when the Outer Circle came into sight, she slowed to a canter and then a walk.

He reined in his mount as he came up alongside. 'You give up so easily?'

'I've achieved my goal.'

His lips quirked. 'Oh?'

'To escape your brother's company.'

He laughed, bold and bright, and Maria couldn't help but join him as they stepped over the cobbled line onto the Outer Circle.

'You thought my goal was to be alone with you?' she teased.

'A man can hope.' They headed to the other side of the road, to where an Alterwood bridge stretched far into the distance across the Inner Circle, linking the land of Celestl to Dromeda, the island in the middle of their world. Or at least, it had been an island before all the water had disappeared.

They stopped beside the makeshift shrines that always appeared near Toll Day, and Elex dismounted, swinging his leg over the front of the saddle and sliding down to land lithely on his feet. He didn't bother holding his horse, apparently confident the beast wouldn't wander off.

'Do the people make shrines in your lands, too?' Maria asked, dismounting and pulling the reins forward over her horse's ears; her mare wasn't nearly so well-behaved as his stallion. She looked down at the woven baskets filled with brightly colored flowers, tiny figurines, and coils of metal. Eventually, they would be carried across the bridge and left outside the Toll

Gate for the Goddess, but she never took in her gifts, even before Dromeda had stopped spinning.

'Yes, they do,' he confirmed, 'and we have those.' He pointed to the brass looking glasses, two on each side of the path leading to the bridge.

He swung one up, positioning the long lens to face down the bridge, and hunched to peer through it.

Maria slipped her arm through her reins, then used the second glass to look as well. Everything seemed normal, the contents of last year's shrines strewn in front of the circular gate made of Alterwood, her family's wand of power in its usual place above, the tip facing the sky, nothing holding it aloft but magic.

'It's different,' he said.

'What is?' she asked, scanning again for anything out of the ordinary.

'The color of your wand is different to ours, and your gate. Ours are darker.'

'Well, of course they are!'

He pulled his eye from the glass and looked expectantly at her.

'Your gate and wand are made from the roots of an Oshe tree. Ours are made from Alterwood.'

'No, they're not,' he said, frowning hard.

'Yes, they are! Why would you think otherwise?'

'I was taught the gates were created equal. That they are precisely the same.'

'I suppose that explains some of Oshe's arrogance if you think all gates are made from Oshewood.'

He scowled, although he was more thoughtful than angry.

'You've never been to another bridge?' she asked.

'Spruce and Laurow don't let just anyone use their looking glasses. Not like here or in my homeland.'

'I've barely ever left Alter, so I wouldn't know,' she said bitterly. Her brothers had been allowed to attend the university in Spruce—one of the few ways the ruling families had worked together during the war—but not her or Pixy.

'Aside from your trespassing in Arow Claw?'

'Come on,' she said, tugging at his arm, 'the others are close.' And she wasn't in the mood for serious things.

He followed without protest, tying his horse next to hers, then following her down the perilous descent into the garden of the Inner Circle. Few routes down existed, and most were, if not treacherous, then not exactly safe, but Maria moved on swift, confident feet, and Elex followed with easy movements of his own.

'Hey!' John called out, just as they reached the bottom of the fifty-foot descent. 'Wait for us!'

'Will do!' Maria shouted back, but one glance at Elex said he was game, and they took off together into the undergrowth.

'Maria!' John bellowed. 'Come back!'

They didn't. They wove through the trees, laughing as they ran, not slowing until they came to a clearing filled with tiny, delicate flowers. The ground was a riot of pink and purple, yellow and red, but they largely ignored the beauty, instead making for the ring of blue fungus growing around the base of a tree on the far side.

'Back off,' Maria said with mock menace. 'I saw it first.'

'Make me,' he laughed, grabbing her arms and pulling her back before releasing her and sprinting for the tree.

'Elex!' she shouted. 'You beast!'

'I do have a reputation to uphold,' he called over his shoulder.

He dove for the ground and picked up a flat stone because in their haste to get away, they'd forfeited the trowels and baskets the servants had brought for this purpose.

Maria rootled around in the undergrowth for her own digging imple- ment, but by the time she'd found one, Elex was triumphantly holding his prize aloft. The triffle was a rough, irregular black ball that fit neatly in his palm. It was a beauty, both in size and quality, which Maria knew because she could smell the rich, earthy scent from where she stood a few paces away.

The fungus around the tree changed from a bluish green to brown, and Maria scowled because that meant in this patch, there were no more triffles to be found.

'Oh, don't look like that, my dear,' said Elex, closing the distance between them with a couple of long, easy strides.

'Don't look like what?'

He gave her an indulgent smile, holding out his hand in offering, the triffle in his palm.

'What are you doing?' The words were high-pitched and breathy, out of her mouth without thought. One didn't just *give* triffles away. It was a matter of pride, of principle, and on a hunt like this, no one wanted to return home empty-handed.

'Offering my betrothed a gift,' he said, and for a moment, Maria thought she saw something uncertain flash across his features. 'Assuming you'll still have me after I snatched this from under your nose.'

Maria looked at it for several long beats, and a strange emotion swelled in her chest. No one had ever given her a triffle before. No one had ever given her anything, really, aside from the odd thoughtless knickknack on her birthday, and she hadn't even received one of those in years.

Not that she needed anyone to give her gifts. Since she'd happened upon the disused still room built into the cliff below her home, she'd been able to trade for anything she needed. Well, after some near-disastrous experimentation and many trips to the library.

'Don't tell me I've rendered you speechless?' Elex gently teased.

'No,' Maria said quickly. 'It's just ...' But what was it, exactly? Something about this situation made her deeply uncomfortable. Perhaps because the idea of receiving without giving in return was foreign? Or maybe he did expect something in return ... Yes, that was it. 'I'm not sure about the specifics of this trade, that's all.'

Elex's eyebrows pinched. He reached a slow hand towards her face, then twirled a stray lock of hair around his finger. 'This isn't a trade.' He tugged gently. 'It's a gift.'

'Is there a difference?'

'Of course!' he said through a laugh, brushing the hair behind her ear, then dropping his hand. 'Maria, I don't expect anything in return.' He pressed the triffle into her palm and wrapped her fingers around it, holding fast as he met her gaze.

'Nothing at all? Because I have some very rare—'

'Don't think I've missed your covert trades. Believe me when I say I want to hear more about them, but not everything is a barter. *This* isn't.' He squeezed her fingers. 'This is a gift freely given.'

'Why?' In Maria's experience, there were few occasions when generosity was as selfless as he purported his to be.

He exhaled a chuckle. 'Because we are to be wed and I am relieved—ecstatic even—to find my future wife is intelligent and canny as well as beautiful.'

Maria rolled her eyes. 'You think if you speak pretty words, you'll wrap me around your finger, is that it?'

'No!' He dropped her hand and stepped back. 'Maria!'

She sent him a quizzical look, all at sea.

He took a long breath, then tried again. 'I know my reputation paints me a certain way.'

'As a brutish, selfish, half-time drunk?'

He raked a hand through his hair. 'I needed for my father not to see me as a threat but also not as someone to bully. It's different in Oshe, not like it is here.'

Her forehead pinched. 'Oh?'

'Alter seems ... peaceful, like no one questions Danit's rule.'

'Because they don't.'

'Well, Oshe is not the same.'

'You fight among yourselves?' *Goddess* ... what was she heading into?

'Yes. My father is a tyrant,' he said, as though that fact should be self-evident, 'although so is your uncle, no matter how well he hides it behind Alter's orderly veneer and courtly ways.'

He said the words with no malice, as though they were so obvious no one could dispute them, but she did dispute them, something visceral pulling tight in her gut. 'He's not that bad!' she said defensively. She disliked Danit, and she especially hated the way he treated the Claws, but the people of Alter were prosperous and happy, and whether she liked it or not, that was his doing, too.

Maria had grown up with the freedom to roam across a Blade where her safety was guaranteed, he'd allowed her use of the still room and to push the boundaries of womanly dress codes, and he was her uncle—her dead father's brother—which meant something, even when he made her rage. Her life could have been a great deal worse—she was under no illusions about that—and she was grateful for what Danit allowed her to have, even if she often wanted to push him off a cliff.

'Yes, he is that bad,' Elex said gently.

'So you would have us fight each other like you do?' she asked, her tone barbed. She was sick of all the fighting, and families should stick together. Hers was a long way from perfect, and she dearly wished Hale would return—the only one who brought a fond smile to her lips when she thought of him—but first families weren't built on love and niceties. They were built on duty and sacrifice and cold, hard practicality. She'd thought Elex understood that. It was the very reason for their marriage, for Goddess's sake!

'I don't want fighting,' he said evenly, 'but if it meant others could lead us, it would likely be worth the cost.'

'Others like you? Because you would be so different ...'

'I would,' he snapped. 'My reputation is not who I am. I want to change things, and I had hoped you might want that too.'

His words scored a direct hit on her heart because she was loyal to her family, but she also wanted change. She wanted the Claws to be the Blades' equals, and for Nicoli to be allowed to dine with her family, and for everyone in Celestl to have enough. She closed her eyes for a beat, taking a moment to let the pain subside. 'How?' she breathed. Even if she agreed that new leaders were the answer—which she didn't—it was an impossible task. The likes of Barron and Danit had armies, money, water ... how could anyone even begin to fight them? Not to mention, changing their leaders could never be peaceful, could never be achieved without violence and death.

'Overthrowing them is the only way.' He watched her carefully, hopeful but resolute.

She puffed out disbelieving laugh. 'They control everything!'

'They don't control me. And when you marry me, they won't control you, either.' He stepped closer, reaching for her.

She stepped back. 'No. You will.'

He froze. 'No,' he said with surprising force, shaking his head. 'I make that promise now.'

Maria scoffed. 'Promises are easily broken.'

'Yours may be, but mine are not.' He studied her, something akin to disappointment taking hold of his features, and she turned away, facing the trees, hiding.

Who was this man, whose words were so at odds with everything she'd heard of him? Or maybe her uncle was right, and he was playing with her like he might a fragile child's toy, maneuvering her into his palm, poised to crush her. But she wanted desperately to believe him. To believe he wouldn't use her as a pawn, that she would be free to do as she pleased when they wed. That she would no longer answer to anyone, never be forced to do another's bidding again.

She turned slowly back to face him, taking him in anew. Still tall and devilishly good-looking, with an easy, balanced stance and broad shoulders most women would swoon over. Who was she kidding—that *she* was swooning over.

She tried to look past his shell. To look deeper. What did he want? What was his game? Could she trust him?

'I suppose I've been conditioned to think of my marriage as a political alliance only. A trade,' she said eventually.

'It is, but it can be more,' he said softly. 'It can include gifts, for example. That is common.'

'Is it?' She was still skeptical. Her father had never given her mother gifts. At least, not ones she'd known about.

'Yes! Especially when a man is to wed a woman he has only just met, and by some great miracle, likes very much.'

Maria softened despite herself. 'I suppose you're right. It could be worse.'

He exhaled a laugh. 'I believe we'll make good partners, Maria, but only if we're honest with each other. Truly honest, open, vulnerable ...' He gave her a pointed look, and she averted her gaze. 'I don't know why you're so suspicious of a simple gift,' he murmured, moving closer, 'but please trust that is all it is.'

'And here I was thinking you were hoping to trade it for a kiss ...'

'Why did you do that?' he said gently, halting his approach.

'Do what?'

'Deflect.'

'I ...' She looked from one of his eyes to the other, not sure what to say. He wanted truth ... the same as she'd asked from him. Why was that such a challenge? 'So you don't want to kiss me?'

'Maria ...'

'This is hard for me.' She folded her arms across her chest, her insides squirming uncomfortably. She closed her eyes and paused a beat, collecting herself. 'My whole life, I've trusted no one, not all the way, not a single soul. And after knowing you for less than a day, you want my deepest truths?'

'You don't trust your mother? Your siblings?'

'No. I mean, I mostly trust them, but they have their own goals, their own tasks set by my uncle. That will always come above their loyalty to me, and rightly so.'

'It will not be that way between us,' he said, shaking his head. 'At least, that is not how I want it to be. I want to trust you all the way and for you to do the same with me. To feel like you are safe to do so.'

Maria wanted to believe him, to believe anything could be so pure and simple, but it went against everything she'd ever known, and her gut screamed at her to run. To lie. To keep her drawbridge firmly up. She cringed. This was what she'd asked for, *wanted*, but his display of weakness tied her insides in awkward knots.

But a small voice railed against that, whispering that maybe it wasn't weakness. Because if they could truly trust one another, it would lead to greater strength, wouldn't it? And hadn't she asked for exactly that? To be his partner? His teammate?

But to trust him meant putting her fate in his hands, exposing her vulnerabilities, taking a leap of faith. And there was no way of knowing whether he would catch her or if she would plummet to a bloody death.

'I'm sorry,' said Elex, pulling away. He drew in a deep breath and ran his hand through his hair. 'I've approached this all wrong.' He showed her his back for several tortuous beats, and then turned slowly, his features in a calm, understanding arrangement. 'Just know I believe you worthy of my trust—I've never been so sure of anything—and I want to earn yours, but I understand it will take time.'

No man Maria knew spoke this way. They laughed and made ribald jokes and tried to talk every woman they came across into bed. Or they were like Nicoli, reserved and serious and intense. But never had she met a man so forthright. So open. So willing to offer her his jugular. Not that she knew many men, and most she did were either servants, her siblings, or men who wanted something from her through trade. But her skin prickled with discomfort all the same.

This was not what she'd expected from the Black Prince. She'd thought she would have to convince him to treat her as his equal over many months. Years, even. She'd expected to need to prove herself time and again for even the smallest fragment of his respect. That she'd have to claw her way into his confidence.

'Would it make you more comfortable if I tried to steal that kiss?' said Elex, tipping his head and somehow transforming in the space of a heart-beat into the self-assured cad his reputation claimed him to be, mischief shining bright in his eyes.

Her shoulders relaxed, and she exhaled the breath she'd been holding. She cocked an eyebrow. 'What would your parents think of me if I let you do that?'

'My father has three wives ... and have you seen Erica?'

'So he's more likely to encourage you to steal my virtue before our wedding night than protect it?'

His eyes widened a fraction. 'You have virtue left to steal?'

Maria's face flamed, and Elex looked immediately regretful.

'Why would you think otherwise? I am not the kind of woman to ... well, I take my duties seriously, even if the men in the first families do not have the same expectations placed upon them. Your sister is not expected to—'

'My sister makes a point of sleeping with at least a third of the men she meets.'

Maria recoiled. 'Oh.'

'You judge her for that?'

'No. I just ... You must think me—'

'It's just sex, Maria,' he said, suddenly close. 'Although some make it out to be some momentous occasion for young women, it is little more than an animal instinct.'

She nodded, her face burning with embarrassment as she tried to flee the cage of his eyes, not sure how they'd reached such dangerous territory.

But he didn't let her escape. He slid a hand to her neck and pulled her back to him. 'I expect you'll get the hang of it with ease.'

The fire spread to her chest, then her belly, as his eyes dipped to her lips, and suddenly he was so close, all-consuming, invading even the air she breathed.

He lowered his face towards her, so close her lips tingled with anticipation, aching to be kissed, her eyes fluttering closed. But he slid sideways, and disappointment stabbed through her, replaced a heartbeat later with raw desire as he grazed the rough skin of his cheek against hers, making her nipples tighten. And then he slid his nose down the curve of her neck and planted a kiss in the hollow of her collarbone, and she exhaled loudly, swaying against him as her hand flew to his hair. She tipped her head back, baring her neck, begging for more, and he nipped her gently, sending a pulsing shockwave to her core.

He pulled back, looking down at her with large black pupils, but he didn't let her go. 'Just as I suspected,' he said, the deep timbre of his voice sending a shiver of pleasure down her spine. He slid a hand across her lower back, the other digging into her hair, holding her for long moments.

Maria pushed her hands as far as she could up under his doublet, stroking her fingers over the hard ridges and valleys of his back through his shirt, nearly weeping at the intimacy ... the warmth. It was a strange reaction, probably, but she'd never been held and her body sucked up the contact like a person starved. She pressed her chest more firmly to his, needing pressure right in the center, and something within her released so that her next exhale came out like a breathy whimper, sensations rolling through her she'd never felt before.

When had she last had prolonged physical contact at all?

Her mother was caring in her own way, but she was not maternal and did not encourage physical affection. Her older brother, Hale, had certainly not been a hugger, and John and Maria had a rivalry that led to naught between them but tit-for-tat transactions. Her sister, Pixy, was a little younger and possessed a kind of impish beauty and potent, magnetic energy that inspired people to write songs in her name. It had made her aloof. Not in a snooty way but for her own protection, and she'd never really cared for people in general. Then there was Danit, who wouldn't know affection if it slapped him in the face.

Maria had never had a consistent nurse or teacher. She was close with her servants, and they were nothing if not loyal, but touching them in any way was not appropriate. So the closest thing she'd had to someone she could hug was Nicoli, although they'd never actually shared more than a brief embrace because that would have stretched the line of friendship they'd kept carefully in place.

'We should return to the others,' Maria said eventually, her fingers tracing back and forth across his spine. She didn't want to go—she couldn't imagine ever tiring of him being wrapped around her—but every part of her itched for more, her body trying to press against him in a way she didn't truly understand. If she didn't put distance between them, there was no telling what she might encourage him to do, and at some point, the others would come looking.

He released her with a kiss to her temple, and cold rushed in to steal the warmth he'd left behind. She made to move away because she wanted nothing more than to return to his arms, her lips still tingling for the kiss they'd never felt, her chest strangely tight. He caught her hand, and she looked up, her pulse thudding loudly in her ears.

'You should fix your hair before we return,' he said with a cocky smile.

'Oh,' she said shyly. He released her hand and tidied his own short locks, then tucked his shirt more firmly into his breeches, Maria biting her lip as she watched him.

She was lucky beyond measure that she was to marry this man; it could have been so different. She could have been betrothed to the painted peacock, the idea of doing this with him so repulsive it made her face scrunch.

'Hey,' said Elex, catching her fingers when she'd finished poking long stray wisps of hair back into her bun, 'everything okay?'

'I was just thinking how lucky I am to be betrothed to you and not your brother. The idea of him is nowhere near so pleasant.'

His lips split into a satisfied smile as he rubbed a slow circle across the pulse at her wrist. 'Pleasant will do for now,' he said, cupping her face with his free hand, then tracing her bottom lip with his thumb, 'but we can do so much better in time.'

Chapter Six
Ava

It was several weeks before Malik came again, and Ava's heart lurched and her stomach sank when he entered the tavern. Strange that she could be both overjoyed and deeply dismayed at the mere sight of him.

They locked eyes for a second, and then Malik headed for the stairs. He'd go to the usual room, one of the nicer ones few had the coin for—not that he ever paid. Ava finished stacking her tray of clean tankards behind the bar, then headed to the kitchen to find Tasha.

It was a quiet morning, less than a handful of customers out front, and Tasha sat at the tired wooden table with Cook. The smell of apple pie wafted around them, making Ava's stomach clench and her mouth water. Her eyes homed in on the apple peelings they were rolling into roses then tossing in their mouths. They wouldn't usually have dared, but Mrs. B was out, and with so few customers, they had little else to do.

'Catch,' said Tasha, throwing a rose of apple peel at Ava. She dropped her empty tray, which clattered as it hit the flagstones, caught the apple, and gobbled it down before anyone could snatch it away. Her jaw hurt as the juice hit her tongue, and she looked hopefully at Tasha, silently begging for more.

'No,' said Cook, standing and scooping the remaining peelings into a bowl. 'Mrs. B will have my hide if she finds out.'

Ava exhaled a sigh. 'Do you think she'll ever forgive me?'

'No,' said the short, grey-haired man.

'Unlikely,' agreed Tasha, with her trademark giggle.

At moments like these, Ava found it hard to like Tasha. If Ava told Mrs. B what Tasha did with Malik, she'd be thrown out, no question. Yet still Tasha delighted in mean acts like that giggle, presumably to remind Ava who was above whom in the pecking order. Ava didn't need reminding. She knew only too well she was at the bottom of the food chain.

She rubbed the copper in her pocket, the one Malik had given her, and told herself that one day she would get out of there and leave everyone who'd treated her cruelly to rot in the stinking Cleve. She didn't yet know how she'd do it, but her daydreams had changed since the disgusting kiss with Malik. She no longer dreamed that someone would rescue her, for she knew deep in her heart the idea was a childish fancy. Instead, she would watch and learn and lie in wait. For one day, an opportunity to leave her life in the Cleve behind would arise, and when it did, she would be ready.

'Everything okay?' said Tasha, interrupting Ava's thoughts. She'd been staring at the table with unseeing eyes. 'The other tray's ready to go out.'

'Can you help me with something first?' Ava flicked her eyes to the ceiling.

'Oh ... yeah ... 'course.' Tasha bustled out of the kitchen, smoothing her hair and straightening her skirts. She unhooked a couple of buttons and tugged down her dress, accentuating the swell of her cleavage so it was impossible not to look at it.

Ava hurried up the stairs after her. Tasha and Malik were already kissing—in the corridor where anyone could discover them—by the time Ava made it to the third floor, one level below the attic, where the staff slept. Well, all except for Ava, who'd been banished to the basement with the beer barrels.

Ava took a long inhale, then settled herself on the floor beside the bedroom door. It was clean enough and free of splinters, and she wouldn't be there long. Tasha giggled as she led Malik by the hand through the open door, and Malik dropped a bread roll in Ava's lap. She snatched it up and held it to her nose, closing her eyes as she savored the fresh, homely scent.

'You can't sit,' Malik sneered. 'If anyone finds you, they'll know exactly what we're up to ... On yer feet.'

Ava stood, inwardly rolling her eyes, holding the roll slightly behind her, protecting her prize, but Malik had already moved on.

Ava sighed as she leaned against the wall, sinking her teeth into the delicious bread, but before she'd had even a moment to appreciate the flavors rolling across her tongue, light, running footsteps sounded on the wooden stairs.

She froze, her whole body suddenly shaky, then rapped sharply on the door three times—the agreed signal.

'Can I help you?' she called, as the intruder's profile came into view, a man stepping onto the landing below, the bread hidden behind her back once more. But when the man looked up at her, any further words shriveled and died in her throat.

He paused, and their eyes locked as they had that day at Mrs. Kelly's shop. Deep blue, with the barest hint of rippling silver.

He'd filled out in the last year and seemed taller, too, his new leather coat and pristine clothes even more at home on this updated body than the almost identical outfit he'd worn the last time she'd set eyes on him. Ava, on the other hand, wore the same dress she had back then, only with more patches. She'd had to scrounge scraps of fabric to sew around the bottom, too, meaning it still fell to her knees, even though she'd grown several inches.

The man paused when he saw her, his assured movements losing some of their purpose, but he checked only briefly, then continued up the stairs.

His destination was clear—the bedroom—and Ava panicked, shooting out a hand and grabbing his arm, pulling him to a stop. He went still, as though shocked she dared touch him, then looked purposefully down at her scrawny fingers. She quickly released him but stepped in front of the door, blocking his way with squared shoulders.

'You can't go in there,' she said, ensuring her voice was loud enough for Malik and Tasha to hear. At least they'd know she'd done her job, that she'd put up a fight.

The unmistakable scrape of a window rolling open came through the door, and the sound seemed to galvanize the man before her. He pushed her, trying to force her aside, but she braced herself, pushing back, at least until one of his shoves sent her bread flying out of her hand to the floor.

'No!' she shouted, immediately abandoning the scuffle to retrieve the precious food. She stuffed it into her pocket, and by the time she'd straightened, the man was hauling Malik back through the open window. Malik had one leg in, one out, and he kicked and shouted, trying to get free, but

when he saw the man's face, he paled, then threw himself to his knees and
groveled.

What the Gods' goodness? The handsome stranger couldn't be more than
twenty, and Malik was the King of the Cleve. Who was he, and why did he
invoke such terror?

'Please,' said Malik. '*Please*. Whatever you want. I'll give you anything.
Please don't take me to him.'

'It's not him you should worry about,' said the man, hauling Malik to
his feet. 'At least not this day.'

Malik seemed torn between complying and fighting, but in the end, he
did little more than shake his shoulders a few half-hearted times to try and
free himself from the man's iron grip.

Tasha sobbed quietly on the bed, not moving a muscle as he hauled her
meal ticket away, but Ava followed them, curiosity moving her feet without
the need for conscious thought.

'Who are you?' asked Ava, following them down the stairs.

The man stopped on the landing and turned to face her. 'It doesn't
matter who I am.'

'It matters to me ... and to him,' she said, pointing to Malik.

The man started moving again, and Ava followed all the way to the
bottom, until he stopped abruptly and shoved Malik face first against the
wall just outside the taproom. He held Malik at arm's length and pivoted
to face Ava, who, standing on the step above, looked him directly in the
eye.

'Do not follow us,' he said quietly, his face close to hers. 'My father is not
a nice man. Believe me when I say you do not want to meet him.'

'But ...'

'Ignore my advice, and I won't be able to help you.'

'Who are you?' she whispered, her head spinning, trying to make sense
of what in the name of the Gods was going on. 'Why do you want Malik?'

His eyes flicked to Malik, then back to her. 'Take my advice,' he said,
then pulled his captive off the wall, but she grabbed his arm.

'What's your name?' she begged.

He shrugged her off and kept moving.

'Please,' she hissed. 'Tell me something!'

He turned his eyes to the door, checking for some threat, but the tap room was virtually empty, and no one looked their way, most of them sleeping, heads hunched over their arms.

The man exhaled a frustrated breath. 'I will tell you my name if you promise not to follow.'

She nodded without hesitation. She hadn't been planning to follow him anyway, so it was an easy deal to make. He shook his head, as though not quite believing he was going to tell her, then leaned in so close there was barely any air between them. He smelled clean, like soap and expensive plants she could have named if she hadn't been torn from the life she'd been born to.

She undoubtedly smelled awful—it had been more than a week since she'd bathed—but then he breathed, 'My name is Kush,' and everything aside from that one word fled her mind.

'Kush,' she whispered, and it was as though the name were a spell, causing their eyes to fuse for a long moment.

'Go and find what's taking him so long,' said a loud, icy voice from beyond the open tavern door.

'Do not follow, Ava,' Kush said, pushing Malik ahead.

'A promise is a promise.'

A short, squat, barrel-chested man stepped inside. He was at least double Kush's age and had the confidence of someone no one trifled with. Ava shied back into the shadows.

'Everything okay?' he demanded, scanning the tap room with calculating eyes.

'Fine,' said Kush, pushing a now sobbing Malik through the door. 'Let's get this over with.'

As soon as they were through, Ava raced up the stairs. It took three attempts to find an unoccupied bedroom at the front of the tavern, but when she did, she flew to the window, hiding behind the heavy drapes as she scanned the street below.

They'd moved a little way up the road so they stood outside Malik's den, his muscle nowhere to be seen. Ava studied the group, Malik prostrated on the ground before a man dressed in an outfit so fine Ava's breath caught in her throat. Gold glinted from the cord edging the man's moss green cape, his boots even finer and lighter in color than Kush's, leather gloves covering his fingers. Energy seemed to radiate from him, so much so he practically glowed, his white-blond hair reflecting the light along with his creamy, unblemished skin. Could he really be Kush's father?

The men spoke for a moment, ignoring Malik, and then the man in the green cape swiped a short cane of twisted wood out from under his arm, pointing it at Kush, the posture promising violence. Ava held her breath.

Kush seemed tense, his jaw locked, shoulders stiff, and the squat man was watching him with judgement dripping from his pores. The thug smiled as Kush stepped over Malik, placing a foot on either side of his prostrated form. Malik screamed, groveling to both Kush and his father.

Kush gave a little shake of his head, then shoved his hand into his coat and held it there for a beat before pulling out a knife. Once the blade was in his hand, he didn't hesitate, reaching down and grabbing Malik's hair, pulling his head back and slitting his throat in a single movement.

Ava gasped, her hand flying to her mouth as she watched blood pour from Malik's neck, spilling across the stained cobbles and merging with the filth. Kush released him, letting him fall like an inconsequential sack to the ground, then walked away, refusing to meet the eyes of the other men. His father gave the squat man a triumphant smile, raising his eyebrows and tilting his head as though some bet had just been won. The man nodded grudgingly, seeming disappointed. Then they followed Kush, leaving Malik's lifeless body behind.

Chapter Seven
Maria

Maria held her triffle high as she and Elex re-joined the others.

'You found one already?' said John, scowling hard.

'And I pipped dear Elex to the post,' she said, throwing Elex a look that dared him to contradict her.

'Much to my chagrin,' he agreed.

'She cheats,' said John. 'That is undoubtedly the reason. How did she do it?'

'Oh, stop being such a lamentable louse,' said Maria, folding her legs beneath her and sitting on the blanket next to John. 'Have you even been hunting?'

'No! As is proper, I offered our guest refreshment first.'

'And after the ride, and that terrible descent, I was glad of a glass of delicious sparkling rosehip,' said the painted peacock, holding up a crystal tumbler filled with light pink liquid.

'It is very delicious,' Maria agreed, accepting a glass from a servant.

'It's impolite for *you* to say so,' said John, rolling his eyes.

Maria raised her glass in salute, a smirk on her lips.

'Why?' asked Elex, unfastening his cloak and pulling it from his shoulders.

'Because it's from a long-lost recipe I discovered in my still room.'

'Your still room?' Elex sat next to Maria, a little closer than propriety allowed, close enough that if she leaned in, she could brush her shoulder against his arm.

'My sister concocts all kinds of lotions and potions and goodness knows what else,' said John. 'It becomes tiresome after a while.' He eyed Maria and Elex's proximity, and his features turned suspicious. 'You two are getting along well ...'

'Mmm,' Maria replied tartly, warning him to move on.

'Maybe she drugged you with a love potion.'

'John!' said Maria, feeling her face flush. 'I do not make potions. I make oils, predominantly.'

'And I knew from our very first conversation that our match was a good one,' said Elex. 'So unless you think she slipped me something the second I met her, I'll trust my own judgement.'

Maria's cheeks flamed harder at that, and she took a long sip of her drink. Alas, when she finished, all eyes were still on her.

'I'm sure you're hoping for similar comradery with your betrothed,' Maria said to John, her tone perhaps more hostile than strictly necessary, but her brother had a special way of getting under her skin. 'Are you not?'

'Of course, in an ideal world. But it matters little, really.'

He shrugged with nonchalance, and Maria scoffed at his bravado. 'If you say so.'

'When does she arrive?' asked Cane.

'Soon,' said John. 'Tomorrow, in time for the ball. Have you met her? You stayed with the Laurows on your way here, did you not?'

'We did,' confirmed Cane, 'and we met her. Sophie ... I think that's her name?' John nodded. 'She seemed a pliant, meek thing. Tall, russet hair, ample curves ... busty.'

'Brother!' said Elex.

'Sounds quite wonderful to me,' said John with a broad smile. 'What about your sister? Is she worried about her engagement?'

Elex sniggered. 'Our sister can hold her own.'

Maria looked down at her hands, remembering what Elex had said about his sister's carnal pursuits. Of course a woman like that wouldn't be worried.

'Urgh,' said Cane, scowling with distaste. 'You should be marrying me.' He looked from Elex to Maria, who balked as his words sank in. 'My brother is a brute, and I feel quite left out of all the fun.'

'Well, Brother,' said Elex, sitting up straighter, leaning in a little closer, 'Maria and I are betrothed, and you are betrothed to the daughter of our father's closest ally. As I recall, you were adamant your existing match was of the utmost importance to the stability of Oshe Blade.'

'And I see now I was wrong,' said Cane, throwing up his hands, 'because the stability of Celestl is more important. It would send a stronger message if the first son of Oshe were to marry the first daughter of Alter.'

'But I am already betrothed to your brother,' said Maria firmly.

'A minor detail.'

'You really don't want her,' said John. 'She's a handful. Willful and argumentative. She backchats like you would not believe ...'

'Still,' said Cane, puffing up his chest, 'I will raise the matter with Father.'

Maria's eyes found Elex's in a silent plea, and she located something bolstering in the warm brown depths—she wasn't sure what, exactly, but some assurance he would deal with it. Her shoulders came down a notch because she trusted that he would, that he was capable and determined enough to do whatever had to be done. Not that it entirely placated the uneasy feeling in her stomach ... but even though she didn't yet trust Elex entirely, she would never trust the painted peacock at all.

Elex shifted even closer to Maria so his torso was slightly behind hers, his legs so close they almost brushed her hip, and draped his cloak around her shoulders. 'You look cold, my dear,' he said, marking his territory.

He propped his arm across the space behind her, and Maria was surprised to find her face didn't flush, her back didn't snap ramrod straight, and her guts didn't squirm ... at least, not in a bad way. In fact, she found she rather liked it, enveloped in his warmth and scent, his formidable strength at her back.

She chanced a glance up at him when the others were distracted with holding out their glasses for more sparkling rosehip, and she found him looking down at her, his chest only a hair's breadth away. She couldn't fight the smile that tugged at her lips at his quiet monitoring, and she nudged his chest with her shoulder, touching him feeling oddly natural. He was all solid muscle and didn't move an inch, but something settled between them in that moment. Something that made her feel as though they might truly be a team.

They lazed on the blanket for longer than they should, seeing as they were supposed to be hunting for triffles. Most of the servants left them to go on searches of their own, no doubt terrified of punishment if there weren't enough for Toll Day. Although, now it was to be called *Blade Day*, should triffles still be part of the fun? They were a gift from the Goddess, after all ...

'It's strange to think this whole place was once under water,' said John, lying back and looking up at the near sheer-sided cliff they'd clambered down. 'It drained three hundred years ago, but you can still see the water line near the top.'

Maria looked upward, finding the line for herself. 'Do you think the water will ever return?' she asked no one in particular.

'No,' said John. 'And our uncle is quite certain it will not.'

'Do you?' Maria asked Elex.

He considered the question, but Cane answered before Elex could. 'Oshe Blade believes it will return when mighty Dromeda spins once more.'

Maria turned her eyes to the center of the Inner Circle, where Dromeda loomed large, the high walls of the Goddess's home visible atop the enormous column of rock that rose from the ground. It was impossible to tell what was behind those walls because they were solid stone all the way around, the only openings the Toll Gates, which hadn't admitted a soul for three hundred years. Even when they had, it had been impossible to see anything beyond, and none of the sacrifices had ever returned to tell their tale.

'You think it will spin again?' said Maria, looking at the fortress for the thousandth time, searching for some tiny clue.

'We have books and records in Oshe that go back to the dawn of time,' said Cane. 'They speak of the Goddess in such reverent tones, it's hard to imagine she would abandon us entirely.'

'Unless she's dead,' said Elex.

'Killed by some slighted god of war,' added Cane.

Of course he would think that, because all that mattered to men like him was brute power.

'What do you think?' Elex asked.

'Like *she* knows anything,' said John.

Maria ignored her brother and focused on Elex, who appeared genuinely interested in her answer.

She shrugged because, of course, no one knew. 'But how would we get triffles if the Goddess re-filled this place with water?' she said, doing her best impression of the stupid air-head John made her out to be.

Elex's mouth split into a sly smile, and Maria's insides contracted at the sight, his face somehow even more handsome than before.

'Oh, people would dive,' said Cane, 'like they used to. We had many in Oshe who were quite excellent at it. We have poems and ballads, even a play dedicated to their exploits.'

'As do we,' said John. He pinned Maria with a glare because he'd discerned what Cane had failed to—that Maria had made a joke at his expense and Elex had sided with her.

Cane frowned, apparently catching on, but Maria had no time—and very little inclination—to continue their conversation. She forced herself to straighten, reluctantly pulling away from Elex's warmth. 'We should hunt! We can't let the servants take all the glory.'

'You already have a prize triffle,' said Elex, cocking an eyebrow.

'You're right. Maybe I'll lie here and doze while the rest of you search in vain for a triffle half as glorious as mine.'

'Maria!' said John. 'One shouldn't gloat.'

'Maybe we should make it interesting ... the last to return with a triffle must complete a forfeit of my choosing?' she said with a devilish smile.

'No,' said John. 'Not after last time.'

'Then for bragging rights,' said Cane, getting to his feet. 'Fear not, dear Maria, I will return before my brother.'

Elex rose, dusting himself off as he watched John and Cane disappear into the trees.

'Do you want your cloak?' Maria asked, hoping very much he didn't.

'Keep it so when my brother returns, the first thing he sees is that you belong to me.'

Maria's chest constricted with giddy delight, although a tiny pocket of space somewhere near her armpit railed against the idea of belonging to anyone. But she'd never had a suitor, let alone two, and although she had less than no interest in Cane, she could admit it was nice to be desired, to be fought over as though she were worth something.

Although, she shouldn't get carried away; it wasn't her they were after but the alliance her hand would buy them, at least in Cane's case. Elex wanted her to believe his motives were pure, but were anyone's motives ever that?

Elex reached the tree line, and she smiled at him when he glanced back, warmth radiating through her blood. She forced herself to wait five full minutes, giving him time to move farther into the woods, then got to her feet and hurried to the ascent up the cliff, her heart beating wildly in her chest.

She had hardly any time, but if she got to the border with Alter, there was a tavern nearby whose landlady often traded with Maria for oils. Perhaps she would take Danit's message to Nicoli. And it was close to the Outer Circle, so perhaps she'd make it in and out before Gabriele's spies knew she was there. The chance was small and apprehension sat heavy in her stomach, but what choice did she have?

She'd taken only a single step up the steep scramble to the top when a cough sounded from behind. She jumped nearly out of her skin, spinning to face the threat as she returned to the ground. She couldn't hide the guilty expression that immediately painted itself across her face when she found Elex's unimpressed form leaning against a nearby tree.

'I'll be back shortly,' said Maria, indignantly. She didn't answer to this man ... not yet, anyway.

'Where are you going?'

'What difference does it make?'

'You want us to be partners ...'

'And you said yourself, trust takes time.' Her words were harsh because she was furious at being so easily discovered. For years she'd slipped away to make trades or gather secrets and she'd never been caught, not once, yet Elex had been here a day and already he'd done so. 'And you obviously don't trust me either, or you wouldn't have followed me.'

His face shuttered, and she instantly regretted her words. 'I want to keep you safe,' he said. 'I heard what that woman in Arow said. I don't know what happened, but it must have been something bad enough to make them turn on you. And there are still soldiers patrolling our lands, and bandits forced to steal because of the war.'

'You oversell the dangers,' said Maria. 'We are quite safe, I assure you. I have handled my own affairs all these years without you, and I am equally capable of doing so now.'

'I would hazard that is false,' he said, pushing off the tree and stalking towards her.

'Excuse me?'

'I've been here hardly any time at all, and your illicit activities were immediately obvious to me. The servants all know, as do the people of Arow Claw, so really the only people you've successfully hidden it from is your family. I would respectfully suggest the only reason you have been able to do so is because they are too self-absorbed to notice. I, on the other hand, am quite absorbed in you.'

Her chest squeezed so hard it physically hurt. 'So you lied to me. You never had any intention of triffle hunting?'

'On the contrary, I have both been watching you and hunting triffles, and as luck would have it, I came across a trove of smaller orbs just over there.'

'Will you gift those to me also?'

He halted his approach, looking as though he might be reassessing his whole opinion of her, which meant that in wounding him, she'd also wounded herself, because she never wanted him to look at her that way again.

'I'm sorry,' she said quickly, unable to meet his eyes. 'I'm angry at myself ... at my failure, and I shouldn't take it out on you. It's hard for me to set aside a lifetime of suspicion, but I do want to trust you.'

He nodded, tension seeping out of his shoulders, and she blew out a long breath of relief.

'My uncle requested I complete a task for him, but it matters not—it's too late in the day to achieve it now.'

'What did he want?' he asked with concern, although his mistrust hadn't entirely abated, and that sent a clench of worry through her. 'Perhaps I can help?'

'Hey!' called John, stepping out of the trees, a triffle in his hand. 'You can't just run away and not tell anyone where you're going! It's irresponsible! The servants would have been looking for you for hours!'

'We weren't going anywhere,' Maria said sharply. 'Elex found a trove just over there.' She reached out and squeezed Elex's arm. 'I'll tell you more later,' she said quietly. 'I promise.' And to her surprise, her words were true.

Their ride home was uneventful, and everyone seemed relaxed, confident Danit would be content with their large haul of triffles, but as soon as they arrived back at the mansion, Maria's maids practically dragged her from her horse and whisked her away, chastising her about being gone so long. She tried to point out she'd had little choice, but they refused to listen, clucking about jewelry, flowers, dresses, shoes, and goodness knew what else.

They bundled her into a bath, dragged combs through her wet hair, and urged her to wash quickly. The dressmaker was already in a bad mood, apparently, having wasted half the day waiting for her to return.

'No one told me!' said Maria, scrubbing the day from her skin as hastily as she could, then climbing out and toweling herself dry.

A maid wrapped a robe around her, while another made short work of plaiting her long hair and coiling it on top of her head. 'That will do,' said the first, ushering Maria into the corridor, shepherding her to the round room used only for fitting clothes.

'Up,' said the seamstress, jumping to her feet as soon as Maria entered. She was a stocky woman with a severe bun of ginger hair and calculating grey eyes.

Maria stepped onto the raised platform, then waited. This seamstress had fitted her since she was a child, and the only thing Maria would get by opening her mouth was a sharp rebuke or a pin in her side.

'A gown of purple and blue,' said the seamstress. It was more of a command than a suggestion, so Maria simply nodded her head and plastered on a smile. Maria could have protested, and if she'd felt strongly opposed, she would have, but blue and purple, although not her favorite colors, were symbolic of the union between Oshe and Alter, and it was the path of least resistance. 'Your hair will be up?'

'Yes,' said a maid. 'Almost as it is now.'

'Shoes?'

'We were thinking these slippers are best?' said the second maid, holding up a pair of cream silk slippers with a slight heel.

'No,' said the seamstress. 'I think these.' She moved to the window seat and retrieved a pair of flat, lavender blue slippers with shimmering pearls sewn over the toe in the shape of the Celestl Star.

The maids cooed over the beautiful shoes, and Maria agreed they were quite breathtaking.

'We have jewelry to match,' said the first maid.

'Yes,' said the second. 'The pearl necklace with the Celestl Star pendant.'

'And pearl studs in her ears.'

'And in her hair!'

'Do you need me?' asked Maria, who would have been quite happy to find something else to occupy her time before dinner.

'We'll tell the gardeners to pick matching flowers.'

'And we'll order matching napkins.'

'The kitchen wants to know if you have any food requests?'

A long pause followed the question.

'Oh, I'm sorry, were you talking to me?' said Maria.

Their faces morphed into matching frowns, and Maria fought the urge to grin. 'Food for when? We'll wed on the bridge, presumably? And then we'll partake in Toll—I mean, Blade—Day celebrations. We'll eat street food like we usually do, will we not?'

'No, we will not,' said a male voice from behind them.

Maria spun, glad she was still wearing her robe, because her uncle glared at her from the door. 'Is there something urgent, Uncle?'

'Out,' said Danit in such a sharp snarl, even the seamstress rushed to obey, and for the first time in her life, Maria stopped to consider the deference afforded to her uncle. Did her maids think him a worthy leader? Was that why they obeyed without question? Or was it fear? None in Alter had the strength to challenge Danit, but how many truly respected him? Did it even matter if the result was the same?

'Uncle?' said Maria, stepping down from the platform.

'Well? Did you get word to Nicoli?'

She bit her lip, steeling herself. 'Elex was watching my every move. I tried to slip away, but he caught me.'

'Elex?' he said, drawing out the word so it sounded sinister on his tongue. 'Your brother reports you are getting on quite well with your betrothed.'

Maria tried for nonchalance. 'I wouldn't trust much from John's lips today. He's bitter I found more triffles, and he's worried about meeting his own betrothed tomorrow.'

'So you deny it?'

'I deny the unspoken part, that my loyalties might be shifting. I am building a rapport with my betrothed—that much is true—but I know my duty and am devoted to this family, to you, Uncle. If John means to suggest otherwise, then yes, I deny it. Strongly.'

Danit appraised her for a beat, silence descending over them, and Maria held her breath, offering a silent prayer to the Goddess that he didn't find anything in her features he disliked. He tutted sharply. 'You will go tonight to Arow and tell Nicoli to come immediately. You will bring him with you when you return.'

'And if I don't return?' said Maria. It could be dangerous travelling at night even in their own lands, let alone in Claw territory where she was no longer welcome.

'You will. He will not kill his only childhood friend.'

'I'm not—'

'You will go after dinner, and that's the end of it.'

'But ... why—'

'Enough,' he barked with such force she clamped her mouth shut, a kernel of fear taking root in her belly.

She gritted her teeth and nodded demurely. 'Yes, Uncle. I will go after dinner.'

Chapter Eight
Ava
AVA'S SIXTEENTH BIRTHDAY

Ava ducked out of the tavern and hurried towards the street that led to the prison. An hour before, Mrs. B had finally relented and thrust a new dress into Ava's hands. Not new, of course, but the oldest, most unattractive cast-off Mrs. B could find.

She'd only done it because Ava had recently turned sixteen and her existing dress was practically indecent, the regulars having taken to asking Mrs. B if the Cleve Arms was now a whorehouse whenever they saw her. Mrs. B couldn't give a rat's arse about Ava's comfort or decency, but she did care about the reputation of her establishment, and after the rumors flying about Tasha, she'd had little choice.

But Ava hadn't washed in almost two weeks, and she'd be damned if she would dirty her ugly new dress the moment she donned it, even if a trip to the stream was risky, given Mrs. B was in today.

A street kid ran towards her, weaving through the bustling crowd with his hand held high, half a pie clutched in his little fingers. Where he'd got such a bounty, Ava couldn't imagine, but Ava threw her new dress over her shoulder, stepped into his path, and plucked it from his hand.

'Hey!' shouted the kid, skidding a little as he came to a halt, distraught. 'Give that back!'

'Make me,' said Ava, taking a big bite, her mouth watering deliciously.

He ran forward, fists flailing, but Ava easily kept him off with an out-stretched arm. She took a second bite of the delicious, buttery, flaky pastry stuffed with succulent meat. It was easily the best food she'd had that year, and as she took another bite, she thought of it as a birthday treat; it had been a long time since she'd had one of those. 'Where did you get this?'

The boy deflated and gave up trying to snatch it back. Ava was stronger than she looked, and at the rate she was eating, the pie would be gone in seconds. His face scrunched as he fought tears.

'Please,' he begged. 'It's not just for me. Someone dropped it right beside me. Said it was the worst pie they'd ever tasted. They left it there! I didn't steal it, I promise!'

Ava decided he was telling the truth. 'Then the Gods have smiled on you twice this day,' she said, handing the remaining food back. He snatched it and took off. 'Next time, hide it!' she shouted after him, but he was already gone.

Ava shook her head as she hurried on, taking a tiny, rarely used path around the back of the prison, then across an acre of scrubland beyond. She ducked into a small thicket of shrubby trees, careful not to get her new dress wet in the barely-there trickle of the stream.

The Gods were smiling on her, too, what with the chance to be clean, a new dress, and a full belly. When had she last had so much to be thankful for?

She washed down the pie with a handful of water before pulling off her old dress. Then she sat in the biggest of the four or so puddles and scrubbed away the dirt from her body as best she could. She shuffled down, lying back and dunking her head, scrubbing at her hair as she looked up at the branches cocooning her from above.

She was soon shivering all over, the water cold, the day overcast, little warmth penetrating the shade of the trees. She used her old dress to dry off, then slid into her new one, the thick, unblemished fabric warm and luxurious against her skin. She tied it closed with the bodice strings and was shocked to see a pillow of cleavage when she looked down. She'd known her breasts were large—they'd grown enough that the fabric of her old frock had stretched tight across them, so much so they'd often popped the buttons—but she'd never seen them on display like this.

She blushed at the thought of others seeing them. What they might think ... or do. Mrs. B wouldn't tolerate any *funny business* inside the tavern, but Ava still had to walk the streets. She had to do so in a moment to get home. She pulled the fabric high, which helped a little, but every time she looked down, there they were.

She told herself it was fine as she hitched up her new dress and carefully squatted to wash her old one. Nearly all women wore similarly revealing clothes. No one would bat an eye. It was something she would have to get used to, that was all. A change. Nothing bad.

She wrung out her old dress, which she would hang out to dry when she got back to the tavern. She would keep it, of course, because in time she would need the fabric to patch her new dress, and she could lay it over herself on chilly nights to help stave off the worst of her shivering.

She stood and stepped towards the round hole that led out of her small haven. She'd been away too long, and the Gods had already given her much that day, which meant her luck would likely not extend further. No sooner had the thought crossed her mind than a figure came through the hole, blocking her path.

They were backlit by the sun, so she could see little more than the outline of a tall, well-built man, and an icy wave of fear rolled through her, then gripped her in an iron clasp.

The man straightened, and Ava gasped in shock as she took in his face—a year older and even more attractive than before, if such a thing were possible.

'Kush ...'

He studied her face, and she fidgeted, then forced herself to stop, imagining what her mother would say.

'You've changed,' he said eventually, his eyes roaming around the confined space.

'Did you watch me bathe?' She awkwardly covered her chest by raising a hand to her collar, feeling exposed as he returned his gaze to her.

'No.'

'Are you here to kill me?'

He stilled. 'Why would you think that?'

'You killed Malik for stealing from the Gods ... at least, that's what everyone said ... and this stream comes from the temple. The few who know of this place are too scared to use the pools for fear of angering the Gods, but I—'

'No one's going to kill you for bathing in discarded water.' He seemed irritated. 'If you walked into the temple and sat in a sacred pool, it would be another story, but what the temple women throw away may be freely used by others.'

'Oh. Well ... good.'

A clumsy silence descended, and Ava wrung her free hand in the fabric of her old dress. She knew she should go, images of a furious Mrs. B flashing before her mind's eye, but she didn't want to.

'Why did you take the pie from the boy?' he asked, his tone laced with accusation.

Her breath stilled as she worked out his meaning. 'You were watching?'

'You stole from him.'

Ava's stomach lurched. 'You're here to punish me for that? I was kind to him. Most would have taken it all and given him a kicking for good measure. I taught him a lesson that will serve him well.'

He tipped his head, considering her words.

Well, if he was here to punish her for a few bites of pie, she refused to take it lying down. 'And you're a fine one to pass moral judgements,' she said. His hair was glossy, his wide shoulders had filled out even further, and his clothes practically shone. 'You killed a man. I only took a few bites of pie, despite my humble circumstances.'

She'd played it over so many times. He'd killed a man. In cold blood. In plain sight of everyone. Then he'd left the body in the street as though it meant nothing.

'Your humble circumstances?'

Really? That was where he chose to dwell? 'Who *are* you?'

'You have clothes on your back and a roof over your head ...'

He said the words more to himself than to her, so she ignored them. 'Why did you collect your mother's washing that day?'

'You have food, and—'

She sprang forward without thinking, pointing a finger, her rabid reaction causing his eyes to fly wide. 'I haven't had enough food since I came to the Cleve, and with Malik's death, you stole my one joy.'

'But you live in a tavern!'

She was so close she could see every flicker and ripple of his dark blue eyes, although they'd lost any hint of silver and were gentler than she'd expected. 'You can't be that naïve,' she whispered, her rage abating.

He held her gaze for a long moment, looking down at her from only a pace away. If a tavern patron had come so close, she would have backed up a step, but it felt different with him. Safe, somehow.

'Why did you kill him?' she whispered, even though she was scared to hear the answer. Killing was commonplace in the Cleve, especially for the likes of Malik, the *why* the only way to separate good men from bad.

He stepped back, clearing the path and giving a small cough. 'You should go.'

'Are you an enforcer? Do you work for the Gods?'

Something about the look on his face made her uncomfortable, although she couldn't put her finger on what it was.

Silence stretched, and he turned his head to look pointedly at the hole until she eventually relented, stepping past him and out into the light.

'Kush ...' she said, turning back, 'I'm—' But by some magic, he was already gone.

CHAPTER NINE
MARIA

A STRANGE ATMOSPHERE HUNG over the banqueting hall as Maria entered for dinner, the floaty layers of her Alter Blade purple dress pooling around her legs. Tonight's meal was less formal, with no procession, although the food laid out still constituted a feast.

Strips of tender, uncooked meat and mushrooms sat on platters, with long forks sitting across every person's plate. When everyone was seated, the servants would place pots of boiling oil before them, so they could each cook their own food to their preferred tastes.

Maria took her seat between Elex and her uncle. Elex squeezed her hand under the table in greeting, while the servants placed elaborate salads and bread pockets puffed up like clouds before them.

'I hope you've had a more restful few hours than I,' said Maria, her voice low.

'Maria!' said Danit, leaning across her, demanding her attention.

'Yes, Uncle?' she said sweetly, straightening and pulling her hand from Elex's as she turned.

'Tell Erica about the triffle hunt.' He was red-faced and almost panicky, a look Maria had never seen him wear before.

Erica, the latest addition to Barron's collection of three wives, was leaning across Danit, her hand placed inappropriately on his thigh. Her dress was so low-cut, Maria wondered if her breasts would fall out if she leaned in any farther, and her pendant necklace kept slapping between her cleavage as she moved forward and back, drawing attention to the area.

'Oh, it was quite successful,' said Maria, resolutely keeping her eyes on Erica's face, even if her uncle couldn't manage the same. 'Elex has quite a knack for it.'

'Elex has quite a knack for most things,' Erica purred, her eyes flashing salaciously.

What in the world did that mean?

'Did you have a pleasant day?' Maria politely enquired, Barron watching them from across the table.

'Oh yes, thank you,' Erica said breathily. 'Danit's home is so very impressive and comfortable, and I was so pleased to see all the wonderful preparations for tomorrow's ball, and the gardens are *so* beautiful, don't you think?'

'Do you not have gardens such as these at your home in Oshe?' asked Maria, genuinely interested. It was to be her future home, after all.

'No,' she said sulkily. 'Barron cares more for brawn than beauty. I am not allowed such things.'

'We have no space for such things,' Barron said firmly, putting an end to the discussion.

Erica bowed her head in deference, although there was something pouty about it, conveying that she didn't agree but knew better than to make a scene.

'What do you like about your home?' asked Maria, but Erica didn't respond. Her attention had snagged on the far side of the table, where Cane hovered over his father's shoulder, a frenetic energy radiating from him.

'Well, Father?' said the younger man. He kept flitting his eyes to Maria, then Elex, then back to their father, and an icy hand clenched around Maria's guts. Whatever this was, it wasn't good.

A cruel smile spread across Barron's lips, perhaps enjoying the dread on Maria's features. 'Yes, I suppose it makes more sense for you to switch. But it will require careful handling. Your current intended has fire in her belly, as does her father.' Barron clicked at his guards, 'Please help Maria to her new intended's side.'

And suddenly Maria was being manhandled out of her seat, Elex looking for a moment as though he would lunge for her, but then he dropped back, adopting a relaxed slouch against his chair, only his balled fists under the table giving any hint that something was wrong.

'Uncle!' Maria shrieked as her grandmother threw back her chair, signaling to the Alter guards with her stick to intervene, but Danit held up his hand, overriding her order, and the Alter guards froze in place.

Barron's men dragged Maria to the end of the table, only releasing her when she was within reach of the painted peacock, who grabbed her hips and pulled her onto his lap. She tried to get up, crying out in surprised disgust, fury raging through her blood, disbelief coursing through her mind. How had this happened? Why was no one doing anything to stop it? He grabbed her with bony fingers and pulled her back down.

'You're mine now,' he whispered in her ear, clamping an arm firmly around her, holding her in place. She squirmed, digging her fingers into his flesh and fighting to get free, willing Elex to look at her with every fiber of her being, silently begging him to save her. He didn't. He lounged back in his chair, a look of sick amusement on his lips, his eyes meeting anyone's but hers.

She clawed her way forward again, trying to gain some purchase with her legs, trying everything she could think of to escape, trying to focus through her haze of terror. This couldn't be happening. She wouldn't marry Cane. She couldn't. But a single glance at her uncle made her halt her struggle, because of course she would; she was loyal to her family and her people. She would do whatever was needed to end the war, and if this was what she had to do, she would do it, no matter the personal cost. But she would be damned if she would do it with a smile.

'Please, keep it up,' Cane grunted in her ear, shifting her a little in his lap, pulling her hips back. She went statue-still as she felt the ridge of his arousal against her backside, and bile rose in her throat. Tears pricked her eyes as Barron stroked her arm, making minute pulses with his hips.

'You're disgusting,' she said, loud enough for everyone to hear, and those who'd begun whispering among themselves went silent, their scrutiny returning in full force. Everyone except Elex, which tore at the fragile kernel of hope that had begun to unfurl deep in her chest. 'Uncle,' she begged, a single tear running free as she turned her pleading eyes on him once more. 'You cannot let this insult stand. I am the first daughter of Alter, and this ... this ... rat treats me like a common whore! In your presence ... in *Grandmother's* presence ... in our banqueting hall!'

Danit tipped his head to the side, considering the predicament carefully, presumably playing over the options in his mind. He could simply go along with this treatment of her, let slide Barron's decision to switch her betrothed, but to do so would convey colossal weakness. Barron should have consulted Danit before making such a decision—the insult was great. If Danit simply nodded his head and let events continue, it would be akin to a dog rolling over at his master's feet.

But the opposite was also fraught with danger. Publicly disagreeing with Barron would embarrass him and seed friction in their new friendship. At worst, it could lead to the dissolution of the pact before they'd even sealed it.

So he would look for some middle ground. Something that allowed them all to walk away with their dignity intact. All besides Maria—Danit wouldn't care about her.

'Come, Danit,' said Barron, holding up his goblet. 'Let us drink. Enough of this tedium.' He beckoned his wife to him, and Erica didn't hesitate before pushing back her chair and rounding the table. She brazenly hitched up her dress, then eased herself onto Barron's lap. He slid his hand over her backside, then slapped it, and she let out a breathy moan of faux protest.

Maria couldn't believe her eyes. Never had her uncle allowed behavior like this inside their home. Never.

Danit's expression was unreadable, but John stared openmouthed, his eyes flicking from his uncle to Maria to Barron as though he couldn't believe what he was seeing.

'Time for bed, I believe,' said Maria's grandmother, rising from her chair slowly this time. 'I will take Maria with me, and I suggest you gentlemen resolve this mess without further embarrassment.'

Barron scoffed. 'You would let an old woman talk to you that way?' His eyes stared at Danit so hard it was a wonder they didn't leave holes.

'Just think what pretty little babies we'll have,' whispered Cane, sliding a single finger down Maria's bare spine.

Maria inwardly shuddered but outwardly refused to give any indication she'd heard or felt him, blocking him out as best she could. The feel, the smell, his words ... she refused to register any of it. Instead, she focused on her grandmother. Danit's mother. Would he let Barron speak to her this way?

She was afforded such high position in their lands that none would ever question her. Danit depended upon her counsel—respected it—as Maria's father had done before him. But never had they faced a slight such as this. No one in their lands would dare speak to Danit—to challenge Danit—in the way Barron had, just as no one would question Dio's place at his side.

Maria looked again at Elex, but he was watching Danit like everyone else at the table. The guards shifted uncomfortably, presumably wondering if things would turn nasty, if the night would end with a pool of their blood seeping out across the floor.

'Maybe I'll make my brother watch as I fuck you,' murmured Cane. 'Wipe that smug expression off his face.'

Maria willed her ears to close to him.

And still Danit said nothing. He picked up his goblet and swirled it in his hand before taking a sip. 'Goodnight, Mother,' he said, looking at Dio for only a moment. 'Thank you for your offer, but Maria will stay awhile.'

Dio looked as though she might protest, but instead she pursed her lips and turned on her heel, her stick clicking aggressively on the floor. She stopped to say something to the guards, but Danit's voice stole Maria's attention.

'I am aware things are done differently in other Blades,' Danit said slowly, his eyes fixed on Barron, 'and for that we must allow our guests leeway when they bend our rules. However, you should know behavior of this sort is not proper inside my home, and I consider it an insult.' He paused, waiting for Barron to respond, and the room collectively held its breath.

All except Cane, who whispered, '*Proper?*' in Maria's ear, his tone snide. 'What prudish land is this?' But he gripped her more tightly, fingers digging into her flesh as though scared he might be forced to let her go, and the movement undermined his bravado, exposing him as the spoilt child he was.

Barron held Danit's gaze for a long time, and Maria willed him to back down, to make this the concession Danit needed. He eventually inclined his head, and Maria nearly wept with relief.

'Of course we would never knowingly offend our hosts,' Barron said with mock curtesy.

Danit nodded as Barron slid Erica off his lap, instructing a guard to bring a stool so she could sit at his side. A fucking stool.

'And I am sure my son is of the same mind,' said Barron, motioning for a guard to bring Maria a stool, too.

Maria's blood boiled. He would make her perch on a stool at his side like a trained dog?

Cane tensed, but there was little he could do other than comply. He released Maria's waist and slid his hands down her arms as she pushed herself off his lap, hating that she pressed into him as she stood. But he didn't relinquish her entirely, grabbing her hand before she could step away.

That, out of everything he'd done so far, made her want to scream the most. It was intimate, holding someone's hand, and her fingers were too sensitive to block the feel of him, especially when he ran his thumb down her palm. She fought the urge to yank her hand away or to snarl, to act like the animal he was making her out to be.

She refused to perch on the stool, preferring to stand, making it awkward for him to continue holding her hand. But somehow that made her even more powerless, tethered to him like a naughty child. Though she was glad the rest of her was free, even if her body could still feel the phantom touch of him.

Danit seemed to breathe easier now decorum had been restored, but there was still the problem of Maria's betrothal, and everyone waited for him to continue. 'I shall allow the switch,' said Danit, 'although we shall require a bigger bride price to cover the ... emotional upheaval my poor niece has suffered.'

'There are no bride prices,' said Cane, scowling hard.

Obviously, Maria didn't say aloud. Nobody replied as Barron and Danit stared at one another, taking their time, turning the interaction careful, giving it the respect it deserved, each of them aware one wrong step could spell disaster for them all.

Barron eventually shrugged and picked up his goblet, waving it around. 'I suppose we can come to some arrangement but not tonight, Danit. For the sake of the Goddess, enough for tonight!'

Danit held his gaze for one moment longer, then nodded, sealing Maria's fate, stealing not only her life but her hope, the promise Elex had represented. She was suddenly lightheaded, her knees buckling so she had little choice but to sit heavily on the stool, almost knocking it sideways, her limbs barely responding to her commands.

She leaned forward, hiding her face, sucking in as much air as she could get into her lungs, but it wasn't enough. There wasn't enough air in the world to help her now. She'd been so close to happiness, and then this weasel, this despicable excuse for a man had snatched it all away, still grasping pathetically onto her hand because it was the only way he could keep her.

'My love?' said Cane, leaning forward, putting his head close to hers. 'Are you ill?'

She flinched away and made a growling noise in her throat.

'Sit up! Show everyone how happy you are!' he said with smug self-satisfaction.

'You think you've won?' she bit out, staying firmly hunched forward, refusing to meet his eyes. 'You think stealing me from your brother makes you a victor? A hero? Something worthy?'

'Maria,' he said, censoriously.

'You are pathetic. Nothing. Not even worthy of fading into your brother's shadow. I realize now why I've never heard of you—because you are not a man worth wasting breath on.'

He made a grab for her neck, but Maria lurched away, the stool toppling backwards, sending her sprawling onto the floor. Cries went up from the table, and many stood, but Maria was too busy regaining her feet and putting distance between her and her disgusting betrothed to look at them, stopping a safe distance away.

'Come back here,' said Cane, his voice shrill. He took a step forward, but every time he did, Maria backed away, keeping the distance the same. 'Now!'

Maria shook her head.

'You will be punished for this. When you are my wife, I will flog you for this insolence.'

Danit paled but said nothing, did nothing, becoming the tyrant Elex had made him out to be.

'Now look here,' said John, who hovered at the other end of the table, on his feet but just barely, like the ground might swallow him whole if he let go of his chair. 'That's a bit much, don't you think?'

Maria's eyes kept moving back to Elex, who still sat as though dinner were going swimmingly, akin to a stroll through the park on a fine warm day. Did things of this nature regularly happen in Oshe? The idea sent a fresh bolt of terror through her blood because Oshe was to be her new homeland, and now she would go at Cane's side. She didn't dare imagine all the terrible things he might do in a land where scenes like this were commonplace.

And that was the sad truth. She would go at Cane's side no matter what she did tonight. Protest was hopeless, and worse, she would pay for her actions. First by Danit's hand and then by Cane's. Perhaps even by Barron's. She looked one last time at Elex, then at her uncle, but they offered no safe harbor in which to weather this storm she'd unleashed.

Her shoulders slumped as she reminded herself that she was the first daughter of Alter. She had one job, and that was to do her duty to her family and her people, no matter how high the personal cost. Tonight she had failed them. She deserved whatever punishment came her way, and she would endure it because her happiness didn't even compare to the importance of peace for her people.

So she overrode every single instinct she possessed and moved at a snail's pace back to Cane's side. When he realized her intent, he smiled like the victorious viper he was, and she bit the insides of her lips hard, willing the pain to keep her tears at bay. And then she perched on the insulting stool and let him take her limp, despair-numbed hand.

CHAPTER TEN

AVA

AVA'S SEVENTEENTH BIRTHDAY

KUSH WAS NOT WHO she wanted him to be. Ava repeated the mantra for the thousandth time as she celebrated her seventeenth birthday. Or more accurately, endured it as if it were any other day, ignoring the usual lewd comments from the regulars slouching over the bar.

One more year and Ava would be a fully-fledged adult, but she still went hungry and still slept in the basement, as she'd done for years. Mrs. B invited Ava to leave any time she raised the topic of payment or moving upstairs, but of course she had nowhere to go. She had no family, no friends, and certainly no Kush. She hadn't seen him in a year, but despite that, her brain was quite happy to fill his absence with pleasant imaginings, no longer of rescue, per se, but of friendship, and sometimes even love.

It was stupid and childish, especially because, despite knowing her circumstances, he'd never once tried to help her nor brought her food nor even paid her a visit. Hence the mantra.

Kush is not who I want him to be. I do not know Kush. Kush killed a man in cold blood. My life is not a fairytale.

But the passage of time made it harder, if anything, to put him from her mind, her fantasy version of him her constant companion. Who was his father? What was his role? And why had he sought her out by the stream?

Tasha's giggle brought Ava back to the present, and she slid a tankard of ale across the bar to a man openly ogling her breasts. They'd grown even bigger since Mrs. B had given her the dress, and they strained the fabric, impossible to hide.

Tasha giggled again, and Ava's eyes found where she sat on the lap of the new King of the Cleve. Tasha had been distraught for days after Malik's death, determined she would never be happy again, but then the new King had emerged and her hunt had begun.

It had taken a while, but he'd eventually succumbed to her charms, and rarely did he select another to accompany him, much to Tasha's delight. Tasha acted as though the title *Queen* was in her future, but Ava couldn't see it. King, as he called himself, would never share anything with anyone, and certainly not that.

The streets had been perilous for days and nights on end after Malik's death, and even when King had emerged as victor, he'd done little to settle things. He liked the chaos, so even now, almost two years later, the Cleve was dangerous, especially at night.

He'd made other changes, too. Mrs. B had tried to keep the tavern reputable, but that didn't suit King at all. And one day, when Mrs. B had ordered Tasha off King's lap, threatening her job if she didn't comply, King had commanded Tasha to stay, his eyes daring Mrs. B to contradict him. And in the face of that, what power did she really have?

King had brought in *dancers*, as he called them, the very next day, and each dancer had been given a room for entertaining guests, changing the nature of Mrs. B's establishment forever. The increased competition meant Tasha was rarely too far from his lap, which meant she rarely did any work, and Ava had had to pick up the slack.

It was good because it kept Ava busy, and it meant she'd escaped with only light gropings here and there, but she'd felt a shift recently, the atmosphere darker where she was concerned, men openly watching as she bustled by. It was only a matter of time before someone tried their luck, and when they did, there was little she could do about it.

Of course, she could run away, but to where? And out on the streets she was more likely to be attacked, not less. So instead she sank deep into the escape of her fantasy world and did her best to stay out of sight, the alternative to the looming pit of despair that would otherwise swallow her whole.

Mrs. B spent most of her time in the kitchen these days, drowning her sorrows and reminiscing about the good old days. Ava had little time for it, and the self-indulgence had diminished the woman in her eyes; she didn't seem half as terrifying now she no longer ruled the roost.

'No!' shrieked Tasha, pulling Ava's eyes once more. 'King!' She shoved him playfully, and he lifted a hand to her neck, wrapping his fingers around it and dragging her face to his. He whispered something in her ear, then shoved her to her feet, slapping her thighs before pushing her in the direction of the bar.

Tasha sauntered over, dressed only in undergarments like the other *dancers,* and leaned forward as though about to share a great secret. 'King's got an offer for you,' she said, giggling again, the sound grating like a cat's claws across Ava's ears. 'An ... intimate offer.'

Fuck.

'He'll pay you.'

'No, thank you,' she said quietly.

Tasha dropped her voice to a whisper. 'You're going to have to do it sooner or later. The more you resist, the more they'll want you, and eventually one of them will just take what you won't feely give.'

'Something to look forward to ...'

'It's not what you think. King doesn't want to fuck you. He wants to ... facilitate your first time,' she said, her smile sick. 'He sees you like a ... oh, I don't know ... a favorite niece or something.'

Fuck. Fuck. Fuck.

'He'll sell you to the highest bidder and even let you have a cut. It's a generous offer, seeing as he could just let them take you. You know he's been protecting you, right?'

'Tasha ...' But she didn't know what to say, shock and repulsion stealing her voice, so she simply stared, her mouth open.

'Is that a yes?' Tasha played with a rag on the bar, flicking the corner back and forth with her pointer finger.

'He can't,' Ava blurted, her mind racing, heart thumping, stomach churning.

'Oh, he can.'

'No ... I mean ... I'm not a virgin.'

Tasha reared back. 'Yer what?' she hissed, then leaned in and lowered her voice conspiratorially. 'Who?'

Ava's face flushed as she looked down at her hands. Who could she say? Everyone knew everyone in the Cleve, and no one would dare lie to King.

'He's not from here,' she blurted. 'You don't know him.'

'But you never go anywhere!' said Tasha, her frivolous mood rapidly souring. 'If you think you can lie to get out of this ... I'm doin' you a favor! King was gonna do it himself, just to put an end to the squabbling among his men, right here at the bar, but I stopped him, for *you*.'

Favorite niece indeed. 'And I'm grateful, Tasha, but he can't sell what doesn't exist.'

She folded her arms. 'Then tell me who.'

'I don't even know how to find him. I've only seen him a few times ...'

'Nooo ...' said Tasha, eyes widening in disbelief. 'Not that uptown guy you were mooning over for months?'

'Huh?' Panic gripped her chest.

'Oh my Gods. It is! Isn't it?'

'Who?' said Ava.

'That one who killed Malik! Ava! How could you do that to me?'

Ava stilled. She pressed her lips together and tried to think of a way out of the hole she'd dug for herself that didn't involve being auctioned to the highest bidder.

'And he left you here after! Bet that isn't how you thought it'd go, is it?' Tasha's features were cruel, jealous. 'Bet you thought he'd whisk you away to a better life, pampered like a princess. Ha! Not for the likes of us, dearie.'

Ava looked down at her hands again because, despite her cruelty, Tasha was still an ally of sorts, and the only thing Tasha would see in Ava's eyes at that moment was deep, black hatred.

Ava forced herself to take a long, steadying breath. She would get out of this. She would escape this hellhole. And Tasha, King, Mrs. B, they would rot in the Cleve for the rest of their lives. The thought was cheering but offered no practical assistance with her current predicament, so Ava fled to the kitchen, mumbling something about needing more flagons, a pitiless giggle floating on the air behind her.

She found Mrs. B sitting at the table shelling peas, complaining loudly about her lot in life. Ava helped herself to one, jumping out of the way when Mrs. B tried to swat it from her hand. 'Put it back,' she snarled.

'No,' said Ava, something having cracked inside her. She still had nowhere to go if Mrs. B threw her out, but King's proposition had changed something. Mrs. B could no longer protect her, and Ava had had enough of working herself to the bone, half-starved, nothing to show for her troubles. And who else would Mrs. B get to work there? She'd have to pull a kid off the street and train them. It would be a hassle, and Mrs. B wasn't driven like she'd been before, not since King's changes had sucked the life out of her.

Ava plucked a fresh bread roll from the cooling rack and sank her teeth into it, feeling liberated as she watched Mrs. B flinch, daring her to do something. Gods, it tasted good, and Mrs. B didn't move from her seat at the table. Instead, she slumped back and turned her eyes away.

'I need to go out for a while,' said Ava. 'It's tense in there, like something's going to blow. I'm scared they're going to hurt me.'

'Too many men with too little to occupy their time,' said Mrs. B, resuming her pea shelling. 'Malik wasn't a good man, but he was doing something good for the Cleve ... overall, anyway. *King*'—she sneered his name—'is pushing us back into the gutter and grinding us into the filth with his heel.'

'And there's nothing we can do about it,' said Ava, helping herself to a bowl of stew. Her stomach gurgled in delight. When had she last had a lunch so wonderful? When had she last had lunch at all?

Mrs. B made a growling noise in the back of her throat as she flung an empty pod into the bowl. 'Take this,' she said, fishing a piece of parchment from her pocket, 'and go uptown. The whores need more herbs, but King doesn't trust them to go themselves, so he sends me instead. It's a long walk, and your young legs will be quicker.'

Thank the Gods. Relief swelled in Ava's chest as she snatched the parchment from Mrs. B's hand. 'Where?' she said, already halfway to the door.

'The apothecary on the other side of the temple. Far end of Alter Lane. Put it on King's account.'

Ava was out of the door so fast her feet barely touched the ground. She raced uptown, for once hardly noticing anything. She slowed as she reached the temple, looking up at the wide, intimidating steps that led to the single black hole of an entrance, tall columns on either side, three circles pierced with a line through the middle carved above. She shivered every time she looked at the place, and she couldn't begin to imagine what Malik had been thinking even stepping foot inside, let alone stealing from the Gods. Although no one could agree on what he'd actually done ...

She found the apothecary easily enough and ignored the judgmental look the woman behind the herb-covered counter fixed her with. The place was dark and smelled of musty lavender, and Ava was glad to step back outside into the fresh, warm air.

She had no interest in returning to the tavern so soon, but she had no coin to spend in other shops, so she wandered the streets, taking in the sturdy, beautiful brick buildings, some attached together in rows, others surrounded by lush gardens. The stone was sandy-colored, the woodwork painted white—nothing like the dreary, flaking buildings she was used to—and the streets were clean and free of sewage.

She meandered around the back of the temple and came across a small collection of single-story houses made of wood. Each had a fence bounding it and was slightly separated from the others. Many had women sitting outside, preparing herbs or cooking or simply sipping tea and chatting in the sunshine.

They seemed relaxed, none of the hustle and bustle of the other streets here, and there were only women, she realized, as she wound farther through. No men.

A few curious eyes flitted Ava's way, and she almost turned back, feeling as though she were intruding on something private, but her feet kept moving, her curiosity too piqued for her to abandon her course now.

She rounded the corner of the temple and found more houses, similar to the others but larger, the women sitting outside older. They all wore the same long robes of light blue, their hair tied back in intricate plaits, and it made Ava feel shabby, her long hair in a lank ponytail down her back—and greasy, seeing as she hadn't washed in at least two weeks.

These must be the women of the temple, she realized. She'd thought they lived inside, but maybe that wasn't so. They seemed happy enough, relaxed, with smiling faces and upbeat tones, and Ava wondered if life as a temple woman was as bad as she'd imagined ... as everyone in the Cleve implied. Perhaps this could be her escape. They took women from all backgrounds, and it appeared the women were well looked after.

But they could never leave. Their whole lives were devoted to the Gods. No husbands. No children. No freedom. Ava shuddered. She would be a fool to swap one cage for another, no matter how well-gilded. At least she could leave the tavern … in theory.

Ava could see the road that ran in front of the temple again now, having completed her circuit of the building. It wasn't too far beyond the last house, which was the biggest of them all and mostly hidden, set back in the trees.

She almost walked past it without looking inside. She hadn't bothered with the last few because every house had been the same. Identical, in fact. Boring. But movement caught her eye, and she turned her head to see the door opening and a man stepping out. A man clad in a long leather coat and fine boots, and who was now so tall he had to stoop to fit through the door. A man who had filled out considerably since last she'd seen him so that hardly any trace of boyishness remained at all.

He sat at the small, round table in front of the house, only his head and shoulders visible above the fence, and a woman joined him, taking the seat opposite. She was older but strikingly beautiful, her ochre skin containing some hint of the glow Ava had seen on Kush's father, her long, dark hair glossy, despite the handful of grey streaks. She was tall-ish and willowy, seeming to flow with the fabric of her long robes, and she seemed at ease as she studied Kush across the table.

Kush also seemed relaxed, leaning back in his chair as he said something to the woman. But then he looked up, perhaps sensing Ava's eyes on him, and every slack part of him went rigid.

The woman turned to look at Ava too, following Kush's gaze, and her face split into a warm, broad smile. She stood, calling to Ava, beckoning her with open arms. 'You're a friend of my son?' she asked as Ava approached, her eyes alight, almost mischievous.

'Uh …' Ava's eyes flicked to Kush, wondering if she should answer. The woman seemed genuine enough, but those who dwelled this far uptown were rarely kind to anyone from the Cleve. What was her angle?

Kush got awkwardly to his feet, seeming unsure for a moment, then said, 'Would you like some iced tea?'

The woman chuckled at her son's obvious discomfort.

'Um ...' Should she stay? Probably not.

'Come sit,' the woman said to Ava with a firm authority she didn't feel she could refuse. 'I'll get the tea.'

Ava did as she was told, desperately trying to make sense of the scene. 'I thought women of the temple weren't allowed children?' she said in a low voice, pinching her eyebrows together.

'They're not.'

'Then how—'

'My father is an influential man.' The words seemed to pain him, and he balled his hands into fists.

'You don't like him?'

He exhaled a laugh, as though there was so much she didn't understand, it wasn't even worth trying to explain.

Silence settled for a beat, and Ava let her eyes roam, but everything was identical to the other houses. 'Do you live here?'

'Oh, he's just visiting me on my birthday!' said his mother, returning too soon with a tray.

Kush looked down into his lap.

'Happy birthday!' said Ava.

'And to you,' Kush said quietly, although he still wasn't looking at her. He seemed ... reluctant.

'Thank you,' said Ava, gratefully accepting a precious glass of iced tea from his mother. A real birthday treat. 'I'd all but forgotten, but how did you—'

'Happy birthday, Ava!' said the woman, sitting beside her and squeezing her arm. 'You are blessed, for the day of our births is auspicious.'

'Uh ... it is?' said Ava, not a clue what the woman meant.

'Mother,' chided Kush.

The woman threw up her hands. 'Okay, okay, I won't spout doctrine. I know how it irritates you. Although why, I can't imagine. Your father—'

'Mother, please.'

'They have a complicated relationship,' said the woman, leaning towards Ava conspiratorially. 'Men can be so funny about things! But Kush diligently visits me every year on my birthday, so I have that to be thankful for. It's the only day his father lets him have off—'

'Mother,' said Kush, banging his fist on the table and making them both jump.

His mother cocked an eyebrow and chuckled. 'Funny,' she mouthed at Ava. 'I'll be inside if you need me. My name's Yella, by the way.'

'Nice to meet you, Yella,' said Ava.

The woman left them, and silence descended. Ava stared at the table, then at her tea, then took a sip, finding the drink tangy and refreshing. When she looked up, Kush's eyes were on her, studying her in the same way she studied others.

'What?' she said.

'Why are you here?'

She frowned at his almost accusatory tone. 'Mrs. B—the one who owns the tavern—she sent me on an errand to ... well ... she sent me on an errand. I didn't want to go back, so I was wandering around, seeing how the other half lives.'

'You didn't know I was here?'

She gave him an incredulous look. 'How could I have known that?'

'People talk.'

She laughed scornfully. 'You're so high and mighty, so far above the people of the Cleve, you might as well live in the clouds. They spoke of you a bit after you killed ... well ... But then things went to shit and everyone was more worried about staying alive.'

He nodded, her words seeming to make sense to him. 'You're thinner.'

She bristled, aware once again of how out of place she was here among these beautiful, well-nourished people. 'And you look like you enjoy three square meals a day. I'm sorry if my appearance disappoints.'

'I didn't mean it like that.' He puffed out a tired breath, then said in a tight voice, 'You look ... like you always do. Just thinner.'

She scoffed. What did that mean?

'You don't get enough food, do you?'

'Not since you killed my gravy train.'

'That's why you were outside the bedroom?'

'Why else?'

'Well, I wasn't sure if ...' He coughed, then took a sip of his tea, an awkward silence washing over them once more. 'It's not safe for you here.'

'Why?'

He looked towards the temple. 'My father.'

'Why would he care about me?'

'He's dangerous.'

'So are you,' she said darkly.

His jaw worked as he flicked his now turbulent blue eyes back to her. He leaned forward, his hands balled into fists on the table, the muscles of his forearms flexing. 'Killing Malik ... that's not who I am.'

She sat back, folding her arms in defense. 'I imagine Malik would disagree.'

He shook his head. 'My father made me do it—part of my *training*.' He practically spat the word. 'I'll never willingly do it again.'

She looked from one of his impassioned eyes to the other and surprisingly found she believed him. 'What are you training for that requires you to kill a man?'

He stayed silent for many moments, disappearing into his thoughts, seeming conflicted. 'Do you have a family?' he eventually said.

'I ...' She curled forward, both inside and out, as though if she pulled herself tight enough, she could block the memories of her parents and her charmed past. The pain of remembering what it was like to belong somewhere ... *to* someone ... what she hadn't known to appreciate when she'd had it, and now she'd lost it.

'You think we're different, but you're wrong,' said Kush, sitting back in his seat.

How could he think that, with his fine clothes and food and mother who made iced tea and powerful father?

'You'd kill too, if your life depended on it.'

She stood abruptly, unsure why his words had touched a nerve. 'I should go.'

He stood, too, and rounded the table, following her as she moved towards the gate. 'You would have, just as I did. I can see it in your eyes.'

She whirled to face him. 'You know *nothing* about me.'

He stepped closer, towering over her, so close she could smell his eucalyptus-scented shirt, and something below that, something like wood shavings and spice. 'Just as you know *nothing* about me.'

He was right, and that hurt more than anything, because she wanted to know him. But she didn't need him. She didn't need anyone. 'Fuck you, Kush,' she said, and then she walked away.

CHAPTER ELEVEN

MARIA

DINNER LASTED FOREVER, AND Maria barely ate a scrap. Cane insisted on cooking Maria's meat for her, not bothering to ask how she liked it, but she couldn't stomach anything anyway, and the overcooked chunks of steak piled up on her plate. Cane didn't seem to notice.

Maria existed in a haze, like a cloud had descended over her mind, making her slow to understand and respond to her surroundings. When people spoke her name, she took longer than usual to turn her head. When someone asked her a question, she had to think hard to find even the simplest answers.

For a brief, perfect moment, a life had stretched out before her with a man she liked. Could have loved. And now it was gone. Snatched away by a petulant child who felt left out of the fun. She couldn't even stand to look at him, let alone work with him, *sleep* with him ... He wasn't looking for a partner. He was looking for a dog to sit on a stool by his side.

Cane slid yet another piece of shriveled meat onto her plate. He picked up a fresh chunk with his short, bony fingers, skewered it, and dropped it into the boiling pot of oil he had all to himself now Dio had left them.

Even Cane's hands were repulsive. Spidery. Small. So unlike Elex's strong, capable hands. He smelled wrong too. A floral, sickly scent masked undertones of stale sweat. Nothing like Elex's woody, musky smell that conjured images of lying in a forest under a starlit sky. Would she ever feel his hands on her again?

Perhaps they could have an affair. Or maybe Elex would steal her back once they reached Oshe; he did have a reputation for brutality, after all ... How she longed for it to be entirely true. There was nothing he could do here. It would be him against all the might of Danit's army, but maybe once they were in Oshe ... Did he even want to, though? He seemed to have already made peace with losing her, and they were only ever marrying out of duty. Perhaps he was relieved he was no longer required to tie himself to another.

Maria tried desperately to think of an escape. She could stick a knife in Cane's heart ... But if she did that here, in Alter territory, it would be an attack on their guests. It would give Barron a reason to start another war, a reason for the other Blades to rally behind him.

Perhaps she could brew a poison; there had been books in the library on such things. She'd never paid close attention, but she knew of substances like nightshade, arsenic, and hemlock.

Although, she'd need to wait until after they'd left Alter to kill him that way, too, which meant marrying the rat. She'd have no choice but to force herself to say the marriage words, endure his disgusting body atop hers and whatever punishment he would choose. Unless she ran away. She could find Nicoli and beg him to hide her. But that would cause a war with the Claws. And it wouldn't be fair on Nicoli or his people.

It was only then she remembered her uncle's demand. She was supposed to go to Arow Claw tonight and insist that Nicoli return with her. A small flower of hope bloomed in her chest, the task chasing away the fog clouding her mind, giving her something else to focus on, a reason to escape the banqueting hall that her uncle might support. Escape now, tonight, was better than no escape at all. She could achieve at least that and worry about her bigger problem once she was out in the night air. Maybe Nicoli would think of something ... some option she'd overlooked. He was a genius, after all.

She tried to hide the swell of hope lifting her shoulders, forcing a dejected look onto her face as she turned towards Cane. 'I'm tired after all the excitement, and we have much to do in the coming days. I must take my leave.'

She began to stand, but Cane grabbed her hand and yanked her back down. 'You don't leave until I say you can, because you are *mine* now. You will leave when I do.' He didn't even look at her as he spoke, so completely assured of his power.

Maria slumped heavily and turned her gaze to Danit, silently asking what she should do. Of course, he offered no help. His expression said only, *Try harder. Find a way. And if you don't, there will be consequences.*

She took a long breath, scrunching her hands into fists. What exactly did Danit expect her to do?

Cane leaned in, waving a piece of bloody meat, specks of red liquid flying into her lap, marring her dress. 'Perhaps I'll join you tonight,' he murmured, 'for there would be no question who owns you after that.' His lips pulled back, baring his teeth in something partway between a smile and a snarl.

'I require the water closet,' she said in calm reply, getting to her feet once more and turning purposefully away, moving out of his range before he had a chance to throw down the meat and make a grab for her.

The window in the nearest water closet was too small to climb through, but she could slip into an antechamber, assuming Cane didn't follow. The consequences of running would be severe, but she had to get to Nicoli, both for her family and for herself.

Cane stood as Maria rounded the table, the scrape of his chair making her glance warily over her shoulder. She thought for a moment he would come after her, but Elex was watching Cane with the kind of smirk on his lips that siblings reserve for one other. 'Scared you'll lose her so soon, brother?' Elex goaded, twisting a napkin in his hands.

Cane's features darkened, and Maria hurried on, getting close enough to freedom that her mouth watered at the promise of the taste. Perhaps Cane and Elex would even do her the service of creating a scene to cover her escape.

'You forgot something,' Elex called after her, pushing back his chair and striding easily towards her, holding up the napkin.

'Do not touch her!' screeched Cane, kicking Maria's stool out of the way and racing towards them, but Elex was already at her side.

He took her right hand in his left, then slipped their joined hands through a circle in the fabric he'd made by loosely tying the two ends of his rolled-up napkin together. He pulled it tight using his free hand and his teeth, then said urgently, 'Tie it again,' as he turned his back on his brother, shielding her to give her time.

'Unhand her!' Cane demanded, grabbing Elex's shoulders and trying to haul him away, the guards stepping closer but seeming confused, not sure what to do.

Maria had no idea what was happening, but she tied a second knot with her own free hand and teeth while Elex fended off his hysterical brother.

'Release her!' screamed Cane, scrabbling to try and get around Elex's much larger torso, but Elex fended him off with his free hand.

Elex looked back, checked the knot was securely tied, then held their joined hands aloft.

Cane's eyes bulged when he saw what Elex had done. 'No,' he breathed. 'No!'

'I claim the right of hand-tying,' Elex said loudly, sliding a reassuring thumb over the back of Maria's hand.

'No!' cried the painted peacock. 'Father!'

Maria half-laughed. She had no idea what was happening. It felt like some frantic party game, but it also felt like they were winning, she and Elex. Like the tables had turned. Like maybe this was a way out she hadn't known existed.

'Guards!' screamed Cane.

The Oshe guards lunged forward, heading for Maria and Elex, and for a moment, Maria's chest cratered because they couldn't possibly fight off every guard in the place alone. But then the Alter guards leapt to Maria's defense, and soon guard was fighting guard, the ring of steel on steel drowning out all other sound, the two of them cocooned together in the middle of the chaos.

Elex lowered his lips to her ear. 'Stay behind me,' he said urgently, 'and whatever happens, protect the binding.'

'Elex?' she breathed. Surely he couldn't mean he planned to fight? They would never make it out alive. One stray sword swing could spell death, and even if they did escape, where would they go? 'What is this?' she asked, looking down at the fabric binding them.

He gently ran his thumb along hers, and for a moment, everything else fell away. 'It's—'

'Enough!' Barron's voice boomed out across the room, and the guards broke apart, circling each other warily ... at least, those still on their feet.

'Father!' said Cane. 'Undo this! I demand it!'

'It cannot be undone,' said Barron, who stood, leaning forward so his hands rested on the table, 'as you well know. Please, if you believe you can take back by force what I handed you on a platter, by all means, go ahead. But I won't risk any more good men over this folly.'

'You still observe this archaic right?' said Danit, who at some point had also risen to his feet. His face was almost beetroot, and he was practically shaking with repressed rage.

'It is not common, but once invoked, it cannot be reversed,' said Barron.

'We must make an exception,' whined Cane. 'The marriage pacts are more important. They supersede some old custom.'

'Enough, my son,' said Barron, waving his hand and sinking back into his seat. 'What's done is done. You had your chance, but it has passed. You will marry the daughter of my right hand, as you have already sworn to do, and your brother will marry this woman.'

Barron looked directly at Maria, something like intrigue shining in his eyes. 'What you have done to put my sons in this state, I cannot imagine. They have never in their lives fought over a *woman*.' He said it with the utmost disdain, like there were many things he could understand fighting over, but not the person one would be tied to for the remainder of their days. But then, he had three wives, so he'd sidestepped the problem of having to like only one woman for any significant duration.

'I have done nothing, sir,' said Maria, her tone too curt to be polite. 'As far as I can tell, their interest has little to do with me. It seems to have more to do with their inclusion in the peace pact.'

Barron nodded, her words seeming to make sense to him. Apparently the peace pact *was* something worth fighting over.

Elex squeezed her hand, presumably trying to convey that her words weren't true for him, but Cane scrunched his face in fury. 'How dare you speak about me that way?'

'Enough, Cane,' said his father. 'You will leave this hall, and do not return until you are in a more civil-minded mood.'

'Father—'

'And if you insult our hosts again, I will send you home. Now apologize and be gone.'

Cane gritted his teeth and did as he was told. He bowed his head in Danit's direction, the movement stiff on account of his obvious rage, and then he turned, complying with his father's command—or at least it seemed that way until he snatched up a steak knife and hurled himself at Elex.

Elex reacted in a heartbeat, pushing Maria behind him and blocking Cane's attack, grabbing his wrist, but he was hampered by his leash to Maria, which deprived him of an arm and limited his movements.

Cane attacked with his free hand, making a grab for Elex's face, but Elex ducked and pulled his knee up, ramming it into his brother's groin so hard he dropped to the floor like a stone. There he lay, rolling back and forth, clutching himself as he whimpered unintelligible words.

Elex moved to stand over him, tugging Maria along behind, and watched for a moment. Then he booted Cane in the side hard enough for his whole body to convulse, eliciting a fresh wave of wailing, along with begging for Elex to stop.

Elex showed no intention of mercy. If anything, he seemed to be winding up to finish what his brother had foolishly started, their father, apparently, having no intention of preventing it. What a strange land Oshe Blade must be.

Elex kicked Cane again, but Maria pulled him back before he could do it a third time. 'No, Elex. You can't kill your own brother!'

Elex spun, looking down at Maria with wild eyes. 'Give me one good reason why not,' he snarled, his voice quiet so only she could hear.

'Because once it's done, you can't undo it,' she said, refusing to cower under the weight of his fury.

'Exactly the point.'

'Because as vile as he is, he's still your brother.'

'He is no brother of mine.'

'Elex, please ... not like this.'

He faltered, looking back at Cane for a beat, and Maria held her breath, not sure what he would do. But when he returned to her, a chink of light shone through the dark ferocity in the depths of his eyes. He nodded once, then pulled Maria towards him, bowing over her and looking down with an intensity that made her breath catch. For a blissful moment, it was just them in a bubble of their own creation, and Maria, although still not entirely sure what had happened, knew she was happy about it.

'Clean up this mess,' snapped Danit, slamming his hand on the table and piercing the moment. Elex inhaled deeply, then turned back towards the table, drawing Maria along beside him.

But just as they reached Elex's chair, John cried out, and then a force tugged Maria back by her hair, nearly pulling her off her feet.

She staggered into the man behind her and fought against his hold, managing to turn enough to confirm it was Cane, hunched and panting hard but sporting a crazed look that turned Maria's blood to ice in her veins. He brandished the steak knife in his hand, aloft and closing fast, but not with Elex—with her.

She had no time even to scream, but Elex yanked her close and spun them, putting himself between Maria and his brother. Instead of trying to stop the attack, however, he used their momentum to keep spinning, grabbing Cane's torso with his free hand and hauling him with them, then hurling him with such force that Cane's feet left the ground, his upper body flying back across the banqueting table.

Boiling vats of oil still littered the table, and Danit immediately sprang back, as did the others in neighboring seats. Cane flailed, then tried to right himself, lowering his hand to the table with the obvious intention of pushing himself upright. But his hand didn't find the table as it dropped—it found a pot of boiling oil and slid inside.

Cane's scream would haunt Maria until her dying breath, she was certain, high-pitched, desperate, filled with terror. Elex pulled her away, so Maria didn't see the moment Cane tipped the oil sideways, splattering his face and torso, some finding the open neck of his shirt. But she heard his screams, at least until he passed out from the pain.

Chapter Twelve
Ava

Ava wasn't sure why she'd reacted so badly to Kush's words. She was nothing like him. She knew that. And she tried not to dwell. But of course, she had little else to think of, so for the next few weeks, she thought of it—and him—almost constantly.

The interest in her from the men in King's gang had calmed after Tasha told them she wasn't a virgin, and as luck would have it, a new *dancer* had arrived the following day, distracting the men for a while. But it wouldn't last forever.

And no one would save her.

Kush couldn't save himself either, apparently a mere slave to his father's wishes, which meant she no longer even had the fanciful daydream version of him to keep her company. Maybe she had no choice but to accept her fate, but the idea of one of those animals on top of her made her want to vomit.

Kush's words came back to her once more: *You would have killed, just as I did*. Perhaps sometime soon she would prove him right, and then she'd really be in the shit.

Ava wiped down the bar one final time, then headed for the cellar stairs. Only King, Tasha, and a couple of King's most trusted men remained, and Tasha could get them anything they needed. But King's eyes tracked her as she left, and it made her blood run cold.

Ava barricaded the door as she usually did, using a length of wood held on either side by the uprights from the bannisters. The door would open a fraction, but not enough for anyone to slip a hand inside and remove the wood. They'd have to smash their way in, which would alert everyone in the tavern to what they were doing. So far, several had tried the door, but, thank the Gods, the barrier had been enough to deter them.

Ava descended the rickety wooden steps and slid her way between the barrels of beer and sacks of grain, the full moon through the small window lighting her way. She checked behind the barrels, made sure the lock on the window was securely in place, then removed her dress and laid it carefully aside, pulling a tattered nightgown from under her straw mattress and sliding it over her head.

The nightdress was a relatively new addition to her wardrobe, acquired when a dancer had been caught stealing and been forced to flee. Ava had made sure she was the first into the dancer's bedroom. She'd stripped the sheets and shoved the nightgown under her dress only moments before the other women had burst into the room, fighting over the remaining clothes and trinkets. Ava had slipped out with the dirty sheets, and nobody had suspected a thing.

The nightdress was sleeveless, with a lowcut neckline, and made of flimsy fabric. She hated the way her cleavage bulged as she climbed under her scratchy woolen blanket. Perhaps if she was flat-chested, the men would ignore her. Or at least not ogle quite so much.

Her head had barely hit the pillow when a light scratching sound came from the window, and Ava's eyes flew open in fright, her heart hammering hard in her chest. No one had ever tried the window. She held her breath as she listened, not daring to sit up, not wanting to give away that she was inside.

Go away. Go away. Go away. She repeated the words as though they might form a magic spell, as though they had power, but they didn't, and a low voice called her name. 'Ava? Ava, it's Kush.'

She sat bolt upright, saw his face through the glass, then scrambled to open the window. 'What are you doing here?' she hissed, as he slid through the small gap feet first.

He landed with perfect balance, then looked around before turning his gaze to her. His eyes dipped to her breasts, then lower, before guiltily returning to her face, and she snatched up her blanket and wrapped it around her shoulders.

'What are you doing here?' she repeated, trying to ignore the strange warmth rushing to her core on account of his appraisal.

'I had an errand to run in this part of town, and I ... wanted to see you. To see how you are.'

'Well, here I am, and I'm fine. Probably *too thin* for your liking, but there you go.' In fact, she'd eaten quite well since her birthday and was filling out nicely, but he didn't need to know that. Although, now she looked at him, he seemed tired and drawn and not at all like himself.

'It's just, I heard—'

Banging came from the top of the stairs, followed by cursing, and Ava shied back. Her frantic eyes found the window, but she didn't have time to get dressed, or even put her shoes on; the wooden barrier was already splintering.

'Help me,' she pleaded, turning desperately to Kush. 'I'm sorry for how I behaved the other day, and I'll grovel all you want later, but I can't fight whoever that is alone.'

He stepped close to her side, and some of her panic abated, but it returned in full force as the wood gave way and King thundered down the stairs.

'I've had it with all this,' said King, his hands going for his belt buckle. 'We're going to finish this here and now. No more questions. You won't be a virgin after what I have planned.'

'No,' said Kush, his voice relaxed and startlingly final. King looked up, staggering a little from the shock and too much whiskey.

'What the fuck?' said King, abandoning his buckle and reaching for a dagger, but before he drew his blade, Kush stepped into the light of the moon, and King squinted hard to make out his features. 'You?' His eyes flicked to Ava's shaded form. 'So it is true? You ... and him?'

Ava clamped her mouth shut. What would Kush say if he found out what she'd let everyone believe? That they had ...

'Looks that way,' said Kush. 'And if you touch her, I'll hang you like a fish from a hook, so everyone knows the consequence if they ever dare think of doing the same.'

Ava thought for a moment that King would fight, that come morning she'd have to clean blood off the floor, that her only dress would be ruined and one of them would be dead on her bed. But then King moved his hand from his dagger and turned for the stairs. 'She's not worth it,' he growled. 'And you be sure to tell the Gods of my kindness.'

King banged the door shut behind him, and Ava's legs buckled, dropping her heavily onto the bed. Her body shook, her teeth chattered, and a numb fog coated her brain. She barely even noticed when Kush sat by her side, wrapping a tentative arm around her shoulders.

She leaned into his warmth, and something about the comfort made tears well in her eyes. She didn't sob, she didn't have the energy for that, but trickles slid down her cheeks whenever she blinked, soaking the fine material of his shirt. She couldn't even bring herself to care, neither about his shirt nor the humiliation he'd witnessed ... what he'd saved her from.

She closed her eyes and focused on taking deep inhales, trying to calm her shaking. Kush's smell of sandalwood and spice was rich and expensive and delicious, another stark contrast between them. No one in her world could smell like him. She probably smelled like a wet dog who'd rolled in decomposing rat remains, not that he seemed to care.

'I heard them talking,' he said. 'They were ... bidding for you ... or at least, trying to convince King to let them. They said ... well ... that you and I had ... that we'd ...'

Ava flushed as he trailed off and closed her hand around the fabric of his shirt, holding onto him, scared he would leave. She shut her eyes tight but refused to let embarrassment cripple her. 'King wanted to auction my virginity,' she said, trying to ignore the squirming, shameful sensation in her guts. 'I told Tasha that I'd ... you know ... with someone. Just to make it stop. I haven't ...' she started, then regretted it, her face flaming.

He squeezed her arm, and tears threatened again, so she quickly blurted out the rest.

'Tasha wanted to know who it was. She wouldn't let it go, and I didn't know what to say. I told her it wasn't someone from the Cleve, and she decided it was you. I had no one else, so ... I'm sorry.' He put his free hand on her head, somewhat awkwardly, and she took a shuddering inhale. 'I'm really sorry. I didn't mean to drag you into all this.'

Her shaking worsened, and he hesitated, then pulled her more tightly against him. 'It's okay. I'm glad I can help.'

She nodded against his chest, and another stream of tears blinked free. They lapsed into silence, the only sounds the drunkards on the street outside, shouting and stumbling, and after a while, Kush's hand began tentatively stroking her lank, greasy hair. She held her breath, not daring to breathe, soaking up every inch of the comfort, the kindness.

'You should lie down,' he said eventually. 'Get some rest.'

She swallowed, then nodded, and he helped lay the blanket over her, covering up the skimpy nightgown and wrapping it under her toes.

'Don't leave,' she said as he stepped back, her eyes flying open in panic.

He froze, reminding her of a rabbit caught in lamplight, but then looked around for somewhere to sit.

'We can share the bed,' she said because beer barrels were her only furniture. He stilled. 'I don't mean ... I just ... You can't sit on the floor; it's cold and dirty.'

Kush looked at his feet for a moment, then closed his eyes. She thought he would refuse, and a pang of disappointment hit her squarely in the chest, but then he didn't just sit on the tiny, lumpy straw mattress, he lay beside her, his chest inches from her back, and warmth flooded Ava's whole being. Relief.

They weren't touching, but he was close enough that Ava could feel his heat, her body minutely aware of exactly how close he lay in the darkness.

'I used to dream you would take me away from all this,' she whispered. Words she would never have been brave enough to say in the light of day. Words she probably shouldn't say under the cover of darkness, either. 'It was a silly, childish thought—a fantasy—but it was a refuge, too.'

He stayed silent for a long while, and Ava thought maybe he'd fallen asleep, but then he blew a long breath against her neck, making her whole body tingle. 'Then I was silly and childish also, because I dreamed you would do the same for me.'

Chapter Thirteen
Maria

HEALERS CAME TO TAKE Cane away, laying him on a stretcher and carrying him off to the infirmary where they'd administer oils and ointments Maria had created. She was glad to see the back of him, unable to breathe freely until his feet disappeared from view, and even then, it was difficult after everything that had happened, and considering she was still tethered to Elex.

The servants made quick work of cleaning up the carnage, and Elex pulled Maria close as they did, seeming reluctant to return to the table.

'Will you send him home?' John asked Barron, his mouth still gaping open, even when the servants were serving their next course. Never had any of them seen such scenes in Alter. Theirs was a calm, civilized Blade, and Maria wondered what her life would be like in Oshe if this behavior was as normal to Barron, Elex, and Erica as it seemed.

'He is permitted to act as he did under the law of hand-tying,' said Barron, as though nothing momentous had taken place before them.

'No,' said John. 'I mean, because of his injuries. He needs to ... to recover.'

'I am sure Alter Blade has adequate healers,' said Barron, selecting a slice of custard tart from a platter in the middle of the table. 'My son challenged his brother, as was his right, but he must live with the consequences. I will not coddle him.'

Maria sucked in a sharp breath. The night's events would filter out through the guards and servants and would be the talk of Alter for weeks to come, yet Barron sat there eating pastries as though it were a run of the mill occurrence.

'Do not provoke your brother again,' he said to Elex, although his voice was mild.

'Yes, Father,' said Elex, but he wasn't even looking at the man. He was looking at Maria.

What in the Goddess's name? Did Elex think this was normal? Was her new life in Oshe to feature regular meals like this? Was this mild compared to what they were used to? It seemed to be.

But at least her life in Oshe, even if it was to be brutish, perilous, and base, would be with Elex and not his detestable brother. Maria's pitcher was half full, not half empty, and she would worry about the rest later.

She leaned in, and Elex stooped so her lips were close to his ear. 'I'm still not sure what this is,' she said quietly, glancing down at their tied hands. 'What does it all mean?'

'I claimed you as my own,' he replied, a little sheepishly. 'If any wants to take you from me now, they'll have to kill me.'

'Elex!' Maria hissed.

'It was the only way,' he said, stroking her long hair back over her shoulder.

'I am not a commodity to be fought over!'

'I know,' he said, then ran his thumb across the palm of her hand in a way that sent shivers down her spine. 'But it was the only way. And I apologize deeply if I was mistaken, but I rather got the impression you'd prefer to marry me over the *painted peacock*. And I could not bear to let you go.'

She couldn't hide the smile demanding space on her lips, and he gently squeezed her waist in reply.

'Father has always had a soft spot for Cane, even if he has little respect for him, but the opposite can be said for me.'

'Why?'

'Because I often refuse to comply with his wishes. He controls my siblings and his wives with gold and favors, but I have gold of my own and men loyal to me. I don't need him, and he doesn't like it. He takes any chance he can to slight me.'

'Even if that means risking my uncle's displeasure?'

Elex shrugged. 'Does your uncle care which of us you marry?'

'No,' she conceded. 'But he would've cared if oil had ended up in his lap, and he won't be pleased a dinner in his home ended this way.'

'Father's testing him. He'll watch closely to see how Danit responds ... if he chooses to respond at all.'

Maria inhaled and gave a little acquiescent shake of her head. *Men.* 'Fine,' she said, sulking a little, 'then I suppose I am glad you claimed me. How long must we stay like this?' She held up their joined hands. 'Not until we wed?'

He chuckled. 'Much as I would like to keep you by my side every minute until then, it need only last until dawn.'

Maria chewed her lip, her mind whirring.

'What is it?' he said. 'I can avert my gaze if you need to use the water closet.'

She exhaled a huff of laughter. 'I am not squeamish about such things.' Danit, who'd accompanied Cane to the infirmary, strode back into the room, snapping at the servants to bring liquor strong enough to burn away the memory of the night. 'He wants me to go to Arow.'

'Tonight?' Elex said, aghast. 'You can't go at night; it's too dangerous!'

'It's dangerous during the day, too, but Danit doesn't care.'

'Then I am doubly glad to have claimed you.'

'He won't be pleased.'

'What will he do?' Elex turned serious, seeming to sense her foreboding. She shrugged.

'Beat you?'

'No. He doesn't do that any longer, but he might destroy my still room, or send away my servants.'

'Then put on a show,' he said with a roguish smile. 'Let the room know you are displeased with my behavior, and I will play along.'

Danit sat heavily in his seat, accepting a drink from a servant.

'You don't think we've had enough drama for one night?' she said, lowering her voice even further.

'Is there such a thing?'

For the love of the Goddess ... 'I don't dare think what my life will be like in Oshe if you find the events of tonight amusing. Do things like this happen often?'

A broad smile spread across his lips. 'More often than they do here, apparently. So you should take this opportunity to practice. I'll even give you notes.'

'Elex ...'

'Maria ...' he echoed, his tone playful.

She bit her lip to hide her smile. It was probably a bad idea, but her uncle would likely punish her anyway for failing to get Nicoli, so she might as well do something fun to offset her sentence, and the evening was already a disaster.

'I don't care how you justify it,' she said, raising her voice just a little, 'you cannot *claim* another person as your own!'

Her words wiped the humor from Elex's lips, and something like fear ran down her spine at the look that replaced it. A cold, hard, impenetrable mask she didn't like one bit. 'What difference does it make?' he said. 'You were to wed an Oshe, and now there is no doubt as to which one.'

'You want our marriage to be like this?' She raised her voice a little more. 'You calling all the shots, expecting me to meekly obey?'

'Yes,' he said simply. 'That is the way of Celestl, is it not?'

Maria made a disgusted noise in the back of her throat.

'Power is king,' he continued. 'Whatever one wants must be taken, not given. If you want my respect, you must do something to earn it.'

'Unbind me. I am tired and wish to go to bed.' Her snappish words came easily after his touching that very real nerve.

'No need; I'll accompany you ...'

John gasped behind them. 'Uncle, will you let such language stand?'

Maria turned pleading eyes on Danit, as though begging for help.

'There is little I can do,' he snarled. 'Anything goes once hands have been tied. If you wanted to get away, then you shouldn't have helped him tie the knots.'

'I didn't know what he was doing! Unbind me,' she demanded again.

Elex tugged her hand, pulling her closer. 'Make me, beautiful.'

She punched his arm, putting real weight behind it, a furious fire raging through her blood, some emotional part of her responding, even if her rational mind knew his words were fake. 'This is the way you wish to begin our lives together? Belittling me? Disregarding my wishes?'

'What else would you have me do?'

'Urgh, a man like you could never understand.' She tried to pull him to the table, planning to quietly ask Danit what she should do about visiting Arow, but Elex held firm. 'If I am to be tied to you all night,' she spat, 'I would at least like the comfort of a chair.'

Elex's smug smile turned wicked, and Maria froze as he moved impossibly close. The whole room was watching!

'What are you doing?' she breathed, a shot of adrenaline punching through her veins.

'Providing you with the comfort of a chair,' he said, sliding his free hand under her legs.

'Elex! I'll fall!'

He moved their joined hands to his neck. 'Not if you hold on.'

Maria couldn't hold anything with her right hand, seeing as their fingers were entwined, but she clutched at him, and by some miracle stayed in his arms.

'Bring a comfortable chair, please,' Elex said to the servants hovering by the door, 'and put it by the fire.' They rushed to do his bidding and soon returned with an armchair most definitely not big enough for two to sit side by side.

'Bring a couch!' Maria shrieked, but Elex ignored her, carrying her to the fire and sitting on the springy, upholstered chair, settling her across his lap, then leaning triumphantly back into the cushions.

'Uncle!' Maria shouted. 'Help me!'

Danit scowled as the servants scurried about, making quick work of cleaning up the mess. 'There is nothing I can do.' He looked away, throwing his napkin irately onto the table before leaning back in his chair.

Maria fought for a while, giving the others a spectacle, but Elex easily held her in place. Eventually she quietened down, and the others returned to their food—some with more gusto than others—while casting occasional glances Maria and Elex's way.

'Bravo, my little hell cat,' Elex murmured in her ear. 'That was worthy of the stage.'

'You did an excellent job yourself,' she said. *Perhaps a little too good.* She shifted, resting her head against his shoulder, and his hand stroked her arm, reassuring and intimate, brushing away the hurtful words until she'd forgotten he'd said them at all.

They sat in silence for a while, Maria savoring him, his warmth and feel and smell. She burrowed in closer, wanting to climb under his skin, needing to erase the night, the feel of Cane, the memory. She wanted to fuse herself to Elex and never let him go, the need making her restless.

'I'm sorry,' said Elex, stroking her back. 'Tonight was … It won't ever be like that between us. And when we return to Oshe, my men will keep you safe, even when I can't.'

Maria was too wrapped up in the relief and elation and utter exhaustion of the night to think too much about the future. 'We have to get to our marriage intact first,' she whispered, wondering what else might happen to jeopardize that.

'After tonight, if my brother—or anyone—tries to claim you before we are wed, I can kill them with no consequences. And anyone considering themselves noble would be honor-bound to help me.'

'Because of this?' She held up their joined hands.

He nodded. 'So long as we remain bound until dawn.'

'Hand tying's a serious business.'

'The old customs are the best.'

'Hmmm …'

'Are you hungry?' he asked. 'Should I get the servants to bring food?'

'Yes,' she said, realizing she was, seeing as she hadn't eaten anything at the table. She called to the servants.

'Shall we cook meat for you?' asked one.

'Yes,' said Maria. 'I don't expect it's safe for a vat of boiling oil to be placed anywhere near us as things stand.'

The servants hid their covert smiles and busied themselves with their task.

'I suppose a private dinner is more pleasant than dining with the others,' said Maria, 'even if we had to work for it.'

'And so much more comfortable,' he agreed, stroking his thumb across her waist.

Her body melted into him, and that same unfamiliar sensation pooled low in her belly, Maria surprised a simple touch could achieve something so complex. She had never been this close to a man, aside from Cane earlier, but with Elex, it was so entirely different.

'Having me atop you cannot be more comfortable than a chair of your own,' she said, playing with the buttons of his cuff, then sliding her fingers along the line of skin at his wrist.

'It really depends what type of comfort you mean,' he said, moving his fingers higher, approaching the underside of her breast, the copious fabric of her layered dress hiding his hand from view.

'Here we are,' said a servant, carrying two plates loaded high with meat and salad. Several more brought a table, another drinks, and the last carried a basket of fresh bread.

Maria cleared her throat and sat up straight. 'Wonderful, thank you so much.'

They left, and Maria looked at the plates, then their joined hands, and giggled. 'How are we supposed to do this?'

'Lean forward,' he said, and as she did, Elex removed his right arm from her back. 'Now lean against the arm of the chair.' It created space for their free arms in front of them, and Elex reached for a plate, placing it on her legs, then handed her a fork. 'Easier to share.'

Maria soon abandoned the fork, finding it easier to wrap chunks of meat and lettuce in the bread with her fingers in the tight space. Their conversation was wide and sweeping, covering their homelands, families, favorite foods, the war, Maria's black market, the exploits that had resulted in Elex's reputation, all with the occasional scowl thrown in for the benefit of the rest of the room.

'And that's when I met your brother, Hale,' said Elex, at the end of a story about his time studying geostronomy at the university in Spruce Blade.

'You know Hale!' she said with a quiet squeal. 'Were you friends?'

'Yes. I like him a lot, especially after he saved me in a brawl.'

'I can't imagine you brawling. Hale, on the other hand ...' A weight settled on her chest. 'Do you think he's truly dead?'

Elex shook his head. 'I can't bring myself to believe that. He was top of his class in astrocal and florology and even pipped me to the post in geostronomy. He had such an interest in all things and was an accomplished sailor. Are we supposed to believe he fell off the edge of the world? Or got lost? It's hard to imagine ...'

'So you think he's, what? Exploring?' she asked hopefully.

He shrugged. 'That's what he set out to do.'

'He set out to touch the edge of the Circle Sea.' Which was stupid and reckless and dangerous.

'And to discover what lies beyond.'

'There is nothing beyond,' she said, gesticulating so fiercely she nearly upset the plate of food.

Elex steadied it, then slowly rubbed the oil she'd smeared across her knuckle with his thumb.

Maria almost forgot to breathe, feeling the intimacy everywhere.

'How do you know?' he said, his voice low, his attention on her fingers.

'How do I ...?'

He lifted his gaze to hers, his eyes dark as the night sky, and her mouth went dry.

A cough from the table reminded her they were not alone, and she shook her head and pulled back a little, exhaling hard to steady herself, Elex still watching her with the same intense look. 'Hale is not the first to be inquisitive. Others have sailed where he planned to, have circled Celestl, and reported there is nothing there.'

'But they never went right to the edge,' Elex countered, picking up his wine, 'for fear of falling.'

'Then by your logic, maybe he is dead.' Her mind recoiled at the thought, refusing to truly believe it.

'Or maybe he heard about the peace pact and delayed his return so as to leave the burden of marriage to his siblings.'

A smile tugged at her lips. 'Now that does sound like my brother.'

Elex leaned back and chuckled. 'I hope to see him again. He's a riot.'

'He's an arrogant pain in the arse,' she said fondly, 'but we shouldn't talk of him.'

'Why?'

'Because Laurow demanded the first son of Alter in the pact. If John's betrothed gets a whiff of the idea that Hale could be alive, the whole thing could crumble.'

'Why does it matter? Is a child of the first family not as good as any other?'

Maria gave him a levelling look. 'Need I explain the laws of succession?'

'Yes, the first son inherits, but—'

'If she marries John, and then Hale shows up, her position is dramatically altered.'

He took a sip of wine. 'It is different in Oshe. And you don't seem concerned to be betrothed to the second son of Oshe Blade.'

Maria smirked. 'Because I am selfish. I care more for happiness than position.'

He gave a cocky smile and squeezed her hand. 'What about your uncle?'

She shrugged. 'Cane might be the first son, but the whole of Celestl whispers about you and your black reputation. Each of you have pros and cons, so it makes little difference which I marry, but John ... I love my brother, but he and Hale do not compare.'

'How casually they play with our lives ...'

'Imagine if another toyed with them as they do with us.'

'It would be a fine way to start a war,' he said. She agreed with a grim nod of her head.

They finished eating, and Elex used the napkin around their hands to wipe Maria's mouth.

She giggled. 'At least it's practical for *something*.'

His eyes dipped to her lips, and her lungs stopped working, but then he looked away, back to the table where the others were making their excuses, retiring for the night.

Danit was the last to leave, a deep scowl etched into his face. 'Remember, Elex, there is always someone watching.'

Maria stifled an embarrassed laugh. 'What does he think you're going to do?'

'I have ideas,' he growled, squeezing her waist. 'And I don't care who watches ...'

'Elex!' She swatted his arm, ignoring the bolts of desire that fired out from his fingers. 'There are servants everywhere!'

'Nothing they haven't seen before,' he said, urging her forward so he could put his arm behind her once more.

She settled against him, and they lapsed into silence, the only sounds the shuffling and clinking of servants clearing the table and the crackling of the fire.

He stroked her arm, pressed his lips lightly to her temple, and then began humming a gentle folk song she hadn't heard since she was a child, his deep, rich tone soothing to her core. The sound rumbled up through his chest, that and the vibrations lulling her until her eyelids became heavy and she could do nothing to resist the unrelenting tug of sleep.

Chapter Fourteen
Ava

Kush was gone by the time Ava woke the following morning, but she felt better and more rested than she had in a long while, for once warm and protected in her bed. She helped herself to a hearty breakfast of porridge and honey, Mrs. B glaring at her from across the kitchen, then got on with her chores.

Perhaps she was imagining that everyone was looking at her differently, giving her a wider berth than usual. She didn't know if King had told them what happened, but it felt different. Like there was a reason for others to be wary of her ... not that she knew why Kush and his father invoked such fear, aside from the obvious threat of death.

Who was the older man? *Influential*, Kush had said. But how? He wasn't the mayor, nor the tax collector. Perhaps a successful merchant or the owner of a market? But he didn't have the look of someone who got their hands dirty, and everyone kept referring to the Gods where he and Kush were concerned. Could his father work directly for them? Impossible, surely. But they'd punished Malik for stealing from the Gods, and Kush's mother lived beside the temple ... had likely been a temple woman herself.

The Gods didn't share the women of the temple with anyone. Had Kush's mother been gifted to his father as some kind of reward? She'd heard of such things. Or perhaps they'd fallen in love and begged the Gods for mercy. Ava preferred it that way, although Kush's parents didn't live together, so perhaps it wasn't such a happy tale ...

She'd ask Kush, and he'd probably refuse to tell her, if she ever saw him again after ruining his shirt and ... everything else.

But she did see him again. She saw him that very night. He knocked on the window when the moon was up, and Ava let him in, her mouth hanging open in delighted astonishment.

'Hi,' she said awkwardly, stepping back to give him some space.

'I brought you something.' He stepped towards her and pulled a small, round stone from his pocket, a playful smile on his lips. 'Open your palm.'

She hesitated for a moment, then did as he said, her heart in her throat as he carefully placed the stone against her skin. 'What is it?'

'A lava stone,' he said, looking expectantly at her, but she had no idea what a lava stone was. 'It generates heat. Look at it and say, *infernon mynon*.'

Ava felt foolish, blushing as she eyed the innocuous stone, but she did as he said, then almost dropped it when it became hot. 'Gods!'

'Just make sure you always say the *mynon* bit. Otherwise, you'll burn the whole place to the ground.'

'Oh ...' She eyed the stone warily.

'And to make it stop, just say, *neidge*.'

'Neidge,' she whispered, and the stone instantly cooled. 'Wow.'

A smile split his face, transforming his tired, drawn features into something radiant. 'You like it?'

'I love it. Thank you.' And she meant it because she would no longer shiver as she slept. It wasn't quite as good as Kush's warmth, but it was the next best thing.

And it was the first proper present she'd had since losing her parents. Every time she thought of them lately, she was filled with a greater and greater sense of loss.

Silence descended, and when Kush showed no signs of leaving, Ava was unsure what to do. 'Would you like to sit?' she tentatively asked.

He dropped down onto the lumpy mattress and shuffled backwards, leaning against the stone wall.

Ava winced. 'Those stones are filthy.'

'I don't care.'

'Well, don't say I didn't warn you,' she said, perching on the edge of the bed.

'Was everything okay today?' he asked, his eyes searching.

'Better than okay. Not a single bad word or slight or elbow in the ribs.'

'They do that to you?'

She scoffed. 'Kush, I'm no one ... everyone's punching bag on a bad day. You get used to it.'

'You are not no one,' he said, shaking his head darkly.

She laughed, then looked at the ceiling. 'Most would disagree.'

'Then most are wrong.'

'Oh?'

'You're ... important.'

She bit back a smile, glad he thought so, but ... 'I'm a tavern girl.' There was no denying it.

He looked at her for a long moment, his features turning sad, and Ava got the impression he wanted to say more, but then he shook off his reverie. 'I had the best night's sleep in a long time last night.'

Ava smiled in shy delight. 'Me too.'

'And I wondered if ... maybe ... we could do it again? I don't mean—'

'Yes.'

He chuckled, and she flushed.

'But I have questions,' she added, a little defensively.

His smile fell away, and shutters slammed closed over his openness. 'I can't promise to answer them.'

'I know. But ... can I ask?'

He nodded stiffly, and Ava thought for a moment. 'What can you tell me? About who you are? Your father? Your training?'

He clenched his jaw and slowly shook his head, looking away.

Ava waited, holding her breath, appraising him the way her mother had taught her, relishing the chance to finally look beyond his veneer. And then their eyes met and held, still and exposed, and to her surprise, he let her see him. More than that, he invited her in.

Her chest clenched as she tried to glean what she could, but he was so complicated. Most people were straightforward, their motivations and desires and personalities. But he wasn't. He was layered and conflicted, like he hadn't yet worked out who he wanted to be ... who he was beyond his father's expectations. Or perhaps she was merely projecting her deductions ... he was so muddled, it was impossible to tell for sure.

'My father is determined for me to be great,' he said eventually. 'He's been training me—shaping me—for years. Killing Malik was a test. He didn't think I was capable ... knew I didn't want to, so he ... if I hadn't ...' He finally pulled his eyes away, hiding some shadow he didn't want to share. 'He allowed me more freedom after that, even if he had his lapdog track me.'

'Still?' said Ava, a pang of fear ripping through her. If they'd followed him here ...

'No. He's not in this—' He stopped himself. 'No.'

He shut down, and Ava was desperate to know why. 'What are you training for?'

'To carry out the will of the Gods,' he said in a tone she couldn't quite place. Was it bitterness? Sarcasm?

'So you're an enforcer?'

He shook his head. 'Not like in the stories.'

So many fairytales featured righteous, sword-wielding enforcers sent by the Gods. To save towns from famine or slay evil leaders or protect the temples from the unworthy.

'Well, not exactly anyway.'

Ava cocked an eyebrow. 'You mean you can't travel between worlds and wield enchanted stones and don't regularly save damsels from tall towers guarded by fearsome beasts?'

'Turns out I prefer cellars.'

Her heart lurched, and a beat of silence expanded between them.

'What's your plan, Ava? You'll be eighteen in a year.'

'So?'

'What then? What will you do?'

She frowned. 'What do you mean? What else could I do?'

'Lots of things.'

'Like what? Other than clean and serve ale?'

'You're clever,' he said sincerely, 'you could do anything, go anywhere.'

She wanted to believe him but knew better. 'What about you? How old are you?'

He hesitated, as though not sure he should tell her. 'Twenty-one.'

'And your plan is to work for your father?'

He shifted uncomfortably. 'I have little choice.'

'Will you work with him forever?'

'We're talking about you,' he said firmly.

She smiled. 'I'm more interested in you.'

He stayed silent for a beat, seeming reluctant, like his mind was at war with itself, fighting a lifetime of ingrained secrecy. 'It's complicated.'

She drew in her shoulders and raised her eyebrows. 'Families are, or so everyone tells me.'

'What about yours?' he said gently. 'Do you remember them?'

She shrugged. 'I remember my parents a little. They were ... experimental academics, or something like that. I remember bits of our house, where they worked, and sometimes visitors would come.'

'Who?'

'I don't know. Usually they would shoo me away and tell me to be quiet.'

'They treated you badly?'

'No! They taught me all kinds of things and listened when I spoke and told me I was special. And then one day, a man in a black cloak said they were dead, took me to Mrs. B, and told me to be good.'

'Who was he?' Kush asked, leaning forward.

She shrugged. 'I wish I knew.'

'Have you ever tried to find out more? About how they died? Or visited your old home?'

She eyed him speculatively. 'Why would I?'

'You're not curious?'

'I don't remember where we lived. All I know is that it was somewhere past the temple, and I can't remember anyone who knew them. I can't even remember their names. I was only six when Mrs. B took me in.'

'What did the man tell Mrs. B?' said Kush. 'What did he promise her in return for taking you?'

'I asked about him once but never again ...' And she hadn't thought of the man in years, ever since it had become clear he wouldn't return.

'You should ask her again.'

'What's the point?'

'Knowledge.'

'Knowledge is dangerous.'

'No, Ava, knowledge is strength. Knowledge keeps us safe.'

She watched him for a moment, not sure what he meant. She couldn't imagine any knowledge that would make her feel that way.

He exhaled slowly. 'We should sleep; I have to go early.'

They shuffled into the same positions as last time, Ava closest to the wall, Kush on the outside, only a whisper of space between them. Ava relished the puffs of warm air hitting her neck, imagining it was his fingers caressing her, her skin screaming out for contact, starved and desperate for the simple joy of touch. But he didn't touch her, and she couldn't touch him, too scared he would run away, that she'd never see him again, that she would lose the new wonder of his company at night.

He inhaled deeply, and she pretended it was because he liked the way she smelled. She'd seen men do that to women—bury their noses in their necks and tell them they couldn't get enough of their scent. Ava probably smelled terrible, given how infrequently she washed, but she pretended she smelled as good to him as his spicy, musky scent smelled to her.

'Tell me a story,' she whispered, wanting to prolong their time awake together, wanting to know more about him in any way she could, wanting the deep timbre of his voice to vibrate through the uncomfortable mattress into her chest.

'A ... story?'

'A happy one.'

He stayed quiet for a long while, and Ava worried he would refuse or that he'd fallen asleep, but then he said quietly, 'Once upon a time, there was a magical tree.'

Gooseflesh pebbled her skin, and she bit her lip as she waited for more.

'The tree was the center of everything, and at the top, in the Clouds, lived the most powerful people in the land: the sorcerers.'

'They wielded magic?' said Ava.

'Yes, and they hoarded their magic, hiding themselves away and coveting power. But one day, a young woman came to the Clouds with her grandmother. The older woman had been hired by the sorcerers to teach their children magic, for she was the most remarkable and inventive sorcerer they'd ever seen. But she had one condition: that her granddaughter could attend the lessons, too.

'The sorcerers reluctantly agreed because, although they didn't like the idea of a commoner infiltrating their ranks, the girl had recently grown into magic that seemed set to rival even her grandmother's great strength.'

'So they coveted her, too,' guessed Ava.

'They did. And after a time, she married into the oldest, most respected family in the Clouds, the family who'd first discovered the tree. But not everyone was happy about the union, especially when she turned herself and her husband into Gods with lives so long they were practically immortal.'

'How?' asked Ava. 'How can someone make themselves into a God?'

She felt Kush shrug, his arm brushing her back in a way that made her shiver. 'The other young sorcerers demanded to know the same thing, demanded to be turned into Gods themselves. Nothing could deter them, and eventually they forced the woman to do it to them, too.'

'How?' said Ava.

'Magic,' he whispered.

'Why?'

'Because they couldn't bear someone else having something they didn't.'

'Typical,' Ava said with a frown.

He sighed. 'They basked in their new greatness for a while, proclaiming themselves Gods to all the worlds and demanding fealty. But the new Gods were scared that the woman who'd made them could unmake them, were scared she would make other Gods, and they didn't want to share their power. They killed her and her husband and retreated to the Clouds where they lived out their days, glad to be the most powerful sorcerers once more.'

After a pause long enough to imply he'd finished, Ava turned her head to see his face. 'That's it? They got away with murder? I said I wanted a happy story!'

'And the new Gods lived happily ever after,' he said, with a wry smile.

'Kush!' She rolled her eyes, then turned back to face the wall, pondering for a moment before saying, 'I'm changing the ending. In my version, they didn't kill her and her husband. Instead, they all lived happily together in the Clouds. They used their new powers for good and ruled justly and fairly forevermore.'

He huffed out a breath that hit her neck hard, and her hair stood on end. 'Happy endings don't exist, Ava.'

'It's a story, Kush,' she said, mirroring his tone. 'Anything can exist in a story.'

He hummed skeptically, and the sound resonated through her. 'If you say so,' he murmured.

'I do say so, because the happiness found in stories is the only happiness I have.'

Kush was gone again by the time Ava woke, and she played his words over in her mind as she went about her chores. She wasn't sure she wanted the answers to his questions about her parents, knew she should probably let sleeping dogs lie, but then she stepped into the kitchen and found herself alone with Mrs. B, and one was out before she could stop herself.

'Who was the man who left me here?' she blurted.

Mrs. B's aging features morphed into something bleak ... something fearful, and Ava's eyes widened. King seizing power had wrought many changes on Mrs. B's face, but never had any of that brought about this expression, and it shocked Ava to such a degree, she took a step back.

'Why would you ask me that? Why now?' Mrs. B gripped the back of a chair, her knuckles white.

Ava paused a beat, then remembered why Kush had asked. 'I'll be eighteen soon, an adult, and I'd like to know all I can about my past.'

'Why?'

'Why not?'

'It's him, isn't it? The boy.' She took a menacing step towards Ava. 'What's he been filling your head with?'

'Nothing!'

'Then *why*?' She practically shouted the word, but her attempt at intimidation only strengthened Ava's resolve. Since she'd started taking food,

Ava had grown stronger, whereas Mrs. B looked suddenly old and far less frightening ... and she was hiding something.

'Because I want to know who I am. I want to know why you took me in. And I want to know what else you've been keeping from me.'

'I took you in out of the goodness of my heart,' she hissed. 'I clothed you and fed you and put a roof above your head. And *this* is how you repay me?'

'You're scared.' It came out like an accusation, although she hadn't meant it to be.

'The man who brought you here was as evil as your parents, but I owed him a debt.'

'Evil?' Ava repeated in a whisper. Her parents hadn't been evil ...

'Playing with nasty things. Dangerous things. They got themselves killed because of it.'

'My parents weren't evil. I remember a house filled with—'

Mrs. B cut her off with a contemptuous, high-pitched noise. 'No one will touch that house with a ten-foot pole. That's how bad—how contaminating—they were. Barely human.'

Ava shook her head. 'I don't understand.'

'Evil,' she sneered. 'Your parents were an abomination. They thought themselves above everything and everyone. Even the Gods.' She cocked her head to the side, fixing Ava with a spiteful, triumphant look. 'But they were wrong.'

Chapter Fifteen
Maria

Maria woke with a start but stilled when she remembered where she was and whose arm was wrapped around her.

'Goddess,' she breathed, Elex's arm tightening as he woke, too. 'We made it!'

'I stayed awake until dawn to be sure,' he said, stretching back as much as he was able. Then he squeezed her tight and lowered his lips, hovering them just above hers.

Maria's body came fully awake in the space of a heartbeat, her lips falling open as she tipped her head back, a charge like lightning skittering through her blood.

He smiled as he watched her, and she closed her eyes, urging him to do it. To kiss her.

But he didn't, and when she blinked her eyes open, she jumped, finding the face of her maid hovering just above them.

'Ma'am, you must come!'

Maria ignored her embarrassment as best she could. 'What's the time?' she said, rubbing her eyes with her free hand, trying to ignore Elex's fingers drawing lazy circles on her waist.

'It's almost nine,' said the maid, 'and the party from Laurow is early! Scouts spotted them on the Outer Circle and they're travelling at speed. They'll be here in minutes!'

'Shit,' said Maria, tugging at the knot binding her to Elex. He helped, and when their hands parted, she sprang to her feet. 'I have to get dressed!'

He nodded. 'Likewise,' he said, standing slowly but showing no sign that he planned to move away from the chair. She smiled as she rushed off, giddy at the feel of him watching her go.

Within minutes of reaching her room, Maria was once again ready to present herself to the world. She wore a sturdy, split-skirted dress in her preferred style with riding breeches beneath, and to honor their visitors from Laurow, it was all a deep burgundy red.

It was good they had arrived early, because Maria could slip away straight after their welcoming committee. With no hiccups, she could get to Arow and back in time for lunch, and no one would ever notice she'd gone.

Maria began lining up with her family at the bottom of the steps in the mansion's courtyard, listening to the sound of approaching hoofbeats. She was distracted as she shuffled towards her spot, thinking of Elex, of how no one could prevent her from marrying him now, so it took her a moment to realize what was happening when Danit stopped her with a ferocious grip on her arm, dragging her to a halt.

'Liar,' he hissed, and Maria started, her face pulling into a questioning frown.

'Don't act the fool with me, niece. Your acting skills are not as good as you think, and you are not yet married to the Black Prince.'

'Uncle, I ...'

'Oh, I believe you hate Cane; you were entirely convincing on that front. But Elex?' He scoffed. 'Remember your duty, girl.'

He released her, and she staggered to the end of the line, taking her place beside her grandmother.

'One day more,' Dio said lightly, clicking her stick on the paving. 'One day more.'

Maria turned her head, but her grandmother was looking forward, her expression polite yet somehow also conveying that she was currently under-stimulated, and Maria half believed she'd imagined the words.

But at that moment, the Oshe family strode down the stairs behind them, and as she turned to look, Maria could once more think of nothing but Elex. He was dressed in midnight blue, and the sight made her start because that was the color of the Claws. Had he done it on purpose?

She forced herself to look away, not to stare, but she chanced a glance at him as he took the space to her right, while the rest of his family lined up on his other side, his brother notably absent, still lying sedated in the infirmary.

'Red suits you not nearly so well as the color of the sky,' said Elex, his voice barely more than a murmur.

'Whereas I like you in midnight blue. Dark, like your reputation.'

His knuckles brushed the back of her hand, and she almost forgot to breathe, which was ridiculous, given they'd been bound together all night. He linked his pinky with hers, and her heart almost stopped at the tenderness, the intimacy, the promise.

The party from Laurow rolled through the gates, the carriages, just as ostentatious as the ones from Oshe, coming to a stop before them.

Laurow guards rushed to open the doors of the first, and a tall, glamorous woman with short, dark hair and olive skin stepped down. She wore a fitted dress made of the finest burgundy silk with a delicate purple scarf around her shoulders.

All in the receiving line offered respectful head bows or curtseys, but the woman didn't stop before any but Barron and Danit. To them, she curtseyed, then told them how happy she was to see them and how glad Laurow was that they could finally put the war behind them and move on as friends.

'We are pleased to hear that, Linella,' said Danit, 'and we are delighted to welcome your daughter, Sophie, into our family.'

Linella turned her gaze to the second carriage, and the rest of them followed her cue. The door swung outward, opened by a burly, burgundy-clad guard, and Maria's jaw almost dropped when Sophie stepped down. She was a tall woman, her skin a shade darker than her mother's, and with long, reddish brown hair, just as Cane had described, although if you asked Maria, there seemed nothing meek about her.

She was swathed in a single length of gauzy purple fabric, draped artfully around her, concealing most of her modesty, although it stretched a little tighter across her large breasts, meaning her nipples pushed against the fabric, virtually in plain view.

Four sour-looking guards formed up around her as she covered the short distance to the receiving line, nothing on her feet but ankle bracelets that jangled as she walked.

Maria caught the stiffening of John's shoulders from the corner of her eye, and she had to exercise every modicum of her self-control not to laugh.

This was his idea of a nightmare, for although he was reasonably rakish, and had certainly bedded many women, never would he have expected his betrothed to arrive wrapped in so few clothes and with so much of herself on display.

Elex tugged on her pinky, and she glanced up at him. He widened his eyes the barest fraction, and then they both turned their attention back to Sophie, who, after bowing her head respectfully to Barron and Danit, stopped before John.

John didn't move a muscle as Sophie sank to her knees before him and lowered her lips to kiss his shoes. She rocked back on her heels and looked up at him from under her lashes, seeming to be waiting for something—what, Maria didn't know, and nor, apparently, did John. Eventually, John held out his hand and helped her to her feet. If Sophie had been expecting some other response, she didn't show it, accepting first his hand and then his stiff invitation to go inside with him.

Maria followed them with her eyes as they climbed the steps, too shocked to speak, just as the others seemed to be.

Danit was the first to snap out of it, just as John and Sophie disappeared through the open doors into the mansion. 'You still observe the old traditions?' he said, his tone containing more than a hint of accusation.

Was this another relic from the past like hand-tying? Had every bride been forced to endure ritual humiliation once upon a time?

'Only on special occasions,' said Linella, accepting Danit's arm and letting him lead her up the stairs. 'And this is a *very* special occasion.'

Maria slipped away as the receiving line broke, heading into the tunnels off the courtyard. Elex was distracted, his father demanding his attention for a moment, but Maria didn't hang around to find out why. This was her only chance to get a message to Nicoli, and she couldn't delay.

She wove quickly through the tunnels, heading for her still room because there was no way she was going to Arow without bribes. Her feet navigated the route without input from her brain, which was busy making a list of all the things she would take, so as she pushed open the door, it took her a moment to make sense of the scene. The carnage that had once been her ordered still room.

Bottles smashed, workbenches turned over, equipment and notebooks missing.

'Fuck,' she said aloud, grabbing handfuls of her hair.

She moved carefully into the room, going immediately for the three secret nooks that contained her most precious things.

'Fuck!' she said again, finding two of them empty, her notebooks gone and all her money. The final nook was, thankfully, intact, and she carefully removed the oils inside, stowing them in her pockets.

She took careful stock of what else remained, finding one of the smallest cupboards still full, hidden behind an overturned bench, along with a handful of vials tucked away at the back of the highest shelf. She had plenty to work with, thank the Goddess, and she didn't let herself think about everything she'd lost.

She combed quickly through the mess on the floor and found a few more salvageable items, but she allowed herself only a cursory search before forcing herself away. She had to get to Arow before her time ran out.

But when she whirled back around, a figure stood in the doorway, and she nearly jumped out of her skin. 'Elex!' she squealed. 'You can't creep up on me like that!'

'Sorry, I thought you'd heard me,' he said absently, a frown on his face as he studied the destruction.

She shook her head, taking a moment to catch her breath.

'What happened?' he asked, stepping into the room and closing the door.

'Danit,' she said bitterly. 'My punishment for last night.'

'But you didn't do anything.'

'He knows I like you, that my protests were false. He's worried I'm no longer loyal to him.'

Elex gave an unhurried nod.

'He's taken my notebooks, money, my most valuable oils, my still ... everything I need. It will take me years to rebuild ... assuming you let me, of course.'

'Maria ...' He stepped forward and pulled her into his arms. 'You may do as you please. I'll buy you ten stills if that's what you need.'

She hesitated before sinking into him, but when she did, the feeling was so good, so much what she hadn't known she desperately needed, she nearly sobbed. Warmth spread through her, but it wasn't only from his touch, it was also the knowledge that she was no longer alone. If John, her mother, or her sister had been the ones in the doorway, they would have shaken their heads and sent pitying looks, then left, this not their problem to solve, but Elex wanted to help her, to replace what Danit had taken ... saw her problems as his own. Relief unwound her long-tense muscles and she molded herself fully against him. 'Thank you,' she whispered, 'but I need my notebooks most.'

'Then we'll get them,' he said without hesitation.

She looked up at him, her heart suddenly running rampant in her ears. 'Danit can't know how important they are. He'll burn them.'

'Maria ...' He took her head in his hands and looked calmly, assuredly down at her. 'We'll get them.'

She buried her face in his chest and held on tight. Why was his kindness causing tears to trickle from her eyes?

'I have to go,' she said, forcing herself away, wiping her face, hardening her heart.

His forehead pinched. 'Why? Where?'

'You know where.' She cast her eyes around, searching for anything she might have missed.

'Arow?'

'Obviously.'

'I'll come with you.'

'It would be more dangerous that way. If they saw you, it would make things a thousand times worse.'

'I'll stay out of sight.'

She laughed but didn't have time to explain the audacity of his state-ment, how badly he'd underestimated the people of Arow Claw. 'They'd find you.'

'They wouldn't.'

'Elex,' she snapped, 'I don't have time to argue. We are to be wed to-morrow, there is a ball tonight in our honor, and if I'm not back in time, there will be trouble. I will go quietly, get the message to Nicoli, and return without delay. That is it.'

'And what if Nicoli hurts you?'

'He won't.'

'Why?'

'Because we've been friends our whole lives.'

'Friendships end.'

Maria tried to push past him, but he stopped her with an arm across her waist before lifting a hand to her neck.

He took a resigned inhale as he looked deep into her eyes. 'Be careful,' he said, his breath caressing her face.

'I will,' she promised, and then he pressed his lips to hers. The kiss wasn't long, but it was deep and tender and comforting, and Maria didn't want to pull away. In the end, Elex was the one to break it. 'I won't be long,' she said, her heart racing wildly. Then, after one final scan of her ruined workroom, she hurried away.

CHAPTER SIXTEEN
AVA

IT HAD BEEN A few nights since Kush had visited, but instead of the usual thoughts of him, Ava played the conversation with Mrs. B over and over in her mind. Had Mrs. B known her parents? Were they truly evil? What had they been doing that went against the Gods?

And then a thought more terrible than all the others: Had Kush's father killed them? If it was something to do with the Gods, it would surely have been an enforcer. Was that why Kush had been interested? Did he know more than he'd let on? And who was the man in the black cloak?

Almost a week after she'd confronted Mrs. B, Kush finally scratched at her window, and Ava wasted no time on pleasantries before launching her inquisition.

'Did your father kill my parents?' she demanded almost as soon as his feet hit the ground, not caring that she sounded like a madwoman.

He frowned, confusion painting its way across his features. 'Why would you think that?'

'Because Mrs. B said my parents were evil, that they did something against the Gods.'

Understanding dawned on his face. 'Oh.'

'Did you know?'

'No!'

He was lying, or at least withholding something, she was sure of it. 'Kush ...'

'What else did she say?'

Ava folded her arms and pursed her lips.

'Can you just tell me, please? And then I'll tell you what I can.'

She narrowed her eyes.

'Ava, please?' His forlorn look thawed her icy resolve, and she threw up her arms in defeat.

'Fine. But you'd better not go back on your word.'

'I won't. I promise.'

Ava told him everything. How Mrs. B had owed the man in black a debt, how her parents had apparently been doing evil, dangerous things, and how Mrs. B had laid the blame for their deaths at the door of the Gods.

'Did she say who the man in black was?'

'No.'

'Why did she think the Gods killed them?'

'She didn't actually say it was them, just that my parents thought themselves above the Gods and that they were wrong ...' She sat on the bed, and he came to sit beside her, taking her hand. 'Do you think it was your father?' she asked in a quiet voice.

Kush shook his head. 'It's ... possible, but if he did, he's never said anything about it to me.'

'Why did you ask about them? My parents?'

'For the same reason you ask about my family: I'm curious.'

Well, he had her there. 'Do you know anything about the house? Mrs. B said no one would touch it because of what my parents did there. Do you know where it is or what happened to it?'

'No, but I might be able to find out.'

He sighed, then pushed her gently down onto the mattress, their positions now habitual, Kush behind Ava, and she closed her eyes and let herself imagine they were somewhere different. Somewhere with meadows and waterfalls and lakes surrounded by flowers. She imagined them married, living in a little house by a pond, catching fish and foraging for berries.

'Where do you go, Kush, when you go away?' She rolled a little, just far enough to see his head resting on his bent arm.

He raised his eyebrows, then shifted onto his back and looked at the ceiling, his side pressing against her body in a way it had never done before. 'To the desert and the mountains and the sea ...'

She turned to face him fully, lying on her other side because there wasn't room for her to lie on her back, too. 'Everywhere ...' He shrugged, and Ava prodded him in annoyance. 'You said you'd tell me everything you know ... so tell me!'

Tension puckered the space between his eyebrows as he refused to look at her. 'I don't know much, Ava. Father barely tells me anything.'

He was so infuriatingly evasive. 'Just tell me!'

He shook his head a little. 'If your parents defied the Gods, it would have been like painting a target on their backs.'

'Like Malik?'

He tilted his head noncommittally.

'You think the Gods sent enforcers to kill them?' she pressed.

'I don't know, Ava! But it's possible.'

'Who were they? What did they do?'

'I wish I had more to tell you ...'

'You wouldn't tell me even if you knew,' she snapped, turning huffily away and staring at the wall. His loyalty was to his father, not her, and she didn't blame him for that, but it was frustrating and hurtful nonetheless.

It took a long time for her to fall asleep, even after Kush shifted into his usual position on his side, reinstating the careful space between them, and in the morning when she woke, he was gone, a pattern repeated many times over the months that followed.

He came to see her once or twice a week, whenever he could slip away without detection. Sometimes he would bring gifts—wonderous flowers she could barely believe existed, small decorative beads in vibrant colors, or delicious morsels for them to share—and he would relay funny stories and strange things people had said. It all sounded so curious ... foreign ... worlds away.

He told her about his mother. How she'd been a temple woman and how it had changed everything when she'd got pregnant.

'But didn't your father get into trouble? I thought the women of the temple belonged to the Gods ...?'

'No, he didn't get into trouble.'

He changed the subject before she could ask more, telling her of his mother's various quirks, like how she insisted on sending her washing to Mrs. Kelly's shop rather than letting the temple workers do it for her. 'She thinks they spy on her.'

'Do they?'

'I doubt it. Although the place is riddled with gossips.'

As the weeks wore on, they eased into a companionable rhythm, point-edly ignoring the moments when their gazes lingered too long, or when the air between them turned heavy and crackled, or when they sat a little closer together than necessary on her bed.

Ava found herself lying awake at night when he was beside her, acutely aware of every move he made and breath he took. But every time she thought he might touch her, hug her, or even brush his lips gently against hers, he pulled away, and her heart broke a little more each time.

It was stupid and fanciful and naïve to even hope he might see her the way she saw him. He was tall and broad and strong and finely dressed and smelled so good and came from a world entirely apart from hers. But then she would catch him staring, or she'd wake to find their bodies touching in the night, and a little bead of hope would swell inside.

But really, what could she expect from him? Even if he did have feelings for her, he was beholden to his father, powerless, just like her. Worse, she was nothing but a tavern girl, and Mrs. Kelly had been right, someone like Kush wasn't for the likes of her. So Ava equal parts endured and basked in their torturous, glorious, unlikely friendship, but on the nights he wasn't there, she buried her nose in the place where he'd lain on her pillow, inhaled his musky scent, and dreamed.

Months later, Kush arrived one night in a dark mood, and Ava shrank back onto the bed, wary. He never seemed to stop getting bigger, and his temper sucked the air from the room.

'What happened?' she asked, her voice little more than a whisper.

'Father ... he ...' He paused, and Ava thought he would shut down like he usually did. He paced to the farthest beer barrel and rested his hands on the wood. 'He's a monster. The things he makes me do ... vicious, vindictive things. I don't know how much longer I can do it.'

'Then don't,' she said, her voice small, just like her hope.

'Ava ...'

'Run away!'

'He'd find me.'

'You don't know that. We could go together!'

He bent lower over his hands. 'I can't, Ava. I just ... can't.'

His words weren't a surprise, but some part of her chest folded in on itself anyway, creating a weight that sat heavily on her heart.

'It's too late for me, but if we're careful, I think ...' He twisted his head to look her in the eye. 'I think I have a way to get you out of here.' He took a step towards her. 'Father gave me ... well ... I have something that could help.'

Ava thought for a moment, trying and failing to decipher his words. 'I don't understand.'

He pulled a flat disc of dull silver metal from his pocket, then strode to the bed and set it down between them as he sat. Ava couldn't tear her eyes away, something about the object calling to her. It was perfectly round, with a series of moving discs of varying sizes set into the metal. Intricate, swirling lines and symbols were carved both on the pieces that moved and all over the rest of the device, but Ava had no idea what they meant.

'What is it?' she asked, looking up at him.

'It's an Atlas Stone. It's used for navigation.'

'Like a compass?'

'More like a map and compass and ... well, we'll get to that.'

'Get to what?' Her mind boggled because she still didn't understand how this small metal disc was supposed to help her.

He took a long breath. 'Do you remember when you asked if I was an enforcer?'

'For the Gods? Yes.' Of course she remembered. The thought was never far from her mind, seeing as Kush had revealed little of his role or what his father was training him for.

'Well, the man who was with me the day I killed Malik, he's an enforcer.'

'Okay ...'

'The head enforcer, and my father's training me to take on that role.'

'Kush, I don't understand.'

He looked at the ceiling, seeming to search for a better explanation. 'Do you remember what you said about the fairytales?'

'That I like happy endings?'

He shook his head.

'That enforcers save damsels from towers? The man you were with didn't seem like that type to me.'

'No, he's not. But the other part was true, about how enforcers ... how they ... how they move between worlds.'

A bark of laughter escaped her, but when his gaze met hers, she clamped her mouth shut, his eyes deadly serious. She glanced at the metal disc. 'How?'

'Only three of these exist, and they're powerful. We use them to do it.'

'Kush ... I—'

'But there are also portals, kind of like doors that link many worlds to a central place, to the Atlas Tree.'

Ava gaped as he continued to talk, the words seeming to spill out of him, sharing secrets he'd kept hidden all this time.

'The Atlas Stones are connected to the tree. When all the dials point to the top,' he said, turning them to demonstrate, 'it leads to the top of the tree.'

'Kush ... I ... Why are you telling me this?'

'Come with me. The Atlas Tree is huge, level after level, big enough to disappear in. You could start a new life there. Get a job. Be free from all this.'

'And where would you be?'

'I would be there too, sometimes ... most of the time.'

'Still working for your father?'

'I can't escape. Even if I ran to another world, he'd find me. But not you.'

'I can't leave,' she said, the words reflexive.

'Ava ...' He took her hand, but she yanked it away.

'A tree, like in your story? I'm not even sure I believe you. How could I? It's ... too much.'

They sat quietly for a long time, then Kush shifted, lying on the bed behind her, shuffling up next to the wall. She eventually lay beside him, but it was uncomfortable, all wrong, because they usually lay the other way, Kush on the edge and her beside the stones.

Ava's mind raced with all he'd told her, and she slept fitfully, waking, unusually, when Kush got up to go. She didn't open her eyes, not sure what she would say if she did, letting sleep tug her back into its clutches, her drowsy mind only just registering Kush's movements. At least until the mattress dipped and his lips brushed her cheek. That chased any hint of sleep away.

'I'm sorry, Ava,' he whispered. And then he was gone.

CHAPTER SEVENTEEN
MARIA

MARIA LEFT HER HORSE at the usual tavern, steeling herself as she stepped across the border into Arow. She couldn't see any lookouts, but then, their ability to conceal themselves was the reason they were chosen for the job.

She travelled quickly over the scrub land that acted as a buffer between the territories of Alter Blade and Arow Claw, then swiftly navigated the twisting, turning streets to Nicoli's workshop.

She was only a street away when Nicoli's cousin stepped into her path, two others behind her, menacing expressions on their faces.

'Gabriele,' said Maria, holding up her hands in surrender, her heart racing, 'I'm not here for any trouble. I told my uncle I was not welcome, but he sent me anyway. I'm here only as a messenger. If you allow me to speak and promise to convey the words to Nicoli, I will turn around and leave.'

Gabriele flicked her long ponytail over her shoulder and smirked viciously. 'No, Maria, that's not how this is going to work.'

Hands grabbed Maria's arms, and she gasped, fear stabbing through her as they forced her forwards. 'Where are you taking me?' she asked, her voice shaky.

'I told you last time we would kill you if you came again,' said Gabriele, who was leading the way, so Maria couldn't see her face.

'You'd kill a messenger? I came only to tell you my uncle requests an urgent meeting with Nicoli!'

'About what?'

'He refused to tell me.'

'So you ran along like a good little mouse.'

'I am under his control,' said Maria. 'You know this. You and Nicoli have seen him punish me many times.'

'Poor little daughter of Alter wants our sympathy,' said Gabriele.

The others laughed.

They pushed her into Nicoli's workshop, and Maria breathed a small sigh of relief. Gabriele could be rash and impulsive, but Nicoli was more level-headed. She was sure he would hear her out, then let her go.

But Nicoli wasn't in his workshop.

'Where is he?' asked Maria, looking frantically about.

'Away,' said Gabriele.

'Please, Gabriele, just let me go. I've delivered my message and—'

'You are not in charge here,' said Gabriele. 'Tie her up, gag her, and put her in the back room.'

'If I'm not home in time for the ball tonight, my uncle will send his army. He'll see this as an act of war!'

'He committed an act of war by sending you here.' Gabriele nodded to the others, and suddenly there was a gag between Maria's lips.

She bit down hard and screamed with frustration, praying to the Goddess that Nicoli would return soon.

Nicoli did not return soon. They tied her to his bed and left her for hours, checking on her only once to give her water and take her to the outside privy so she could relieve herself.

Maria wracked her brain for anything she could do, but she could barely move and couldn't speak. She tried to tease apart the knots at her wrists, but her captors had been careful and she couldn't even touch the loops.

So in the end, all she could do was lie back and stare at the ceiling, wondering how long it would be before she was missed.

Her uncle would doubtless send a squadron to retrieve her, and then everything would truly go sideways. Couldn't Gabriele see this would only harm the people of Arow?

The sun was setting by the time Nicoli finally returned. The pact ball would already be underway, and her uncle would be spitting feathers. Elex

would have told Danit where she'd gone, would also be angry and itching
to do something, so the only question was whether they would wait until
morning or abandon the ball and come tonight. But if they waited until
morning, Maria might be late for her own wedding, putting the whole pact
in jeopardy.

Urgent whispers slid under the door, and although she couldn't make
out the exact words, she could decipher enough to know Nicoli wasn't
happy with his cousin. Hopefully that boded well for Maria.

The door banged open, and Nicoli paled when he saw her lying on his
bed. He rushed to untie and ungag her, then helped her to sit.

'Why did you come?' he asked, kneeling beside her, features forlorn.

'Danit gave me no choice. He wants to speak with you. He said it's
urgent.'

'We told you not to come here.'

Maria's blood flared hot. 'I came as a formal messenger, and you detained
me. *You* should not have done *that*.'

'Well, you've delivered your message, and now you must go.'

'You think it's that simple? You've forced Danit's hand, held me too
long for me to wave off my absence, and not only have you caused embarrassment for my family but also for the first family of Oshe! Even if my
uncle were willing to overlook it—which you know he will not be—my
betrothed is honor-bound to defend me. Your cousin's actions cannot be
undone. If I were you, I'd prepare for an attack, and believe me, I don't say
that lightly.'

'Then go now and placate them. You're good at that.' His words were
dismissive and accusatory.

'Do not sneer at me as though this were my fault. I have not changed. I
have been a loyal friend to you and the Claws. You are punishing me for
my role in a pact I had no say over. Now you've invited the wrath of the
Blades, you look to place the blame on my shoulders? You see all too clearly
the shortcomings of my actions but don't think yours have consequences
of their own?'

Nicoli dropped his head. 'Gabriele should not have done this, but Arow
does not deserve to be punished for her failings.'

'Then come with me to my uncle. We'll find some story to explain my absence, apologize, and—'

'I cannot.'

'Nicoli! Why?'

'I will not bend the knee anymore. They treat us as though we're worthless, but we do have value, and my people have been persecuted enough.'

'But the Blades control the water ...'

'They do, but you said it yourself, the Claws control the turbines that keep Celestl turning.'

'You would put the whole world at risk?' Her stomach leapt into her throat as though she was plummeting off a cliff. He wouldn't. Nicoli wasn't like the men who ruled their world. He was good and kind and cared about his people.

'I would do no such thing; your uncle and his like do that.'

Maria took Nicoli's hands. 'We can end this peacefully,' she pleaded, holding on to his limp fingers, willing him to meet her halfway.

'Peacefully for whom? The Claws don't live peaceful lives, no matter how luxurious yours may be perched atop your moated mansion. You don't see the harm your people cause, and if we have to make it visible to change things, then that's what we will do.'

'Many will die.'

He wrenched his hands away. 'Many people die already from lack of water, and I will not pretend otherwise.'

Maria shook her head, knowing she couldn't change his mind, trepidation seeping into her soul. She squared her shoulders. 'Then tell me how I can help.'

He stood and turned away. 'Run along back to Elex Oshe and attend your wedding like a good little princess.'

'Nicoli, I am not your enemy,' she said bitterly, pleadingly.

'If you can still say that tomorrow, I might just believe you.'

Chapter Eighteen
Ava

Kush had been absent for almost a month, and Ava worried he would never return, causing her mood to turn sour. So much so, Mrs. B sent her out on countless errands, just so she didn't have to tolerate the darkness.

'Uptown with you today,' said Mrs. B. 'The girls need more herbs. And if you're pregnant—if that's what's put you in this black temper—ask them to help with that, too.'

Ava scowled hard. 'I am not pregnant.'

Mrs. B cocked an eyebrow. 'Pity. He might start paying if you got with child ...'

Ava made a disgusted noise as she stormed off.

'Something to think about,' Mrs. B called after her.

Ava was so preoccupied with thoughts of Kush and other worlds and escape that she didn't notice King until he was right on top of her. 'Trouble in paradise, little Ava?' he said, ruffling her hair as he passed.

'Fuck off,' she said under her breath, but the thought had crossed her mind more than once that if Kush never came back, King and his cronies would realize eventually, and then Ava would be in deep water once more.

Her feet made the trip to the apothecary without conscious direction, and then they led her to the temple, to Kush's mother. She'd told herself she wouldn't go, but somehow there she was regardless.

'Ava!' said Yella, who was knitting out front despite the chill in the air. 'I wondered when I would see you again.'

'It's nice to see you,' said Ava, with a polite smile. 'I was passing.'

'Sit! Would you like tea?'

'No, thank you.'

'Both of you in one day! It's Kush's birthday; he visited earlier.'

Ava's heart lurched as she sat in the closest chair. 'He did?'

'He was sad. He's been so happy for months, visiting me so often. I was grateful to the Gods, but recently, I haven't seen him, and today, he wasn't himself.'

'Why?' said Ava, picking at a loose thread on the cuff of her dress.

'I thought maybe you could tell me.' The woman's gaze turned hawk-like, and Ava pulled back.

'I haven't seen him,' she said quickly.

'Ah, then we have our answer!' Yella said, seeming delighted.

Ava stood abruptly. 'I should go.'

'Oh, wait,' said Yella, putting down her knitting. 'I have something for you.' She rushed inside and returned a moment later with a thick woolen scarf. 'I made this for you.'

'I ... um ...'

'Here, try it on.' Yella wrapped the drab thing around her neck. It was brown and shabby-looking, so it wouldn't be out of place in the Cleve. No one would covet it, either, and it was so deliciously warm, covering her exposed chest and neck.

'Yella,' said Ava, pressing it to her skin with both hands, 'it's too much, I ...'

'Pish,' said Yella, waving a dismissive hand.

'Thank you.' Tears filled Ava's eyes.

Yella hugged her. 'You are most welcome.' But she gave Ava a strange look when she pulled back. 'Something about you feels so familiar to me. I thought it the last time, but ... have we ever meet? Did you perhaps come to the temple as a child?'

The very notion made Ava's guts roil; her parents had hated the temple. 'No, I don't think so. And Kush is older than me, so I suppose you would have left the temple before I was born.'

She gave a light, tinkling laugh. 'Oh, child, I never left the temple. I still worship the Gods. I still partake in ceremonies.'

'Oh. Sorry, I didn't—'

'Don't apologize!' She tapped Ava lightly on the arm. 'Now off with you before you freeze. It's making me cold just looking at you. I think next I'll make you a hat.'

Something about Yella's comment set Ava on edge, but she couldn't put her finger on what. The woman had been so warm and welcoming, had knitted her a scarf, and had been thoughtful enough to make it drab and dull, but some part of Ava didn't trust her.

Not that that was unusual. Ava didn't like people in general. Some she could tolerate, so long as she didn't have to spend too much time with them, but she would *choose* to spend time with very few ... only one, in fact, and maybe now she'd lost him.

She looked longingly at the window, as though she could summon him with her thoughts, but of course he didn't appear. 'Happy birthday, Kush,' she whispered just before she fell asleep, making do with the warmth of her lava stone and her scarf.

A scraping sound woke Ava, and she held her breath as a figure slid through her unlocked window, his shoulders so broad now, he only just fit through. She wanted to go to him, to throw her arms around him and sob with relief, but her body was frozen in place, terrified he'd come to say goodbye, that he didn't want to see her anymore, that he'd saved some princess from a tower in another world and liked her better.

But then he lay beside her in the dark and placed a light hand on her arm. Despite sleeping close, they rarely touched on purpose, and it sent something live and vibrant coursing through her. 'Ava?'

She rolled onto her back, expecting him to pull away, their faces so close their breath mingled. But he didn't. Instead, he looked down at her, his eyes soft and warm and inviting.

'I thought you'd gone for good.'

'I'd never do that,' he said, leaning farther into her space. 'I'll always come back to you.'

'Where have you been?'

He pulled away a little. 'Everywhere. I've been transporting enforcers to so many places.'

'Why?'

'Father never tells me.'

'Happy birthday.'

'How did you ...?'

'Your mother.'

He tensed. 'You saw her?'

'She said you'd been there.'

'You shouldn't visit her.'

Hurt stabbed her heart. 'You're embarrassed?'

'No, Ava. It's not safe.'

'Why?'

'Because there's a risk she'll tell my father. If he finds out about you ... that I spend so much time here ...'

'Oh.'

'You're the only person I can trust, Ava. The only person that I ... I have to keep you safe.'

The blue light of the moon cast half his face in shadow, but as their eyes met, it set a bobbin spinning in her chest, coiling so tight it almost hurt, and her lips parted on a breathy exhale.

Her hand moved of its own accord, pressing itself to his hard chest, the feel of him under her fingers making her lips tingle, her skin suddenly too small.

He swallowed, and the bob of his strong throat somehow made the space between them unbearable, so she crept closer, rolling until more of her body pressed against his.

He stiffened. 'Ava ...'

She stilled, waiting, willing him to come closer, praying to every God that he would. He turned his head away, and a shock of panic clenched her heart. 'Don't leave,' she breathed, barely resisting the temptation to take hold of his shirt.

'I'm not ...' he said, turning back, looking down with conflicted, stormy eyes. He lifted a hand to her cheek, running light knuckles across her skin, and her eyes fell closed as she savored the contact.

He moved his hand to her hair, his thumb swiping gently back and forth across her temple, and every fiber of her being focused on his touch. She opened her eyes and watched him watching her, his chest rising and falling heavily, while her lungs stopped working altogether.

'Kiss me,' she whispered, his lips so close, only a hand's distance away.

He didn't move, but his thumb kept gliding back and forth and his eyes slid to her mouth, lingering there.

She'd never been kissed, not properly. The thing with Malik didn't count, and she hadn't wanted it, but the same could not be said for Kush. Every part of her ached for him to close the space between them, to brush his lips against hers.

'We can't,' he said eventually, but he didn't move away and he still caressed her, making it hard for her to think of anything but *more*.

'It's just a kiss.' And the forbidden idea had hung in the air between them so many times over the many months they'd shared a bed.

'It's dangerous,' he breathed, the flex of his fingers against her scalp sending sparks skittering through her blood, making it race.

'You kissed me goodbye. On the cheek.'

'I ...'

'Please, Kush. I know you feel this too.'

He rested his forehead against hers and trailed his fingers across the skin behind her ear.

It pulled something tight at the base of her belly, making her arch. 'Kush ...'

'We shouldn't.' He slowly shook his head, but with each small sideways movement, his lips came closer until only the barest sliver of air separated their skin.

'Kush ...' she begged. 'Please.'

It took several torturous heartbeats, but then the air was gone, replaced by a barely-there press of his lips. A soft hum escaped her as relief seeped into every part of her soul, and as he kissed her again, she slid her hand into his thick, soft hair and pulled him more firmly to her.

He groaned into her mouth, and something inside her turned feral at the sound, so she parted her lips, and Kush didn't hesitate before deepening the kiss, probing his tongue into her mouth.

She pulled him with her as she rolled onto her back, needing more. More contact, more pressure, more everything.

She'd never wanted anyone, but she wanted nothing in the world apart from him, and it wasn't enough. She wanted to rip open her skin and pull him inside, clutching at him with her arms and hooking her leg around his hip to try and make it so.

But she was too greedy, and he broke the kiss, although he didn't pull away, his head hanging beside hers, his breathing ragged in her ear. 'We can't do this,' he panted. 'Ava, we can't.'

She took his hand and lifted it to her face, kissing the fleshy part of his thumb, her lips still needing contact. The smell of eucalyptus floated up from his cuff, and she inhaled gluttonously, then gently bit his skin, swiping her tongue across his flesh, needing to taste him.

Kush's eyes turned hooded, and he canted his head, then he groaned as she bit him again, her nipples tightening at the sound, pressing through the thin cotton of her nightgown, so sensitive it almost hurt.

She slid his hand down to cover her breast, and he made a choked sound, then moved them, turning her and pulling her back against him, wrapping his arms tightly around her, pressing his lips to her hair. 'We can't,' he breathed.

'Why?' she asked in a voice so small, she was almost surprised he heard. 'We just ... can't.'

She exhaled a long breath and tried to still her racing heart, to stamp out the inferno of lust raging through her, telling herself it wasn't a rejection. They were wrapped together as they'd never been before. That meant something. He wasn't pushing her away—quite the opposite—and she pressed as close to him as she could, the rise and fall of his chest caressing her back, both of her arms hugging his tight. But it was more difficult than ever to ignore the hard bulge against her backside that she'd felt the barest hint of so many times before.

Kush woke Ava in the morning, long before the sun was due to rise, with the light brush of his lips against her forehead.

'I'll try to come tonight,' he said gently, pulling away.

She blinked herself awake and pushed up on her arms to find Kush standing halfway to the stairs, holding the center of the Atlas Stone between his thumb and first finger. He used his other hand to flick it so it spun, their eyes locked for one final heartbeat, and then he was gone.

Chapter Nineteen
Maria

It was full dark by the time Maria made it to the boundary between Arow and Alter, and she didn't like what awaited her there one bit.

Elex, Barron, and Danit stood before a squadron of mounted cavalry, Danit mid-speech, telling his men they would teach the Claws a lesson they would not soon forget.

Nicoli had refused to say another word, then kicked her out. He'd told his cousin to make sure she got home safely, but Maria hadn't seen a single person as she'd wound her way through the streets. Then again, she'd been preoccupied.

What had Nicoli meant about her becoming his enemy tomorrow? Something to do with her wedding? Or Toll Day ... Blade Day? Had the Claws planned a protest? The very thought made her sick.

She understood their impulse to say enough was enough. They were second-class citizens in the eyes of the Blades, but her uncle and his peers would show no mercy, and their armies were battle-hardened and spoiling for a fight. They hadn't seen action in months, not since the peace pact had been agreed, and they would be only too delighted to defeat a common foe, regardless of the fallout.

But if the turbines stopped spinning, everyone would die. There would be no more water to fill the lakes that sustained them, and it would be a bloodbath before the end.

'Uncle!' Maria shouted, running for him. 'Uncle, I'm fine! I had to wait to see Nicoli. There's no need for any of this.'

'He kept you waiting?' said Danit, whirling towards her with fury in his eyes.

'He was out of town and only just got back. I thought it better to wait ... The matter seemed urgent.'

'You thought it more important than the ball to mark your own marriage?' His voice dripped with disbelief.

'I didn't think I would have to wait so long, but I left it too late and realized I would miss the ball regardless, so I decided to stay.'

'And risk insulting your betrothed?' said Danit, pointing to where Elex stood beside his father. Elex's expression was guarded, and Maria willed him not to jump to conclusions, to wait and hear her out.

'I would never want to insult my betrothed, but you said it was urgent...' Her uncle wouldn't want to air any of this in public. 'I hope you'll forgive me,' she said to Elex.

He nodded curtly and stepped forward. 'I'll escort you home.'

'Won't we all be going home?' asked Maria, her heart in her mouth. 'Now I'm back, there's no reason for this.'

A cold veneer covered Danit's face. 'Where is he? Where is Nicoli?'

Maria faltered. 'He ... couldn't come.'

'Couldn't?'

'I'm not exactly ... I think ...' Maria searched desperately for a legitimate excuse. 'I think there was something he had to finish before the celebrations.'

'Something more important than speaking with me?' said Danit.

'It seemed like it was out of his hands. Probably to do with maintaining—'

'They need to be taught a lesson once and for all,' snarled Danit.

'They don't,' said Maria, her tone placating. 'They haven't done anything wrong, and it's the eve of Blade Day. Attacking a Claw now will forever taint the peace pact. It's all anyone will remember.'

'You're worried this will overshadow your wedding?' said Danit, a sneer on his face.

'Of course not! But—'

'Take her home,' Danit said to Elex, waving a dismissive hand. 'And do not let her out of your sight until you are wed.'

'Uncle! That is not appropriate.'

'I decide what is and is not appropriate, child. And anyway, you might as well save your appeals for your betrothed. Your wedding is in a matter of hours. After that, you're his problem, not mine. Maybe he can do with you what I have never been able to.'

Maria didn't rise to his bait, much as it angered her. It was true, in a few hours she would belong to Elex, not Danit, but at least with Elex there was hope of a different kind of life. Perhaps a life where she could help the Claws ...

'Anyone you kill tonight will become a martyr,' said Maria, part of her surprised to find herself speaking, raising her voice so the soldiers could hear. 'This will be the legacy of Blade Day: death and destruction and oppression. The slaughter of innocents. You do not face a well-armed force on horseback. You plan to pull men, women, and children from their beds like barbarians!'

Danit slapped Maria hard across her cheek, and her head snapped to the side. She cried out in surprise and clapped a hand over her face as though that could somehow stop the stinging.

Elex was at her side in a heartbeat, shoving Danit back, putting himself between Maria and her uncle. Elex towered over Danit, making him seem small and insignificant. 'The only reason you're not flat on your back on the ground is out of respect for the peace pact,' Elex growled, 'but if you ever touch her again, make no mistake, that is where I will put you.'

Danit paused a beat and then laughed. 'Run along, children. Leave the adults to their work.'

Elex shook his head, then turned his back and followed Maria to her horse. She slipped a vial of orange oil into the usual nook, ensuring it remained out of view, then accepted Elex's help mounting. By the time he'd mounted his own steed, Maria was already galloping away. She would have to slow soon or risk her horse breaking a leg with only the dim light of the moon and stars to guide them, but the small freedom eased the vicelike grip of injustice around her chest a fraction.

Elex caught her as she slowed, and he leaned over to see her face. 'Does it hurt?'

She gave him a level look. 'Of course it hurts.'

'He's a bastard; I'm sorry.'

'It's not your fault. I knew I was playing with fire, but he's never hit me in front of people before.'

'He hits you behind closed doors?'

'Not since he found a better means of control.'

'Your still room?' She nodded, and they rode on in silence for a few moments before Elex said, 'I found this note after you left.'

He handed her a sliver of parchment, and she read it by the light of the moon. *Be a good girl, and I'll give back your toys.*

'Well, I'm guessing after today that won't be happening.'

'I'll buy whatever you need,' he said softly. 'You don't have to do what he says any longer.'

'No, just what you say.' She immediately regretted her sharp words. 'I'm sorry. I'm ... Thank you. I'm just ...'

'What really happened?' said Elex, changing the subject in a way that told her he'd already forgiven her, and her heart swelled. 'I can't believe you really just sat around waiting for Nicoli.'

'I did, actually,' she said with a smirk, 'just not voluntarily.'

'They kidnapped you?'

'Nicoli wasn't there to start, and he wasn't happy about it when he got back. It was his cousin, Gabriele—she's always hated me. Nicoli freed me, but by then, the damage was done. I'm sorry I missed the ball.'

Elex's features were playful when he turned his eyes on her. 'Devastated as I am not to have whirled you around the floor, I think I'll survive.'

Her heart lurched. She'd never craved such a thing before, but she would have loved to dance with him amid the pomp and splendor of the filled ballroom. 'Unless my uncle and your father start a war that kills us all ...'

'The Claws have no army. How would they fight?'

She scowled at him, so he quickly continued, 'I'm not saying I agree with the attack, but how could there be a war if the Claws have no way of standing up for themselves?'

'They control the turbines ...'

'But they rely on those too!'

Maria shrugged. 'I don't know, but Nicoli said something ... I told him I wasn't his enemy, and he implied something was going to happen tomorrow that might change that.'

'Our wedding?'

'He wouldn't say more.'

'What else could it be?'

'The Claws don't just control the turbines but also the flow of water around Celestl ... the pipes.'

'If he messes with any of that, his own people will be hit hardest,' said Elex. 'The Blades would cut the supply to the Claws in a heartbeat. It doesn't make sense.'

'I don't know,' said Maria, 'but Nicoli has always had a militant streak. He's quite brilliant but idealistic, and my uncle has never treated him or his people well.'

Elex exhaled a frustrated breath. 'It's all madness.'

'Uncle won't back down.'

'Nor my father, not after the ball tonight; it's a matter of pride now.'

'And if Nicoli won't either, everyone is at risk. I just wish I knew what Nicoli had planned,' said Maria, as they crossed the bridge over the moat into her family's home. 'That we could *do* something.'

Soldiers rushed forward to ask if she was alright.

'I'm fine,' said Maria. 'It's a long story, but Arow did nothing to hurt me.'

'Expect wounded men before dawn,' Elex added grimly. 'Danit plans to attack regardless.'

No one detained them further as they rode up the cobbled switchbacks to the mansion, jolly stone buildings with bowed glass windows pressing in on either side. Most contained shops with flower boxes and pretty signs out front, and Maria wondered how Elex's home compared.

'It's nothing like this,' he said, when she inquired.

'Go on,' she pressed.

'It's cold and austere. No flowers, dark colors, buildings designed to keep people out rather than welcome them inside ... even the taverns. I've always thought the roofs curve in a pleasing way, our style different to Alter's, and I'm fond of the scale of it—it means it's far easier to hide than it would be here—but most of the buildings are made of wood, not stone, and many are rotting because the owners can't afford to maintain them.'

'Your father doesn't help?'

'That is not the way of Oshe, and Father doesn't care for pretty things—with the exception of women. He couldn't give a damn how it looks.'

'It's amazing, how we're the same and yet so different.'

They handed their horses to two stable girls and headed inside, surprised to find a pair of kissing bodies curled up on a couch by the fire in the entrance hall.

'John?' Maria cried, and he sat bolt upright, his face flushing scarlet.

'What are you doing here?' asked John, Sophie sitting up lazily beside him. She still wore the same sorry excuse for clothing she had earlier, but unlike John, she didn't look embarrassed at all, despite having been caught in a highly compromising position.

'You won't tell anyone, will you?' said John, smoothing his hair and making an effort to unrumple his shirt.

Maria's eyes flicked to his other hand, which was tied to Sophie's. 'You ...' she said. Her brother had handtied his betrothed? Presumably for no good reason.

'Other suitors were trying their luck,' said John, 'so I took a leaf out of Elex's book.'

'There are no other suitors with a valid claim,' said Maria. 'Only—'

'Yes, well,' said John, growing even more flustered. 'What happened? Why did you miss the ball? It was mortifying.'

Maria scowled. 'I was in Arow, delivering a message for Uncle.'

'Oh?' said John.

Elex, realizing they would likely be there a while, dragged over a couch from the window. He and Maria sat, their legs pressed together on the small seat, Elex's arm stretched out behind her.

Maria recounted the bones of the story, glossing over the part where Gabriele had kidnapped her, partly because John had a big mouth, but also because she didn't know if she could trust Sophie.

'Uncle's going to attack them?' asked John, leaning forward.

'I tried to stop him.'

'And the bastard hit her,' sneered Elex, his eyes dipping to her cheek.

John gaped. 'With you there?'

'In front of everyone,' said Maria. Had they attacked the Claw yet? How many would die because of her uncle's senseless pride?

'It will be terribly difficult to cover up that mark on your face for the wedding,' murmured Sophie.

'Hmm,' said John, clearly caring about that not at all. 'The officiate wanted to talk to us earlier.'

'But now it's going to be first thing in the morning.' Sophie pulled a tiny feather off her dress and dropped it to the floor. 'He was a little put out, but he seemed nice.'

'Did he?' John leaned back in his seat and shifted to face his betrothed.

'Oh yes,' said Sophie, placing a hand on John's leg. Their eyes held for a moment, and Maria and Elex shared a knowing smile. Sophie broke the intimacy and turned her gaze on Maria. 'And can I just say, I'm so glad to meet you, Maria. I've always wanted a sister.'

'Uh ... thanks,' said Maria. She'd never met someone this gushy, and it was off-putting somehow. 'So, what are we going to do?'

'About what?' asked Sophie.

'Stopping the bloodshed,' said Maria.

Sophie tittered. 'It's not for us to get involved; it's a matter for our parents.'

Maria worked hard to prevent her mouth from falling open.

'Yes,' agreed John, 'you're right, my dear.'

Silence settled for a beat, and then Elex got to his feet and held out his hand to Maria. 'We should get some sleep ahead of our big day.'

Maria accepted, then wished the other two a good night. It took all the self-control she possessed not to start raging within earshot.

'Well, they seem perfect for one another,' she hissed as soon as they'd rounded a corner.

Elex shook his head as he walked, and when they reached the foot of the sweeping double staircase, Maria stopped dead, a thought pushing its way into her head. 'Did you tell my uncle where I'd gone?'

'Yes,' he said, looking her dead in the eye. 'I deflected for as long as I could, but after the dancing had begun and you still weren't there, I was worried. I planned to slip away and take a few guards with me, but your uncle was watching and if I couldn't go after you, someone had to.'

'You shouldn't have told him,' she said, knowing it was unfair to take her anger out on him but doing it anyway.

He faltered. 'I had little choice.'

'See you in the morning, then,' she said, heading up the stairs. But he followed her, keeping pace easily with his long legs.

'I'm not supposed to let you out of my sight, remember?'

His words sent a zing of awareness up her spine, which then spread down her arms, making the hairs stand on end. 'You take orders from my uncle now?'

'Seems stupid not to when his purposes and mine align.'

She whirled to face him, and he stopped a step below so their eyes were in line. 'You like the idea of locking me up?'

His features darkened. 'Do I get to be inside or outside this hypothetical prison?'

She punched his arm. 'Don't.'

He smiled. 'I'm so glad I get to marry you, my little hell cat.'

'Don't change the subject.' But she softened a little, glad he appreciated her ferocious side.

'You don't like the idea of being locked up with me?' he said in a low, seductive tone, and the air around them suddenly stilled, becoming charged. 'Because soon you won't have much choice. You'll be mine ... and I'll be yours.' He lifted his fingers to her face and ran his thumb across her bottom lip.

She shivered. 'Elex ...'

'Yes?'

Her eyes fluttered closed as he gently tugged down her lip, sensation pooling between her thighs. She reached for him, and then his lips were on hers, capturing her breathy moan in his mouth.

Chapter Twenty

Ava

Ava's Eighteenth Birthday

Kush didn't come back that night. Or the next night. Or any night for months, and on the eve of her eighteenth birthday, she'd begun to lose hope of ever seeing him again.

Mrs. B had become increasingly erratic, nice to Ava one minute and horrible the next. It was as though something weighed on her, but Ava had no idea what. Perhaps the situation with King and his men ...

King had certainly begun to weigh on Tasha, who had lost her usual sparkle. She never giggled anymore, and King spent more time with the other girls than he did with her, which meant Tasha spent more time with Ava. The arrangement didn't suit Ava, because it meant Tasha had noticed Kush's absence and Ava worried Tasha would tell King, desperate as she was to reclaim his favor.

'He still buys me oranges, you know,' Tasha said defensively, watching from the bar as King pulled a *dancer* onto his lap—his end-of-night selection. 'They're my favorite.'

Ava didn't reply; Tasha had said the same many times, clutching desperately to her only scrap of hope.

'When'd you last see him, then?' asked Tasha, tearing her eyes from King and narrowing them at Ava, looking for someone else's misery to detract from her own.

'Oh, I don't know,' said Ava, wiping the scarred wood even though it didn't need wiping. 'A few days ago, I think.'

'Hummm,' said Tasha. 'Really?'

Ava shrugged.

Tasha narrowed her eyes further.

Ava put down the rag and squared her shoulders, going very still as she stared her down. 'Is there something you want to say, Tasha?'

Tasha gave a little nervous laugh. 'What's got you all in a tizz?'

'Mrs. B,' said Ava, which wasn't entirely a lie.

'Oh, Gods, what has got into her?' Tasha filled a pitcher with ale and pushed it across the bar, switching it for the empty a *dancer* handed over.

'No idea,' said Ava. 'Maybe all this has finally cracked her.'

Tasha raised her eyebrows. 'So when's he coming next?'

'He'll be here tonight or tomorrow,' said Ava. 'He won't miss my birthday.' Or more accurately, he wouldn't miss his mother's birthday, and Ava had plans to visit the temple first thing in the morning. She wiped the bar one final time. 'I'm going to bed.'

'Night,' said Tasha, her eyes back on King.

Ava couldn't help but feel a little sorry for Tasha. She was stupid to think a man like King would ever settle down, especially with someone like her, given the way he'd treated her from the start, but Tasha had nothing else. She was stuck here, working for erratic Mrs. B, with no money, no prospects, and no way of getting out.

At least Ava had Kush—if he ever came back—and his offer of the Atlas Tree—assuming it truly existed. The idea was becoming more tempting by the day.

Ava descended the stairs to the basement and nearly screamed in fright when a figure stood up from her bed.

'Ava,' said Kush, his voice hoarse, his left arm in a sling across his chest.

'Kush!' She resisted the stupid, girlish urge to run to him, her sensible, guarded, hurt parts winning out. 'Where have you been?'

She stopped three feet from him, but she couldn't see much, the moon hidden behind clouds. He pulled something from his coat pocket, muttered words under his breath, and a light ignited in his hand.

'What is that?' asked Ava, examining the smooth, oval-shaped object that was now giving off a soft, orange light.

'It's a glow stone,' he said, then collapsed awkwardly onto the bed, dropping the stone onto the mattress as he leaned back against the wall. He clamped his eyes shut and ground his teeth.

'Kush! You're hurt!'

'I'm fine.'

'What happened?' she asked, sitting beside him and taking his hand.

'I'm sorry I couldn't some sooner.'

'It's okay. You're here now.'

He lifted the back of her hand to his lips and pressed a kiss against her skin.

'What happened?' she whispered.

He sighed heavily. 'Father's expanding the Federation.'

'The what?' She lifted her head and looked into his eyes.

He tipped his head back against the wall, gaze on the ceiling, lost in his own thoughts for a moment, then he inhaled a deep, laborious breath. 'The Atlas Tree links many worlds through portals, but only some belong to the Federation of the Gods.' He moved his head off the wall and looked down at his hands. 'The Federation allows free travel and trade, which works well for the most part, but it's also a way for the Gods to expand their influence.'

He paused, glancing up at her, and she leaned in, nodding a little to encourage him to continue.

'Each Federated world must agree to worship at least one God, pay fealty to them, and build a temple in their honor. In return, they get free access to the other worlds, and the Gods protect the portals and enforce the rules.'

Her mind scrunched as it failed to understand. 'But why do the Gods want to expand? Don't they have enough already?'

'Nothing's ever enough for them, and the worlds he's sending me to have already refused Father once ...' Kush seemed to sag a little, bone weary, his exhaustion sucking all the life from the room. 'Convincing them is not easy.'

'They did this to you?'

'This and much more. The last attack was so bad I only just made it out alive. I've been recovering in the temple for weeks, bathing in the healing pools every day. They whispered about who would tell Father if I didn't make it.'

'Kush ...' She squeezed his hand. 'What can I do?'

He shook his head. 'I'm fine now. I just need a little more time, but I wanted to see you. And I think ... I think I found your parents' house.'

'What?' Her spine snapped straight and she gripped his hand harder. 'How?'

His eyes softened as he watched her reaction, but the press of his gaze was somehow even more intense than usual. 'It's at the end of High-Water Road, half a mile past the temple on the other side of town. It's all by itself, surrounded by a high wall and with a solid gate that wouldn't budge when I tried to open it.' A tired curve of amusement formed on his lips. 'A man saw me and warned me to be careful. He said the house is haunted and spelled and that bad things happen to anyone who tries to enter.'

Ava sat back. 'I need to see it. To try for myself.' She thought about heading there that very second, but Kush was injured, he was already half-asleep, his eyes falling closed, and it was dangerous on the streets at night. She'd waited this long ... a day or two more could hardly hurt. So instead, she helped his head find the pillow, threw her thin blanket over them both, and curled herself around him.

'Happy birthday, Ava,' said Kush, as the first shards of morning light sliced lines across the floor.

'How are you feeling?' she asked, almost giddy at waking up beside him, the best birthday present she could imagine.

'Better for being with you.' But his words seemed sad, laced with melancholy.

She kissed him. Not a long kiss, but soft and lingering, and she bit her lip as she pulled back, nervous to see what he would say.

But he didn't say anything.

'I want to do it,' said Ava, then quickly continued because Kush's eyes flew wide. 'Move to the Atlas Tree.'

'Oh.' His face fell, and her heart dropped; he'd changed his mind.

When he'd first proposed the idea, she hadn't seen how her life would be any different there than it was at the Cleve Arms, but the long months without him wouldn't have happened if she lived in the Atlas Tree. He could have come and seen her without raising suspicion, without making a special trip.

The thought of becoming like Tasha or Mrs. B made her shudder. Even when women carved small wins for themselves in a world tilted against them, the rug could be pulled from under their feet at any moment. She didn't want her life to be like that. She wanted to be with him.

And the Atlas Tree would be an adventure. Maybe she could even find someone willing to teach her skills she could use to get a proper job, a good one. Or maybe they had jobs wielding magic. She could learn, she was sure of it, and her chest gave an excited squeeze at the notion.

Until she looked once more at his face.

'What is it?' she asked, a flutter of panic lifting off inside her chest.

'It would never work,' he said quietly. 'I was foolish to suggest it, to ever think I could protect you.'

'You've changed your mind.'

'No!'

'But you said—'

'Father has spies everywhere inside the tree and in every temple. They've been feeding me information that might help secure allegiances, and thank all that is good and just in the world that you refused my offer the first time, because otherwise he would already have you.'

A ball of ice fell into Ava's stomach, freezing her from the inside out. Her lungs ceased to function, refusing to draw in enough air. She had no escape ... She would be stuck in the Cleve forever.

'You should go to your parents' house,' said Kush. 'You can't stay here, and their house is empty. Perhaps you'll be able to get in. Or perhaps we can use the Atlas Stone.'

'You didn't try that before?'

'I was being watched, and it's not that simple. I don't know the coordinates ... We'd need to find them, and the wards might—'

The door at the top of the stairs flew open, and Ava sprang to her feet. A great clattering accompanied Mrs. B as she rampaged down the stairs, her hair in scruffy disarray, eyes wild.

'Take it,' she snarled, thrusting a small, copper-colored package into Ava's hands. 'Take it and get out.'

Ava swung her head to look at Kush, wondering why Mrs. B hadn't moderated herself in front of him, but he wasn't there. He must have used his stone and fled. *Coward.*

'Your parents were filthy sorcerers, power-hungry, ungodly, and it has pained me to have you under my roof for so very long. But I have fulfilled my end of the bargain, and now we are both free. So get out.'

The flicker of panic caused by Kush's words was nothing compared to the clawing, raging fear that filled Ava now. She'd never seen Mrs. B this way, and even if the woman hadn't been kind, she'd never treated Ava like this: with abject hatred.

'But ... I don't have anywhere to go.'

'Not my problem. Go. Now. Before I call King's men and get them to get rid of you for me. Just be grateful I'm letting you keep my dress.'

Shame and embarrassment and loneliness joined Ava's fear, and tears welled in her eyes as she quickly got dressed. Then Mrs. B grabbed her and hauled her up the stairs.

This couldn't be happening ...

'Why?' Was all she could manage as they ascended the steps at a rapid pace. 'Why are you doing this?'

'Because if it hadn't been for you, I would have taught those pieces of shit a lesson a long time ago. You can't imagine what I've endured, watching them, bowing and scraping to their pathetic whims, *dancers* in my tavern ... well, not any longer.'

Mrs. B dragged Ava through the kitchen and threw her out of the back door, which she shut and locked behind her. Ava sucked in a shaky breath, trying to collect herself, trying to process what was happening, trembling hard as she attempted to work out what to do. She had to move before she was discovered, before anyone realized what had happened—that she was alone and vulnerable. She hurried out into the street, her feet carrying her to the first secluded ally she could find.

She pressed her back to the wooden wall of a seamstress's shop and crouched, concealing herself as best she could while trying to avoid the worst of the filth. The streets were already getting busy, and she couldn't bear for anyone to see her, not like this.

She put her trembling hands together in her lap and was surprised to find one contained a package, remembering now that Mrs. B had thrown it at her before forcing her up the stairs.

The small bundle was wrapped in a material Ava had never seen, copper in color, and more like metal than fabric or parchment. A strange twine secured the wrapping in place, made of different kinds of strands—wool, reed, metal, and others she didn't recognize—all twisted together.

She wiped the tears from her eyes, then carefully untied the package, sliding the twine into her pocket before unfolding the slinky metallic layer.

It slid apart, flowing like fine fabric, and she laid the open wrap across her dress, running her eyes over the items inside, trying to make sense of them.

The first was a small, thin knife—a scalpel—a dazzling silver color and embossed with intricate swirling patterns. She picked it up and turned it over in her fingers, sliding the metal guard down to reveal a wicked blade. She didn't like it much, so she slid the cover back up and moved on.

The second object was chunkier, although about the same length and made of wood. Four different types of wood wrapped around each other in a spiral that tapered at each end, held together by pointed metal endcaps, one end silver, the other gold. She'd never seen anything like it and couldn't begin to imagine what it was for.

The third and final item was a scrap of sturdy, cream fabric. She flipped it over, revealing a drawing, and gasped when she realized what it was: a circle with other circles inside—the face of an Atlas Stone.

She studied it, noting the locations of the various dials but not having the first idea where the coordinates would lead. The package contained no note or explanation, and she wondered if she could persuade Kush to take her there, her curiosity so thick it was a wonder she didn't choke on it.

Ava turned the items over, studying and restudying each in turn, then carefully stowed them in her pockets. They were obviously important, so why had Mrs. B kept them from her all these years? What were they for, and who were they from? The man in the black cloak? Her parents? What did it all mean? How was she supposed to use them?

She could dwell on her questions later, but she had only one person in the world she could turn to for help. She prayed that when Kush had disappeared, he'd gone to his mother's to wish her a happy birthday and that he was still there. If he wasn't, it could be months before he returned and learned what Mrs. B had done.

But as she ran through the streets towards the temple, the city sluggishly coming to life around her, she recalled again and again the moment Kush had abandoned her, sewing a seed of doubt about him in her mind. What if Mrs. B had attacked Ava? Or if it had been King's men? Why hadn't he stayed?

Her blood, already set to combust after the events of the morning, burned hotter with each passing step. Maybe he didn't care after all …

Ava finally reached Yella's house, hot, sweaty, and breathing hard, but her worry eased a little when she saw Kush at the table outside.

He started, getting gingerly to his feet when he saw her, hampered by his injuries. 'You can't be here,' he hissed, his voice low and urgent, eyes wide with fear.

'Why did you leave me?' She half shouted the words as she came to a stop. 'Mrs. B threw me out.'

'You have to go.'

'Go where? I have nowhere to go.' Shame and embarrassment made her face flame even hotter, but she refused to look away; let him see her discomfort.

'Father's—'

The front door swung open, and a man with a feline smile stepped out, dressed in a green cape similar to the one Ava had seen him wear before and carrying the same stick of twisted wood, which she could see now was topped with a purple orb that seemed to ripple in the light. 'Ah,' said his deep, smooth tone. 'I thought I heard voices. And Kush, you brought me a present. Well done, my boy.'

Kush's spirit fled in a whoosh, and he deflated before Ava's eyes as Yella stepped out of the house, too, her eyes flitting back and forth with salacious interest.

'I wondered for a while,' his father continued, 'whose side you were on. When I got here this morning, I was a little alarmed when your mother told me she hadn't seen you. She also told me of a girl you liked to see when you were here, and it didn't take much to put two and two together. I thought maybe you'd betrayed me, but ... here you are.' He spread his arms wide, just like his smile.

Kush wheeled slowly to face his father. He nodded deeply but said nothing.

What the fuck?

The older man ignored his son, eyes locked on Ava. 'You're special, Ilyavra. Did you know that?'

Ava stilled. No one had called her that in so long, she'd almost forgotten the name Ava was a nickname.

'Your parents were special, too. They were great sorcerers—perhaps the best that ever lived. What they could do ... it baffled the mind! And I witnessed it all. Can you imagine what that was like? The joy? The *rush*. We were close friends, your parents and I. Inseparable.'

'Until they died,' said Ava, her tone icy. All she knew about this man was that he was powerful and deadly and that he'd put Kush in danger. His own son.

'Yes, well, we were all so very sad about that, but you will continue their legacy. We will, together. We'll honor their mighty memory.'

A part of Ava wanted to bite his hand off. Pepper him with questions about her parents and learn all she could because, aside from a couple of childhood memories, all Ava knew of them was that they were dead and what Mrs. B had told her. But Mrs. B's version hadn't been quite so complimentary.

Power hungry.

Ungodly.

Mrs. B had agreed with him that they were sorcerers, but she'd branded them *filthy*, not *special*.

Ava had learned a lot working in a tavern, mainly that almost nobody could be trusted, even parents with their own children. She'd seen and heard things that made her glad to be an orphan, and if this man treated his own son as a tool to be abused, he wouldn't hesitate to do the same with her. People were mostly vile when it came down to it.

'And now you're of age—on a most auspicious day—it is time to claim your legacy. Everything that was once theirs is now yours. Their house, wealth, knowledge, magic. I've waited a long time for this day.'

Ava cast a glance at Kush, who was watching her, but his face gave nothing away.

'We will go to their house now, without delay.'

'But how will we get in?' said Ava. 'It's protected, is it not?'

It was knowledge Ava shouldn't have had, and Kush's father narrowed his eyes. 'You can get in, Ilyavra. It is your house now, and it will teach you about your parents' powers ... their work ... work you *must* continue.'

'Why should I believe a word you say after what you made Kush do in the Cleve?'

Yella gasped, a hand flying up to cover her mouth. She fell to her knees and prayed at the man's feet, begging for Ava's forgiveness.

Ava watched her with confusion. What was she doing?

The man didn't seem to think it was strange. He smirked, tilted his head to one side, then stepped forward and swung his hand at Ava's face so fast, her only reaction was to close her eyes against the pain. But the pain never came.

Kush stood beside them, his uninjured hand holding his father's wrist.

'Kush,' his father growled. 'Step aside.'

Ava moved farther behind Kush, using him as a shield, and wracked her brain for a way to get away. This man was evil, and she wasn't about to hand over her parents' house and legacy, certainly not without understanding why he wanted them. But how? And even if she could escape, where would she go?

She pressed herself against Kush's back, and his father chuckled cruelly. 'My son has a crush. Not a bad choice, I concede, given your lineage, but it's not to be, I'm afraid.'

Ava pressed her forehead against Kush's long leather coat, which was draped over his shoulder on the injured side, the pocket flapping open. And inside the pocket sat his Atlas Stone.

She didn't stop to think before reaching carefully inside and retrieving the cool metal disc.

'You know, he told me he couldn't find you. But now I see he's been keeping you to himself, keeping you safe, planning to bring you to me on this special day.'

Was that true? Had Kush known who she was all along? Who her parents were? Had he been lying since the beginning, only pretending to care so he could deliver her to his father? She looked down at the Atlas Stone, working out what she needed to change so the dials would match the coordinates from the drawing Mrs. B had given her, because they were the only ones she knew. She prayed she'd remembered them right.

'But he's a fool if he thinks he can get between you and me.'

'I won't let you hurt her,' said Kush. 'There's no need to—'

'Fire! Fire in the Cleve! Help!' The shouts came from the street beyond the temple, and all of them turned their eyes towards the flurry of activity there. Ava didn't want to think what that meant, so instead she used the distraction to double-check the coordinates, then pinched the disc between her thumb and forefinger.

But what about Kush? Should she take him with her? Was he on her side or his father's, or was he playing some other game? He'd told her to leave. Had seemed shocked and fearful when she'd arrived. But he'd also kept secrets all this time, secrets about her ... her past ... her parents.

'Out of the way,' said Kush's father with the casual assurance of a man used to being immediately obeyed.

'Only if you promise not to hurt her.'

He knocked Kush sideways with a brutal shove, then followed it with a swipe of his stick so hard he fell to the ground, grunting as he landed on his bad arm. Ava cried out but didn't dare move and assumed his mother would help him. But Yella stayed on her knees, not a scrap of compassion on her features as she watched her son fall. And then she prostrated herself on the ground before the man who'd hurt him. 'Forgive him, my Lord,' she groveled. 'He's not himself. The pain made him do it. He will take your punishment gladly. And do not think badly of me for his impertinence. I taught him respect. I did ...'

She kept going, but it was as though Kush's father couldn't hear her. He sneered at his son, chastised him for his weakness, then turned back to deal with Ava.

But when he saw what she held in her hand, his composure cracked. He lunged for her, but it was too late because she was already spinning the metal between her fingers. 'I'm sorry, Kush,' she said, her heart splintering at having to leave him with this cruel man. But if he heard her, she couldn't tell because, in less than a heartbeat, she was gone.

Chapter Twenty-One
Maria

MARIA BLINKED THE SLEEP from her eyes, disoriented because of the darkness, trying to work out what had woken her at this un-Godessly hour. But then there was a clattering from the stairs, along with shouts and urgent voices. That would be it.

Elex stirred, too, and Maria froze. Maria had agreed to let him spend the night in her room and even share her bed, but they'd done little more than kiss, much to her body's chagrin.

Elex was up and pulling on his breeches before Maria had time to object. She followed, throwing back the heavy, down-filled covers and reaching for the same dress she'd worn the day before.

'Happy Toll Day,' said Elex, dropping a kiss on her nape as he helped with her laces. She closed her eyes at the staggering sensation and sucked in a deep breath, trying to center herself. But that only served to heighten his smell of earthy, woody things.

'Happy Toll Day,' she breathed when he finally stepped away.

They finished dressing, then cracked open the door and listened hard, but aside from shouts and the sounds of urgent movement, there wasn't much they could discern.

They hurried along the plush purple carpet of the wide corridor, then down the stairs and out into the courtyard, John and Sophie already there. Thankfully, Sophie had finally found a cloak to cover her near-nakedness.

'What's happening?' Maria had never seen a commotion like it, with guards rushing this way and that. During the war, the fighting had always happened on the borders, safely away from the homes of the first families, and if scenes like this had existed, she'd never seen them.

'Arow's fighting back,' said John, clearly surprised the Claws could.

'How?' asked Elex. 'They don't have an army ... or weapons.'

'Turns out they have both,' countered John. 'Our forces ran headlong into an ambush last night. Uncle and Barron staged a tactical retreat and called for reinforcements. Many died.'

Maria threw up her arms. 'What are they even fighting for? To teach the Claws a lesson? What lesson? Why are they doing this?'

John shrugged. 'Nicoli refused to meet with Uncle—a serious slight.'

'And we must keep these people in their place,' added Sophie. 'A sharp shock will do them good.'

John nodded, and Maria turned away before she inadvertently blew up the pact and started a war between Alter and Laurow.

'Blade Day celebrations have been postponed until at least tomorrow,' sighed John, as though that should be top of their list of concerns.

'Including our weddings.' Sophie pouted.

Despite herself, Maria felt a pang of loss. Not because she thought her wedding more important than the plight of the Claws, but because as soon as she wed Elex, she would no longer answer to her uncle.

'The water!' shouted a stable girl in a high-pitched voice, her head poking through the gate. 'There's no water for the horses!'

Maria's stomach fell. *No water.* Words that would fill any in Celestl with dread because only so much of it fell from the sky and those who controlled it held the only cards that mattered.

'A pipe must have burst,' John said calmly. 'You there'—he motioned to the nearest commander, who had gold bands adorning his purple uniform up to his elbows—'go and—'

'Kitchen 'as no water!' shouted a new voice, this time a small boy whose head poked through a window near the ground.

'Oh, for fuck's sake,' said John, as everyone shared terrified looks. 'It will be fine!'

'Sir,' whispered a maid, who'd crept up unnoticed behind them, 'there's no water for our guests. We can't draw 'em baths.'

'Fuck,' said John. 'You don't think ...'

'That the Claws would destroy the pipes they built to carry water from the lake to our house?' said Maria.

'The same pipes carry water to them,' countered John.

'Not the same ones, actually,' said Dio, surprising them all with her presence. She seemed enthused by the chaos. 'Many pipes spread out from a pump house near the lake, one of which leads here, and one to Arow Claw.'

'But ... it would be an act of war!' gasped Sophie.

'Whereas marching our army into their territory was ... what, exactly?' Maria scoffed.

'It's not the same!' said Sophie.

Dio sent her a withering look but otherwise ignored her, and so did Maria. She looked up at Elex, whose features were unreadable, then she turned to the commander John had summoned, who was standing ramrod straight awaiting instruction, his buttons so highly polished they reflected the light. 'Check the pipes,' she ordered. 'Start with the ones inside the cliff and work out. Maybe the problem's here. Maybe it has nothing to do with the Claws.'

'Unlikely,' said John.

'Possible,' said Elex.

John huffed, then led Sophie inside. 'We'll be in the library if anyone needs us.'

Soldiers traced every pipe inside the moat and checked over each pump that pushed water from the bottom of the cliff to the top. By the time the sun was high in the sky, they'd completed their search but found no trace of the problem.

'Shit,' said Maria when the commander finished reporting to the group assembled in the library.

'Should we check the pipes outside the moat?' the man asked.

'Yes,' said Maria at the same time John said, 'No.'

Maria rounded on her brother.

'We should wait for Uncle,' he said.

'We don't have the time,' said Maria. 'We need to know the cause of the problem, and we need to know it soon. Before we run out of water.'

'And we need to know which pipes are affected,' said Elex.

Maria nodded, catching his meaning. 'Yes. We should check if the Claws' supply is off, too, or just ours.'

John waved a hand. 'Fine. But if Uncle disagrees, I'm blaming you.'

The commander nodded sharply, then spun on his heel, and Sophie ordered breakfast sandwiches while Dio followed the uniformed man out.

Elex pushed to his feet and browsed the shelves, doing a good job of feigning calm, but Maria could see the frustration simmering just below the surface. She sat staring into space, wracking her brain for something useful she could do, trying to block out John and Sophie's ramblings as they discussed their wedding ad nauseum.

They were debating whether Sophie should have a flower crown for the third or maybe fourth time when Danit and Barron stormed in, looking ragged and furious. No doubt they'd had no sleep and would consider their inability to quash Arow in a single strike humiliating.

'Uncle,' said John, as the older men stormed into the library.

Sophie paused with the teapot in midair. 'Tea?' she offered perkily.

'Is it true?' demanded Danit. 'They've shut off our water?'

'It looks that way,' said John.

Maria tutted. 'We don't know that. It's true that something has happened to the water, but it could be a burst pipe or a blockage.'

'Then we must check,' Danit snapped, gripping the back of a chair with white-knuckled hands.

'Already underway.' A cocky smile accompanied John's words, and Maria sent him a disparaging look.

'Fucking Nicoli,' spat Danit.

Of course, because this is all entirely his *fault.*

'Are we officially at war with the Claws?' asked Sophie, biting her lip and giving Danit doe eyes.

He scowled but seemed unsure.

'Yes,' said Barron. 'I will send word to Oshe, and your mother should do the same to Laurow,' he told her.

'I'm sure she will be happy to,' she said, bowing her head. 'And our marriages?' She looked up at the two older men from under her lashes, and they turned to one another, considering her question.

'We thought it pertinent to wed as a matter of priority,' John said keenly. 'To bind the Blades as planned.'

Sophie's face turned grave. 'It's especially important now, don't you think?'

Maria watched on in horrified wonder. Would Barron and Danit be so easily swayed by Sophie's full lips and big eyes?

'Yes,' Danit agreed, nodding slowly. 'I'll send for the administrator.'

'We'll do it here?' asked Elex.

'No! Of course not! We will ride for the bridge.'

Elex frowned hard. 'Then the better course is to wait. We'd need to take every soldier we have, and even then, our safety won't be guaranteed.'

Maria knew he was right, but she had to fight to keep the disappointment from her features. She was as desperate to wed as John seemed to be.

'Scared, son?' drawled Barron.

'I only intend to have one wife,' Elex shot back, 'and it's my job to keep her safe.'

'Touching,' said Danit, 'but fear not, the Claws have bigger fish to fry.'

Maria's stomach bottomed out. 'Like what?' she whispered, although she feared she already knew.

'Commander!' Danit hollered.

The commander appeared with a sharp, 'Sir,' snapping his feet together as he came to a halt.

'Go to the pump house and shut off the pipes that carry water to the Claws, as Nicoli has somehow done to the ones that lead here, then send word to the other Blades to do the same.'

The commander hesitated for a split second, then barked, 'Sir!' before marching away.

Maria's mouth fell open in shock, taking a moment to collect her wits. They didn't even know it was the Claws' doing! 'They'll turn off the turbines,' she said, her eyes flicking from Barron to Danit and back again.

'No, they won't,' said Danit, 'because if they do that, they die.'

'And if they don't care?'

Danit waved his hand, swatting away her concern as though it were a fly. 'Prepare for your weddings, all of you; you will marry today as planned. Leave the rest to us.'

Chapter Twenty-Two
Ava

Colossal darkness punctuated by shooting white lights, that was all Ava could make out, and even that was almost too much to take in. Then she landed hard on her feet, still clutching the Atlas Stone tight in her hand.

She closed her eyes for a beat, giving her head time to settle, then looked about. She was in a tunnel of sorts, mostly enclosed all around, but with holes here and there through which a faded light shone. It showed Ava things she didn't understand. It seemed as though the walls were formed of tree branches—

The sound of running feet interrupted her thoughts, and Ava shoved the Atlas Stone into her pocket and looked for a place to hide, but there was nowhere suitable. So she ran from the noise, all the time casting about for an alcove or hole big enough to climb through. She was contemplating one, trying to determine if it was big enough, when a voice behind her called out her name. 'Ilyavra!'

Her head snapped around to where a short, skinny, ginger-haired man with round glasses hurtled towards her. She didn't recognize him, but she did recognize one of the men in the group behind who were chasing him—the enforcer who'd been there when Kush had killed Malik.

Fuck.

'Run!' shouted the short man. 'Run, or you're dead!'

Ava ran. She ran faster than she'd ever run before, but the men were closing swiftly. Her shoes were far too small and not made for speed, and the heavy fabric of her dress wrapped around her legs.

As they rounded a corner, the short man caught her and yanked her sideways. She expected to slam into the tunnel wall, but to her surprise, they sailed straight through into another tunnel that looked exactly like the first.

The man held her upright with surprisingly strong hands, then glanced down at a circular contraption attached to his palm with leather straps around his wrist and fingers. A dial spun bizarrely atop the symbol-covered metal plate, and Ava could have sworn she saw the dial hand extend and then shorten, but before she could look more closely, he dragged her forward five paces, then shoved her through the tunnel wall once more.

He repeated the process four or five times, then pulled Ava at a fast walk to the end of a tunnel, to where a spiral staircase hugged the edge of an enormous, bark-covered tree trunk.

The place was deserted, but he said not a word as he led her up the stairs to a landing, then along another corridor made of roots and branches, although in this one she could make out far more details, seeing as it was lit by glow stones.

Leafy green plants spilled from urns atop decorative stone plinths set out at regular intervals. The man stopped beside a plinth that looked to Ava just like all the others. He glanced up and down to make sure they were alone, then twisted the urn a quarter to the right, followed by almost a half-turn to the left, then another turn to the right.

Nothing happened, but he grabbed Ava's arm and pushed her towards the wall. She slipped through, meeting no resistance, and gasped when she reached the far side.

She'd entered a sitting room of sorts, with walls made of thick branches and vines, many lined with shelves full of bottles, each with a label strung around its neck. A rectangular table stood off to one side, surrounded by mismatched wooden chairs and stools. There was a sink in the corner, along with a tap above it that had been stuck into a living branch.

The only other furniture consisted of a couple of dressers piled high with junk, four worn armchairs arranged in front of a large balcony with a cozy rug on the floor between them, and a few pot plants that had seen better days.

She moved to the balcony, which occupied the whole of one wall. They were high up in the air and overlooked an almost circular area that seemed to be an enormous, hollowed out tree trunk. It reached up another few stories before disappearing into a canopy of leaves. Layers of balconies ringed the space, all higgledy-piggledy and with rails of twisted wood. The nearest were close enough that, with the right running jump, Ava could probably escape to the next one if she ever had cause. Not that she would want to, seeing as the fall was at least four floors—too far to be worth risking.

Although, the bubbling pool at the bottom, nestled in a garden filled with tall plants swaying gently in the breeze, would probably provide a soft landing ...

'Begeezers,' said the man, collapsing into an armchair. He did a full body shake, then rubbed his hands together. 'That was close.'

'Who are you?' said Ava, studying him properly for the first time. He had short, curly hair that was a shade lighter than full ginger, and round, wire spectacles sat over his green eyes. A shirt poked from the neckline of his green woolen jumper, and he wore strange mustard-colored trousers with little ridges set into the fabric that Ava had never seen before. Ava wondered if he also had no choice but to wear clothes others had cast aside.

'I'm your uncle, Billy,' he said, opening his hands and tipping his head at a jaunty angle.

'My ... uncle?' she said slowly. He looked nothing like how she remembered either of her parents, and he didn't look old enough, although she had only vague memories of her parents now.

'Well, not your actual uncle but your spiritual uncle. Your parents were like family to me.'

'They were?' Her heart stuttered, and she took an unconscious step forward.

'Absolutely!'

'Well ...' So many questions ran through her mind, but suspicion overruled all else. 'In the tunnels, earlier, how did you know who I was? How did you know I'd be there?'

'Oh, do sit; you're making me uncomfortable.'

Ava reluctantly sank into the armchair opposite Billy's, perching on the edge, and he smiled broadly as he watched her.

'Now,' he said, curling his legs under him and wiggling a little to get comfortable.

'Wait ... are you the man who left me at the tavern? After my parents were ...'

'Murdered?' His features darkened. 'No. But that man is the reason I knew where you'd be today. Happy birthday, by the way.'

'Thank you?'

'I had to hang around for hours. Wasn't sure if you'd ever turn up, and then Var's cronies appeared and I had to leg it. The man who took you to the tavern—he's called Novak and, well, it's a long story, but one way or another, he told both Var and me that if you were going to show up, it would be there, and it would be on or after your eighteenth birthday. If only you'd come ten minutes earlier, it would have been much more civilized.'

'I'm ... sorry?'

'Although, I suppose if you'd shown ten minutes later, it would have been much worse ... on balance, we'll let it slide.' Billy threw his legs over the side of the armchair, crossed them, then drummed his fingers on the top one. Apparently he wasn't one to sit still.

Ava frowned in thought. 'Who is Var?' she asked.

Billy's fingers paused mid-air. 'Who is Var?' He lifted his back off the chair's arm and twisted so he faced her more squarely. 'Var? As in, the God? One of two that pretty much run the place these days?'

'Uhhh ... why would a God care about me?'

Billy shook his head a few times in quick succession and let out a disbelieving titter. 'Why would ... Oh, that's a good one!' He was unable to speak due to his quiet chortling. 'I'm sorry,' he said, putting his hand on his chest. 'It's just—' A bark of laughter burst free. 'So funny!' He took a deep breath and closed his eyes, exhaling a satisfied, 'Ahhh ...'

Ava waited patiently because she still didn't know what she was dealing with, but she would have very much liked to throw something at him.

Billy swung his feet to the floor and leaned forward. 'Ava, my dear, Var cares about you because you are the only person in all the worlds who knows the location of his soul.'

CHAPTER TWENTY-THREE
MARIA

THE RIDE TO THE bridge felt all wrong. The fields were empty, devoid of life, as was to be expected at sunset on Toll Day, but silence had replaced the sounds of work, not the usual shrieks of jubilation.

Danit had decided against carriages, so they could be nimble in case of *nasty surprises*, and Sophie and John rode ahead of Maria and Elex. An enormous flower crown stuffed with burgundy roses sat proudly atop Sophie's auburn hair, and her outlandish dress—another construction of sheer fabric in the purple of Alter Blade—almost touched the ground as she rode. Maria's dress seemed understated in comparison, even though the copious swathes of demurely cut blue and purple made it difficult to ride, her favorite pearl hair pins inconspicuous nestled against her blonde locks.

Elex, Cane, and Barron wore black uniforms trimmed with the light blue of their Blade, John and Danit were in Alter purple, while Erica and Sophie's mother had selected full, flowing dresses in their respective home colors.

Maria kept casting furtive glances at Cane's cloth-wrapped hand and the livid raw splotches on his neck and face, this being the first time any of them had seen him since the hand-tying. He kept his head down, not making eye contact with anyone, although none but Sophie and John had much to say and the administrator looked positively ashen.

Maria soon blocked her brother's incessant chatter, her mind whirring with thoughts of the Claws and Nicoli. Would he truly turn off the turbines and doom them all to death? Maria couldn't imagine it, but he'd also made it clear he would bend the knee no longer ...

'What I can't work out,' said Elex, riding close and pitching his voice so only she could hear, 'is why your uncle was so desperate to speak with Nicoli? What did he want, and why was it so urgent?'

'Urgent enough to start a war ...' agreed Maria.

'And why did Nicoli wait until now—until the Blades were all but united—to fight back?'

She'd been turning the same questions over in her mind. 'The Claws want the respect of the Blades. They want to be treated as equals ... to be valued.'

'But the Blades have the upper hand.'

'The water,' said Maria. 'It always comes back to that.'

'So what's changed?'

Silence settled over them, and vexation rolled off Elex in waves. Maria was equally restless, seeing as her only useful part in settling the turmoil was to wed, and she hated not being able to see the full picture. To make matters worse, she'd heard nothing through her network, which was unusual, putting her further on edge.

'I don't know what's changed,' she said eventually, 'but Nicoli's a genius. He wouldn't make a declaration of war lightly, so he must be prepared ... must have some trump card.'

'But how could he retaliate without jeopardizing his own people?'

'Maybe he's willing to.'

'They'll die.'

'And so will we.'

'A game of chicken? It's too reckless.'

'He most likely blocked the water to Alter Blade this morning,' said Maria. 'Was that not reckless?' The guards had found the pumps in the pump house working fine, happily pushing water down the pipes that led to the Claws, but not through the pipes that led everywhere else. From those, water cascaded through the overflow mechanism and back towards the lake, the route through the pipes blocked, and even though Maria wanted to believe the best of Nicoli, it was too much of a coincidence. In fact, it was so blatant it was brazen.

'And then your uncle stopped the water to Arow. You said yourself, Nicoli's a genius, he knows the Claws will run out of water before the Blades do.'

'Maybe,' she replied, but she knew she was missing something—she had to be. Even if Nicoli was willing to risk Claw lives, he cared deeply about his people. 'Or maybe he has another supply of water ...'

'Impossible,' said Elex. 'The only supply falls into the lakes.'

'Perhaps he's devised a way to make sea water safe to drink.'

Elex laughed. 'Is he a magician as well as a genius? A small amount is possible, but on a scale big enough to sustain the Claws? And how would he hide it?'

Their party bunched up as they approached the lake, the level low—as was usual before a fall—the sunset deluge due at any moment. They let the horses drink, fanning out along the shallow edge, only the administrator's voice interrupting the horses' quiet slurping.

'Must we delay so long?' he said, a little too aggressively, an air about him of a timid mouse who'd finally plucked up the courage to talk. 'I must return to the temple. This situation is—'

'If you keep wagging your tongue, you'll lose it,' Danit snapped.

The man clamped his mouth shut, and although a tiny, unkind part of Maria applauded Danit's sentiment—everyone's nerves were jangled given the circumstances—she also understood the man's urgency. Danit had sprung the change from Toll Day to Blade Day without warning, and the temple's purpose was to oversee all administrative matters in Celestl on behalf of the Goddess.

They were an independent entity, answering to no one but their creator. Although, seeing as the Goddess had abandoned them and they had no army, they had no physical power. But they controlled Celestl's records, hoarding them in their crypts, and the sanctity of the temple was a line none had ever dared cross.

'On to the bridge,' said the commander from the head of the group, and they quickly formed up behind him, all of them keen to keep moving while they still had sunlight to guide them.

It wasn't far now, and Maria would be glad to get there. The atmosphere was so strange ... charged, the place absent of anyone but their travelling party. But it was too quiet, even so.

The soldiers at the front, some fifty feet farther on along the lake, led them off just as the click of the fall mechanism sounded. Maria looked up as the usual wall of water thundered down from above, as breathtaking and terrifying as ever. It slammed into the middle of the lake with a huge splash, sending water almost to where Maria's horse stood.

'Well, at least that's reliable,' said Elex.

'So long as the turbines keep turning,' Maria countered.

But moments after the words had left their lips, an almighty jolt threw them sideways, and the horses stumbled and snorted as they tried to keep their balance. Maria's horse recovered quickly, and she scanned her eyes over several unseated guards as she tried to work out what the Goddess's name was going on.

But then her eyes snagged on movement, and terror gripped her. 'Fuck,' she breathed, as she watched the enormous, plummeting mass of water slide sideways, heading for the edge of the lake.

No, she realized, that wasn't it. The water wasn't moving, it was that the ground hadn't stopped as it was supposed to, and if the fall's breakneck speed was any indication, the ground was turning faster than it usually did.

'Watch out!' Maria screamed. 'Turn around!' Her horse pranced in fear, but Maria barely noticed, easily keeping her seat through the jinks and backsteps, her eyes glued on the water. It was nearly at the shore, exactly where the vanguard was struggling to control their mounts and help their fallen friends.

Maria's horse reared high up in the air, kicking its front legs and scream-ing in fright, and Maria leaned forward to stay mounted. By the time it was back on all fours, now rooted to the spot and trembling, spray enveloped the soldiers, swallowing their screams and spinning horses. Maria was soaked in an instant, and she desperately fought with her mare, trying to make her move, to turn back the way they'd come.

The waterfall hit land, and clods of dirt and stones flew everywhere, water pounding the earth, then bouncing back up into the sky. Parts of men and horses came next, the impact of the fall pummeling them to a pulp, ripping flesh from bone, and Maria's heart stopped. Her horse finally relented, taking a great flying leap into a dead gallop away from the threat, and it was all she could do to cling on, registering only that the water was moving in an arc away from the lake.

It seemed to last a lifetime, or maybe time slowed as the horror unfolded, her horse seeming to travel no distance at all, the roar of water deafening, the freezing spray marring everything in fog, projectiles flying everywhere. But then, just as suddenly as it had started, it stopped. The torrent ceased, and for a moment, everything turned calm. Then the land slowed violently. So violently, Maria's horse fell, and she was thrown from the saddle, hitting the ground and rolling fast until she lost momentum.

She looked up at the big, blue sky, her head throbbing, ears ringing, the usual scent of wildflowers after the deluge replaced by the stench of wet earth and fear. She took stock of her limbs, wiggling her fingers and toes to make sure she still could. She breathed a sigh of relief to find everything intact and was building the strength to roll over and push to her feet when rustling in a tree just behind her caught her attention.

She tipped her head back to see Nicoli leaning out of the canopy, watching her carefully, his face full of concern. But then he was gone, replaced by Elex's worried features, his hands examining her for damage then hauling her into his lap.

'Nicoli,' she breathed, and he stilled, his arms tensing around her.

He leaned back, looking in her eyes. 'It's Elex,' he said gently.

It was hard to form words, and she scowled as she tried, her head pounding. 'In the tree. Nicoli. Here.'

Elex put her down and lurched to his feet, spinning to scan the nearby trees. 'I can't see him.'

Maria tasted blood in her mouth, her head still too foggy to think.

Elex returned to her side and helped her up. 'We have to get out of here; it's not safe.' He lifted her easily into his arms and carried her towards his horse.

'The others?' she croaked, gingerly turning her head, and was rewarded with a severe bout of pain. She closed her eyes, waiting for it to subside, and eventually managed to squeeze Elex's arm and say, 'Put me down. I'm fine. We have to help the others.'

He reluctantly lowered her to her feet, making her stand still and let him check her eyes before slowly releasing her. She tried to take off at a run towards the carnage, but her legs buckled beneath her, and she would have collapsed to the ground if Elex hadn't been there to catch her. Another bout of pain lanced through her head, and she closed her eyes, waiting for the spinning to settle before trying again.

'I'm fine,' she said, pushing him off.

'Just go slowly,' he said, sliding his arm around her waist. 'I'll help you.'

She looked for John and Sophie, and she was glad to find them huddled together near the lake, their limbs intact.

Barron and Danit were also unscathed, already screaming bloody murder in between barking orders. But the same could not be said for the commander or half a dozen of the guards who'd been at the front of their party. Their remains were barely recognizable, some with limbs detached and floating in red-stained puddles, others arranged on the ground with arms and legs at odd angles.

The fall had destroyed trees and nearby buildings, too, and Maria couldn't believe the destruction, the ground scarred, precious water running away to who knew where. Wasted.

'Those bastards have stolen our water!' cried Danit. 'They've stolen our water!'

'Nicoli,' she said to Elex, scanning the area to find her best friend. 'This was what he meant.'

Of course he couldn't shut off the turbines, but he'd changed how they worked so that the land kept turning while the water fell. That happening once might not make too great a dent in their supply, but if it continued, the water levels would fall dangerously low.

But the Blades still controlled the flow of water through Celestl and reducing the Blades' supply meant even less for the Claws. What was his plan?

'He's in the tree at nine o'clock,' said Elex, pulling her to him, making it easier for her to look without anyone noticing.

Maria picked out Nicoli's serious features among the lush, green leaves. Their eyes met, and he sent a mock salute. She nodded because even after this, she refused to see him as her enemy, and the fact he wanted her to made her resolute.

Chapter Twenty-Four

Ava

Now that was laughable. The idea that Ava, a lowly tavern girl, knew anything about anything, let alone the location of a God's soul ...

'I don't,' said Ava.

'Well, no, probably not yet. But only you have the means to find out.'

'And when you say his soul ...?'

Billy hummed in thought. 'It's ... well ... I guess it's ... the thing that makes him who he is? His life force. His essence?'

'And somehow that's not inside him?'

Billy gave her a look that implied she might be a few strings short of a guitar. 'Not all of it, no.'

Ava frowned. 'Is my soul inside me?'

He sucked in a dramatic breath, then sprang to his feet. 'Urgh ... what's your poison? *Tipsy? Woozy? Inebriated? Carefree? Cloud Nine?*'

'Ummm. I ... water?'

He cocked his head.

'Please?'

'I mean, the others are more fun ...' he said, walking to the tap. '*Inebriated* especially has a pleasant sweet and sour thing going on. But water will do for now, I suppose. Filtered through great old Atlas herself and tapped at source. Considered a delicacy in some parts.'

'Oh,' said Ava. 'The water comes from ...'

Billy pouted. 'From the tree! We're in the ... You know what the Atlas Tree is, right?'

'Sort of?'

'Really, what did your parents teach you in the seven whole years you lived with them? Wait, six? Was it six or seven?'

She fixed him with a death stare. 'To read and add up?' And she was rusty on both. Other than that, Ava wasn't really sure.

Billy handed Ava her water, then returned to his seat, having poured himself a large measure of something called *Patient and Polite*. The liquid was clear, but he dropped a small tablet in the top which eddied to the bottom, leaving a trail of pink in its wake.

He swirled the crystal tumbler in his hand, then put it under his nose and inhaled deeply. 'Not my favorite, but desperate times ...' He took a long sip, closed his eyes as he rolled the liquid around his mouth, then sat back as he swallowed. 'Right ...' He threw his legs over the side of the chair once again and made a ticking sound as he looked around the room.

His ceaseless shifting made her restless, agitated. 'Can you just tell me what you know?'

He stilled, swiveling his eyes to look at her, his glass halfway to his lips. 'Well yes, obviously that is the plan.'

Ava scowled. 'Now?'

'Okay, okay,' he said dramatically. 'No foreplay, fine. Well, I first met your parents when they were nothings and nobodies,' he said, leaning his head back and looking at the curved ceiling. 'Well, that's a lie. Your mother was nobody, but your father, he was somebody, if you catch my drift. They weren't even together back then, but your father was considered quite the catch among the magical families, and *everyone* was after him.' He raised his eyebrows salaciously.

'The magical families?'

He huffed. 'The Atlas Tree was discovered many many many many many years ago by a very famous sorcerer called ... oh ... hang on ... I always forget his name. He was called ... urrrr ...' Billy screwed up his face. 'Rupey! Yes! Your father was named after him, in fact.'

'Right,' said Ava.

'Now Rupey,' he said, twisting so he could point a finger at Ava around his glass, 'was your great great great ... lots of greats grandfather. Which is why, incidentally, your father was such hot property back in the day.'

'Um ... what?' That couldn't be right.

'Mmm hmm,' he said through a mouthful of drink. 'But here's the thing: your father was only *almost* brilliant. Your family had been devoid of the dazzling bright-as-the-sun variety for so long it was getting hard to cover it up, and people were starting to talk.'

'Why would anyone care?'

He gave her an incredulous look. 'They ran the joint!'

'The ... Atlas Tree?'

'Of course! But never fear, because your mother's family—now, there's a story. Came from nothing—your maternal great grandmother was an absolute cracklejack—and suddenly, she was *everywhere*. She weaseled your mother into the premier circle, and by the time anyone realized what she was up to, it was too late to stop her.'

He swung his legs to the floor and leaned his elbows on his knees. 'Do you know how hard that circle was to infiltrate?' He paused, seeming to require an answer.

'Ahhh ... no?'

'It was impossible. *Impossible!*' He chuckled to himself and lifted wistful eyes to the ceiling. 'Ahhhh. Well, anyway, there she was, your mother. Just walked into Advanced Portal Preening one day—one of the many lessons us children of the sorcerers had to endure—and stole the show. Your father never looked sideways at anyone else again. We were all spitting.' He flopped back into the armchair and tipped his head, leaning it against the cushion so he was once more staring at the ceiling. 'Those were the days.'

Ava watched him for a while, trying to process everything he'd said, while he remained resolutely focused on the branches that formed the ceiling above their heads.

She eventually began to fidget, wondering where to put her empty glass. She settled on leaving it on the floor by her seat, and when it seemed Billy had no intention of continuing, she said carefully, 'So my family were sorcerers and they used to live here? In the Atlas Tree?'

As she said the words, Kush's story came back to her, hitting her like a blacksmith's hammer. He'd told her about a tree and sorcerers and a woman and her granddaughter ... A rushing noise filled her ears, and she had to lower her head to fend off the fuzziness billowing at the edges of her mind. He'd been describing ... he can't have been ... had he been ... the same story? Her breaths became rapid unruly puffs.

Billy made a sucking noise, popping his lips as he came fully upright. 'Yep.'

'My family were sorcerers ...' she said into her knees.

'Mmm hmm. Top of the tree. No one higher.'

'They led the others?' She lifted her head, the fuzz making her sway.

'Well, yes, basically.'

'Were they ... good?' She ducked her head back down.

'At running the show?' He barked a laugh. 'Gods, no! Well ... they're the reason we even have Gods, of course.'

Ava frowned because Kush had said that, too, about how the couple had found a way to make Gods. She felt suddenly nauseous. The couple ...

'Well, here's the thing. Sorcerers are power-hungry blighters. They—or rather, we, for I should say, I hail from a long line of formidable sorcerers myself—always want more. And here's the other thing, your family fluffed their feathers at the top of the tree for such a long time'—he pointed a meaningful finger at the ceiling—'making no friends, rubbing their superiority in our faces, refusing to share the wealth, that it was inevitable someone would take them down eventually.'

Ava tried to focus on breathing while Billy stood and moved towards the shelves, pausing and turning his torso back towards her midway. 'Of course, it backfired.'

'What? What backfired?' She wasn't sure she understood any of the story, her thoughts muddled in the face of his onslaught.

He took a loud, flouncy breath. 'The takedown!'

'The ...'

'Your parents stole their souls!' He poured himself a measure of something light blue called *Had Better Days*, then leaned against the dresser, cradling the tumbler against his chest.

Ava's heart leapt into her throat. 'Why?'

'Because they were a little bit better at playing the game than everyone else ... until, of course, they weren't. Made the mistake of fucking over even their closest friends: B, Novak, me ...

'Novak was still *just* compassionate enough back then to save you, Ilyavra, and called in a favor with B, but it seems even his compassion has run out. He sold you out to Var in exchange for his new role as Master of the House.'

'Master of the ... wait. B? Mrs. B?'

'Yes. Prickly fish that one.'

'Prickly fish?'

'Prickly fish, don't you agree?'

'But ... she knew my parents?' Ava's stomach bottomed out. Her whole life Mrs. B had lied to her ...

'She was one of their closest friends. But as I said, they screwed her too, like the cheap little Cleve rat she always was.' He smacked his lips. 'Best not tell her I said that. Sore spot. The only reason she took you in was because she owed a debt to Novak and he didn't want to look after you himself, especially seeing as it was dangerous, of course.'

'And now he's ...'

'Master of the House, yes. In exchange for telling Var's men where to find you.'

'What does that mean?' asked Ava. 'Master of what House?'

He pinched the bridge of his nose as though in great pain. 'The House of Portals. Novak controls trade and travel through all portals—Bridge and Unfederated. He's practically a God himself again, except, of course, he's not.'

Ava just stared, very few of Billy's words making much sense. 'Gods are created,' she said quietly, more to herself than to him, trying to sort it all out in her mind.

'Oh, yes, well ... hmm, no. First we must be clear about what we *mean* by that word. Everyone who lives in the Clouds these days calls themselves a God, whether they have long lives or not. They just can't bear the idea of being lesser, even though they are ... well, sort of ... depends on one's perspective, I suppose. But although creating a new God is theoretically possible, no one knows *how* any longer, not since your parents ... well. No one except you, that is.'

'But I don't—'

'Yes, yes, you know nothing.' He waved a dismissive hand. 'That is very much apparent. Anyway, your parents wanted to keep their discovery under wraps, but it got out, and then all the sorcerers wanted a piece of immortality. Led to all sorts of nastiness, and in the end, they turned some of the other young sorcerers into Gods. Oh, it was all fine for a while, but then ... well ... they added a kicker, as was their way.'

'A what? My parents were ... they were Gods.'

He clicked his fingers at her. 'Come on, dear, keep up. Yes! Your parents were the *first* Gods. They devised the method.'

'The method for ...'

'Eternal life, of course. God-making!'

Kush's story ... it *had* been about her parents ...

'They tied a person's soul to another world's timeline. It was a quite remarkable innovation, but the toads wanted to keep it to themselves. And then, when forced to share, they held everyone hostage—well, their souls.'

'How?'

He went still and fixed her with an intense look. 'By hiding which other worlds their souls were tied to.'

Ava bit the insides of her lips as she slowly pieced together the story. Her parents were powerful sorcerers, they'd discovered how to tie a piece of their souls to another world, which somehow gave them long lives and turned them into Gods. The other sorcerers were jealous and forced her parents to tie their souls, too. Mrs. B was a liar, and the man in black's name was Novak, but he'd sold her out to become Master of some House. *Brilliant.*

It sounded insane but maybe not quite as insane as using an Atlas Stone to travel between worlds. And if she'd done that, perhaps the rest might just be true as well.

'Now,' said Billy, 'let's talk about you.'

Chapter Twenty-Five
Maria

Eventually carts were called and the dead and injured were hauled away, by which time the women were shivering in their soaked flimsy dresses. Maria was better off than Sophie, whose dress was practically see-through, and even with John's cloak around her, the poor thing trembled with cold and shock.

Their group was a sorry sight, like drowned rats who'd been plucked from the water, rolled in dirt, then shaken about before being set free. Not that anything about the situation felt like freedom, and Maria's head still banged with pain.

'We will continue,' said Danit, sliding a hand over his bald head, unwittingly smearing dirt more thoroughly across it. No one bothered to tell him, and Maria wondered just how terrible she looked. They were sure to be quite the picture, reciting their vows looking as they did. Not that she cared. It was funny, in a perverse kind of way.

Maria mounted a borrowed horse because hers had bolted. She didn't dare ask whose she now rode or whether they'd lived or died.

'Move!' Danit shouted as the stragglers mounted up. He wanted the marriages out of the way so he could retaliate against the Claws, Maria had no doubt.

Sophie shared John's horse, her flower crown nowhere to be seen—replaced by a splattering of dirt—John's arms wrapped firmly around her, and no one even blinked at the impropriety. They trudged the short distance to the Outer Circle with not a word uttered between them, the silence different to before, more varied, the riders preoccupied and introspective and perhaps tinged with fear.

A gasp pulled Maria back from her thoughts, and the sight ahead made her guts churn anew. People lined the road, sitting along each edge wearing their Toll Day finery and watching the mounted group as they crossed. They sat in eerie stillness, even the children, eyes fixed on the bedraggled group.

The road was less crowded than it ordinarily would have been during the Toll Day procession, maybe because no one from Alter Blade had turned out. These people were all members of the Claws, and she wondered if her uncle had told their people to stay away or if they'd somehow known not to show.

It was ironic because the pact was supposed to bring their world together, and yet here they were, more divided than ever before. Even during the war, the Blades had called a ceasefire for Toll Day, and the celebration had been a collective exhale of relief.

The short ride to the bridge was uncomfortable, and the guards glanced nervously left and right, but Maria didn't feel hostility from their audience, only curiosity and perhaps a note of triumph.

She hadn't bothered hiding the mark on her face where her uncle had slapped her. She'd wanted the world to see him for who he really was, but now they wouldn't even notice it amongst the blood and dirt and sodden, soiled fabric. Nicoli's slap had been more terrible by far.

They dismounted at the wooden bridge, leaving behind the guards and horses, only the three families and the administrator walking the last mile across the void to the Toll Gate. Silence enveloped them still, perhaps because they were glad to be alive, or maybe it was just that the shock had stolen their tongues. Maria was glad of Elex's steadying arm as they crossed the bumpy wooden surface, still a little wobbly on her feet, her head pounding.

'Oshe and Alter first,' Barron barked the moment they reached the gate. Danit nodded in agreement, not giving Linella, John, or Sophie an opportunity to protest.

Maria took a slow, deep inhale, careful not to go too fast due to the pain in her head, and paused a moment to consider how this simple act would change her life forever.

She followed the line of twisted roots that ran from under her feet, stretching up into an arch over the top of the perfectly circular door before her: the Toll Gate. The door was made of Alterwood, and on the front was carved the star of Celestl. The same symbol was on all four of the gates, or so she'd been told.

The arch of roots had sprouted delicate white spring flowers, and Maria reached up and brushed her fingers across one as the administrator took his place. He carefully positioned himself under the Wand of Alter—four long, thin sticks twisted together and tapering to a point at each end—which hung in the air, suspended by magic, or at least, if it wasn't magic, no one could discern how it was done.

The administrator cleared his throat, and Elex took Maria's hand. She found him looking down at her, the hint of a smile on his lips, and her chest constricted as she smiled back.

'I must start by asking—'

'Make it quick,' snapped Danit. 'We have more important things to do.'

The administrator did his best to ignore Danit, clearing his throat before starting again. 'I must start by asking if any here present knows of any reason why these two should not be joined in marriage.'

He paused, a pregnant silence settling over them, and just as Danit took a deep, angry inhale, Cane stepped forward. 'Me! I do.'

Barron rounded on his oldest son, his eyes fierce, like a deadly hunter with prey in its sights.

'It should be me, Father,' said the painted peacock, puffing himself up despite new injuries from the waterfall and his general state of dishevelment. 'I am the oldest, and I—'

Barron moved with startling speed for a man of his size and age, shoving his son so hard he fell. Cane cried out in surprise, scrambling for purchase, trying to get back to his feet, but he went still when the older man moved to stand over him.

'Take your horse and ride back to Oshe,' Barron commanded in a voice that promised violence. 'Do not stop and do not speak of the reason for your return to anyone. This is a grave embarrassment to me, your people, and your betrothed. Pray her father does not discover your actions, or dire consequences will befall you, and I will be powerless to stop them. Not that I would try. I would rejoice in them, for your judgement is lacking and you could do with a lesson you won't easily forget. Erica will accompany you.'

The peacock paled, stuttered an apology, then scuttled away without a backwards glance. Barron tipped his head impatiently, indicating Erica should hurry up and follow him. She hesitated for a beat, seeming as though she might protest, but then pasted a fixed smile on her lips and did as he bade without uttering a single word.

Maria shuddered. Had Erica chosen the course of her life, or had she been forced into it? Either way, for a woman so fiery, being treated like a pet dog must smart. Maria released the breath she'd been holding and found her legs wobbly once more. Erica's life had so nearly been her life. If Elex hadn't claimed her as he did …

Elex squeezed her hand and ran his thumb across her knuckles, doing what he could to reassure her, but it did little to quiet her unease.

'Continue,' she said to the administrator, needing for this to be over, to be bound to Elex and not any other man.

The administrator did not make the usual opening remarks, nor did he lecture them on marriage or say any of the other unnecessary words that so often took time at weddings. He only requested they each confirm they were free to enter the marriage, asked them if they took the other as husband or wife, then, when they confirmed they did, declared them wed.

It was strange, really, that so few words, said in such speedy fashion, could alter Maria's life so completely. She answered to Elex now, would live with him, fight with him, sleep with him. The thought brought heat to her cheeks, and he smiled knowingly as he stepped into her space and kissed her.

She should have been embarrassed, their families looking on, but she couldn't bring herself to care. She was free of them, and Elex was kind and reasonable and didn't see her as a pawn.

She reached up to touch the wand when he pulled away, not sure why, exactly, but because it seemed right. He did the same, closing his hand over hers, and they stood there for a moment, staring into each other's eyes.

'Enough,' said Barron. 'Maria, you are a member of Oshe Blade now and answer to me, so move, both of you. We have another marriage to suffer before this day is done.'

Maria froze, Elex having to pull her to the side. Of course, she'd known Elex ultimately answered to Barron—and therefore so did she—but she'd been so wrapped up in him, so eager to get away from Danit, that she hadn't fully considered what it would be like in her new family, the dynamics and chain of command.

The stark reminder that she was not free and never would be sent her fleeting joy tumbling down into her guts. There it cracked open, hatching dread.

Elex pulled her close and kissed her temple. 'We don't answer to him,' he whispered, and she hugged him tight, willing his words to be true. She wished they were alone, that they could leave and hide away, just the two of them, but she still had a duty to her old family to perform, to her brother.

The administrator pulled a piece of parchment from his leather satchel, then a quill and ink pot. 'Could I ... ah ... ask for assistance?' he said, looking for someone to hold the ink. Maria had forgotten about the marriage contract.

Elex stepped forward, then Maria, who offered her back as a writing desk. The administrator worked as quickly as he could, but it was awkward and took time that Danit and Barron were not happy to give.

Elex signed, then Danit, who cursed when the ink stained his fingers. He seemed not to realize that was the least of his worries if he was concerned about the general state of his attire.

'I hope she's fertile,' said Barron, eying Maria as the administrator put the parchment away—she wasn't required to sign the agreement that bound her to Elex for the rest of her days. 'Because otherwise all this is for nothing.'

'She'll bear fruit,' said Danit. 'None of our women have ever failed in that regard.'

'Nor ours,' said Linella. She pushed her daughter forward and whipped John's cloak off her shoulders so that Sophie stood practically naked, the wet, ripped fabric doing little to conceal her flesh. 'Now, as you said, Barron, let's get on with this.'

John stepped forward, clearly conflicted about Sophie's lack of coverage, but then she looked up at him as though he'd put the stars in the sky and he lost any hesitance.

Maria had to hand it to Sophie—if she'd been forced to stand naked in front of this group, she wouldn't be taking it nearly so well, but Sophie acted as though nothing were amiss. Perhaps in Laurow they cared little about such things.

Indeed, somehow the couple seemed excited despite the tragedy that had befallen them, the worry over the water, the fact the Blades were now at war with the Claws, and their half-drowned appearances. Maria hadn't looked like that when it had been her turn, had she?

But as the administrator faffed about, putting down his satchel and getting into position, the *thunk thunk* of running footsteps resonated through the bridge behind them, and they all whirled to face the sound. What now?

A tall, well-built man with dark hair approached, but he was too far away to make out any details. He seemed familiar, something niggling at Maria about his gait as she watched him run. And then it slipped into place just as John breathed, 'Hale?'

Hale stopped short, still too far away for them to see his features. He hesitated, took a step forward, paused, then turned, starting back the way he'd come. But it was too late, Linella shrieking his name before he could really get going.

'Hale Alter!' she screamed. Then she rounded on Danit. 'You *lied* to us. You swore he was dead!'

'And I truly thought he was,' said Danit, so visibly off kilter that Linella backed off. 'Hale!' cried Danit, turning back to Linella once Hale was moving in their direction, albeit far more slowly than before. 'We will fix this mess at once.'

'You promised us the first son of Alter,' Linella hissed, 'and my daughter will marry no one else.'

Danit nodded shakily. 'We will straighten this out ... fear not.'

'Hale!' breathed Maria, rushing to him and hugging him around the waist. 'We thought you were dead!' She held back tears as Elex and Hale clasped forearms.

'Hello my old friend,' said Elex.

Hale smiled cockily. 'You mean brother?' His eyes darted to Maria, and Elex put an arm around her waist.

'*Brother*,' said John, barging in and elbowing Elex out of the way, his face a furious mask. 'Why are you here?'

Maria gave Hale an angry shove that was nonetheless full of sisterly affection. 'Why have you been gone so long? Where have you been?'

Hale scanned the whole group before returning his gaze to them. 'It's a long story,' he said, dismissing them in the way of older brothers. 'Uncle,' he continued, nodding his head at Danit. 'I saw an Oshe man fleeing ... He seemed injured. And then a woman who refused to utter a word, and I thought ... well, it appears I had nothing to be concerned about.'

'But why are you here?' John bit out, hands balled into fists at his sides. 'Why now? Why today?'

Everyone ignored him, and Danit stepped forward, his legs seeming unsteady, face white as a sheet. But despite his apparent frailty, Maria recognized the white hot rage in his eyes. She'd seen it only a handful of times, and it never ended well, which was why it was such a surprise when Danit said slowly, 'It is fortunate timing, all things considered.'

Maria gaped, wondering if she'd heard him right.

'Yes,' agreed Linella, nodding briskly. 'Fated by the Goddess. A few minutes later and Sophie would have already wed John.'

Hale appraised Sophie for a long moment, then met her eyes and held them. 'What a shame that would have been,' he drawled, none of them missing his sarcasm. Sophie's whole body trembled, whether due to the cold or Hale's rudeness, Maria didn't know, but Hale eventually dismissed her, too, then asked, 'What happened to you all?'

Sophie sucked in a sharp breath and pulled herself up straight, snapping back to her usual sultry self, the transformation staggering. 'It's a long story,' she said, pouting at him in the exact same way she'd been pouting at John since she'd arrived in Alter. 'I'll tell you everything on our ride home, just as soon as we're wed.'

Hale huffed a condescending laugh. 'No.'

She paused a beat, blinked, then continued unperturbed. 'But you must marry me! The pact states that I am owed the first son of Alter.'

He folded his arms across his chest. 'The pact can say whatever it wants, but I did not agree to wed, so if I were you, I'd marry my brother and be glad you've escaped me.'

Sophie slid her hands calmly together and let them fall in front of her, Maria struck that she was able to act in such poised fashion, especially given her exposed state. 'My father will not let this stand.'

Hale stepped slowly into her space and looked haughtily down at her, a look Maria wanted to chastise him over. This man was different to the brother she'd known. He was wilder somehow, his edges no longer the smooth lines of a first son. They were rugged, chipped by the sea.

'What's your father going to do?' said Hale. 'Restart the war?'

Sophie cocked her head to one side. 'Yes.'

'Your father is too busy drinking and whoring to do much of anything.'

'Enough,' said Danit. 'Hale, you will not speak to our guests that way.'

'Apologies, Uncle,' he replied, dropping his head a fraction. He spun and grabbed the cloak Linella clutched in her hands, then tossed it irritably at Sophie before striding away. 'Now, if we are done here, I have—'

'We are not done here,' said Linella. 'We are far from done.'

'Let us return to my home,' Danit said placatingly. 'We will all feel more level when we are washed and fed, I am sure.'

Linella looked as though she might object, but the tide had already turned against her, Barron on the move, Hale right behind him.

John tried to take Sophie's hand, but she shrugged him off. His face fell. 'Sophie ... but ...'

'Do you want this back?' she asked, holding out the cloak to him.

John looked aghast. 'No! Of course—'

She cut him off with a shake of her head, then slung the thick velvet sheet over her shoulders and turned her back as her mother stepped close to Danit.

'If this pact means anything to you,' Linella spat, 'you will keep your word because my daughter will marry the first son of Alter or no one at all.'

***

They made it back to the mansion with no further incident, Maria glad of the hot bath the servants had drawn for her, even if it was a callous use of their now-limited water supply. Maria reasoned that the water was wasted either way, filled with salts and oils as it was, so she might as well enjoy it, especially after the day they'd had.

The servants left her to soak away her aches, and Maria was glad for a moment of reprieve, the throbbing in her head finally subsiding. They'd found the mansion in a state of disarray when they'd returned, on account of the dead and injured soldiers, the large Blade Day dinner that Danit insisted go ahead, and the underlying fear about the water.

Every spare pair of hands had been sent to haul water up from the moat, but the supply there would not last forever, and the mood was ominous.

They shouldn't have had to transport the water by hand, of course, but no one knew how to switch the pumps across to the moat, and asking the Claws wasn't exactly an option.

Hale had disappeared somewhere along the journey, and Maria wondered if he'd headed straight back to his boat, planning to set sail for wherever he'd been hiding all this time until the mess was over—she'd be sad if he did. Or maybe he'd gone in search of Nicoli. They'd become friends too, over the years. Perhaps Hale hoped to broker a peace ... wishful thinking, no doubt, but why had he chosen this particular moment to reappear?

The servants eventually returned, forcing Maria from the cooling water and into a freshly steamed dress the color of burnt orange—not another in light blue or purple, thank the Goddess. It had capped sleeves, but she waved away the light blue shawl they offered to cover her bruises, instead selecting a gauzy one in midnight blue. She secured it with a silver broach the shape of the Celestl Star, the Blades picked out in gemstones and the Claws in shimmering pearls.

The servants paled and shot each other worried glances but weren't brave enough to question her choice of color.

Maria was disappointed to find herself seated apart from Elex at dinner—presumably a demonstration from her uncle that he still had some power—but they shared plenty of long looks and smiles across the table, and Maria's thoughts regularly strayed to *later* ...

She was glad to find Hale hadn't abandoned them and was engaging Elex in quiet, animated conversation. Sophie—who'd been placed beside John at Maria's end of the table—kept casting longing glances at Hale's broad, rugged form.

'If only we all had reason to be as giddy as you,' said Sophie from her seat opposite Maria.

'He's an ass,' said Maria, but Sophie refused to tear her eyes from Maria's older brother. He'd never exactly been affable, but his time at sea seemed to have stripped him of any polish at all. What little Maria could hear of his conversation made him appear even blunter and more brooding than before.

'He's delectable,' said Sophie, 'and he's mine.'

Maria reared back in surprise, then remembered to hide her emotions.

'Your uncle agrees,' Sophie added, eyeing Maria speculatively.

Maria didn't point out that until Hale had appeared, Sophie had apparently thought John delectable. She also refrained from mentioning that it was one thing for her uncle to exert control over Maria and John, but quite another for him to do so over Hale.

Hale was dangerous to Danit. Leading Alter Blade was Hale's birthright, and Danit only ruled at Hale's behest. Not to mention, Hale was more than their uncle's match physically, if it ever came down to it, and Hale would easily persuade their army to follow him, a younger, better-looking, more inspiring leader than Danit, on top of the fact that the position was rightfully his. Danit walked a fine line, especially as this new version of Hale seemed less reasonable than the old one.

'Sir,' said a guard, approaching Danit at the table. 'The land failed to stop again at the Sunset Fall. There is even more destruction around the lake.'

It was confirmation of what they already knew because they'd felt the ground speed up and then slow back to its normal speed. It had thrown many off their feet, although perhaps not so vigorously as the first time.

Danit tried to dismiss the man with a casual wave, but he was already speaking again. 'We found flaps inside one of the water pipes. We believe they are supposed to be used for maintenance, but in this case, the Claws have utilized them in a hostile manner. They closed the flaps as a way to shut off our supply, seeing as they obviously couldn't do it from the pump house—even if they could have got access, it would have been too easy for us to fix and—'

'Get to the point, man,' snapped Danit, circling his hand.

'Sorry sir, yes ... We can restore the piped water by discovering the locations of all the other flaps and forcing them open. Or perhaps we can even find the mechanisms designed for opening and closing them and use those, which would be preferable, seeing as it would lead to less disruption.'

'Very good,' said Danit, cutting him off before he could continue his long-winded impart. 'Send word to the other Blades in case they haven't already discovered the same.'

'Sir,' said the soldier, snapping his feet together and lowering his head in a sharp, deep nod, then wheeling for the exit.

'It won't be much good if there's no water to pipe,' said Linella. 'The levels were already falling, and now this?'

'Linella!' Barron exclaimed, but it was too late, everyone had heard and pricked up their ears.

'What do you mean the level was already falling?' said John.

'Linella,' said Danit, 'you are dangerously close to contravening the pact.'

Linella shrugged. 'The pact is, as of this moment, dead. My daughter should have married Hale earlier today, but seeing as she didn't, you have broken the terms, and I am now free to say what I wish.'

'*I* didn't break the terms,' said Danit. 'Hale did.'

'Makes little difference to me. Sophie and Hale must wed, or the pact is done.'

Sophie nodded her agreement as her eyes found Hale, who lounged in his chair, seeming disinterested, as though it didn't concern him at all.

'But ...' said John, spluttering wildly, his trademark cockiness having deserted him, 'I have ... we've ... I've taken liberties!'

Maria covered her mouth with her hand, hoping to appear scandalized but really trying to stifle her smile. The room paused at the admission, and Sophie froze but somehow kept her composure.

Hale barked out a laugh. 'Good for you, brother. I didn't know you had it in you!'

'Hale,' growled Danit.

'We didn't ... I didn't mean ...' stammered John.

But Hale had already lost interest. He leaned back in his chair. 'I believe you have information to share, Uncle?'

'As do you,' said Danit. 'Like where in the Goddess's name you've been all this time.'

Hale's casual demeanor remained, but his face set into a stubborn mask that hadn't changed one bit since they were children, the purse of his lips the only sign he was preparing for battle.

As dearly as Maria wanted to hear her brother's story, she knew he wouldn't budge—he was nothing if not obstinate—and Maria's mind was more concerned about Linella's revelation. 'What do you mean the water level is dropping?' she said into the silence of Hale and Danit's standoff.

Danit, to his credit, took the olive branch she offered, turning his head away from Hale's silent challenge, although he didn't deign to answer her question directly. 'We must find a way to collect the water that falls outside the lake.'

Barron leaned forward, his fists balled on the table. 'And cut off every last drop that flows to the Claws.'

'We already have,' said Danit.

'They'll die!' said Maria. 'Innocent people ... children ... babies ...'

'And it is all down to Nicoli and his ambition,' said Danit.

'He's not the one shutting off their water,' countered Maria.

'But he is the one playing with ours.'

'That's why you wanted to see him, isn't it? Because you knew the levels were dropping and you needed his help. No one else can solve the problem, just like no one here even knows how to pump water up from the moat!'

'Your fondness for that man is a problem,' snarled Danit. 'If I were your husband, I would take you in hand.'

'But the fact remains,' said Elex, 'if the water is truly declining, we do need his help.' Maria could have kissed him.

Linella folded her arms across her chest, a malign look on her face that made Maria shudder. 'And it's speeding up, the decline.'

'Linella!' snapped Danit.

'Marriage,' she countered. 'I don't see much in the way of you trying to solve that problem, either. I'm wondering what good you are to any of us, in fact.'

Maria looked from Linella to Danit to Barron, and not one of them seemed surprised. 'You all knew,' she said. Silence settled, no one denying it. 'That's the real reason for the pact, isn't it? You're not done with war, it's just that a greater threat forced you to set aside your differences.'

'And Nicoli has proven we were right to,' said Danit. 'The Claws are a threat to all Blades.'

'They just want fairness!' said Maria. 'Recognition. Respect.'

'Wealth,' spat her uncle. '*Our* wealth.'

'But without water,' said Barron, sitting back in his chair, 'they'll come begging for mercy soon enough.'

Maria knew Barron's theory was right, even though it hurt to think that way. But Nicoli was not stupid, which meant either he didn't need water from the Blades or he had something else up his sleeve. Both options filled her with dread.

'It won't be so simple,' said Hale, steepling his fingers. 'Nicoli is—'

'Out,' said Danit, pushing back his chair and getting to his feet. 'All of you, out.'

The servants scurried away, and the few senior guards seated at the table did the same, but Maria looked at Hale, waiting to see what he would do before she moved. Everyone did.

Eventually, Hale stood, refilled his goblet with wine, saluted Danit in a way that was anything but respectful, then sauntered to the door. Everyone aside from Danit, Barron, and Linella followed.

Maria took Elex's offered arm as they met near the door, following Hale into the library that had been decorated with lavish garlands made of lush green foliage and bright flowers to celebrate Blade Day. They sat on a couch, arms wrapped together, Maria glad to be reunited with her husband.

Hale took an armchair, and Sophie claimed the couch beside it, as close to Hale as she could possibly manage. John took the other end, and Sophie scowled at him despite the large gap between them.

A bowl piled high with triffles sat on a low table in the space between them, and Maria smiled, thinking of all the ways she might use hers.

'Sophie,' John said quietly, reaching for her hand, but she recoiled.

'We are no longer betrothed,' she snapped.

It was only then that Maria realized Sophie's scandalous clothes had been replaced with something almost demure, her hair seeming softer, falling around her shoulders in loose waves, her makeup less pronounced. Why the sudden change?

'You said you—' said John.

'It matters not what I said. We were betrothed then, we are not now, and that is the end of it.'

'Sophie!' John protested. 'We're hand-tied, and I'm sure if you spoke to your mother ...'

'No.'

'But—'

'Enough,' she sneered. 'Stop whining like a brat.'

Maria's eyes widened as sickly-sweet, coquettish Sophie vanished for a moment, replaced by someone sensible, a little mean, and in possession of an impressively straight backbone. Maria liked this version of Sophie rather better, even if it exposed her previous falsehoods when it came to her feelings for John, for there was no doubt in Maria's mind which brother Sophie truly wanted. Maria refused to judge her for that because wouldn't Maria have been forced to lie if she'd been engaged to Cane from the outset?

Hale lifted an eyebrow as he watched the exchange, and Maria wondered if he was beginning to regret his out and out refusal. But much as Maria would have liked to explore the topic further, unfortunately, they had more pressing matters at hand.

'We need to meet with Nicoli,' said Maria, knowing it was dangerous to say that in front of John and Sophie but deciding to do it anyway.

'Why?' said Hale.

'To put an end to all this.' *Obviously*.

'Wasn't it him who did that to your face?' said Hale. 'I heard—'

'Of course not! Nicoli has never lifted a finger against me, which is more than can be said of our uncle.'

Hale nodded in understanding. As a boy, he'd experienced his fair share of beatings at Danit's hand. 'Either way, Nicoli is responsible for many deaths today and going forward; that is no small thing.'

Maria sighed. 'We have to stop this! The people of the Claws are no different to us, and there's plenty to go around if we would just learn to share!'

'How?' said Hale, resting his arms on the sides of his chair like a king on his throne. Maria found the posture highly irritating, even if he had a point, because it didn't matter a jot if they wanted to stop the bloodshed if they had no means to.

'Nicoli will have a plan.'

Elex squeezed her arm, and she looked up at him in confusion because it was almost a pinch.

Hale smirked. 'Keep your knickers on, old friend. We have no way to contact Nicoli, and if he and Maria were in love, they would have run off together years ago.'

Maria's face flushed as she glared at Hale. 'Your manners haven't improved then, brother.'

'I've been aboard a ship filled with seasoned sailors ... You thought that would improve my comportment?'

Sophie chuckled, and John's features turned so dark, Maria had to cough away a laugh of her own.

'I'm going to bed,' said John, pocketing a triffle before heading to the door. 'The company here is lacking, and I for one won't run cap in hand to our enemy.'

'Remember triffles can't be used for love!' Hale called after him, then threw a meaningful look at Sophie as though warning her of the same.

'We're going to bed, too,' said Elex, leaning forward and reaching for the triffle bowl. He handed one to Maria, then helped her to her feet. 'The way I see it, unless we can convince our relatives to abandon their vendetta against the Claws, Maria's right: meeting Nicoli is our only hope of bringing the violence to an end.'

Hale inclined his head in what Maria took to be reluctant agreement, but as they wished him goodnight, leaving him alone with Sophie, his expression turned comical, terror staining his stern mask.

'Don't let the night bugs bite!' Maria called over her shoulder, a small part of her wanting to stay and force her brother's story from him ... but knowing Hale, that would not be a quick affair, and as Elex impatiently tugged her from the room, she giggled, thoughts of anything but him flying from her mind.

Chapter Twenty-Six
Ava

THEY DIDN'T TALK ABOUT Ava, much to her relief. Billy sat back in his chair once again and promptly fell asleep, dropping his—thankfully empty—tumbler in his lap.

Ava waited for several minutes to see if he would wake, and when he didn't, she put his tumbler in the sink along with her water glass and explored the place.

She combed over every inch, looking in every cupboard and on every shelf, but there was nothing interesting, only plates and cutlery and the like.

She stepped out onto the balcony and walked its full length, sliding her hand along the railing, but when she came to the corner, where the rail should have turned back towards the wall, her hand kept sliding. Her brain jolted as what she felt and what she saw diverged, and then something shifted in the air and she could suddenly see that the balcony continued for another two feet, a second room leading off it.

She hesitated, wondering if exploring further was a good idea. She looked guiltily back at Billy, but he was sound asleep, his mouth open, breathing heavily.

She poked her head into the new room and found only an empty bedroom with a large but plain bed, a dressing table littered with lotions and potions, and a full-length mirror.

At the back of the room, another door stood open, and she went to it, finding it led to what she assumed was a bathing chamber. But it was the strangest bathing chamber she'd ever seen, for despite the indoor privy—quite the luxury compared to what she was used to—there was no bath, and there were strange holes in the floor below a metal pipe with an end that looked like a sieve. It was foreign and yet elicited a feeling of distant familiarity, of comfort ... a memory, maybe?

A noise came from the other room, and Ava jumped, rushing back the way she'd come.

'Where is she?' demanded a woman's voice ... a familiar voice. Ava's blood stilled as she halted just in time to stay hidden, listening hard.

'Ahhhh,' Billy said around a yawn. 'BeeBee!'

'Don't call me that.'

'It's such a ... well, it's ... refreshing to see you, at least.'

All the blood in Ava's body rushed to her head, and she had to bend double to keep from blacking out, her vision blurring. It was true then, what Billy had said.

'Where is she?' the woman asked again, a hint of concern leaching into her tone.

Ava straightened up and stepped into view, her feet moving of their own accord, her brain barely able to keep up.

'You little snake ...'

Ava braced herself for physical pain as Mrs. B rushed towards her, but she diverted to a pot plant on a dresser at the last moment. 'You swore you'd look after them!'

'They're alive, aren't they?' said Billy, stretching his whole body into a star shape.

Mrs. B rushed to the sink and filled a pitcher with water, then moved around the room, giving each of the plants a long drink.

'Mrs. B,' said Ava. 'You—'

The woman scoffed. 'Did I ever once mention a husband?'

Ava flinched. 'Um ... I thought maybe he was dead? Or had left?'

Mrs. B's nostrils flared. 'My name is B. Drop the Mrs.'

'Okay,' she said slowly. 'Sorry?'

'Another irritation by your hand,' B snapped. 'At first I thought it was funny—the spoilt little girl showing me deference—but then everyone else started doing it, and soon it was just another burden you'd saddled me with.'

Ava's eyebrows pinched—she could hardly be blamed for that—but she held her tongue.

B took a step closer, looking younger and more refreshed than she had earlier that day. Impossibly so. 'Who even are you?' B asked venomously. 'I mean, are your parents actually your parents? I've always wondered because I can't say I've seen much evidence ...'

'B,' said Billy, 'I know it's been a hard few years, but no need to be mean. And she looks like her mother. She's got that weird button nose thing going on, and those eyebrows ... her grandmother's eyebrows.'

'Well, I'm not convinced,' said B. 'The Gods have trouble conceiving; maybe it's all a ruse. A way for them to fuck with us from beyond the grave.'

'You've got issues, my dear B,' said Billy. 'Paranoia isn't healthy ... and you know only too well whose child she is.' He waggled his eyebrows.

B shuddered as she looked away, facing the balcony. 'What the fuck is that?'

'I never liked the real view,' said Billy. 'I prefer it this way ... more intimate ... less intimidating.'

'What?' breathed Ava.

Billy rolled his eyes. 'Out yonder is a colossal heap of, well, bark. I hate it, so I painted something nicer on top. A vast improvement if you ask me.'

Ava's mind reeled, but before she could ask a follow-up question, B said, 'Gods, I came close to jacking it in at the end there. *King* ...' She paused for a long while, and Billy closed his eyes, waiting for her to continue, patient aside from the smallest bounce of his index finger on the arm of his chair. 'But then I'd really have been in the shit.'

'Novak is a stickler,' agreed Billy, eyes still closed.

'And ... well ... you know ...' said B, with a long sigh.

'What?' said Ava.

B whirled and fixed her with sharp eyes, looking almost as though she'd forgotten Ava was there. 'None of your damn business.'

Billy shot Ava a conspiratorial sideways glance, clenching his teeth and pulling his lips wide. 'He sold her out, though,' said Billy.

'Novak?' said B, going very still for a moment, her arms in midair.

'Mmm hmm.'

B selected a bottle of something called *Shit Show* from the shelves and took a swig straight from the bottle.

'But you don't drink?' said Ava, having never seen the woman touch a drop before.

'Wrong,' said B, taking another long pull.

'You're looking marvelously well, though,' said Billy.

'Borrowed some robes and snuck into the healing pool in the temple before coming through the portal.'

Kush had talked about the restorative pools, but Ava hadn't realized they could do something like this ... Mrs. B looked years younger.

'I needed it, I can tell you. Although, burning the Cleve to the ground was perhaps even better for my health.'

'You did what?' said Ava.

'Don't *you* judge me; you're the one who caused all this. I needed that pool after what I've had to endure.'

'No, I mean, about the Cleve?'

'Scummy, horrible hole in the ground,' she said, then took another swig. 'Wasn't always like that,' she added wistfully.

'What did you do?'

'I burned it to the ground,' she repeated slowly. 'Was I not clear the first time?' She looked at Billy and shrugged as though saying, *See? How* could *she be their daughter?*

A bolt of nauseating panic hit her stomach. 'The tavern?' said Ava, undeterred because Mrs. B had been horrible to her for years; she was used to it.

'The whole fucking place. Used your lava stone, actually—assuming I have Kush to thank for that?'

Guilt tinged Ava's panic even though she knew it wasn't her fault. But how many people were hurt or homeless because of her stone? 'But where will everyone live? How will they survive?'

B scoffed. 'Well obviously I didn't burn the *whole* place to the ground. Just the tavern and the bits belonging to King.'

'What about Tasha and Cook and the dancers ...?' Her voice came out shrill. She might not have liked any of them, but she couldn't bear the thought of them all being dead.

'Don't fret, Ava, I'm not a complete monster. They all got out alive.'

She exhaled heavily—that was something, at least. 'But what will they do now?'

She shrugged again, this time a frivolous hint to it. 'Whatever takes their fancy. The more interesting question is what *you* will do now.'

This woman seemed both the same and entirely different to the one Ava knew. Like her color had been muted before, hidden behind a filter, but now she'd been exposed, vital, bright, and full of life—if still brutal.

Ava had never wondered about B's life before the tavern ... She'd assumed B had always lived there, that there had been no life before. But now she wanted to know. Desperately.

How had this woman gone from being a close friend of her parents to someone who hated them enough to call them evil and treat their daughter so badly?

'Why did you throw me out like that this morning?' asked Ava, feeling the crater in her chest again, the isolation.

'It was fun!' B said simply, clearly not giving a damn.

'Although, she nearly got caught,' said Billy, pouring himself a measure from a bottle called, *Pleasantly Buzzed*. 'Which would have been—'

'Regrettable?'

'A complete fucking shit show.'

'Does your boyfriend know you're here?' B asked Ava.

'Her boyfriend?' said Billy, rounding on Ava and touching his chin to his shoulder.

'Kushnalim de Var regularly visits her bed.'

'You sneaky little dark horse,' said Billy. 'I thought we were friends.'

'It's not like that,' said Ava, her face flushing. 'And no, he doesn't know I'm here. Is he okay?'

'He's the son of a God,' said B. 'He'll be fine.'

'The son of a ... what?'

'Wait, you haven't told her?'

'Oh, I've told her,' said Billy. 'It's just a lot, you know?' He turned to face her. 'Ava, you and Kushy are both children of the Gods—some call you demi-Gods ... Do you dig that?'

Ava just stared at him. Right, her parents were Gods, had created the method, had turned other sorcerers into Gods, too. She'd chosen not to think too much about that, but Kush was ... Var was ... it made sense, she supposed; Var had said he knew her parents.

'Well, we can work on the branding later, but,' said Billy, sitting in his chair and beckoning for Ava to take the one opposite, 'it means you and Kush-Kush have even more in common!' He rested his chin on his fist. 'Tell me everything.'

'He betrayed me,' she said, her voice barely more than a whisper as she sat in the chair.

'Really?' said B, drawing the word out, making it quite clear she didn't believe her. She sat in another of the armchairs and watched Ava like a hawk.

'I don't want to talk about it,' said Ava, curling her legs under her.

'It will make you feel better,' said Billy.

'I doubt that.' Kush had certainly lied to her, at the very least by omission, but—

'Var might even allow them to marry!' said Billy, as though he'd had an epiphany.

'Nope,' Ava said silently and immediately regretted it.

'The optics would be bad,' agreed Billy, although he still seemed to be considering the idea.

'Hmmm,' agreed B. 'There are so few children, though ...'

'What do you mean?'

'Well, that was the other thing,' said Billy. 'Something about tying their souls to alternate worlds made it hard for the Gods to have kids. Although, it's difficult to know how many they have for sure because the Gods all live in the Clouds now, keep themselves to themselves, so ... who knows?'

'The Clouds?'

'At the top of the tree, where your parents used to live.'

'Oh.'

'So,' said B, sitting straight and turning businesslike, 'what are you going to do, Ava? And what was in that package from your parents?'

Billy turned curious eyes on her. 'There was more? Aside from the Atlas Stone?'

'It didn't have an Atlas Stone.'

'Then, how ...?'

'I stole Kush's.'

'Ha!' said B, and Ava caught a gleam of something like respect in the woman's eyes. 'Maybe you're not a lost cause after all. And that explains why Var was in such a rage at the temple earlier.'

'He was?'

B nodded. 'Rampaging about, shouting and screaming, very unhappy with Kush. Very unhappy with everyone, in fact, so I slipped away before I could get caught in anything unsavory.'

'Did you see Kush?'

B shook her head.

'He was injured, and Var ...'

'Var won't kill him,' said B, but the words didn't make Ava feel any better. If Var was willing to send Kush into dangerous worlds where others might kill him, he didn't value his son's life that highly. 'What was in the package?' B snapped impatiently.

Ava scowled. B didn't get to talk to her that way anymore. Sure, Ava was in a strange place, had no friends and nowhere to go, but she got the impression they wanted something from her, which meant she had leverage, and she had plenty of questions of her own.

'Who are you?' she asked. 'And what do you want from me?'

'What was in the damn package?' said B. 'Tell us!'

'No.'

B's eyebrows pulled menacingly together, but Ava had endured similar looks for years and B didn't scare her any longer.

A high-pitched noise came from Billy, one of delight, and it further strengthened Ava's resolve.

'You were friends with my parents?'

Billy swung his head dramatically towards B.

'I was.'

He swung his head back to Ava.

'You all grew up together?'

Billy started another head swing, but B snapped, 'Oh stop it, Billy!'

He gave a little shake of glee before relenting.

'In a manner of speaking,' said B.

'Were your family sorcerers too? Like Billy's?'

B clenched her teeth. 'No.'

Billy looked straight ahead, eyes wide, but Ava didn't stop.

'Then how did you meet?'

B looked as though she was preparing to swallow something nasty. 'Novak is a distant cousin of mine. He brought his friends to my parents' tavern one day to mock us and rub his high standing in our faces.'

'But it backfired,' interjected Billy, 'because B and your mother hit it off.'

B's eyebrows lifted a fraction. 'She'd come from a lowly background herself, and didn't like what the others were doing. She even invited me to spend time with them, determined to make Novak's plan fail.'

'Novak was spitting,' purred Billy. 'Especially as he only did it to impress the cool kids.'

B tipped her head to one side. 'Maybe ... Not that that made it any easier on me. But you're right, he'd worked his arse off to get into their inner circle. It had taken him years, and I got there in a single day.'

'And all because of him,' Billy said with a satisfied smile.

'Your parents bought their house in Santala shortly after that,' said B, 'and based themselves there half the time.'

Billy rubbed his thumb and forefinger together a few times in a quick, rhythmic pattern. 'They liked to be away from prying eyes. The top of the tree is luxurious but exhausting—spies and social climbers everywhere.'

'Eventually it fell apart,' said B. 'Your parents were power-hungry fools, just like all the so-called Gods. I retreated to the Cleve and tried to forget about them ... until you showed up.'

'So,' said Ava, shifting uncomfortably in her seat, 'what do you want me to do?'

'We're more interested in what you *don't* do, actually,' said Billy, then knocked back his drink.

'I don't understand.'

He shrugged as he swallowed. 'You're the only one who can get into your parents' house, and we don't want you to.'

'Oh,' said Ava, disappointment crashing through her. It was all she had, her only link to her parents, and they wanted her to abandon it? Abandon any hope of finding out who she was? Who her parents had been?

Billy traced the rim of his glass with his index finger. 'And in return, we'll look after you. Help you build a quiet life away from the glare of the sun.'

Ava felt suddenly weary. She'd thought she was finally on a meaningful path after years of standing still—even if it had taken B kicking her out to set her on her way—and they wanted her to just ... ignore who she was?

'It will be a good life,' Billy continued. 'And you'll have the freedom to do whatever you want: sorcery, geometry, portalry ...'

'But what about Var?' she asked, not quite saying what she meant.

Billy nodded. 'He'll search for you, of course. We'll have to be careful and change your looks and accent, but the tree is a big place; we can hide you well enough.'

'And Kush?' she said quietly.

'No,' said B, resolutely.

'But he betrayed you!' Billy said in a singsong voice. 'Soooo ... silver linings?'

'And if I refuse?' Ava's voice was smaller still, her energy seeming to have melted away.

'Oh, darling,' said Billy, a warning edge to his tone he hadn't used before, 'don't do that. We do so want to be friends.'

'Be thankful we're giving you the choice,' said B. 'We could have just killed you.'

'BeeBee!' exclaimed Billy.

Ice spread through Ava's veins, and her whole body started shaking. She collapsed forward, losing control of her limbs, convulsing hard. She could see and hear just fine, but she couldn't make anything do what she wanted it to.

B and Billy both jumped to their feet and were crouched at her side in a heartbeat, one of them tipping her head back, the other checking her pulse.

A few silent moments passed, then B rocked back on her heels. 'Stone sickness.' They sent each other matching forlorn looks. 'I'm assuming Herivale is still hard to come by?'

'Controlled by Hunter,' said Billy, 'and Var will be watching the stock ... he saw her use the stone.'

'Fuck.'

Chapter Twenty-Seven
Maria

As soon as they crossed the threshold out of the library, the space in Maria's mind closed in on itself, leaving room only for Elex. His gaze raked up and down her body in a way that made her shiver, and then he moved, throwing her over his shoulder and taking off for the main stairs at almost a run.

He took the steps two at a time, seeming to feel her additional weight not at all, and Maria resisted the temptation to shriek as she bounced around. She didn't want to draw anyone's attention, least of all the servants.

Elex burst into Maria's room and shoved the door closed behind them, turning the key in the lock before sliding her down his body and holding her to his chest. He was barely even breathing hard, she realized, in the split second before he covered her mouth with his. And then all thought was gone, no room for anything but sensation and desire.

He kissed her like a man starved, pulling at her lips with strong, firm strokes and digging his hands into her hair. He slid a hand to her breast and squeezed, and Maria held on to him for dear life as a gasp of pleasure escaped her.

Elex leaned back, watching her as he swept his thumb back and forth across her nipple through her dress. It was stiff and aching after only a handful of caresses.

'Elex,' she breathed, desperately tugging him back to her, growing more demanding by the second.

He kissed her again, his tongue exploring hers, and Maria met him stroke for stroke, forgetting she didn't know what she was doing, because her body seemed to know just fine.

Maria's legs hit the back of the bed—she hadn't realized they'd been moving—and Elex held her upright, his nimble fingers making short work of her buttons and laces, her dress sliding to the floor moments later.

She wore no brassiere—support sewn into the dress—so she stood before him in only a scrap of skimpy lace. Her maids had giggled when they'd handed her the undergarment, and Maria had turned crimson, but they'd assured her Elex would like it.

It seemed they were right because after his eyes snagged on her small, round breasts, they skimmed down across her tapered waist and lingered on the generous flare of her hips. He set his hands on them, slid his thumbs beneath the lace, and pressed into the creases just beneath her hip bones. She nearly collapsed at the intensity of the sensation skittering out from his touch.

He dug his fingers into her backside as he pushed down with his thumbs, moving lower with each press. She bucked and made a noise she'd never heard before. He exhaled sharply and tugged her against the hard bulge of his groin.

She pulsed her hips, the feel of him so utterly divine she could think of nothing but that, needing more. He growled into her neck, then pushed her away and turned her, sliding a hand across her waist and tugging her to his chest.

He slid his fingers into the lace, Maria vibrating as he crept slowly towards where she wanted him most . He skirted her most sensitive flesh, and she moaned, lifting a hand to his neck and clutching him as she tried to press into his fingers, greedy for more.

He touched her again, and she moaned his name until he pressed a finger against her and curled it in a way that made her head tip back. 'Goddess,' she breathed. 'Elex ...'

A loud bang came from outside their room, and Maria's head snapped round, but the door handle remained still. A low curse came through the wood, then footsteps moved away.

Elex kissed her nape, nibbling and sucking and almost convincing her to forget the world again, but something nagged at her, a worry that wouldn't let her go.

'Don't stretch it out,' she said, spinning to face him. He kissed her neck, and she gasped, then grasped his thick hair and forced his head up so she could see his face. His eyes were glassy and full of promise, and her insides contracted at the sight. 'Not the first time. I'm still scared they'll take you from me, but once we ... consummate ... they—' She moaned as he pinched her nipple. 'Elex, please. I can't be parted from you.'

He briefly flicked his eyes to the door, her words finally getting through to him, and then he slid her underwear over her backside and let it fall to the floor.

He reached for his own laces, making quick work of the fastening, then freed his length. Maria's eyes went wide. She knew the theory of coupling but had no practical knowledge, and she felt suddenly vulnerable and so very naked in the face of all his clothes.

'Elex,' she said, hesitantly, 'I ... Why aren't you naked?'

He exhaled heavily as he pumped his hand slowly up and down his shaft. 'Because I was impatient to see you,' he said, resting his forehead against hers.

Her fingers worked to open the buttons of his doublet, but he quickly took over, sending first that and then his shirt to the floor.

Maria slid tentative hands to his waist and tugged down his breeches. He kicked them off along with his boots, and then he pressed his naked flesh to hers. She was utterly unprepared for the feel of it, the heat, the ecstasy. Such a simple thing, their bodies touching everywhere they could—thighs, stomachs, chests—but the intensity, the intimacy, sent flames burning through every part of her, racing through her blood before gathering between her thighs and in her breasts, everything pulling tight.

He pushed her down onto her bed and drank her in for a beat, two, then settled his weight on top of her, kissing her as his length nudged at her core. She gasped as he found her opening, feeling a slight stretch as their bodies aligned, and they both paused, Elex looking down into her eyes, studying her as he gave her time to acclimatize.

Maria tipped her hips, encouraging him to push farther in, impatient, but he hesitated. 'Do you want children?' he asked, his voice gravelly.

She let out an exasperated huff. 'I have little choice.'

'But do you *want* them?'

'Yes. Do you?'

'Yes,' he breathed, 'but not yet ... not now.'

'But then how will we ...?'

'There are herbs.'

Several conversations popped into her mind, words she hadn't understood until that moment. Women asking if Maria could procure them herbs, then acting strangely when she'd asked why they would need the black market for those. Then how her maids had giggled as they'd discussed herbs earlier that very evening while getting her ready for dinner. They'd thought she was out of earshot, but even so, she had neither understood nor cared to enquire further. How she wished now she had.

'I haven't got any,' she said, dismayed.

'It's okay,' he said, pushing in a little farther, the sensation making her eyes roll back in her head. 'I'll pull out before the end.'

'But ...' Her eyes flew open. 'Will it count?'

He chuckled. 'Oh, it will count, and we don't have to share every detail with the world,' he said with a wry smile.

She tried to turn her face away to hide her embarrassment, but he chased her with his lips, showering kisses across her face until she turned her head and offered up her mouth.

She gasped as he pushed fully inside her while he grunted into her neck, and her body pulsed around him, the stretch taking her almost to the point of pain.

'Elex,' she breathed as he gently pulsed his hips. 'It feels ... It's ...'

'Does it feel good?' he asked, looking down with such intensity.

She closed her eyes, his attention overwhelming. 'Yes. But ... I ...'

He stroked his fingers down her cheek as he began moving again. 'Pay attention to what you like—that's all you need do. Your body will tell you what it wants, and your only job is to tell me. To be honest ... not to hide.'

She bit her lip and nodded but still couldn't open her eyes.

'My little hell cat,' he said, going still, 'look at me.'

She did, but she didn't know what to say, making his nickname for her seem even more ridiculous than it usually did. He moved in and out, and she moaned again, her body liking very much what he was doing, although she didn't have the words to tell him.

He pulled out slowly, then pushed back in at the same agonizing speed. 'I like this a great deal,' he said. 'Do you?'

She nodded, arching her back as he did it again. And then he took her nipple into his mouth and sucked.

'Fuck,' said Maria, clawing at his back. 'Elex ...'

When he next looked down at her, he seemed to be losing the strict hold he had over himself, his eyes filled with a lustful haze, his breathing ragged, and she opened her legs wider, obeying her body's command to pull more of him inside.

The more he moved, the less she could think, chasing the strange tingling feeling building inside her that intensified every time his pelvis pressed to hers.

She moaned his name and cried out to the Goddess, then made noises that seemed detached, like they came from someone else.

'Fuck, Maria ...' Elex breathed. 'I don't ... I can't ...' And then something exploded inside her, and she clung to him as a wave of sensation sped through her, followed by another and then another. But before it stopped, Elex pulled away, getting off the bed and leaving her clenching around nothing, desperate and confused.

'Elex,' she whispered as he quickly returned, pulling the bedding atop them as he climbed in, wrapping himself around her. His skin was soothing, but it did little to quash her lingering worry. 'What was that? Did I ... did I do something wrong?'

'Oh, my perfect little hell cat,' he said, rolling her, then pressing his lips to hers. 'You didn't know?'

'Know what?' Her tone was shrill, her heartrate rocketing.

'That was how it should be every time we couple. What it is my job to make you feel. I should have told you what to expect, but I thought ... well ... Things are different here.'

Maria didn't know much, but from the snippets she'd overheard, no other man spoke of coupling in such terms. 'Elex, don't mock me!'

She tried to shove him off, but he caught her hand and pinned it above her head, heat flashing in his eyes. 'I am not mocking you,' he said, his tone low and dangerous. 'That was completion, and you should feel it every time.'

'But ...' Maria was so confused. 'That's not what men speak of when they ...'

He nodded in understanding, then paused a moment, brushing a few stray strands of hair off her face. 'Not all men understand the art of coupling. They think it's a single player game ... about their own pleasure and little more. But it's a team sport, and I get little satisfaction unless I know I've sated you.'

'Oh,' she said, realization dawning. 'So it's the same as all other things in marriage.'

He slid his fingers down the valley between her breasts, a questioning look on his face as he pinched her nipple.

She gasped.

'How so?' he asked, cupping her breast and kneading.

'Men have skewed things in their favor.'

He moved his lips to her neck, sucking there as he rolled and pinched her, stoking hot desire between her legs once more. He pulled his head back to look at her as he slid his fingers down across the swell of her belly, all the way to the ache at the apex of her thighs. 'Not in our marriage,' he said, pressing his fingers to her sensitive flesh.

Maria arched, the tightening sensation back, tugging her insides taut. She tipped her hips, urging his fingers to move faster and press harder, and he dipped his head to her breast, nuzzling her before flicking her nipple with his tongue.

'Mmm,' she gasped, digging her hands into his hair.

He sucked hard while continuing the delicious torture with his fingers, and Maria's encouraging moans filled the room. He released her breast and covered her mouth with his, his kisses deep and rhythmic, his tongue matching the pace of his fingers. And then the feeling inside her grew, spreading, lifting, making her frantic, and she pulsed wildly against his fingers, desperate for more.

He covered her torso with his, positioning himself between her legs once again, then slid his shaft inside, setting off an explosion that had her crying out as her body clenched around him.

And this time he didn't leave before it was over. He pulsed in and out, working in tandem with his fingers, sending wave after wave of pleasure through her until she collapsed back onto the bed and threw her arms out wide, small zings of pleasure still rippling out from where they joined.

Elex pulled out and grabbed a handkerchief from the nightstand, finishing himself off with a few quick slides of his hand. He lay beside her, and she rolled into him, resting her head on his chest as he wrapped her up tight in both arms, cocooning her against the rise and fall of his chest, engulfing her in his big, solid arms.

As the thud of his heartbeat pulsed against her ear, she felt safer than she ever had before, the thought releasing a rushing sensation in her chest. He stroked gentle circles on her back, and she breathed him deep, the smell of him heady, like a dewy forest at dawn. And as she drifted into a deep, contented sleep, she was happier still because she knew she'd meet him in her dreams.

Maria woke to Elex brushing kisses down her spine. They must have rolled in the night, but even his lips couldn't chase away her need to pee.

'Be right back,' she said. 'Don't move.'

He captured her lips as she tried to extract herself, and then somehow she was in his lap, straddling him as he leaned back against the headboard.

'I really have to use the wash closet,' she said, putting a finger over his mouth so he couldn't kiss her again. 'Do not move.'

He reluctantly released her, and she raced for the adjoining bathroom. She was as quick as she could be, but on her way back, her eyes snagged on a small leather pouch on a shelf by the door. She picked it up and hurried back to bed, the cool air biting her naked skin.

She climbed between Elex's legs and leaned back against his huge chest, and for a moment she could do nothing but savor the warmth and comfort. He angled her head so he could kiss her again, and by the time she pulled away, they were both panting, something hard and uncomfortable digging into Maria's lower back.

'Did you bring me a present?' he asked, brushing his lips across her ear.

She'd all but forgotten the pouch. 'It was in the bathroom,' she said, pulling it open. A neatly folded note sat inside, which they read together: *Herbs*.

Elex carefully sniffed them, then set them on the nightstand. 'Yep.' He snickered. 'Who left you those?'

'Someone who will expect something in return, no doubt. How do I take them?'

'You steep a pinch in boiling water and then drink it down, leaves and all.'

'How long do they take to work?'

'A few hours,' he said, walking his fingers up her abdomen to her breasts. He cupped both, one in each hand.

'Then we should find some boiling water.'

'There's plenty of time,' he said, squeezing gently. 'And I want to know what you're going to do with this.' He reached over and plucked her triffle off the nightstand, holding it in his palm.

She almost squealed in delight, having forgotten all about the triffles, and snatched it up like an excited child. 'I don't know what to wish for,' she said, studying it carefully. 'I already have so much.'

He kissed her temple. 'Peace?'

'That's too big and you know it.'

'Then peace and quiet for a while?' he said with a chuckle.

'Probably also too much to hope for.'

The triffles could only work small magics, and even then, many were convinced they did nothing at all, citing coincidence and wishful thinking as explanations when wishes came true.

'Would you be cross if I wished for a meeting with Nicoli?'

Elex entwined his fingers with her free hand. 'Of course not. I don't believe your uncle's goading ... or your brother's.'

'Good, because I never saw him that way.'

'I know you care for him.'

'He's my oldest friend, and he's taught me so much. He's fascinating and curious and clever. Why my uncle and your father treat the people of the Claws as lesser, I will never understand.'

'Nor I,' said Elex.

Maria took a bite of her triffle, the sour flavor like a mix of lemon juice and grapefruit rind that made her wince as she chewed. She swallowed quickly, wishing over and over again to see Nicoli soon, and when it was done, she gratefully accepted the water Elex handed her. Once she'd washed it down, she looked up at him expectantly.

'I think I'll save mine,' he said, placing it back on the nightstand.

'Elex, no!'

She twisted in his arms and made a grab for his triffle, but he pushed her down onto the bed, pinned her with his weight, then set about ravaging her once more.

When they eventually made it out of bed, Elex accompanied Maria on her rounds, as she liked to call them, and today, more than ever, she was excited to see what they could learn.

Their first stop was her still room, and she stopped dead in the entrance, shocked to find it tidy, devoid of shattered glass, and with the salvaged items lined up neatly on a workbench.

'Elex,' she said. 'Did you ...'

He pressed his chest to her back and kissed her temple. 'I had to fill my time with something while you were off chasing Nicoli.'

She narrowed her eyes and shoved him playfully, and he pinched her waist. 'Thank you. Really, I ...'

'You're welcome.'

'At least I still have these,' she said, picking up a burner and a pot, then pulled the leather pouch filled with herbs from her pocket.

Maria worked quickly, preparing the contraceptive tea with deft, practiced fingers, then drank it all down as Elex had instructed. Then she collected up her last remaining vials, handed a few to Elex, who dutifully tucked them away, and slid the rest into her pockets.

Out of habit more than hope, she scanned the room one final time, refusing to let herself cry on account of how empty it was ... all the work she'd lost. But she had Elex now, and soon she would leave Alter and be free of her uncle entirely.

'We'll get you a new still,' he said, seeming to read her mind, 'and anything else you need.'

She smiled up at him, squeezing his arm, then turned for the door, but as her eyes roamed over a low shelf that had once been a secret compartment, she realized there was something inside. Several somethings, actually.

She rushed to the nook and crouched to take a closer look, pulling out a notebook and four vials of her most precious oils, a scrawled note sitting atop the stash that read, *You're welcome. D.*

'Dio!' Maria exclaimed. 'She must have found out what Uncle was planning.' It was just one of many missing notebooks, but it was one she'd had since the beginning of her stilling adventure, so it held a special place in her heart.

'She seems like a wily old thing,' chuckled Elex.

'To put it mildly. Danit might be her son, but I'm not sure she likes him all that much. They play these little games from time to time.'

'If only games like that were all we played in Oshe ...'

Maria jumped up and tucked the notebook and vials into her dress, refusing to let anything ruin her jubilant mood, including thoughts of her brutal new home. She grabbed Elex's hand and dragged him behind her into the corridor, practically skipping on account of the tiny victory.

'Will our adventures take us to the kitchens?' Elex asked lightly.

She spun and looked up at him, batting her eyelashes. 'Hungry?'

They crashed together, devouring each other as though they hadn't already kissed themselves senseless a dozen times since sunrise.

'We should focus,' Maria said between kisses.

Elex didn't stop. Instead, he pushed her back against the wall and kissed her harder. 'I haven't been like this since ... ever. I want to carry you to a cave and pin you under me until you're round with child.'

'Elex! I literally just took the herbs.'

'They only last a month.'

'Elex!' She finally pushed him away. 'You told me you don't want children yet.'

'You're right,' he said, straightening and smoothing his hair. 'Was your triffle wish to drive me mad with lust?'

She giggled. 'Nope, and we should get moving.'

He slid his fingers around hers, holding tight until they heard voices, at which point she slid her hand through his arm—a more appropriate display of intimacy, especially for members of the first family. Ordinarily, Maria would have hidden in an alcove and listened for useful tidbits, but Elex was much too big to hide, so they walked on and wished the servants a good morning as they passed.

Their first stop was the kitchen, and Maria pulled a cloth from the pile near the entrance and hung it over the door handle of a small, private dining area reserved for the head chef. The chef didn't materialize, but his daughter did, carrying two plates piled high with bacon, eggs, sausages, and crusty bread warm from the oven.

Maria placed a vial of rosemary oil on the table, and the girl snatched it up before retrieving a bowl of pureed tomato and a pat of butter. She paused before leaving them. 'One of the guards was in here before. Said they have a new prisoner ... all hush hush.'

Maria put a second vial onto the worn wooden tabletop.

'Pleasure doing business with you,' said the girl with a lopsided grin.

They scoffed their breakfasts as though they hadn't eaten for a week, then headed out of the mansion.

'Dungeons?' suggested Elex.

'Stables,' said Maria. 'They see who comes and goes. The prison guards are hard to crack, and it's better to go in prepared.'

Maria swung open the door to the end stable, glad to find her horse happily munching hay. 'You made it back after dumping me, then,' she said, stroking the horse's neck.

'Trotted back in right as rain,' said a voice through the wooden partition.

'Sounds about right,' said Maria, pushing a vial of vanilla essence through one of the many small holes. She sent a second after the first, and the stable girl started talking.

'They brought a prisoner in this morning, early. I'm right sure it was Nicoli.'

'What?' Maria breathed. 'How do you know?'

'Saw 'is face. Guards weren't right pleased, but I made out I 'ain't seen an' off they went right quick after.'

'He's in the dungeons?'

'Think so. Don't know for sure. Oh, an' your 'orse likes that peppermint one, she does.'

Maria stifled a smile as she pushed a vial of peppermint oil through a gap, glad she had one to offer.

They took the circuitous route to the dungeons, making four or five more stops to trade before winding through the tunnels to the cells. They were the level below Maria's still room, right in the center of the cliff with only one way in and out.

'Might be best if you hang back a bit,' said Maria, and Elex nodded, but as they approached, Hale's voice bounced off the stone walls.

'Hale?' said Maria, as they rounded the final corner.

'Sister,' said Hale, frowning. He seemed to be making small talk with the only guard in sight.

'What are you doing here?'

'Could ask you the same thing.' Hale nodded to Elex, then slid his eyes back to Maria, his features a warning.

The wooden door nearest them flew open, and Danit spewed out into the corridor. 'What the Goddess are you doing here?' he demanded, something about him more volatile than usual. Maria shied back, moving closer to her husband, because Danit's mood was the kind where someone was liable to take a thrashing.

'We came to see Nicoli,' she said, seeing no benefit in hiding what they knew.

Danit's eyes drew together. 'Why would you think he's here?'

'You're saying he's not?' said Hale.

'Don't get involved, boy.'

Hale chuckled. 'I'm going in to see him now, and if Maria would like to come, I see no reason not to let her. She's Nicoli's closest friend, and if he's going to cooperate with anyone, it'll be her.'

Danit looked for a moment like he might protest. 'I want a full debrief the moment you're done,' he said, then stormed away.

Maria raced for the door and swung it open, distressed to see Nicoli chained by his wrists and ankles, lying in a star shape on the floor. He was shivering, and a puddle of his own urine surrounded his lower half.

'Get him up,' Maria barked to the guard. 'Find him fresh clothes and put him in a cell with a bed.'

'I'm sorry ma'am, but I—'

Hale plucked the keys from the man's belt and stepped into Nicoli's cell. 'There are blankets on the back wall,' said Hale, trying the first key, which didn't fit.

Maria found the blankets and also a pile of rags that only a street urchin would call clothes. She snatched them up, then raced down the line of cells—all empty—and selected the one that was most clean and comfortable.

Not that clean and comfortable were words that could be used to describe the place. It was damp and dank and dark and stank of human waste. But the one she'd selected was the best of a bad bunch.

'This one,' said Maria.

Elex and Hale helped Nicoli inside, and Maria stepped out as they cleaned him up.

'Where's the water?' she asked the guard.

He said nothing but clearly knew he was beaten and nodded to a bucket in the corner behind him. Maria filled two tankards before returning to the cell.

She froze as she entered. Hale and Elex were wrapping Nicoli in scratchy, threadbare blankets, and the skin they were covering was littered with cuts and bruises, just like his face.

'Goddess,' breathed Maria. 'Nicoli! What happened?'

'Is it not obvious?' he said, wincing as his split lip cracked open.

'How did they catch you?'

He shrugged. 'It was early this morning. I was laying low in an old burrow, and a guard fell through the roof and landed right in front of me.'

'Fuck,' said Maria, turning to Elex. 'The triffle! This is all my fault. I wished to see you.'

'Triffles don't do anything,' said Nicoli, although his voice was perhaps softer than before. 'There is no such thing as magic.'

'Then why did that guard fall through the roof? You must admit, it's hardly likely.' And he'd never been able to explain how the wands hovered in mid-air, either, although it wasn't the time to reopen that old can of worms.

Nicoli inhaled deeply and said, 'Coincidence,' on the exhale. 'Not that it matters now.'

'Uncle said you refused to speak with him?' said Hale. 'That you would only talk to me?'

The words were a stab in Maria's chest because, not so long ago, Nicoli would have asked for her. Maria handed Nicoli the water, then moved back to stand beside Elex.

'Tell me what you saw,' Nicoli said to Hale, his bright green eyes regaining some of their usual glow. 'Did you make it to the edge?'

With all the goings on of the previous day, no one had pressed Hale about his adventures, and the thought sent a mix of exasperation and guilt swirling through her. Hale had hardly been forthcoming, but then, she hadn't exactly made her brother her priority.

'I'll happily tell you everything,' said Hale, 'as soon as you tell us what's going on between you and our uncle.'

Nicoli awkwardly took a sip of water, his hands and face both swollen. 'That man is a parasite on Celestl.'

'Yes,' said Hale, 'that's nothing new, but water falling where it shouldn't ...?'

Nicoli scowled. 'He wants to wipe us out. The water level is dropping, and your uncle thinks the solution is to destroy the Claws and for everyone who lives in them to move to the Blades.'

'But ...' said Maria, 'that doesn't make any sense!'

'Of course,' said Nicoli, 'because his real goal is to secure those of us who are useful as subjects and exterminate the rest; the dropping water level is a flimsy cover.'

'He wouldn't,' breathed Maria. 'I have little love for my uncle, but he would never kill all those people.'

Nicoli tried to shrug but winced and stopped halfway. 'You don't have to believe me, but it's the truth. I told him I was done helping him ... fixing broken pipes and maintaining the turbines. It's our own fault, I suppose;

we've let ourselves become second-class citizens, have endured it meekly for too long, but this is the final straw, and if we don't act now, we'll cease to exist entirely.' He gingerly crossed his arms. 'I for one shall watch with interest to see how well the Blades fare without us.'

'And what do the Claws want?' asked Hale, crossing his arms over his chest.

Nicoli sent him a hard, unwavering look. 'To be equal to the Blades. Nothing less will do.'

Maria closed her eyes for a beat. It wasn't that simple! 'Uncle sent word to the other Blades. By now the water to all Claws will have been shut off. How long can you last?'

'How long can the Blades last? That is the real question. The Claws are used to suffering.'

'But the Blades still have water,' countered Hale.

Nicoli shook his head. 'With the water falling outside the lakes, the level will continue to drop, and after a short time, your crop yields will decrease, you'll be forced to ration water, and your people's lives will worsen day after day, with no solution in sight. They'll worry and whisper and consider that perhaps treating the Claws with respect would be a better course.'

'The Blades will take over the turbines,' said Maria.

Nicoli scoffed. 'And do what with them? None of your people know how to work them. They'd more likely break them than put them back to how they were before, and then where would we be?'

He wasn't rattled by any of it, or if he was, he was hiding it well. 'You speak like the Claws are immune somehow.'

'Your people think the Claws are stupid, but we are not.'

Maria frowned. 'You have reserves or another way to siphon off water.' That could be the only explanation for his nonchalance.

'We are prepared.'

'Well, the same can't be said for the Blades,' said Elex.

Nicoli raised his eyebrows and tipped his head. Of course he knew that only too well ... Was happily using it to his advantage.

'We're not your enemy, Nicoli,' said Maria, imploring him with her face and tone and eyes. 'We three want to help the Claws.'

Nicoli's proud smile turned into a sneer. His eyes flicked to Elex before returning to her face. 'You couldn't even help yourself. You talk a good game, but when it comes to it, you bury your head in the sand just like the rest of them.'

'That's not fair,' she snapped, his words kindling a fire in her chest.

'No? Then tell me, what use could you possibly be to us?'

'What use could any of us be alone?' said Elex, moving closer to Maria's side. 'It's only together we have a hope.' Nicoli exhaled a hiss, but Elex seemed unperturbed. 'To make the kind of changes you say you want—that we all want—there is only one way.'

The air seemed to rush from the room, leaving a pregnant silence in its wake.

Nicoli sent Elex a hard stare. 'You don't have the stomach for it.'

'No?' said Hale, pushing off the wall. He stepped out into the corridor, checked for eavesdroppers, then swung the door almost shut. 'You question the resolve of the Black Prince?'

A shiver travelled down Maria's spine at the reminder of his brutal reputation. Elex had been nothing but kind to her—deferential, even—but it couldn't all be lies.

'I've heard the stories,' said Nicoli, 'but what I've seen with my own eyes doesn't give me much hope, and the solution that's needed ...'

'Patricide,' Elex said evenly. 'Or are you too scared to call it what it is? The only way to change the Blades is to change the leaders. And for Oshe, it wouldn't just be my father we'd have to kill but my older brother, also.'

Nicoli looked at the ceiling, clearly unconvinced.

Hale stepped forward, and Nicoli's eyes hastily found the potential threat, a wary look shuttering his features. 'Or do you question the strength of my stomach?'

Nicoli looked Hale up and down but said nothing, clenching his jaw tight.

'Hale is the rightful ruler of Alter,' said Maria, trying to keep her voice steady as wings of panic flapped in her stomach. 'We could start here, peacefully ... force Danit to step down. If the other leaders see us cooperating with the Claws, showing them the respect they deserve, they might fall in line.'

Nicoli threw up his hands. 'And rainbows might float down from the sky.'

'She's right, though,' said Hale. 'I am the rightful ruler, and that would be a start.'

Nicoli scoffed. 'Your uncle will slit your throat while you sleep.'

'Not if Hale slits his throat first,' said Elex.

Maria rounded on her husband, gaping. 'And will you do the same? Violence to end violence?'

'I'll do what needs to be done.' His tone was resolute but tinged with sadness. 'Peace for our people is worth almost any price.'

'And what about the pact?' Maria looked from Elex to Hale and back again. 'What about that peace? Because if we do this, the road is long and winding. Cane is back in Oshe, and if he takes power, this could become Alter and the Claws against three war-hardened Blades.'

'For now,' said Hale, 'we should assume the pact is still in place. Danit's sent riders to the other Blades to find out more.'

Maria gave a disbelieving laugh. 'But it's not in place. Linella's already said as much, seeing as you refused to marry Sophie.'

'A threat to try and force my hand,' Hale said dismissively, 'nothing more. The riders should return by dinnertime; we should assume nothing rash before then.'

'It changes nothing either way,' said Nicoli. 'The pact does not include the Claws.'

'Which is why we need a new solution that does,' said Elex. 'A new pact.'

Nicoli huffed in condescending fashion. 'Dreams and fancies.'

Hale's face screwed tight. 'So what exactly is your plan if not to reach peace with the Blades? Do you wish to do what Danit plans in reverse? To wipe the Blades from the face of Celestl?'

'Of course not!'

'Then a pact is the only way to end this,' snapped Hale.

'Which will almost certainly require a change in leadership,' added Elex.

Nicoli raised his eyebrows and gave a defeated half-shrug, finally conceding the point, and Maria exhaled a growl of furious disappointment, her whole body pulling tight with frustration. Why did it have to be like this?

Hale strode to Nicoli and helped him to his feet. 'But in the meantime, we need to get you somewhere safe.'

CHAPTER TWENTY-EIGHT
AVA

FOR THREE DAYS, AVA had no choice but to lie and wait while B and Billy tried everything they could to find Herivale, the only cure for Stone Sickness. It was common, they'd told her, for this to happen the first few times anyone traveled by stone. But seeing as there were only three stones in existence and two of them were missing, controlling the supply of Herivale was just one of the ways Var was using to try and locate the other two.

'It only grows in a single world,' Billy had said. 'Unfortunately, that world is part of the Federation, and we all know who controls that ...' He'd given her something to help with the worst of the shaking, and her symptoms came and went a bit. Sometimes she could even sit up and utter a few words, but most of the time she could do little but lie still and hope they found a way to save her.

'Your body isn't sure where it's supposed to be,' B had told her, 'and eventually, all the fluctuating takes its toll, and it just ... gives up.'

Cheering news.

Surely this couldn't be the end. Not so soon after she'd finally discovered who she really was and found out there were countless worlds to explore with endless wonders to discover. Perhaps she'd never get the chance, but most of all, she didn't want to die without seeing Kush again ... if his father didn't get him killed first.

Her mind conjured images of him often, and she wondered what Var had done to him. She hoped he was okay, but she knew he would be suffering—maybe worse than she was—and hated that it was her fault. She'd stolen his Atlas Stone and saved herself without hesitation, leaving Kush behind to suffer the consequences.

But he had lied to her; he'd withheld the truth of who he was, who she was, and the real reason he'd sought her out.

Had he meant to betray her to his father all along? She didn't want to believe it, and his shock had seemed genuine when she'd turned up at his mother's house, but it was a possibility she had to consider.

If forced to choose between Ava and Var, which way would he go? Var was his security, his provider, his father, and Ava was ... none of those things. She was a burden, at least aside from her ability to access her parents' warded house ... It seemed that had value.

But could she even get inside, let alone find their secrets? As B had said, she'd never shown much promise.

Although B had also told her not to worry, seeing as the Gods wouldn't let her die. Without her, they had no hope of ever finding their souls, which meant, if it came to it, they would give her the Herivale she needed. That was comforting, at least as a last resort—her body wouldn't wither away and die, and she might see Kush again—although she'd almost certainly become their prisoner, too. What was worse: death or that?

The door clicked softly shut in the other room, and Billy whispered, 'Well?'

The quiet clink of a bottle floated to where Ava lay, then their voices, hushed and urgent.

'Kush is back,' said B, 'but he's mezzed up to the eyeballs. I could see it from fifty feet away.'

'Shit,' said Billy.

'He's our only hope,' said B. 'No one has Herivale stashed, and everyone's too scared to even put out feelers. I tried to call in favors from every person I could think of but ... nothing.'

'We could ask Novak,' said Billy.

B barked out a sharp, derisive laugh. 'He sold her out to Var once already. You think he'll hesitate to do it again?'

'Then you're right,' said Billy. 'Kush is our only hope.'

'Unless we try Var directly ...'

It was Billy's turn to laugh, his somehow even meaner than B's.

'Fine,' said B, 'then it's settled; I'll ask him.'

'Why you?'

'He came to the Cleve. He knows who I am.'

'He knows how badly you treated Ava ...'

'He knows I would have drawn attention to her if I'd shown her favor, and he doesn't know you at all.'

'Urgh, fine,' said Billy, the words followed by a thud that Ava assumed was him throwing himself into a chair. 'I'll just stay here, then ... maybe enjoy some scintillating conversation with my guest.'

Chapter Twenty-Nine
Maria

ELEX USED HIS TRIFFLE to aid Nicoli's escape, even though Nicoli rolled his eyes, insisting again that magic wasn't real. 'No harm in covering all bases,' said Elex and swallowed it down.

In any case, they locked the guard in a cell and got out without incident, Maria sending word to the stable girls to saddle up four horses, bring them hooded travelling cloaks, and meet them by the moat. It cost her dearly in oils, meaning she was almost out, but they did as she bade.

They rode as fast as Nicoli could, keeping to the trees as much as possible, Nicoli directing them to a safe house near the border between Alter and Arow.

'Inside, quickly,' said Nicoli when they arrived at a rambling old farmhouse that looked like one good gust of wind would knock it down. 'Your uncle has scouts patrolling the whole border.'

One side of the building had already suffered a cave-in, but they left the horses in a barn that looked sturdy enough, and inside the intact part, they found a hive of activity that stopped dead the moment they entered.

'It's okay,' said Nicoli. 'They rescued me. They want to help.'

'Themselves, maybe,' said Gabriele, embracing her cousin. He winced. 'Shit! What did they do to you? Come.' She led him to the long wooden table, thrust a pack of food into his hands, then pulled out a chair. 'Do you have wounds that need treating?'

Nicoli shook his head. 'Sit,' he said to the others, then pulled an apple from the bag and took a big bite.

Everyone else went back to work, albeit a little warily, dividing crates of food into smaller parcels, then placing those parcels into everyday packs or saddlebags that wouldn't arouse suspicion.

'What's your plan, Nicoli?' asked Maria, taking the seat beside him. 'What next?'

'No,' said Nicoli with a determined shake of his head. 'Hale's story first.'

Hale shrugged from his seat opposite. 'In truth, there is little to tell. I wish there was more, but—'

'You reached the edge of the world?' asked Nicoli.

Hale nodded.

'And?'

'Nothing.'

'Impossible.'

'It's the truth,' said Hale, holding up his hands. 'The water hovers against the boundary. From a distance, it looks as though it falls over the edge, but up close, it's not like that at all. The boundary absorbs the energy of the water so it doesn't lap back and forth. It just sits against the edge.'

'Did you touch the edge?' asked Nicoli, seeming to have forgotten his apple.

'Yes,' said Hale, 'but I wouldn't do so again. It sapped my energy, and if my first mate hadn't pulled me back with the rope he'd insisted on tying around my waist, I'm sure I would have died. Even so, I spent weeks recuperating. To start, I could do nothing but lie in my bunk and sleep.'

'Are you okay now?' asked Maria, looking her brother up and down.

'More or less,' he said with a less than reassuring smile.

'So that's it?' said Nicoli. 'Could you see through it? Beyond the boundary?'

'Nope,' said Hale. 'It seemed to simply reflect our world back at us, showing ripples and my crew and ship. We sailed the full perimeter, and it was the same all the way around.'

Nicoli blew air through his teeth. Maria knew it had long been a dream of his to claim some other territory for the Claws, ideally a place with abundant water and far away from the oppression of the Blades. 'Fuck!' he growled, hurling his apple core into the empty grate of the fire. He leaned forward and clutched handfuls of his hair. 'Fuck.'

'Then we choose violence,' said Gabriele, 'because escape is not an option, and there is no other way.'

Maria wanted to protest Gabriele's words. She didn't want anyone else to die, but she couldn't imagine Barron or Danit ever giving an inch, not when they had the upper hand.

'I'll declare myself leader,' said Hale.

Maria nodded. 'And I'll support your claim, whatever that's worth.'

The corner of Elex's mouth pulled up into a smile. 'I'm sure Sophie will too, and her mother, assuming—'

Hale shot his friend a warning look. 'I'm not marrying her, but I'm not above using their ambition to our advantage.'

Maria shook her head, hating the way of the world because she didn't want to use Sophie in that way, but she couldn't deny it was the strategic move.

'And of course I'll support you,' said Elex, 'but father won't, and nor will my brother.'

Hale inclined his head slowly, the cogs of his brain whirling behind his eyes. 'We'll wait to hear news from the other Blades and regroup when we know more. Perhaps we can convince Spruce to join us ... tip the balance in our favor.'

Gabriele made a skeptical noise.

'But everything will be harder if the Claws keep attacking,' Maria said to Nicoli, and the room held its breath, all attention shifting to him.

Nicoli paused, then exhaled loudly. 'I refuse to adjust the turbines, but we won't do anything else for now. Time is our friend, and the Blades will realize soon enough it is not theirs.'

Hale took the seat beside Sophie at dinner that night, much to her obvious surprise, but she needed only a moment to recover, delight replacing her shock. She leaned into Hale's space and batted her long eyelashes as she hung on his every word.

John had disappeared, no one having seen him since he'd stormed from the library, and although Maria was worried about him, at least his absence meant he was spared the display.

Danit eyed Hale suspiciously from his usual seat in the middle of the table, although he didn't comment, his eyes flitting around the rest of the group before nodding to the servants to bring food.

Dinner was sizeable, as usual, but far simpler than the banquets they'd shared until then, and Maria wondered what Danit was playing at. It wasn't like him to skimp, especially when they had guests, so she had expected him to roll out every luxury until they'd gone, especially given how unhappy Linella was. It concerned Maria that their supplies might already be running low.

Maria nibbled on a slice of rosemary bread but couldn't bring herself to eat much more, her stomach in knots, even Elex's reassuring presence at her side doing little to settle her nerves.

Something in the air felt wrong ... Perhaps it was that Linella was being uncharacteristically silent, engaged in watching Hale and Sophie as she was, or maybe it was just that tensions were running high for everyone, given the general state of things.

'Our prisoner seems to have disappeared,' said Danit, his tone light but his jaw clenched.

'Yes, I freed him,' said Hale.

Maria held her breath. Hale wouldn't make a bid to lead yet, surely ...

Danit sat back at the revelation, seeming unsure. His eyes flicked to Sophie before returning to Hale. 'Why?'

'Why did you lock him up?'

Danit scoffed. 'You really need ask?'

'There was no need to beat him half to death,' said Maria.

'There it is,' said Danit. He looked at Elex. 'I'll say it again: you should be careful when it comes to Nicoli around your wife.'

Elex took Maria's hand under the table and squeezed. 'What news from the other Blades?' said Elex, his refusal to take Danit's bait making Maria's chest swell with pride.

'Some of the marriages went ahead, some did not,' said Danit, 'and they all report decreasing water. If only we had some advantage we could leverage to make them stop this nonsense with the falls ... I don't know ... perhaps something like having their leader in our custody.'

'What of Pixy?' asked Maria. She and her firecracker of a younger sister weren't always the best of friends, but she couldn't bear to think of her stuck in the middle of this mess.

'She did not marry.'

'Why?' said Maria. 'Will she return to Alter? And Mother?'

Danit shrugged. 'The messenger didn't think to inquire.'

'And my sister?' asked Elex, turning to his father.

'Unclear,' said Barron.

Elex frowned, and Maria was equally confused. How could it be unclear?

'Your sister seems to have disappeared,' Barron added.

Elex nodded, as though that made perfect sense.

Hale leaned back in his seat. 'And the Claws. What news?'

'Crying blue murder,' said Danit. 'Demanding we turn the water back on.'

Linella shook her head. 'They're lying. They should already be begging for our mercy, but not a single one has come crawling.'

'And we're using more water than we can capture,' said Danit. 'We're digging channels, trying to save as much as we can, but even so, it's only a matter of time before we run out.'

Barron slammed his palm on the table, making Maria jump. 'They must have water hidden somewhere.'

'They must,' agreed Danit, leaning his elbows on the table, his chin resting on his joined hands, 'and we must find it.'

'You and I can ride out tomorrow and oversee the search,' said Hale.

Danit recoiled. 'I do not take orders from you, boy,' he said with a snarl, going very still as he stared Hale down.

Hale watched him with the quiet respect of a hunter stalking dangerous prey. 'Perhaps it's time you did.'

The air whooshed from the room. Would Hale really stake his claim here? Now? With no preparation? Maria's head spun as the whole place froze, waiting to see what would happen with rapt attention. And then suddenly, as though responding to the same silent cue, the two men stood violently from their seats, squaring their shoulders as they stepped away from the table.

Maria's stomach plummeted with disappointment. It had never been this way in Alter. Altercations at the dinner table were never about anything more consequential than which pie was their favorite. And it spoke volumes that Danit was engaging in the spectacle, this not his usual style at all, the stress apparently getting to him.

It was comical, really, Hale at least a head taller than Danit, broader, fitter, and younger. He'd spent the last two years at sea, whereas Danit had spent the time at banquet. Not to mention, Hale was their rightful leader.

But Danit was a snake, which was why Hale stepped back a pace when Danit stepped forward.

Danit halted his approach, a feral smile on his lips. 'Scared, Nephew?'

A scraping noise drew everyone's attention to Dio as she pushed back her chair and got slowly to her feet. Her cane clicked on the flagstones, and then she stepped between the two men. 'Never in all my long life have I been so embarrassed by my family,' she said, looking first at her son, then her grandson. 'There is a time and a place for such things, and that is not here and not now and certainly never in front of a room full of honored guests.'

Both men faltered in the face of Dio's quiet, furious conviction. She embodied the strict rules of conduct that had been hammered into every member of the Alter family since birth. She seemed to hum with repressed rage, yet even so, she maintained her decorum.

Maria held her breath, willing the men to seize the gift Dio had offered, the branch on which to climb down from this madness.

But in the end, it was Barron who saved them, and no one would ever know what would have happened if matters had been left for Danit and Hale to deal with by themselves.

'I leave for Oshe tomorrow,' said Barron, continuing with his meal as though nothing were amiss. 'Come, join me for a drink! Let us toast my departure!' He held his goblet aloft, and after a moment's pause, Danit snapped the line of tension stretching between him and Hale, wheeling away and returning to his seat, a forced smile on his lips.

The room collectively exhaled, Hale and Dio sharing some look—although Maria couldn't see their faces—before they returned to their seats, too.

'My son and his new wife will join me,' Barron continued, 'so I suppose I will be generous and allow a toast to them, too!'

Elex didn't even hesitate. He lifted his goblet and inclined his head as though nothing would give him greater pleasure than to return with his father to Oshe, but Maria's insides clenched. Leave Alter? She'd known the day would come but hadn't expected it so soon. The idea of packing her things and riding away, of leaving her still room and her family ...

Elex squeezed her leg, and she schooled her features. This was her job, her contribution to the world, and it was not a surprise. She would do what she must, and she would be thankful to be doing it with him.

A large party rode out early the following morning, all of them glad to escape the oppressive mansion, a black mood having descended over everyone, including the staff.

Barron, Elex, and Maria would travel as far as Laurow, where they would stay with Sophie's family for the night before continuing to Oshe the following day. The others would hunt for the water the Claws were using to sustain themselves, a group that included both of Maria's brothers, as well as Sophie and Linella.

John had reappeared earlier that morning, refusing to tell them where he'd been. In fact, refusing to say much at all. He kept flicking covert glances at Sophie, but she resolutely ignored him, his mood souring further with every passing look. He kept apart from the others, his shoulders hunched and a serious expression on his face that didn't suit him at all.

'We'll follow the pipes,' said Danit. 'That's how they're stealing our water, I'm sure of it. Every route, no stone unturned.'

No one answered, and silence settled until they reached the carnage by the lake. The area, usually so serene, with lush green grass, cultivated flowers, and pruned trees, was mutilated and broken, a great gash slicing the ground where the water now fell, debris scattered everywhere.

Danit nodded stiffly to Maria when they'd come to a stop, for this was where the two groups would separate. 'Be good, niece,' he said, and that was it. He didn't even wait for Maria's response before shifting his attention to Barron.

Maria turned to Hale, who reached out an arm and clasped hers. 'Safe travels, sister,' he said, then to Elex, 'Good luck with this one.'

Elex chuckled. 'I think you need more luck than I, my friend.'

Hale lifted his eyebrows and shook his head a little, refusing to acknowledge the source of his woes, who hovered hopefully nearby.

'If only it were Hale who were leaving,' said John, joining them. 'Or better yet, if only he'd never returned.'

'How kind you are, brother,' said Hale.

'You can hardly blame Hale,' said Maria. She lowered her voice. 'But John, perhaps you had a lucky escape? If Sophie doesn't return your affections ...'

'And she only wants me for my title,' said Hale. 'You're quite welcome to her.'

'Do not speak about her that way,' John hissed.

Maria took a long inhale. 'John, it pains me to see you like this. It's as though Sophie has bewitched you, and I pray to the Goddess that you come to see the truth in time ... that you find another who feels for you what you feel for Sophie. Perhaps even someone who doesn't manipulate and lie.'

John sneered and turned away, and it felt wrong to leave with things so strained between them, her brothers arguing, John's easy smile and self-assurance nowhere to be seen.

Maria turned her eyes to Dromeda, that great looming presence in the center of their world. The home of the Goddess, if she still lived. At least it would look the same in Oshe as it did here; she could take some comfort from that.

'We must go,' said Barron. 'We have a long road ahead.'

'Safe travels,' said Danit as Maria took one last look at the lake, her home atop the cliff in the distance, the land that was all she'd ever known. She resigned herself to her fate and caught Elex's eye as she urged her horse into a walk. He smiled reassuringly, and her heart gave a little squeeze. She could take comfort from her husband also, and for that she was overwhelmingly grateful.

Maria turned her gaze forward, to the road that led to her future, and tried to ignore her feelings of unease. It was probably just the fear of the unknown, of leaving everything she held dear—including her notebooks, which would take years to replicate—and the thought of facing Cane again, this time in his own territory, which was by all accounts a brutal one.

'Everything okay, hell cat?' said Elex, his voice low.

'Just feeling unsettled; I suppose it's only natural.'

He nodded, and they rode on in silence, but they'd travelled not even a hundred feet when shouts went up all around them, and Maria's stomach dropped. Her horse skittered, and she searched for the source of the confusion, scanning for Nicoli or other members of the Claws but finding no trace.

Elex seemed similarly perplexed, but then one word stood out from the rest, shouted by many, repeated again and again. 'Dromeda!' Maria turned her eyes once more to the center of their world. Her mouth dropped open at the sight, her eyes practically popping out of her head.

'Dromeda's moving!'

'The Goddess has returned!'

'Dromeda's moving!'

'The Goddess has heard our calls!'

'Rejoice!'

'We are saved!'

'The Goddess has returned!'

Maria froze, turning over the implications in her mind. With Dromeda spinning, the turbines would be needed no longer. They had to be lifted, or they'd break under the strain ... but more importantly than that, in a single moment, the Claws had lost their only advantage.

Danit and Barron turned their heads to one another, their eyes locking across the short distance, and they laughed.

'The Goddess smiles down upon us this day, my friend!' shouted Barron, urging his horse back towards Danit.

'We can finish them!' called Danit, almost giddy.

'Finish them?' Maria breathed, her heart pounding. Dromeda was moving. The Goddess had returned ... maybe. Would the inner circle fill with water once more? If it did, the Claws would have access to their own supply. Things would be so different.

A dull thump pulled Maria's attention from her thoughts to where Danit was tipping forward in his saddle. Then he lost his grip entirely and toppled to the ground, an arrow protruding from his back.

'Uncle!' she shrieked, urging her horse into a gallop. She flew from her saddle, feeling frantically for a pulse, but she couldn't find one, no matter how hard she tried. It was too late—he was gone.

'Shit,' said Hale from somewhere nearby, still atop his horse, and when Maria looked up, she saw why.

Nicoli had climbed down from a nearby tree, a bow in his hand. 'You will not *finish us* as though we are vermin!' he shouted.

'Not a step farther!' said John, drawing his own bow and pointing it at Nicoli.

'Shoot him!' screamed Barron, close enough that Maria could see the whites of his eyes. 'Shoot him!'

Maria moved without thinking, putting herself in the open ground between John and Nicoli, then backing up towards where Nicoli stood.

'Maria!' roared Elex, but although he dismounted, he didn't follow.

'You can't kill him!' said Maria, just as a sea of Nicoli's people materialized from behind rocks and buildings and dropped out of trees.

'Retreat!' yelled Barron, spinning his horse and kicking wildly, his guards scrambling to obey.

But before he'd made it ten paces, Barron fell sideways off his horse, a dagger protruding from his neck, Elex's arm still locked in the position it had been in when he'd thrown the blade.

'Elex,' Maria breathed, her mind racing, trying to make sense of it all. Elex ran to his father's side, crouching to check for a heartbeat, then retrieving his dagger.

An 'omph' forced its way from Maria's lips as Nicoli pulled her flush against him. He must have run forward while everyone was distracted.

Elex stood, his features grim, turning darker still when he saw Maria pinned against Nicoli. 'Let her go,' said Elex, walking calmly towards them.

'No,' said Nicoli, whose arms around her middle bore the scars of her uncle's mistreatment.

'He won't hurt me!' said Maria. 'Just let him walk away.'

Elex stopped beside John and Hale, while Sophie and Linella stood behind, holding the horses.

'You think you know me so well?' Nicoli whispered.

'I do know you so well. You're my best friend. We've known each other since we were children, and you can't expect me to believe you've been hiding your true self all along. You are steadfast, always have been; it's one of the things I love about you.'

Nicoli hissed.

'We will support you,' said Maria. 'Danit and Barron are dead. Hale now leads Alter. Dromeda may be spinning once more, but that changes nothing for us.'

'It changes everything,' Nicoli spat, while Hale snatched John's bow out of his hands.

'What are you doing?' snarled John. 'Traitor!'

Hale let out an exasperated breath as he turned back to Nicoli, dismissing his brother. 'Release her,' he said, sounding more irritated than worried. 'There is no threat to you here.'

Nicoli backed up a step, pulling Maria with him. 'You'll never let us go. I killed Danit!'

'I killed Barron,' said Elex. 'If that's not proof we're on the same side, I don't know what is.'

'We have no time for this,' said Hale. 'We need to lift the turbines and decide how to deal with the other Blades. We cannot fight among ourselves.'

'How do I know you're telling the truth?' said Nicoli, tightening his grip on Maria, although his voice was strained, as though his injuries were catching up to him.

'Nicoli,' she said, lifting her hand to his arm and turning her head as far as she could, trying to look him in the eye. 'You know Hale. You know me. We freed you from our uncle's dungeon only a matter of hours ago! We want to help, but we need to get ahead of this. There are too many witnesses.' She eyed Sophie and Linella, then the guards, trying to work out which of them would run to Cane with tales of patricide. 'We have to contain this, then devise a plan. We are your friends; work with us.'

Nicoli released her, shoving her forward a step. 'Get everyone out of the Inner Circle,' he shouted, then fled, limping as he ran.

'Shit,' said Hale, letting him get away. 'He's right!'

Maria paled. If it filled with water, anyone down there would die.

Hale barked orders to the soldiers, sending some to the Inner Circle and others to transport the dead bodies of Danit and Barron back to the mansion. He ordered everyone else back there too, and by the time he was done, the people of the Claws had melted away into the trees.

Elex wrapped Maria in his arms, and she nuzzled into him. 'Never do that again,' he murmured into her hair.

She looked up at him. 'You killed your father.' It was like the realization had only just hit her: Elex had killed his own father in cold blood.

'He would have raised an army and united the Blades against your brother and the Claws. I did what was required.'

Was that true?

'We'll accompany his body back to Oshe and come up with a story to tell my brother and our people.'

A story ...

'The guards may be a problem ...' Elex glanced around at the soldiers. Many had escorted Erica and Cane home, but at least a dozen remained.

Would they arrest Elex on the journey back to Oshe? Would they tell the painted peacock the truth? Or were they glad to see the back of their cruel leader?

Elex had thrown his knife with no hesitation, and it had hit its mark with deadly accuracy. She didn't know him at all ... What else had he done? What else was he capable of? The thoughts sent shards of ice sliding down her spine.

'I'm sure you'll want to return to Laurow, Linella, and tell your husband the news.' Hale's voice cut through Maria's inward spiral.

'Oh no,' said Linella, who had watched all with hawk-like eyes. 'I will send a messenger to my husband, but Sophie and I will remain by your side. You two are to be wed, after all.'

'I am no longer the first son of Alter,' said Hale. 'John is.'

Linella scowled. 'Your people signed a pact, and that pact is not complete until *you* marry my daughter.'

'The pact promises her the first son. That is now my brother.'

'Not at the time of the agreement.'

'That is of little consequence.'

'Not to me.'

John turned hopeful eyes on Sophie.

'No,' she mouthed, shaking her head. She squared her shoulders. 'Hale is the man I was supposed to marry. I will wed him or no one at all.'

John clenched his jaw and turned away.

Hale rolled his eyes, then said, 'Sophie, it's nothing personal, but you need to be reasonable.'

'No,' said Sophie, crossing her arms. 'You need to honor the pact or face the consequences.'

Linella and Sophie seemed oddly unfazed by everything that had happened. The deaths, Nicoli, Dromeda. It was as though nothing could shake them. Was that not strange?

'The pact is dead,' said Hale. 'Alter will no longer treat the people of the Claws as lesser. We must create a new pact that includes the Claws, or I fear we are at war once again.'

'Then we will include our marriage in that pact,' said Sophie. 'I see no reason for my family to exclude the Claws if the terms are such.'

Hale lifted an eyebrow, as though reassessing Sophie, as though her words had garnered some respect.

'And you must marry someone in the end ...' added Linella.

'I must do no such thing,' said Hale. 'Sophie will marry John; it is a perfectly reasonable solution. You get the first son you were promised, and we are assured of your alliance in helping bring peace to Celestl.' Hale looked around, clearly searching for John.

'Your brother's gone,' said Sophie. 'Didn't you notice?'

Maria looked around for John but found Sophie was right. He'd probably run off somewhere to sulk, as he had after Blade Day, and she wondered vaguely where he liked to hole up.

'No doubt due to his disappointment,' said Hale, 'because you made him believe you had feelings for him when it is plain for all to see that you do not. And after this further refusal, he'll need even more time to lick his wounds, but do not look to me for a husband, because I do not take liars to my bed.'

'Or maybe the Goddess stole him away now she has returned because she knows you and I are meant to be together.' Sophie smiled sweetly, but there was something harsh in her words, something that once again made Maria question the soft face she showed the world.

Hale stared at her for a beat, perhaps also noting the same, but then he dismissed her, turning away. 'We will return home and regroup,' he snapped.

Maria moved close to Sophie as the others readied for departure. 'I believe you have the measure of my brother,' said Maria, because although she wasn't sure if she liked Sophie, and she certainly didn't trust her, it wasn't a bad idea to keep her on side. Perhaps Hale had forgotten in the heat of the moment, but insulting Sophie and her mother was not the strategic path. And besides that, Maria's words were true—Sophie had riled Hale in a way few others had ever managed. Sophie turned away, but Maria caught the wolfish hint of a smile she tried to hide, and despite everything, it made Maria beam.

Dromeda's quiet, persistent movement caught Maria's eye as she mounted her horse, the terrible magnificence of the once more spinning center stealing her breath. And despite the grizzly scene, the death and loss and the likelihood of more to follow, she couldn't help but feel a new sense of possibility ... of hope.

Her uncle was gone, Barron was gone, and her husband and brother—Alter's new leader—both shared her dreams for the Claws. They could finally change things, and more than that, Maria might finally have a voice.

Chapter Thirty
Maria

Maria slammed the door when they reached her room, her insides a storm of emotions, frustration and anger and other things she couldn't think clearly enough to put a name to. She'd been endlessly chastised by both her brother and her husband on the ride home, who'd worked as a team to dress her down and make her feel small.

Elex took in her flaming features and was on her in a heartbeat, kissing her, sucking her bottom lip, pressing up against her. 'I've never seen you look this way ... It's—'

'No,' she said, fighting the building lust and pushing him away. 'How could you?'

He drew back. 'Um ...'

'You killed your father!' It wasn't the real reason for her anger, but it was better than admitting the truth, that she hated how he and Hale had spoken to her, how she'd been on the outside of their team.

His eyes became two smoldering embers, ready to ignite. 'And you protected the man who murdered your uncle. You would have taken an arrow for him!'

His words burned. 'Are you jealous? Is that it?' The idea lit a new kind of fire in her, but she pushed it aside. 'I would have done the same for you.'

'Would you?'

'Yes!'

He hissed and turned away.

'Elex, Nicoli is my oldest friend, and John would have shot him.'

'John could barely hold the bow steady.'

'Unlike you.'

He spun back to face her. 'Meaning?'

'You killed your father in cold blood, with a knife thrown to perfection.'

'Nicoli did the same to your uncle.'

'My uncle planned to wipe the Claws from the face of Celestl!'

'And my father was a saint? Had no part in that plan?'

Maria clamped her jaws tight because he was right; Barron had been just as keen as Danit.

'I told you my reputation is accurate; I never pretended otherwise.'

'Well, I didn't know the extent of it ...'

His eyes bored into hers. 'You regret our marriage so soon?'

'Of course not!'

'And yet you think me a villain? Accuse me as though I've committed some unforgivable act?'

'No, that's—'

'Barron would have rallied the armies of the Blades and marched against the Claws if he'd escaped, and Danit would have been his martyr.'

She knew he was right, and she didn't dare think what other atrocities Barron had committed, but she didn't know how to admit the true reason for her anger, how to break down her walls and let him in, how to be vulnerable.

'If you wish to stay when I leave tomorrow,' Elex said quietly, his anger dampening, 'I won't force you to come. Whatever you think of me—'

'No!' Panic flooded her, and silence descended as they took each other in. Maria sat heavily on the bed, gripping the edge with both hands as she sucked in a long, centering breath, her heart racing wildly. 'I want to start this conversation again.'

'It didn't hurt enough the first time?' His tone was hard, but it had a hint of vulnerability, too.

She lifted her eyes to meet his and finally let him see her own pain. 'I don't care that you killed your father, not really. I don't dare think of the atrocities he committed, how many lives he took ... what he did to you ...'

Elex frowned as she trailed off.

'I do care about the way you and Hale treated me. You think my actions reckless, and for that, I'm sorry, but I am not a child to be chastised and belittled. You told me we were partners—equals—and yet at the first test, you sided with my brother and treated me as though I answer to you. Like some child needing punishment. Like I am naïve ... stupid, even. Like the promises you made to me never even existed.'

Her voice cracked, and Elex looked down at her, staring for several long moments as though her words were taking time to burrow deep into his brain. She refused to look away, letting him see how much it hurt.

'Fuck.' He ran a hand through his hair, then sat beside her on the bed, sliding his fingers through hers. Her chest squeezed tight with hope.

'I'm sorry,' he said, brushing his thumb back and forth over hers, looking at the floor. 'Hale and I are old friends. I suppose we fell back into old habits, and what you did ... I was ...' He trailed off, seeming to search for the right words. 'I've never felt this way before.' He turned his head to meet her eyes. 'I was scared ... terrified, and I could do nothing but stand and watch. Anything I did would have made things worse, and I couldn't bear it ... the thought of losing you.'

Maria stifled a sob.

'If Nicoli had hurt you, or John ...'

'They never would.'

Elex looked away, clenching his jaw.

'But I'm sorry too,' she breathed. 'I didn't stop to think.'

He swallowed, then gave a small nod.

'But you have to trust me. If we're partners, that means trusting I know what I'm doing.'

Elex launched to his feet. 'You can't ask me to stand by while you put yourself in danger! You must also be a partner to *me*.'

Maria pursed her lips, holding tight to the angry retort that wanted to fly free.

'What would you have done if our roles had been reversed?'

She forced herself to consider his point. How would she have felt if Elex had put himself between an archer and their target? Especially if the target had been another woman ...

She lowered her head. 'You're right. I'm sorry ... I suppose we both have things to learn ... and I don't think you're a villain, Elex. I would never think that.'

His features shuttered. 'In many ways I am.'

'Not like Danit or Barron.'

'I've done much worse than I did today.' He sat and looked her squarely in the eye. 'I need you to know who I am because I refuse to hide it from you. And if we are to be a team, you need to know all I'm capable of.'

Maria pulled his lips to hers, needing the press of his skin, his strength and warmth and scent. 'I want you as you are,' she whispered between kisses. 'I want everything. I don't want you to hide.'

'Everything?' He pulled her onto his lap and pressed his forehead to hers, his hand cupping her cheek.

'Every sordid part.'

He kissed her again, and a groan rumbled through his chest. 'I want the same from you,' he said, moving his lips to her neck.

'Yes,' she said, without hesitation. 'Anything.'

'We're a team.'

'And I'm lucky to have you.'

He pulled back, then waited for her to open her eyes and meet his hungry gaze. 'We are lucky to have each other,' he said, sliding his thumb across the sensitive skin below her ear.

Her chest clenched hard, and her eyes fluttered closed as he kissed her softly. She slid her hand under his shirt. 'And I've taken the brew of herbs ...'

She looked up at him from under her lashes, and his features turned feral, pupils blowing wide. He bit the tip of her finger, almost to the point of pain, and she moaned. 'Then we should put them to good use.'

Maria and Elex spent the rest of the day avoiding the world. There was little peace for them beyond the door of Maria's bedroom, and all their possessions had already been packed for their journey back to Oshe, which would now start the following day.

But by the time the house quietened down for the night, Maria had grown restless. Happy as she was in Elex's arms, she was not made to be idle, and nor was he. They'd missed lunch and dinner, and they finally heeded their stomachs and snuck into the kitchens.

They rummaged in the cupboards and cold lockers for leftovers, filling their arms with bread, pies, and fruit before climbing back up the stairs. But as they reached the first floor, instead of turning left towards her bedroom, Maria led Elex right, then through an enormous pair of ornate double doors.

'Where are we?' Elex asked, as Maria fumbled around in the dim light of her lantern. She dumped her food on a table, then quickly lit several more lanterns, turning them up so they shone brightly, illuminating all four corners of the room.

'Danit's office?' said Elex, taking in the large desk near the window at the far end, the walls lined with books, and the vast round table beside them, big enough to comfortably seat twenty.

'Danit's office,' Maria confirmed, through a mouthful of steak pie.

She left her remaining food on the table, then nosed about, opening the cupboards at the bottom of each bookcase, scanning the shelves and searching like a person possessed through the full-length cupboards at the back of the room.

'Yes!' she cried, relief flooding her as she found her still tucked away on a high shelf, along with sieves and strainers, flasks, measuring devices, and temperature gauges. 'It's all here!'

Elex helped her pile the equipment by the door, and then she rifled through the desk. It appeared as though no one else had yet searched the place, and Maria was tempted to read every document, which she would, just as soon as she found her notebooks.

She pulled open each drawer in turn, then the cupboards, then the leather satchel that hung from a coat stand nearby, until all that was left to search were the concealed compartments at the back. Danit had never told Maria about them, but she'd once hidden in this very office when her father had still been alive and seen him open one of the secret spaces.

Her father had caught her and sworn her to secrecy, and she'd kept her word, never telling another soul about them ... until now.

'How are you at forcing locks?' she asked Elex, looking up at him from where she knelt before the desk.

'It's not my forte,' he said, smiling like a shark as he came to her side, 'but I'm sure we can get by.'

'Then it's lucky for us I took this from around Danit's neck earlier,' she said, a shy grin taking hold of her lips as she held up a small key on a thin chain.

'Maria!'

'What? He no longer needs it.'

Elex shook his head, but pride lit up his features. 'Go on then.'

Maria unlocked the first compartment but found little of interest. Deeds of ownership for Alter, the mansion, and various other assets, maps, contracts, but no hint of what she was looking for.

She held her breath as she swung open the false back on the second side, and whooped in delight when she pulled out the pile, her notebooks sitting atop the stack.

'Thank the Goddess,' she breathed, rolling back on her heels, then sitting on the floor. She flicked through them, ensuring everything was there, then began scanning the other documents.

'What the fuck?' came Hale's voice from the door. 'Elex, what the fuck are you doing in my office?'

'Calm down, brother,' said Maria, standing to make herself known.

'Oh,' said Hale, 'and it all falls into place. What are you doing here?'

'Taking back what's mine,' she said, holding up her notes.

'And?' he pressed.

'And nothing,' said Maria. 'At least, nothing yet. I haven't begun my search in earnest.'

Hale strode to the desk and started rummaging through the stacks of paper, too. 'You take that side, I'll do this, and Elex'—Hale handed him a pile—'you take those.'

They searched but found nothing of note. It was all ledgers and letters, not a hint of subterfuge, scandal, or anything else interesting, at least until Maria shoved everything back into one of the secret compartments and a tattered old scrap of paper fluttered out.

She picked it up off the floor, her eye drawn to the names at the bottom, her interest more than piqued when she saw Nicoli's surname—*Enki*—scribbled there. But it wasn't his name before it, just like it wasn't Danit's name that preceded the name *Alter* on what seemed to be an agreement of some sort.

'Goddess,' said Maria, her eyes scanning the page. 'Look at this!'

She thrust the agreement into Hale's hands, and he went slack-jawed as he read. 'Fuck,' he said, handing it to Elex.

'The Claws are siphoning off water,' said Elex.

'And storing it on Alter land ...' added Maria.

'Paying us for the privilege,' said Hale, reaching for a map and spreading it on the desk.

'There,' said Maria. 'Near where the river runs into the sea.'

'Near your turbine,' said Elex.

'Which makes sense, seeing as no one's allowed near it,' said Hale, 'aside from our own soldiers and members of the maintenance team.'

'The Claws have been stockpiling water for years,' said Maria, 'and Nicoli never once even hinted ...'

'None of them did,' said Hale. 'Assuming anyone aside from Nicoli knew.'

'If they didn't before,' said Maria, 'they must now. This is why they don't care we've shut off their piped water. But how do they transport it to the other Claws—or even to Arow—without raising suspicion?'

'Boats,' said Elex. 'I bet they're doing it by boat.'

Hale nodded. 'Although the Blades control the ports.'

'Only the ones in Blade territory,' said Maria. 'The Blades haven't inspected the ports at the Claw tips in decades, and there are plenty of smugglers' coves.' Maria had used those too, from time to time, but her brother didn't need to know that.

'The Claws have been quiet—docile even—for such a long time, I suppose no one saw the need to inspect them,' said Elex. 'I was told stories of how the Claws used to raid the Blades for water, but they haven't done that in our lifetimes.'

'Because they struck this deal?' said Hale, tapping the agreement with the back of his hand. 'But where do the Claws get the money? According to this, they pay us to store the water, and it's not cheap.'

'Or maybe they don't,' said Maria. 'The Claws charge us to maintain our turbine. Maybe the amounts balance out. Or maybe we do pay them for that, just less than the other Blades.'

Hale nodded, considering it. 'Which would keep the coin counters at bay.'

Elex tapped his fingers on the desk. 'And it explains why Danit needed to speak with Nicoli so desperately.'

'Because the other Blades noticed the water level dropping,' said Maria, 'and knew something was amiss.'

Hale folded his arms. 'Danit probably planned to threaten Nicoli into taking less.'

It certainly sounded like something Danit would have done. 'But it's over now,' said Maria. 'The falls are back to normal, and with Dromeda spinning, the Inner Circle will likely fill. That means the Claws will have plenty of water and won't need their secret stash, although Nicoli won't be happy to lose his leverage over Alter.'

Hale frowned. 'He still has leverage. He could still blackmail us, threaten to expose Alter's decades-old deal with the Claws.'

'Not if you expose it first,' countered Elex. 'You had nothing to do with it, and it only has power if you cover it up.'

'But if they find out, the other Blades will never agree to work with the Claws,' said Maria. 'They're paranoid enough about the Claws stealing from them as it is. What will they do if they find out their suspicions were true all along?'

'Hardly stealing,' said Hale, 'considering the sums they pay.'

Maria scoffed. 'Not sure the other Blades would see it that way, and there's a danger they'll unite against Alter for our part, too.'

Elex began straightening the documents on the desk. 'But if the Inner Circle remains empty, the Blades will keep their advantage, the lakes the only supply.'

'And the Claws will still be dependent on the Blades for water,' agreed Maria, 'and unable to play their turbine trick now the Goddess has returned.'

Elex placed a glass paperweight atop of the stack of wrinkled parchment. 'And in that case, they'll want to keep their stash.'

'Meaning a new pact that includes the Claws would be far harder to broker,' added Hale.

'Why?' said Maria. 'The other Blades have no reason to blame the Claws for the falling water levels if we don't tell them about the stash.'

Hale exhaled loudly. 'That really would leave us open to blackmail.'

Elex perched on the edge of the desk. 'But why are their levels dropping at all? If the only stash is in Alter, why are the other Blades feeling the effects?'

Hale threw up his hands. 'Fucking Nicoli! They must have agreements with all four Blades!'

Maria shook her head. 'Or it's all linked somehow, so less water in Alter means less across Celestl as a whole?'

'Unlikely,' said Hale.

'But not impossible,' said Elex.

Maria huffed out a frustrated breath. 'Well, let's hope the Inner Circle fills, then it doesn't matter how many stashes they have or don't have.'

'No sign yet,' Hale said on an exhale.

Elex pushed himself off the desk. 'Perhaps we'll have a front row seat as we ride to Oshe tomorrow.'

'Perhaps ...' said Maria, her shoulders slumping because she had no desire to go to Oshe Blade, especially now Cane ruled.

'Better to go now,' said Elex, catching the true cause of her dejection, 'before Cane has a chance to scoop up all my father's allies and turn them against me.'

'A cheering thought,' she deadpanned.

'In truth,' said Elex, 'I'm itching to return. Many in Oshe rely on me, and I can't let my brother hurt my people or carve out a stronghold ... but ... Maria, if you want to remain—'

'I don't.'

He stepped towards her. 'I would understand—'

'Stop,' she snapped. 'How would it look if you returned without me? And if I stay here, your brother would be well within his rights to summon me anyway, seeing as all in Oshe formally answer to him now. I'm coming with you, and that's the end of it.'

Elex nodded, seeming relieved as he reached for her hand.

Hale's eyes flicked to their joined limbs, but Maria couldn't decipher his reaction. She wondered if it was jealousy, if Hale, too, wanted to find someone to share his life with …

Hale held up the document and turned away. 'And I'll track down Nicoli so we can discuss this and agree a plan for a new pact. I'll send word when I have it.'

Maria and Elex shared a simple breakfast of porridge and fresh berries with Hale and Sophie, their group shockingly diminished compared to the previous day, the conversation stunted and perfunctory.

Hale seemed pre-occupied, and Sophie kept casting furtive glances at him as though worried about something. Maria wondered what could possibly have happened, especially seeing as it had only been a few hours since they'd said goodnight to Hale.

'Your mother's usually up and about by this time, Sophie,' said Maria. 'Is she alright?'

'She's up and gone,' said Sophie. 'A messenger returned from my father in Laurow. She's meeting with him now.'

'I do hope your father will support a new pact with the Claws.'

'As do I,' said Sophie, glancing again at Hale.

Hale turned his head, and his and Sophie's gazes met for a long moment before he looked away. Something Maria couldn't read passed between them, but it was thick and heavy, and Hale certainly seemed less hostile than before.

'John is still missing,' said Hale. 'Keep a lookout for him on your travels.'

'We will,' said Elex.

'Where could he have gone?' said Maria. John was a creature of habit and he rarely left Alter. He had no close friends in the other Blades or the Claws, he'd never attended the university like Elex and Hale, and he had no discernable hobbies.

'My guess is he went deeper into Alter,' said Hale. 'I've sent a warning to Nicoli at the turbine, just in case John shows up seeking revenge.'

'You think that's where Nicoli went?'

'Almost certainly. He'll want to ensure the turbines have been properly lifted and assess any damage. Ours is closest, so it makes most sense for him to have gone there first.'

'We should be off, Maria,' said Elex, downing his thick, strong coffee, then abandoning the small cup.

'May the Goddess protect you on your journey,' said Sophie, putting her hands together and nodding her head.

Maria had never seen anyone aside from a handful of administrators do that, and it did something strange to her insides, sending unease skittering through her. 'You truly think she's returned?'

'How could she not have?' said Sophie with a little shrug.

'Then you think the Toll Bells will chime?'

'Toll Day is past. The next Tolls are not due for ninety-nine years.'

Maria prayed she was right, but something in her gut wasn't convinced. Maybe because if the bells chimed, it was likely Maria's neck on the line. Would Sophie's own people not be forced to sacrifice her? Or was there another from her family who would be sent to the Goddess, never to return?

'Has the Inner Circle filled with water?' asked Maria, wondering if it had happened while they slept. Surely that would be a sign.

'No,' said Hale, still distracted.

'Nicoli seemed convinced it would.'

'It could happen at any time. I've issued an order to keep our people out of the Inner Circle.'

Hale had *issued an order*. How strange to think of her brother as the leader of her people. Of course she'd known, in theory, that Hale would one day rule, but it had all happened so quickly. Only a few days ago, they'd wondered if Hale were dead, and now here he was, issuing orders.

They said their goodbyes, Maria sad so many of her family were absent—or dead—and she wished she'd had more time with Hale. She put the thoughts aside, not one to dwell on what couldn't be.

'I'll do what I can to support you,' Elex said to Hale, 'although my brother won't make it easy.'

'And I'll keep you updated,' said Hale. 'Good luck.'

The party rode hard—Maria, Elex, and the twelve remaining Oshe guards—having decided not to stop at Laurow for the night. Hale had refused to marry Sophie once again, and although it was unlikely that Laurow would detain them—or worse—it was better not to chance it. And regardless, Elex wanted to limit Cane's time to organize.

So they rode the fifty miles at a steady, loping canter, which allowed Maria plenty of time to take in the scenery. The Outer Circle did not change much as they travelled around it, nor did the Inner Circle, but she observed many changes in the land to their right, some subtle, others jaw-dropping.

First came Arow Claw with its topsy turvy wooden structures, then Laurow, where the lofty stone buildings featured scroll-topped pillars of a kind not generally seen in Alter.

Her eyes went wide as they passed the temple, an enormous stone building which sat across the border between Laurow and Laush Claw. Tall, vine-wrapped pillars stood atop wide, shallow steps, lining the entrance to the building that held all the formal administrative records of Celestl. The man who'd presided over their wedding was probably in there right now, fretting over the Goddess's possible return.

Maria wondered what secrets the building hid from the world, but the administrators claimed it had been the first construction in the whole of Celestl, made by the Goddess herself, and only those devoted to a life of service to the Goddess were ever allowed inside.

They passed the temple, then stopped to rest and water the horses a little farther on, beside Laush Claw.

Maria was glad to dismount for a while, happily stretching her aching legs, walking a little way along the dirt road of the Outer Circle, but she had to work hard not to stare at the buildings and streets of Laush.

'It's terrible, isn't it,' said Elex, from just behind her.

She jumped, not having realized he was there, but couldn't tear her eyes from the mess and squalor. Arow Claw was ragged, yes, and poor, but it was also mostly clean and orderly. The same could not be said for Laush.

Rubbish and other filth marred the dirt streets, and children played in the rubble of collapsed buildings, deftly avoiding the piles of decomposing waste.

Wooden buildings rotted, stone buildings had missing windows and doors, smashed glass littered the ground, and the smell ... Maria had never experienced anything like it, some mix of rotting fish and human waste.

Adults sat idle, some swigging from bottles and heckling the children, others watching Maria and the rest of their party with keen interest, but none seemed to have much purpose.

'Why is it like this?' she breathed.

'They don't have a Nicoli or a Gabriele or anyone with the strength to lead. Nicoli keeps all four Claws in water, but there's only so much anyone can do if they're not willing to help themselves.'

Jeering and laughing filled the air, and Maria turned her head to find the cause of the commotion. An old stooping man in a tattered military uniform was being pushed out of a dilapidated tavern near the road. Men and women shoved and slapped and mocked him but didn't go so far as to push him off his feet.

The man hobbled onto the Outer Circle, his mouth moving all the time. Maria assumed he was talking to himself, even if she couldn't hear him. His arms gesticulated wildly, and then he folded them across his chest, huddling in on himself before throwing them out again, holding them high in the air as he stumbled on.

He came closer, until Maria could hear the words spilling from his lips, even if she didn't understand any of what he said. 'Hells bells! Ding dong! Ring rong! Goddess of Dromeda likes to romina. Steal the children. Wands go boom. Goddess of Dromeda what is wrong with ya! Ding ring. Bells sing.'

'Can we help you?' asked Maria, taking a tentative step closer.

The man's head turned to face her with menacing speed, eyes bulging in his weathered face, and Elex was beside her in a heartbeat.

'It's okay,' she whispered so only Elex could hear.

The man studied them with glassy eyes, and then his head snapped back, face turned up to the sky. His voice became a low, otherworldly drone as he said, 'Toll Bells ring when the Goddess returns. Water will come. Prepare. Prepare.'

The man collapsed to the ground, and Maria rushed forward, but Elex grabbed her and hauled her back before she could get to him.

'No,' he whispered in her ear, 'we are not far from Oshe, and you cannot be seen helping this man. Things in my homeland are not like they are in Alter; charity is weakness when done this way.' He called the guards over, and they rolled the man onto his back, avoiding getting too close.

'Dead,' pronounced the most senior guard, showing not an ounce of compassion.

Elex nodded. 'Take him to the temple. We'll wait here.' He drew Maria back to where their horses and remaining guards sat under the shade of a Laurow tree, its big, flat leaves fanning out above them.

Maria accepted a flask of water, then sat beside Elex on the grass a little way from the others. 'What do you think it means?' she asked, her voice coming out as a whisper.

'The old man?' said Elex, before taking a mouthful from his own flask.

'He said the Toll Bells would ring.'

'He did,' Elex said slowly, watching her with questioning eyes. 'And if I said the same, would you take my word as gospel?'

'He seemed ... I don't know ... possessed or filled with magic or ...'

'Maria,' he said, squeezing her leg. 'He was an old, half-mad, half-drunk, half-dead ex-soldier. People in that condition say a lot of things we should not heed.'

'Then you don't think the Toll Bells will ring?'

'Is that what you're worried about?'

'I'm not worried, I'm just ...' She plucked a blade of grass and rubbed it between her fingers. 'What if the Goddess has returned?'

'Like Sophie said, even if she has, the bells aren't due to ring for ninety-nine years.'

'And if the Goddess decides otherwise? She's been absent ... What if she requires the wands and our sacrifices sooner? Who's to say she can't change the rules as it pleases her?'

'Even if she does,' said Elex, stroking his thumb across her cheek, 'you won't be the one to go.'

Maria shrugged off his touch. 'Someone has to! And if not me, who? My sister, Pixy? And what about Sophie and your sister and whomever Spruce decides to send? And who knows what the Goddess does to sacrifices once she has them ...'

Elex held her gaze for several long moments. 'The bells won't ring, my little hell cat.'

Her insides screwed tight. 'You don't know that.'

He looked at her with soft eyes. 'We can't worry about things that might never come to pass, especially when we have plenty to deal with that already has.'

She turned her head for the thousandth time towards Dromeda. She'd always been curious what it would look like when it spun, but now it did, she liked it not at all and wished it would stop.

Although, Elex had a point, so she did her best to shake off the looming dread squatting at the back of her mind and focused on the present. 'Then tell me,' she said, 'what kind of reception will we get in Oshe Blade?'

His spine straightened, and the seemingly unconscious movement sent a spark of dread through Maria's blood. Was it really that bad?

'Ideally we'll avoid any kind of reception at all. I'm hoping we can slip into the city and make it to my quarter before my brother gets wind of our arrival—assuming he's there.'

'The city?'

'Oshala. Our home is not like your mansion. We too live atop a cliff, but it's bigger—much bigger. A whole city sits up there, and a place that big is impossible to control like your family does their home.'

'You kept saying it was different, but I didn't think ...' Tendrils of fear coiled around her lungs.

He pulled her closer and wrapped his arm around her. 'It's more dangerous than Alter, I won't deny it, but I've carved out a place that is my own, that's protected, and you will be safe there.'

'How?'

'I have a whole gated quarter, and my people are loyal to me.'

Maria's mind boggled. 'Your father let that stand?'

'He had no choice,' he said with a dark but mildly guilty smile, 'because my quarter controls the water.'

'Elex!' said Maria, then exhaled loudly. 'It always comes back to that.'

He gave her arm a gentle squeeze.

'So the plan is to sneak in, then hide away?' she said, not loving the idea of being so cowardly—not to mention rude—but not quite hating it either.

'That's the plan.'

'But there must be guards stationed at the gate?'

'I'll admit the plan isn't perfect, but there's only one route in and out of Oshala—across the bridge. The guards search every cart and barrel, so there's no hiding.'

'Fuck,' said Maria. 'Your home sounds vile.'

Elex tipped his head to one side and appraised her. 'Oh my little hell cat, don't pretend you're not intrigued. You and your still and your secret trades will fit in just fine.'

She couldn't help the swell of pride in her chest, and she nudged him with her shoulder. 'If I don't get killed or captured first.'

'We just have to get across the bridge and into my territory.'

'Well, I suppose we don't have much choice.'

'And if my brother tries anything, I still control the water.'

'Urgh!' said Maria, pushing away from him and launching to her feet. 'Why must it be like this?'

'You could still return home,' he said gently. 'It's not what I want, but Oshe is dangerous, especially if my brother has returned and already knows Father is dead.'

'That isn't what I meant,' she snapped. 'I won't run at the first obstacle, but that doesn't mean I'm not cross at the world and the people who run it.'

'I know,' he said quietly, 'but maybe we can change things.'

She laughed cruelly. 'And maybe rainbows will float down from the sky,' she said, echoing Nicoli's words to her. It was hopeless. Perhaps Hale could change Alter for the better, but if Oshe was even half as bad as the picture Elex painted, then how would they ever achieve anything?

'Don't underestimate the impact each of us can make,' said Elex. 'Look at Nicoli, at what he's achieved despite the odds. We'll take it one step at a time. First, we'll get in unnoticed, and we'll figure out the rest from there.'

CHAPTER THIRTY-ONE

AVA

B AND BILLY HAULED Ava into a wheeled chair, then B pushed her through a series of dark corridors made of roots and branches, while Billy scouted ahead. It was twilight, the place was deserted, and it was all Ava could do to keep herself in the chair, her muscles feeling as though she'd gone twelve hundred rounds in a boxing ring.

'Wait,' hissed Billy, holding up his hand. B froze, and so did Ava, booted footsteps sounding from somewhere up ahead. But after a few moments, he beckoned them on.

They went forward like that, along corridors and through portals, starting and stopping, Ava's heart in her mouth, adrenaline rushing through her veins every time Billy's urgent tone floated back to them. By the time they arrived at the place she was to meet Kush—in what was little more than a wooden alcove off a corridor made of tree branches—she could barely keep her head up and shivers wracked her body.

'This is it,' said B, her voice low, eyes flitting around like a skittish horse. 'We'll be close.'

'Don't let him take you,' said Billy.

'And don't give him the Atlas Stone,' added B, looking Ava directly in the eye.

'As soon as he gives you the Herivale, call and we'll come.'

Ava still couldn't speak, nor could she nod, so she narrowed her eyes as best she could and blinked.

She fell asleep while waiting for Kush, her head lolling forward from pure exhaustion, only the makeshift strap across her torso keeping her in place, but the sound of stumbling, scuffing feet woke her, and she opened her eyes to find Kush—or at least some diminished version of him—limping towards her.

He was a mess, shoulders hunched, arm still in a sling, and badly favoring his left leg. But none of that shocked Ava in the way his eyes did when they met hers—they shimmered silver. *Mezzed up*, isn't that what B had called it? Not that Ava knew what that meant. She'd thought the rippling silver was a sign of magic, but he didn't look magical now.

Kush dropped to his knees before her and rested his cheek against her thigh, seeming to need a moment to recover from his exertion. Then he pulled a glass vial from his pocket, yanked the stopper free with his teeth, rested the bottle against the corner of Ava's mouth, and carefully applied the viscous contents to the inside of her lower lip.

The Herivale was gritty against her teeth and bitter when her tongue brushed over it, but after a few moments it turned sweet, and she ran her tongue back and forth, lapping up every last taste.

Ava's fatigue evaporated almost immediately, and her limbs became normal once more. Better than normal. She felt light and energetic and … angry.

'You lied to me,' she hissed, although she didn't dare raise her voice or move because she didn't want B and Billy to take her away. Not yet.

'I didn't tell him about you,' he said, his head back in her lap. 'I never would have.'

'You mean your father?' She laughed cruelly. 'The *God*?'

He winced. 'We don't have much time,' he said, his good hand reaching up to take hers.

She planned to snatch it away, but the scratch of something cool against her palm made her reconsider—a piece of parchment, she realized, as she closed her fingers around it.

'The two that brought you here are lying,' he said, finally lifting his head and meeting her eyes. Beyond the shimmer of silver, he seemed sad and hurt and broken. A shadow of his former self.

'Kush,' she said, lifting tentative fingers to his face. 'What happened?'

He leaned into her touch and closed his eyes. 'There's no time. You need to use the stone. Escape this place. Find answers.'

'What are you talking about?'

'They all want your parents' secrets, and when they have them, they'll kill you. You're too much of a threat.'

She shook her head with tiny movements, rejecting the idea. 'B and Billy wouldn't ... They were friends of my parents. They—'

'No, Ava.' He pulled back a little, his features turning serious, solemn. 'They killed your parents.'

The words hit like physical things, her stomach cratering as though he'd punched her. 'No ...' It couldn't be true ...

'There's no time,' he said again, squeezing her fingers. 'Go to the place on the parchment. I'll come when I can.'

He began to pull away, but she latched onto him, clung to him. 'Kush ...' Tears welled in her eyes. She leaned forward, and he rested his forehead against hers, rubbing back and forth with small, light movements.

'It's going to be okay,' he breathed, his breath caressing her lips.

Two fat tears rolled down Ava's cheeks as she blinked her eyes closed. She held them closed for a moment before looking back into his gaze, her hand still on his cheek. 'But I can't trust you, either. I can't trust anyone, it seems.'

'But staying here means trusting them.'

'Kush ...'

He kissed her, the press of his lips all too swift, detonating an explosion in her chest that hurt so much it stole her breath. 'You're a survivor. You have the stone. You'll be safe there.' His eyes flicked to the parchment he'd placed in her hand.

He heaved himself to his feet and staggered back a pace, and Ava looked down at the drawing of an Atlas Stone.

'Go, Ava,' he said, raising his voice to be heard above the sudden sound of rushing footsteps. 'Now.'

She pulled out the stone, her heartbeat frantic as she turned the dials to match the drawing.

'Guards!' screamed Kush, who'd pulled himself up to his full height, finally looking more like himself. 'Go,' he mouthed, then turned to where B and Billy had stopped a pace away. 'Murderers,' Kush said as he lunged for them. 'Guards!'

Ava didn't think any further, feeling oddly calm amid the sounds of running feet and shouts and Billy calling her name. She pinched the stone and spun it between her fingers, and in an instant, all of it was gone.

Chapter Thirty-Two
Maria

Maria was sore and bad-tempered by the time they reached the border with Oshe. The line between it and Laush was stark: one side chaos, the other ordered, albeit rundown and a little wild.

In Alter, they made an effort to keep the grass that edged the Outer Circle low and had planted trees and flowers and created spaces where people could congregate, but that didn't seem to be the case in Oshe, the grass long and dancing in the gentle breeze.

The few buildings Maria could see from the road looked ready to tumble to the ground, their style less angular than the buildings of her homeland and more squat, the rooves curling up a little at the edges.

They cantered on along the road until they came to Oshe Blade's bridge, where they stopped one final time to rest. It was much like the bridge of Alter, although again, it felt shabbier somehow, the brass of the looking glasses dull, the grass long, Toll Day offerings littered about.

Maria looked once more to Dromeda, and it soured her mood further. She hated the unknown of it all. Would the Toll Bells ring? Would the Inner Circle fill with water? Had the Goddess truly returned? There was no trade she could make to find out. She could only wait like every other person, and it made her want to scream.

They mounted up and were about to leave when a group of excitable teens appeared at the top of a path leading down into the Inner Circle.

Maria gasped in shock. 'Stay out of there,' she called to them. 'It's not safe!'

'Why?' asked a girl.

'Because it could fill with water at any time,' said Elex.

The group eyed them warily, but the girl seemed cockier than the rest. 'There's too much bounty down there to pass up.'

'Even better if others aren't willing to risk it,' added one of the boys.

'You could die,' said Maria.

'But we're getting rich in the meantime,' said the girl with a boastful smile.

They scampered away, and Maria watched as they disappeared into the long grass, heading for a small collection of houses a little farther along the road, pockets no doubt stuffed with triffles and other treasures.

Maria exhaled heavily as they rode out.

'We can't save everyone,' said Elex, but his words didn't help at all.

They turned off the Outer Circle onto a much smaller track that led to the ominous-looking cliff of Oshala in the distance. Elex hadn't been lying when he'd said it was much bigger than the cliff her home sat atop, but it was also dark and foreboding and stark against the flat of the surrounding land, and their Toll Bell's tower protruded like a needle into the sky. Maria's apprehension worsened with each passing stride.

Water suddenly fell from the sky on the far side of the cliff, the mighty cascade impressive even across the distance, and Maria gasped as mist rose behind the city, framing it.

'Goddess,' said Maria. 'It's right beside your home!'

'The lake sits below the cliff on the far side,' said Elex. 'It's quite something to experience from Oshala's edge.'

Maria's blood ran cold at the thought of standing halfway up the fall as the water rushed down.

'Hopefully there isn't too much damage from Nicoli's stunt,' Elex continued. 'It won't have done much to the cliff itself, I don't think, because of the direction the water travelled, but there is a village I fear may have been destroyed.'

Death everywhere, and all for what?

They rode on in silence, the city increasingly unwelcoming as the details came into view. Erica had claimed there were no flowers, and she hadn't been lying. The buildings were in various states of repair, some crumbling, others freshly painted, all intermingled beside one other, making for an unsettling tableau.

Beside the main cliff stood a smaller pillar of stone with a spiral path that climbed its perimeter, and at the top, a bridge stretched between it and Oshala, guards stationed at both ends, already tracking their movements.

'So much for sneaking in,' said Maria.

'There are more than usual.'

'Oh good.'

Elex tensed, and that ratcheted Maria's trepidation higher still. 'Elex?'

'Yes?' he said, whipping his head around to look at her.

'What's going on?'

He faltered, then reluctantly said, 'Those guards are not friendly to me. It could be a coincidence, but it makes me think Cane's already made moves.'

'What will they do?'

Elex shrugged. 'I guess we'll find out,' he said in a low voice, Maria leaning closer to hear. 'Even if we wanted to, we can't turn back now. They would follow us, and there are guards in our party who would side with Cane over me. Our only option is to act as though everything is normal and that we're returning home as planned.'

They wound their way up the spiral path, Maria feeling quite nauseous by the time they dismounted and left their horses with the stable hands at the top.

'The horses live here,' said Elex. 'There isn't space inside the city.'

The ornate carriages that had transported the Oshe family to Alter were lined up there, too. Maria wouldn't want to be the one to have to drive them up and down the cliff. It had been bad enough on horseback.

Maria took Elex's proffered arm as they stepped onto the bridge, which didn't sway so much as bounce a little as they walked, the motion doing nothing to quash the unease in her chest.

They'd almost made it across, the guards still at their backs, when Cane stepped into view on the far side, blocking their path. He was flanked by four others—two men and two women—Erica the only one Maria recognized.

'Brother!' Elex said warmly as they stepped off the bridge, halting before the group. 'It is good to see you.'

Cane held up his bandaged hand. 'I wish I could say the same.'

'I come bearing sad tidings,' said Elex.

'Father is dead,' said Cane. 'I am aware.'

'He will be missed,' said Elex.

Cane sneered. 'I am sure.'

'Alter is making arrangements to send his body,' said Elex.

'Why?' said Cane. 'That is not our custom. What use is a body once the life has left it?'

'It is a gesture.'

'And that is no use to me either,' said Cane. 'Your wife, on the other hand ... now, she is a different story.'

Elex tensed, pulling Maria close. 'I see you have been reunited with your betrothed,' he said lightly, nodding his head at the woman to Cane's right. 'Opal.'

'My betrothed no longer,' said Cane.

'I am his wife,' said the short, blonde woman with hazel eyes, stepping up beside him.

'As am I,' said Erica, doing the same.

The two women were strikingly similar. The same long golden hair flowing past their shoulders. The same short stature and affinity for low-cut clothes. The same haughty, provocative stance. They could have been sisters.

Maria had to work hard to prevent her mouth from dropping open. She flicked her eyes away, which meant she caught the moment the two older men behind Cane shared a dark look. *Interesting*.

'You have two wives?' said Elex, slowly.

'I couldn't have Erica banished,' said Cane. 'Father wouldn't have wanted that for his favorite wife.'

'No, of course not,' said Elex. 'A good idea.'

Opal was the daughter of Barron's closest ally—Maria remembered that much—meaning presumably one of the men behind Cane was her father. Elex had predicted his father's old guard would rally behind his brother, as there was no other option that would keep Oshe united, and they were, at their core, greedy.

Perhaps that was why Opal's father had agreed to Cane's taking two wives, his daughter's happiness less important than stable trade. Although, could anyone ever be happy married to Cane? Perhaps Opal would like for him to take a score of wives so she would never need see him.

'Come, brother,' said Cane, 'let us escort you to your home. I am sure you are eager to return.'

Elex faltered, as though planning to refuse, but then Cane gave him a half smile, and Elex moved, keeping Maria tucked into his side.

'Something's wrong,' Elex whispered. 'He's too confident.'

'Why?'

Elex shrugged.

Why was nothing ever easy?

Elex pulled back and dropped Maria's arm as they entered the city proper, passing houses and shops and taverns packed with people straining to get a look at them. He slid his hand up her back and took hold of her neck, the possessiveness making her shiver.

She glanced up at him, and the change was staggering, so much so she stumbled, but his hand was unrelenting, urging her on.

If she hadn't known better, Maria would have thought him cruel ... frightening ... not the kind of man she would want to find herself alone with. He refused to look at her as they made their way across the city, making it appear to onlookers that he cared not a jot for his new wife but also leaving no doubt in anyone's mind to whom she belonged.

Maria told herself he had to be that way, that she would be safer if others thought Elex didn't care for her, but it still stung, and she found her eyes flitting back to him at every opportunity.

Maria was so preoccupied, she almost forgot to observe her surroundings as they wound through the streets. She noted the lack of flowers and plants, the general shabbiness and crowds of curious faces, but she couldn't stay focused on anything, too troubled by the feel of the place, its sinister undertones putting her on edge, and the smell ... something she couldn't place ... reminiscent of ash, maybe. It was so unlike her home it made her want to weep.

They didn't stop until they'd reached the far side of Oshala, where a large cluster of buildings stood behind a wall, separated from the rest of the city. Elex tensed when the open gate came into view, and Maria's heart fell through her chest.

'This is your quarter?' she whispered.

'I don't think I can claim that anymore,' he said. 'But whatever my brother has planned, I still have many friends in this city. We are not yet out of moves.'

'Welcome home, brother,' said Cane, giving him a wide, self-satisfied grin as they stepped through the gates. 'Or more accurately, welcome to Erica's home. She has grand plans to create a garden to rival those she saw in Alter.'

Elex said nothing.

'You may go,' Cane continued, waving a hand, 'but your wife will stay with me for a while. I should like to give her a proper welcome to our homeland.'

'As you wish,' said Elex, while panic flared like a lightning bolt through Maria's blood.

Elex turned to face Maria, sliding his hand around to the front of her neck as though he planned to choke her, even though his grip was gentle. 'Do as he says, wife,' he said, squeezing a little, 'and do not embarrass me. But remember, brother'—he flicked his eyes to Cane—'if you touch her, the law says I can take your hands clean off.'

'I would never dream of doing such a thing,' said Cane in an overly sweet tone. 'We shall treat your wife with the respect her rank deserves.'

Elex pulled Maria towards him so hard she crashed into his chest, the impact forcing the air from her lungs. He steadied her with a hand on her back, then used the hand that had been on her neck to twist her hair around his fist. He tugged it, forcing her head back until their eyes met, and what she saw in them was hard and unyielding, both terrifying and strangely reassuring.

He kissed her with harsh, deep movements, then moved his lips to her ear, Maria's senses struggling to keep up with it all. 'Sit tight, my little hell cat, and whatever you do, do not try to escape. Oshe law allows him to punish you harshly if you do.'

And then he was gone, and every part of her felt his absence. But the image of her grandmother filled her mind, the woman's spine ramrod straight, stick in hand, a determined gleam in her knowing, azure eyes, and Maria had no doubt what she should do, what Dio would do in Maria's shoes. Maria had survived her uncle for all the years before Elex, and she would survive this, too. They would prevail—she knew it deep in her bones.

So she took a long, centering breath, then turned to face the enemy. 'Many congratulations on your marriages and also your new role, brother,' she said. 'If you would be so kind as to show me to my room, I've had a long journey, and I should like to freshen up.'

Thanks for reading *Bride of Stars and Sacrifice*. The story continues in *Daughter of Secrets and Sorcery,* book 2 in the *Cruel Goddess* series. READ NOW!

If you enjoyed *Bride of Stars and Sacrifice*, I would really appreciate a review on social media or wherever you buy books. This helps others find my stories in this algorithm driven world. Thank you for your support.

And for all the latest updates, sign up to my newsletter (where you'll also get a free story!):

https://hrmoore.com/blog/cruelgoddess/

CONNECT WITH HR MOORE

Find HR Moore on TikTok and Instagram: @HR_Moore

See what the world of *Cruel Goddess* looks like on Pinterest:
https://www.pinterest.com/authorhrmoore/

Follow HR Moore on BookBub:
https://www.bookbub.com/profile/hr-moore

Like the HR Moore page on Facebook:
https://www.facebook.com/authorhrmoore

Check out HR Moore's website:
http://www.hrmoore.com/

Follow HR Moore on Goodreads:
https://www.goodreads.com/author/show/7228761.H_R_Moore

ACKNOWLEDGEMENTS

Thanks, as always, to my wonderful beta readers and general cheerleaders, Alice, Elise, and Steph, to the phenomenally talented Patcas for the stunning cover art, Rosie Venner for the gorgeous map, my brilliant editor, the utterly wonderful and endlessly kind Vela Roth for your time, wisdom, general guidance, and positivity, and as ever, to all my inspiring FaRo author friends for telling me when to STEP AWAY from the terrible ideas and nudging me towards the good ones. And most importantly thank you, thank you to all my wonderful readers. Without you, this journey would be a shadow of itself.

TITLES BY HR MOORE

The Relic Trilogy (complete):
Queen of Empire
Temple of Sand
Court of Crystal

In the Gleaming Light

The Ancient Souls Series (complete):
Nation of the Sun
Nation of the Sword
Nation of the Stars

The Shadow and Ash Duology (complete):
Kingdoms of Shadow and Ash
Dragons of Asred

Stories set in the Shadow and Ash world:
House of Storms and Secrets
Of Medris and Mutiny

The Cruel Goddess Series:
Bride of Stars and Sacrifice
Daughter of Secrets and Sorcery
Book 3 – coming soon

http://www.hrmoore.com

Printed in Great Britain
by Amazon

59956535R00163